# The Elizabethan Collection

2 dramatic tales
set in the turbulent and passionate
times of
The Virgin Queen

*SWEET TREASON*
**by Marie-Louise Hall**

*THE DESERTED BRIDE*
**by Paula Marshall**

**Marie-Louise Hall** studied history at the University of London, where she met her husband. Now living in rural Aberdeenshire, her ambition since marriage has been to find time to write. This is not easy. Writing has to be fitted in between working for her husband's management consultancy, acting as a taxi service for her teenage son and looking after the four-footed members of the family who often appear in her books in one guise or another. They include: an English thoroughbred horse (allergic to straw), a very large German draught horse (who thinks he's a medieval warhorse), three delinquent donkeys, five assorted cats and one very un-pedigree dog.

**Paula Marshall**, married with three children, has had a varied life. She began her career in a large library and ended it as a senior academic in charge of history in a Polytechnic. She has travelled widely, has been a swimming coach, and has appeared on *University Challenge* and *Mastermind*. She has always wanted to write, and likes her novels to be full of adventure and humour.

*Look for*

AN UNCONVENTIONAL HEIRESS

*Coming from* **Paula Marshall**
*April 2003*

# The Elizabethan Collection

Marie-Louise Hall & Paula Marshall

MILLS & BOON®

*MILLS & BOON and MILLS & BOON with the Rose Device
are registered trademarks of the publisher.*

*First published in Great Britain 2003 by
Harlequin Mills & Boon Limited,
Eton House, 18-24 Paradise Road,
Richmond, Surrey TW9 1SR*

THE ELIZABETHAN COLLECTION © Harlequin Books S.A. 2003

The publisher acknowledges the copyright holders of the
individual works as follows:

Sweet Treason © Marie-Lousie Hall 1994
The Deserted Bride © Paula Marshall 1998

ISBN 0 263 83674 6

*024-0103*

*Printed and bound in Spain
by Litografia Rosés S.A., Barcelona*

# SWEET TREASON
## by Marie-Louise Hall

Dear Reader

I have always been intrigued by the younger members of Elizabeth I's first court who grew up in the turbulent and dangerous era between the death of Henry VIII and Elizabeth's. Alliance with the wrong faction or adherence to the wrong faith led both their contemporaries and elders to the block or to the stake. Youth was no protection.

Elizabeth herself was questioned on treason charges at fifteen by her own brother, her cousin Lady Jane Grey was executed on the command of Mary Tudor before she reached her seventeenth birthday. And even when Elizabeth was crowned few expected her reign to last, especially after another cousin, Mary Stuart, declared herself Queen of England – a deliberate invitation to English Catholics to depose or assassinate the new queen.

Many of the young nobility who took their place at Elizabeth's first court had already experienced the shadow of the axe and it seems to me that their only certainty can have been to live for the moment – and trust no one. But even the most cynical are not immune to love and it was from this thought that the rebellious Seraphina Carey, her sometimes despairing family and the disillusioned Earl of Heywood sprang into life.

Young, passionate, reckless, courageous and occasionally badly behaved, Seraphina was my first heroine, and remains my favourite; I hope she becomes one of yours.

*Marie-Louise Hall*

# Chapter One

Richard Durrant, Earl of Heywood, lay motionless in the musty loft of the near-derelict cottage, praying that the dust from the mouldering hay he lay upon would not make him sneeze. Through a hole in the rotting floorboards, he stared into the room below.

The only light came from a poor-quality candle that spluttered and smoked on a rickety table. Four men huddled about the table, as if hoping to gain a vestige of warmth from the paltry flame. Their faces, pale as the small white ruffs at their throats, shone pallidly in the candlelight in contrast to their sombre travelling cloaks which merged with the shadows. It gave their heads a disembodied look, as if they'd lost them already, Heywood thought grimly.

His brown eyes darkened as he glanced from face to face. Tregarrick, Wharton, Southwick and Malgreave. Until an hour ago he would have sworn they were all true Englishmen. He grimaced at his own thoughts. The last few years should have told him that religion, spiced with fear and greed, was a potent enough brew to make clowns of the sounds of men.

The old tyrant, King Henry, would turn in his grave if he knew how his children had wrecked England with their religious see-sawing! First, priggish, Protestant Edward, now pious, Popish Mary, persecuting and burning their own people…turning one man against his neighbour. It was little wonder the economy was in ruins and the army a humiliated shambles after the débâcle at Calais…

A sharp scuffling from the deep shadows outside the wavering circle of light made all the men below jolt and reach for their swords.

Heywood's hawkish mouth lifted at the corners in a humourless smile. God willing, they'd become more familiar with that sound soon enough. The Tower was infested with rats, as he remembered all too clearly from the days he had spent in it, along with Robin Dudley and the Lady Elizabeth Tudor.

'Just rats…' Tregarrick, the craggy-faced Cornishman, said with disgust. 'The devil knows why we had to meet in this flea-ridden plague pit. If she's not here by the time the candle has burnt another finger-width, I am leaving and she can find someone else to do her work.'

The others muttered agreement, self-consciously pushing their half-drawn blades back into their scabbards. Above their heads, Heywood caught his breath. She! That was a possibility he and Cecil had not even considered…they had been searching for clues to a man's identity. He bit his lip. A woman. Who better to get close to a future queen? But who…supposing she was already among Elizabeth Tudor's attendants?

His hands clenched. He must find out who she was; time was ebbing away as fast as Mary Tudor's life.

'How fares the Queen?' Malgreave, the youngest of the men, asked Tregarrick.

'She's dying. There can be no doubt this time,' Tregarrick growled, echoing Heywood's thoughts. 'I saw her last week and I would not give her until Yuletide.'

'She still shows no sign of changing her mind about the succession?' Wharton, a burly, heavy-featured man asked curtly.

Tregarrick shook his grey head. 'No. She won't disinherit Boleyn's brat, even though she knows her to be a heretic.'

'Why the devil not?' Wharton said harshly. 'She's sent Bishops to the stake for the sake of the true faith and yet she balks at this. I don't understand the woman's mind!'

'She's a Tudor first, Catholic second. In the last resort she'll put the interests of the state before her own conscience,' Tregarrick answered tersely. 'She thinks that to give the crown to Mary Stuart will result in civil war. She says the English will not stand for a Scots queen with a French dauphin for a consort.'

'Perhaps she is right...' Malgreave said nervously. 'Elizabeth might be a bastard in law, but none would deny she is King Harry's daughter. Could we not bargain with her, offer out support in return for a guarantee to be able to worship as we please without fear of reprisal or persecution?'

'Aye, I had thought the same.' Tregarrick sighed. 'If there was any other way.'

'Jesu! You both talk as if you're still wet behind the ears!' Wharton sneered. 'What of your families? Malgreave's wife is kin to Bishop Bonner, is she not? And yours, Tregarrick, was she not among those set to spy on Boleyn's brat when she was held at Woodville?' He shook his head and laughed derisively. 'The only bargain Elizabeth Tudor will strike with you, m'lords, will be for your heads! Do you really think the heretic daughter of Henry Tudor and Nan Boleyn would keep her word? Your families and your estates will be the first to feel her talons!'

'You may be right,' Malgreave stammered. 'But sometimes I think it may be better to lose my estates than see England ruled by France.'

'And better to lose your wife!' Wharton sneered. 'Bonner's kin will be the first to be shorter by a head if the Protestants get their way! If I had known that I was to be surrounded by fools I'd have had naught to do with this mess and take a blade to the heretic bitch myself!'

'Are you calling me a fool?' Tregarrick rasped, his hand going to his sword.

'My lords, be calm.' The priest, Southwick, spoke quietly for the first time. 'You must put your differences and doubts aside for the sake of the faith. It is God's will we do here; remember that, and we cannot fail.'

There was a grudging murmur of agreement from all but Malgreave, who dropped his gaze to the mud floor, sunk in his own thoughts.

Heywood smiled as he glanced at the young man. A weak link in the chain…that was exactly what they needed. A little reassurance and Malgreave should prove most helpful—his smile set as he heard the scrape of metal against metal. The door latch was being lifted. She was here. He stared at the barely discernible outline of the door as intently as the men below. At last he would have the name William Cecil most needed...the link with France.

Holding his breath, he watched as the door swung inwards with a squeal of rusted hinges that set his teeth on edge. He caught no more than a glimpse of a cloaked figure silhouetted against the paler darkness of the night sky before the door closed, and the candle guttered in the sudden draught, plunging the room into absolute darkness.

With overstretched senses he registered the sibilant rustle of silk petticoats and a faint, delicious perfume, a blend of spices and musk overlaying the smell of damp and hot tallow. The seconds seemed to stretch for hours as he listened to Tregarrick swear and fumble for flint and tinder. Come on! He willed impatiently, and then cursed silently as the candle flared back into life. He was no wiser to her identity than he had been in the darkness.

She was shrouded in a black cloak and veil. All that was discernible of her face was a pale blur behind the thick black gauze of her veil.

'You're late,' Tregarrick said curtly.

'I had to be sure I was not followed,' she replied crisply, without a hint of apology. 'You should be grateful for my discretion, m'lord.'

Her voice was cool, young, with a soft west-country lilt; Somersetshire or Wiltshire bred, Heywood thought, running through the great families of those counties in his mind.

'I'd be more grateful to get our business over and get out of this ague trap,' Tregarrick rasped. 'Have you got the orders from France? When we are to act?'

'Patience, my lord,' she admonished. 'We do not act until the Queen is dead. In France they still hope she might change her will and name the Queen of Scots her rightful heir. But, if not, I shall arrange for the administration of the poison before Boleyn's brat can be crowned. Your task, m'lords, will be to ensure that there is no opposition to Mary Stuart's landing. She is insistent there must be no focus for a Protestant rising. Since one of our number has died, Tregarrick must now see to it that Lady Katherine Grey is held under close guard, lest she be tempted to follow her sister's example and be a nine days queen. Such details as you will need are here.' She brought a small leather pouch out from beneath her cloak. Stripping off her gloves, she opened it.

The Earl stared down at her hands, small and pale gold in the candlelight. She wore only one ring, but it was distinctive, a coiled dragon fashioned from glittering stones, either rubies or emeralds; it was impossible to be certain in the poor light. A coiled dragon...his brow furrowed as he tried to recall where he had seen it before.

'There are instructions here for each of you,' she said, taking out four parchments from the pouch and handing one to each man. 'Read them now, then give them back to me.'

The four men hunched closer to the candle and read in silence.

'Is there aught else you would know?' she asked, as they handed back the slips of parchment. Tregarrick and Southwick shook their heads.

'But you should know that Malgreave here is having doubts,' Wharton growled. 'Methinks he would like to leave us.'

'I cannot believe that,' she laughed softly. 'He knows that he can only be released from his oath by death, don't you, sir John?'

Her voice was soft, honey-sweet, but the threat was unmistakable.

Heywood's hand crept down to the dagger in his belt; Cecil might insist on discretion, but he could not stand by and watch murder being done.

'Of course he does,' Tregarrick growled, as Sir John Malgreave seemed incapable of speech. 'And I'd remind you all that my daughter is his wife and he would do naught to harm me. You need not fear he will blab, whatever his doubts, will you, John?'

Pale-faced, Malgreave shook his head.

'Good, then let us consider the matter closed.' The woman's tone allowed for no argument.

The four men watched sullenly as she picked up the slips of parchment and held them in the candle-flame until they flared.

'Can we go now?' Tregarrick rasped, when she had ground the ashes into the floor.

'Yes. Please do, my lords. It may take you a little while to catch your horses. I turned them loose in the woods, in case any of you should be so foolish as to try and follow me.'

'You...' Tregarrick began furiously and then thought better of it and stormed out, closely followed by the others.

She was clever. Too damn clever, thought the Earl, as he dropped silently down from the loft a minute or so after she had left the cottage. Her perfume still hung in the air. It was a warm, feminine scent, spicy and sensual. It didn't suit her. She was cold, ruthless. There was nothing womanly about her.

Pressed against the damp stone wall beside the small, shutterless window, he watched her cross the moonlit clearing outside. Her grey gelding was tethered to a fallen tree. Hampered by her skirts, she clambered awkwardly on to the tree-trunk. The gelding moved restlessly as she freed the reins from a branch and threw them back over its head. It shied as she placed one foot in the stirrup, leaving her sprawled across the saddle with her legs flailing beneath her petticoat; revealing ridiculously high-heeled silk slippers more suited to a masque than to riding. Heywood's mouth twisted. It seemed she was vain as well as cruel.

'Stupid beast!' she cursed loudly and clutched at its mane for balance as it skittered in circles.

Not so cool now, the Earl thought with a grim smile as she hauled herself upright in the saddle. The grey went stiff-necked and poker-backed as she jerked back on its mouth and kicked it forward at the same moment. 'Poor beast,' Heywood muttered. Clever she might be, but she was no horsewoman. He stepped back from the window as the grey lurched into an unbalanced canter and disappeared among the trees. Picking his way to the table he felt across its surface, and smiled as his fingers found the leather pouch. With luck, it was all he needed.

After listening carefully at the door he slipped outside. The others were making enough noise for an army in the woods, cursing and swearing as they blundered into branches and brambles. It would be easy enough to pass unnoticed.

He whistled softly. A moment or two later his bay mare trotted obediently out of the trees on the far side of the clearing and an ugly pied hound rose from where he had lain hidden beneath a patch of bracken.

'Well, Tumbler, let's see if you are as good at sniffing out a traitor as game.' The Earl held out the leather pouch to the hound. The dog nosed at it for a moment and then began to cast for the scent in ever-widening circles. The Earl turned to mount his mare, and then grinned as the hound gave a small squeak as he found. More than once he had been mocked for keeping a hound with neither looks nor voice, but Tumbler's nose more than made up for his deficiencies in other respects, and in this case his silence was an advantage; the last thing he wanted was for her to realise that she was being followed.

As usual, the hound did not disappoint him. An hour or so later he stood in the stables of the Rose Inn, staring at the grey gelding as it crunched contentedly on a mouthful of hay.

'A widow, you say? I could have sworn it was my

sister's beast,' he said to the coachman beside him. 'Can you describe the woman who brought him there? What's her name?'

'I don't know, m'lord' The man shrugged. 'It was the maid who hired me the day before yesterday; she didn't give me her mistress's name, and, for what they were paying, I wasn't going to ask questions.'

'I see…' The Earl sighed. This wasn't to be quite as easy as he had anticipated. He had hoped to find out her name and be gone before there was any chance of being recognised himself. He doubted that the woman he'd seen at the cottage would make the mistake of assuming his presence at this inn to be coincidence. 'You said she had a maid with her?'

'Aye. A Wiltshire girl with hair the colour of straw, and freckles. Pretty, not that you'd even look at her beside the other one.'

'Other one?' the Earl asked with interest. 'There is another lady with the widow?'

'Aye, a real little beauty, just like the statue of Our Lady in the church. Hair like silver-gilt and eyes as blue and clear as the heavens. She arrived with the widow, but she's asked the innkeeper's lad to take her back to Linton by pillion tomorrow. She's frightened of horses, never rides by herself, but he's not complaining. Here—' the man's face grew anxious '—you don't think she's your sister, do you? I wouldn't want the lad to get into trouble by helping a runaway.'

'I am sure you wouldn't,' the Earl answered reassuringly. 'But I doubt she is my sister. You said little; my sister is tall, about to my jaw.'

'No, the fair 'un wouldn't come above your shoulder.' The groom scratched his head. 'But the one in widow's weeds is tall, m'lord. I'll wager she's the bird you're trying to net.'

'Perhaps. But I must be sure before I confront her. Discretion is everything in this matter. If my sister's betrothed were to discover that she had run off to join another man...it would be most unfortunate. You understand?'

'Yes, of course m'lord.' The coachman's eyes widened as he saw the coin the Earl flipped idly in the air. 'If there's any way I can help, sir.'

'Have you a suit of clothes I might borrow?' the Earl asked. 'My sister is not the only one who can don a disguise.'

Seraphina stared listlessly out of the window into the inn's courtyard below. In the October dawn it looked like she felt inside—grey and empty. Her husband was dead...and she felt nothing. Nothing. But then Edmund had killed her feelings for him long before he had so nearly killed her, in fact.

She picked up her hand-mirror from a table and grimaced at her reflection. Where she was not black and blue, her skin was as white as her linen chemise. Her normally glossy red-brown hair was lank, her grey-green eyes dull. She touched a purple bruise on her cheek tentatively with her fingertips, and then winced.

There was a light tap on the door of the chamber. Putting the silver-backed mirror down, she reached instinctively for her veil—it wasn't there. 'Wait!' Her

voice was sharp with panic; she did not wish to be
recognised, nor for her injuries to be seen. Tongues
would wag and the last thing she needed now was to
be the subject of gossip.

'Seraphina, it's only me.' The voice was gentle,
feminine.

'A moment, Grace.' With painful slowness she got
up and went to open the door.

'I came in to wake you earlier and found your
gown and cloak were damp; I took them to air before
the kitchen fire.' The fair-haired young woman put
down her bundle of garments on the bed as Seraphina
shut the door behind her.

'Thank you,' Seraphina said, feeling a stab of guilt.
Grace was always so kind, so efficient. She should
have thought about the gown being damp last night,
but she had been so tired. 'You should have asked
Bess.'

'She is still sleeping. You let her take liberties, Seraphina.'

'It is not like Bess to be a slug-a-bed,' she answered defensively, knowing Grace was right. She
was not as firm with servants as she should be, but
Bess was as much a friend as maid; they had grown
up together.

Grace's perfect rosebud mouth pursed a little, but
she said nothing as she picked up Seraphina's loose
black gown and held it out for her.

Gingerly, Seraphina eased herself into it, her breath
catching as she lifted her arms into the sleeves. She
winced as several of the gashes on her back reopened
with the movement.

Grace made a grimace as she saw the bright scarlet soak through the linen strips bound across Seraphina's back and into the white linen of the chemise. 'Anyone would think you had been riding half the night!'

'I feel as if I have.' Seraphina laughed raggedly.

Grace sighed and shook her head. 'These should be healing better by now; why not rest here another day or two?'

'No.' Seraphina spoke through gritted teeth as she lifted her arms again to ease them into her gown. The longer she stayed here, the more likely it was she would be recognised And that was something she wished to avoid. 'No,' she repeated. 'I want to go home. It is only another day's journey from here.'

'If you survive it.' Grace frowned as her eyes skated over Seraphina's drawn face. 'I cannot leave you like this; perhaps I should travel on to Mayfield with you.'

'No. You must go back. Someone should be at Sherard House to oversee things until Edmund's heir arrives,' Seraphina answered, a little too emphatically. Grace had been unfailingly kind, yet she found her company oppressive. Not that it was Grace's fault. It was just that she could not look at Grace's ethereal beauty and not be reminded of her husband. Beautiful, charming, cruel Edmund, with his spun-gold hair and ice-blue eyes.

'You *are* eager to be rid of me.' Grace's finely plucked brows rose.

'I did not mean…' Seraphina began guiltily.

'You need not apologise.' Grace smiled at her as

she fastened the ties that held the front of Seraphina's loose gown together. 'I realise that you must wish to forget everything about Sherard House.'

'Never your kindness. I know we have differed on some things, but I hope we shall always be friends,' Seraphina protested. 'I did not mean to sound ungrateful. It's just that you have done more than enough for me. It was you…' She hesitated. It was the first time she had dared to bring herself to speak of the night Edmund had died. 'It was you who stopped him, was it not?'

There was another strained silence.

'Yes.' Grace's pale blue eyes were intent, almost wary, as she raised them to Seraphina's face. 'I am surprised you remember. I thought you were unconscious.'

'I was near enough,' Seraphina replied flatly. 'But I can recall your face bending over me and the sense of relief I felt.'

'Not as much as I,' Grace said half audibly, her eyes momentarily distant and cold. 'I thought he'd killed you.'

'He tried hard enough,' Seraphina answered bitterly.

'No! You must not say that…' Grace was aghast. 'He never meant to harm you. What happened was a moment's temper—'

'A moment's temper.' Seraphina shook her head in disbelief. 'Do you think that was the first time he had raised his hand to me?'

'Perhaps…' Grace began hesitantly '…at times you gave him reason—'

'A thousand at least!' Seraphina cut in with a jagged laugh. 'It seemed it was a crime to wear a pretty gown, to ride in the park without permission or to smile at one of his friends!'

Grace's clear blue eyes clouded. 'It was his nature to desire perfection in all things, and you—'

'Were a far from perfect wife.' Seraphina's wide mouth twisted as she finished the sentence for her.

'That is not for me to judge,' Grace murmured apologetically. 'But when you wed you promised to obey, and a husband has the right to punish his wife—'

'Right! To take his whip to me? To cut my back to ribbons? Dear God!' She could not contain the rage that welled up in her. 'How can you say that when you have never been wed? There was nothing right in the way he treated me and I hope he rots in hell!'

Colour rose and faded in Grace's cheeks, but for a moment she said nothing. And then she sighed. 'Try and forgive him; such hatred is a sin—'

'If I am guilty of all the sins Edmund accused me of I am doomed to hellfire already!' Seraphina laughed mirthlessly, wincing at the pain which flared across her bruised ribs. 'One sin more or less is not likely to make much difference.'

'Seraphina!' Grace inhaled sharply, her voice anguished and her face very white. 'You must not say such things. It makes me afraid for your immortal soul.'

'I'm sorry.' Seraphina sighed as she saw the telltale

glitter of tears in Grace's blue eyes. 'You are the last person I would offend. It is just when you defend Edmund—'

'How can I not?' Grace made a helpless gesture with her hand. 'He was more like a brother to me than a cousin; he gave me a place in his house when the rest of my family would have seen me starve.'

'Yes.' Seraphina agreed slowly. 'Sometimes I used to think that he regretted you were so near in blood that he could not wed you instead of me.'

'I doubt it,' Grace answered curtly, after the most fractional of hesitations. 'We were too alike. Now let us talk no more of what is past; sit and rest, while I rouse that maid of yours and send her in search of breakfast.'

'I am not hungry.'

'Nonsense,' Grace said briskly. 'If you must travel, you must eat. I will not be long.'

'Where is the man? How long does it take to harness horses?' Bess complained loudly as she stood beside Seraphina outside the inn. 'And that loafer on the mounting-block is no better; he's been twisting that hay rope for ten minutes and it's no longer than when he started. And he keeps staring at you! Shall I go and tell him to keep his eyes to himself?'

'No, it doesn't matter,' Seraphina answered through tight lips. Her back and ribs felt as if they were on fire, and such impertinence seemed entirely irrelevant. She glanced at the ill-clad figure in the greasy woollen cap without interest, noting merely that his clothes seemed too small for his powerful frame, and his face was so dirty you could scarce define a feature. But when he looked up suddenly from his work, she found herself taken aback by the directness of his golden-brown gaze as his eyes seemed to stare into hers. She jerked her head away, suddenly very glad of the protection of her veil. Bess was right. He was impertinent; the coach came clattering out of the barn, blocking her from his sight.

'About time!' Bess greeted the hired coachman derisively. 'Don't just sit there; get down, man, and help—can't you see she can scarcely stand?'

Seraphina let Bess guide her towards the coach, and then she halted, swaying slightly and cursing herself for a fool. 'Bess, I have left my box of papers inside. Please, get it once; I must not lose it.'

'As soon as you are settled, m'lady—'

'No, do it now!' Pain and anxiety made her sharp. 'Whatever happens it must not be lost. Go. I'll manage…'

Her face rigid with disapproval, Bess did as she was asked. Seraphina inhaled and lifted her foot with painful slowness on to the step of the coach and then, as she glanced back, she groaned.

'M'lady?' The coachman put a hesitant hand on her arm.

'Crecy? Where is he?'

'The grey…' The man looked sheepish. 'I'm sorry, m'lady, I forgot; I'll get him—'

'No! You load the boxes, I'll ask the stablehand to get him. It will be quicker,' Seraphina answered tersely. Grace had been right; she was not fit to travel.

She could think of nothing but the fact that the sooner they left, the sooner she would be home.

She was halfway across the yard when she knew she had been foolish not to get in the coach at once. There was either something wrong with her legs or the cobbles. The ground was pitching and falling beneath her feet at every step. She was too hot, suffocating beneath the veil. She blinked as she took another lurching step. The mesh of her black veil seemed to be getting smaller, denser, wrapping tighter and tighter about her face. She could not breathe. The man on the mounting block had stood up, and was moving towards her. But his image was blurred and out of focus. She stumbled to a halt and fumbled at the neck of her cloak with panic-stricken fingers, trying to loosen the veil. She was drowning in this bottomless darkness, falling, falling…and then someone caught her, snatching her out of the abyss, and then the dark was not frightening any more, just a blessed respite from pain which she slipped into willingly.

The Earl looked down at the limp bundle in his arms and frowned. She was lighter than he had expected; her hands and wrists, so white against the black of her cloak and gown, were frailer than he remembered from the night before. But it had to be the same woman; he had followed her here; the horse was the same. And the perfume which eddied up from her velvet cloak was unmistakable. It had been pure instinct which had made him move to prevent her from smashing her skull upon the cobbles. And now he wondered why he had bothered; she deserved no better. His mouth curled with distaste as he dumped her on the ground and reached for the edge of her veil. At least he had the opportunity to see her face without her knowledge. That the faint was genuine he had no doubt. His wife had faked enough of them for him to know the difference.

'Take your hands off her, you clod-pated oaf!'

Before he had so much as lifted the veil an inch he found himself reeling sideways from a blow to the head, delivered by the tow-haired maid.

'What have you done to my lady?'

Regaining his balance, the Earl bit back the blistering retort which came to his lips. He was supposed to be a stable hand, he reminded himself, and was, therefore, far inferior in rank to a lady's maid.

'Didn't do nothing,' he muttered sullenly, in as close an approximation of the local accent as he could manage. He scowled as he rubbed his jaw, reflecting that he had taken lighter blows in a tavern brawl with soldiers. 'She just keeled over...'

'Then don't stand there gaping,' Bess answered, without giving him as much as a glance as she bent over her mistress. 'Get into the inn and fetch help; tell them to send for a physician. Go on, you great half-witted loon!'

The Earl retreated hastily and slipped into the stables. He had no intention of going into the inn where the other woman of the party might see him or the landlord start asking awkward questions. He dared not risk discovery at this stage; Cecil had stressed that discretion was essential and he had already exceeded his instructions. He leant against the wooden partition and swore softly. He had been so close.

'Is it your sister, m'lord?' the coachman asked, as he led the horses back into the stables.

'I had not the time to be certain.' The Earl shook his head. 'But perhaps you can help. You say you are travelling west. As soon as you are released from your hire, go to the White Horse Inn and tell the innkeeper of the widow's destination. Have this as evidence of my good faith—' He tossed him a purse. 'There'll be another waiting for you at the White Horse.'

'Thank you, m'lord.' The coachman grinned as he weighed the purse in his palm. 'You'll know their bolthole soon enough, depend upon it.'

# Chapter Two

'Are you telling me you discovered nothing of use? Malgreave! Tregarrick! They're naught but small fry; we need to know who this damn woman is!' Sir William Cecil thrust his quill back into the ink-pot with such violence that ink splashed on to his fingers. 'For all we know, she could be waiting on the Lady Elizabeth as we speak!'

'I don't think so.' The Earl tipped back his chair and rested his expensively booted feet upon the edge of Cecil's writing table. 'In fact, I would lay money upon it—'

'You mean you know where she is?'

'And who.'

'What?' The word hissed through Cecil's teeth. Then, as he saw the gleam of amusement in the Earl's eyes, he drew himself up in his chair. 'You had best tell me all, m'lord, and quickly.'

Cecil listened to the Earl in silence, and when he had finished, remained sunk in thought for several minutes, his chin upon his hands.

'The Carey girl...' he said at last. 'If you had not

been my source, m'lord, I should never have believed
it. Henry Carey's daughter...' He shook his head.
'You say she has gone home to her parents. Mayfield
is the last place I should have looked for a traitor.'

'My thoughts exactly, sir.' The Earl shrugged. 'But
I cannot think her parents have any knowledge of her
treacherous activities. Lady Katharine was one of
Anne Boleyn's favourite ladies, and Lord Henry was
kin to her. I cannot see them raising a hand against
Queen Anne's child.'

'Nor I.' Cecil nodded agreement. 'The Careys have
been loyal to the Tudors since Bosworth. And they
stand to gain more than most when the Lady Elizabeth succeeds. Being kin to the Boleyns, they're
bound to be shown some favour.' He pulled thoughtfully at his beard. 'But Henry Carey was meant for
the old church before his elder brother died, and he
did wed his only daughter to Sherard, a staunch Catholic.'

'I see naught in that but political necessity,' the
Earl said. 'They've been out of favour since Queen
Mary came to the throne. You know how she regards
any that were close to the woman who displaced her
mother and made her a bastard. They probably rushed
into the match when it looked as if the Queen was
with child and that there would be a Catholic succession. I know of half a dozen other Protestant families
who made similar matches in the last year or so.'

'Aye, no doubt you're right.' Cecil pulled at his
beard thoughtfully. 'It is the daughter we must concentrate upon. What else do you know of—what's her

name?—something outlandish; I can never remember...'

'Seraphina,' supplied the Earl. 'It means the burning one.'

'Appropriate indeed, if she does prove to be our traitor.' Cecil laughed coldly. 'She could indeed burn.'

'True.' The Earl agreed without the least sign of humour. He had seen and heard enough of burnings for the thought to sicken him.

'What else do you know of her?' Cecil asked abruptly.

'Little enough, except...' The Earl shrugged his muscular shoulders and wondered how to relate what he had learned of Seraphina Carey to a man who was something of a prude.

'Except what, m'lord?' Cecil prompted impatiently.

'That she is a wanton and was unfaithful to her husband with every man that caught her eye...including her husband's groom.' The Earl's mouth twisted contemptuously. 'It seems she was as willing to betray her husband as she is her country.'

'And yet she had adopted his faith so fervently that she is prepared to take part in treason?' Cecil frowned. 'It does not make sense.'

'Do women ever make sense?' the Earl asked cynically, rubbing a hand over his close-cut black beard. 'The moment Elizabeth succeeds, we should arrest the chit, and drag the truth out of her.'

'And think what confidence that will inspire in the Lady Elizabeth's rule!' Cecil said sarcastically. 'The noble families of the old faith are already tempted to throw their weight behind the Stuart claim, because they fear Elizabeth may seek reprisals against them for her sister's persecution of Protestants! The Careys are related to half the nobility by blood and the rest by marriage! Arrest one of them without evidence that will convince the world of their guilt and you'll start a panic that could lose Elizabeth Tudor her kingdom. You're letting your prejudices fuddle your reason! Wantonness will not do as proof of treason!'

The Earl stiffened and his face set into a cold mask. Had the allusion to his late wife been made by one of his own rank, he would have challenged Cecil there and then—

'My lord.' Cecil sighed as his pale eyes followed the Earl's right hand to his sword-hilt. 'I meant no insult, but you know I am right.'

'Yes.' The Earl exhaled upon the word and unclenched the hand which had tightened upon his sword. 'I know we can't afford to alienate the Careys and their faction until Elizabeth's government is established and Catholic and Protestant alike realise they have naught to fear from her, so long as they are loyal to England... But what the devil are we to do about Sherard's widow! We cannot just let the matter rest; the danger to the Lady Elizabeth is too great.'

Cecil frowned thoughtfully. 'While Queen Mary lives, we have a little time and we must use it well. You must watch her closely, but avoid arousing her suspicions at all costs. If the French are alerted and use a different contact, we will be in an even worse position.'

'But how am I to watch her?' the Earl objected. 'I can scarce bribe the family servants to spy upon her!'

'I neither know nor care.' Anxiety made Cecil uncustomarily sharp. 'But it must be done; marry the girl if you have to!' He sighed impatiently. Then his pale, intelligent face relaxed into a smile. 'By heaven! That's the answer! Who has more right to oversee a woman's activities than her husband?'

'Sir, you know my feelings on marriage!' The Earl dropped his feet to the floor with a thump that made Cecil flinch. 'You cannot ask that of me!'

'But I can, can I not, Richard?'

The cool, pleasant voice came from the door which stood a little ajar. A moment later it opened to reveal a young woman with golden-red hair.

Both men got to their feet and made a deep bow, but the Lady Elizabeth Tudor waved them up impatiently.

'Well, Richard?' Her finely plucked brows lifted as she smiled at the Earl.

'Your Grace knows I will do anything to see you safe upon England's throne—'

'Then it is settled,' the Lady Elizabeth said sweetly, her dark eyes mischievous as they rested upon the Earl's thunderstruck countenance.

'But there must be a better way—' The Earl glanced at Cecil, hoping for support, and found none. 'The family might refuse my suit—'

'Stop clutching at straws, m'lord. The Careys will leap at the match and as for the girl—' Elizabeth grinned at him wickedly '—you're handsome enough and more than practised enough to turn the head of an eighteen-year-old girl.'

'Eighteen! God's breath, is that all? I did not expect her to be so young.'

'Why not?' the Lady Elizabeth asked tartly. 'I had to defend myself from charges of treason when I was but fifteen and my cousin Lady Jane lost her head at sixteen. Eighteen or eighty, it makes no difference, you should know that, Richard. Your late wife's youth did not make her incapable of deception and deceit, did it?'

The Earl's tawny eyes darkened to near black. That was a barb he could have taken from no one else without striking them. 'No, Your Grace,' he said stiffly. He had forgotten how sharp the Lady Elizabeth's claws could be. Sometimes he found it difficult to believe that she was only twenty-five, three years younger than himself.

'Well, m'lord, do not look so cast down. If she continues to dabble in treason, you will soon be a widower again.'

'And if she does not?' the Earl growled. 'I am shackled to a woman I have no desire to wed.'

Elizabeth laughed, her dark eyes shining. 'You could always try staying out of her bed. I am sure we could fashion an annulment for you then. It worked well for my stepmother from Flanders. You might find chastity a new experience for your jaded palate.'

'Thank you for your kind advice,' the Earl said drily, refusing to rise to the bait. 'May I go now, with your leave, madam?'

'Of course,' Elizabeth answered graciously. 'Where are you going?'

'Courting, Your Grace,' the Earl grated.

'Courting? Don't you mean wooing, m'lord?' Elizabeth corrected him with a taunting smile.

It was a smile that did little to improve the Earl's temper. It lingered in his mind as he shut the door carefully and then gave vent to his fury, swearing volubly as he stormed down the corridor. He was damned if he would marry again, not even for Elizabeth Tudor. One way or another, he would discover Seraphina Carey's secrets without having to step before the altar. The resolution cheered him a little and his grim, weathered face cracked into a smile. Eighteen and wanton with it; what was he worried about? Bed her he might, if he had to, but wed her he would not.

'You are fortunate, Seraphina; these cuts have knit more cleanly than I feared,' Lady Katherine Carey said dispassionately, as she smeared herbal ointment across the red weals and fading bruises which marred her daughter's white skin.

'Fortunate,' Seraphina echoed hollowly, pushing aside a wayward strand of fox-red hair from her face. 'If this is fortune, Mother, may God protect me from more of it!'

'Seraphina,' Lady Katherine sighed. 'It did not seem such a bad match at the time,' she murmured, half to herself.

'An excellent choice from your point of view, Mother.' Seraphina smiled bitterly. 'Was it not thoughtful of Edmund to die just when it seems that the Queen is not with child by dying? A Catholic alliance would have been exceedingly awkward when the Lady Elizabeth succeeds.'

'Seraphina!' Her mother paled. 'Do you think I care nought for anything except politics and wealth? Surely you cannot believe I should have countenanced the match if I'd thought he would ill-use you in a such a way?'

'I don't know.' Seraphina shrugged, her eyes cold as they met her mother's gaze. 'You made it clear enough at the time that the family took precedence over my happiness.'

'Yes,' Lady Katherine admitted, 'but I thought you were well enough suited; you said yourself you were grateful that he was young and comely, I even thought you were a little taken with him—'

'You need not remind me of my own foolishness,' Seraphina cut in icily. 'There has not been a day this last twelvemonth when I have not recalled it.'

'Daughter, if you would but tell me what went amiss—' Lady Katherine pleaded. 'Let me help—'

'You can help by leaving me in peace. I have no wish to speak of him—ever!'

'Seraphina...' Lady Katherine said helplessly and then stopped as her daughter's maid came out of an anteroom with a clean white linen shift.

'Have you finished, m'lady?' Bess asked hesitantly, seeing the expression on the older woman's face.

'Yes,' Lady Katherine replied defeatedly.

'There is a basin of warm water for your hands by

the linen chest,' Bess said as she dropped the shift over Seraphina's head.

Lady Katherine made her way slowly into the adjoining room. Bess had placed the pewter bowl of warm water and a square of clean linen on the wide stone windowsill. As she washed her hands she stared out unseeingly at the serene parkland which surrounded the manor of Mayfield. Her brow furrowed as she dried her hands meticulously on the square of coarse linen and wondered if she should have put Heywood off again. But how could she? She had used every excuse she could think of in the last three weeks, and the tone of his last letter, with its reference to the Lady Elizabeth's wishes, had been more insistent than polite. Her frown deepened. It was the third of November; he would be here in two days…and she still had not had the courage to tell Seraphina.

'Her back is mending nicely.' Bess broke into her thoughts as she came in and took out a mourning gown and white silk chemise from a clothes chest.

'Aye…' Lady Katherine nodded, 'but not her spirit. She jumps and starts at every shadow; she does not even go near her horses. If she would storm and rage at me for marrying her to Sherard, or weep, I'd be happier than to see her so cold, so bitter…and so afraid.'

'I'm sure in time, m'lady—'

'There is no time,' Lady Katherine answered wearily.

'M'lady?' Bess gave her a puzzled glance.

Lady Katherine gave a small shake of her head. She must tell Seraphina before word got out among the servants. She sighed heavily and sat down upon the window-ledge, her head bowed as she turned the piece of linen over and over in her hands.

'M'lady…can I help?'

Lady Katherine lifted her face 'Watch her closely for me, Bess. Yesterday, she was by the banqueting house upon the roof, right by the parapet, and for a moment…and when she finds out what I have to tell her…'

'Oh, my lady, not do even think such a thing!' Bess crossed herself instinctively.

'I can not help it, Bess. I lost five of my six children to the sweating sickness when you and Seraphina were but infants…and I cannot count the number of times I have begged God to spare my last child. If I were to lose her as well…' Lady Katherine's voice tailed off.

Bess's pretty, dimpled face crumpled in sympathy. 'Don't fret so, m'lady. You have been so kind and patient; I am certain Lady Seraphina will soon be herself again.'

Lady Katherine took a sudden sharp breath and stood up. The crumpled piece of linen fell unnoticed from her hands as she relaxed her clenched fingers.

'Of course! Why did I not think of it sooner!' Some of the tension left her face. 'I am a fool, Bess, anxiety must have fuddled my wits! Thank you, Bess!'

'For what?' Bess's cornflower-blue eyes were puzzled.

'For reminding me how to manage my own daughter! You shall have a new gown for it!' Lady Katherine replied, as she swept back into her daughter's bedchamber, leaving a bemused Bess to follow with her weighty armful of velvet and silk.

Lost in the maze of her own thoughts, Seraphina stood impassively while Bess fastened her petticoats and black silk kirtle about her tiny waist. She winced as she raised her arms to allow Bess to draw on her heavy black velvet gown.

'You must take care to be a more obedient wife to your next husband,' Lady Katherine said, watching her coldly. 'You always were an undutiful child; perhaps you have now learnt your lesson.'

Obedient! Seraphina jolted in disbelief. How could her mother be so callous? She wheeled to face her, tugging the half-fastened laces of her gown from Bess's fingers and sending another wave of pain across her back.

'How dare you say I—I deserved this?' Her green eyes were iridescent with anger as she met her mother's impassive gaze. 'You are no better than Edmund; the only difference is that you punish me with your tongue instead of with your hands!'

'I should not be so sure of that, Daughter!' Lady Katherine hissed coldly.

Both of the younger women stared at her. Seraphina was white faced and tight lipped, and Bess open-mouthed at Lady Katherine's harshness.

'Leave us!' Lady Katherine gestured sharply to Bess.

After one fleeting glance at Seraphina's ashen face, Bess caught up the skirt of her blue worsted gown and fled.

'Have you no feeling for me, Mother?' Seraphina demanded; as the heavy oak door shut behind Bess.

'Feelings! You have always felt too much.' Lady Katherine was icily dismissive. 'What matters is duty. You are a Carey, your father's only heir. You owe it to him to produce a grandson and to your brothers and sisters—God rest them.'

'My brothers and sisters! I thought you would not forbear to mention them!' Seraphina laughed mirthlessly. Henry, Ann, Kate, Edward and Thomas. She knew them only as the sad little list of names on the family tomb. And yet they had always been present in her life. All through her childhood they had been held up to her as examples, against which she had always felt lacking. Resentment and anger made her reckless as she met her mother's disapproving stare. 'I can scarce believe that I came from the same womb as those paragons of perfection. No doubt you wish that one of them had survived in my place, Mother; I wish I had died with them, then you might at least love me a little!'

Lady Katherine gasped as if she had been struck and went as pale as her daughter.

Seraphina instantly regretted her words, knowing that she had been unfair. However harsh her mother had been at times, she knew she was loved by both her parents. Shocked by her own outburst, she groped for the words to make an adequate apology, but her mother forestalled her.

'Ungrateful, undutiful child! How dare you say such a thing?' Lady Katherine's voice cracked across the room like a whiplash.

'Undutiful?' Seraphina flared, the impulse to apologise forgotten as she smarted at the injustice of the accusation. 'How can you say that? Did I demur when you instructed me to marry Edmund?'

'This is past.' Lady Katherine was icy. 'I am speaking of the present, but since you are evidently out of humour we will discuss these matters later.'

'You may discuss them all you like, Mother, but do not expect me to talk of marriage! I have had sufficient of it to last me a lifetime!'

'You should give some thought to it, even if you will not speak of it,' Lady Katherine said, with a dangerous calm which Seraphina knew only too well. 'The Earl of Heywood has asked for your hand.'

'The Earl of Heywood!' She stared at her mother in disbelief. 'After what Edmund did to me, you would have me wed *him?* 'Tis common knowledge he despises women except for one purpose…and there are some who say his first wife did not die of any natural cause—'

'Idle gossip by jealous tongues!' her mother snapped. 'You know nothing of him except rumour. And even if it is true, it matters not. We cannot refuse a man of the Earl's position and potential influence and you know it.' Lady Katherine added implacably, 'If you wed the Earl, the whole family will benefit once the Lady Elizabeth becomes Queen; he is a favourite of hers…'

'Isn't Mayfield enough for you? We lack for nothing!'

'And what about your Ashley cousins, Ann and Jane? They too suffered because of my association with Anne Boleyn. After five years of exile from court, my sister can scarce scrape together the money to put cloth on their backs. Marry the Earl and you will be in a position to get them a place at court and find them husbands.'

'So that is the price of my happiness! A rich husband apiece for Ann and Jane!'

'You must learn to make your happiness out of what God gives you,' Lady Katherine retorted. 'Once you are wed, I dare say you will get on well enough.'

'That is what you said when I wed Edmund!' Seraphina's voice cracked as memories, vivid and terrifying, flashed into her mind. At Sherard House, she had screamed for help. No servant had dared intervene, because it was a husband's right to treat his wife as he chose. If Grace had not ordered the door broken down she would have been dead. And now she almost wished she were. She lifted her eyes to her mother's face. 'I will not wed him,' she stated flatly. 'I will not.'

'You will do as you are bidden.' If Lady Katherine was moved by the desperation in her daughter's voice, she gave no sign of it.

'Then you send me to my death! I should rather kill myself than wed again!' The words wrenched themselves of their own volition from Seraphina's lips, and she could scarce believe she had uttered them.

Neither could her mother, judging by the shocked expression upon her face.

'I did not mean—' Seraphina began hopelessly.

'I trust not. Disobedience is sin enough!' Lady

Katherine grated. 'I shall await you in the solar; when you have remembered both your manners and your filial duty, you may bring me your apology.'

'Then you will have a goodly wait,' Seraphina seared, her hands clenching on the velvet skirt of her gown until her knuckles were white. Pointedly, she turned her back.

Lady Katherine hesitated, a flicker of uncertainty passed over her face, and one of her hands reached out tentatively towards Seraphina. Then, as she studied the straightbacked, defiant form of her daughter, she withdrew it, a half-smile coming to her lips. She turned and left without another word.

As the door closed behind her mother, Seraphina picked up a pewter candlestick and hurled it. It struck the door with a resounding crash. And then she crumpled, falling to her knees on the rushes, her head in her hands as she began to cry, in gasping, painful sobs.

Outside Lady Katherine leant against the doorframe and uttered a small, silent prayer of relief.

'Everything all right, Kate?' Lord Henry Carey asked his wife a moment later as he stepped out a room further along the gallery.

'Never better,' Lady Katherine assured her spouse. 'Seraphina threw a candlestick at me when I told her she must marry Heywood. And now she is weeping at last, God be praised!'

'Amen to that!' Lord Carey's scholarly face lit up with relief. Although he was more than a little absent-minded and inclined to live in the world of his books, he was very fond of his daughter. 'I was beginning to fear…' He broke off and sighed.

'So was I.' Lady Katherine's eyes met her husband's in perfect understanding.

'Kate?' Her husband's smile faded. 'You're crying…'

'Nonsense.' Lady Katherine scrubbed at her eyes with her hand as her husband put an arm about her shoulders. 'It's just this match with Heywood. It is too soon. It cannot be easy for her…'

'Mmm…' Lord Carey frowned. 'You are sure that he will—well, be kind?' He coughed in embarrassment, having always left such matters to his wife. 'We could put him off.'

'And offend the Lady Elizabeth, who has suggested it?' His wife shook her head. 'We cannot risk it, Henry; you know as well as I the family needs royal favour. And besides, my brother likes him well enough, and if he is half the man his father was I think there is naught to fear, for all his reputation.'

'Aye,' Lord Carey agreed. 'Robert Durrant was a good man.' He smiled and his blue eyes took on a faraway look. 'D'you know, once I thought that I might lose you to him.'

'Robert Durrant!' His wife laughed, her face softening. 'You were never in danger of that. If I had wed Robert Durrant, our house would have been like a galleon with two captains.'

'True,' Lord Carey said gravely.

'You do not have to agree with me, Henry! Am I such a termagant?'

'Yes.' Her husband smiled. 'Now, I remember

what I was coming to ask you. I have a letter to write. Where have you put my spectacles, Kate?'

'Your spectacles are where you left them.' Lady Katherine sighed with affectionate impatience. 'On top of the clothes press in our bedchamber.'

'Thank you, m'dear,' said Lord Carey, turning back towards the room he had just left.

'And don't get ink on your sleeves; it will not come out of the velvet.' Lady Katherine called after his re-treating figure without much optimism.

Then, gathering her heavy, fur-lined overgown around her, she swept through the long gallery with a smile on her face, humming the tune of a galliard that she had danced in front of King Henry when she was a girl. Seraphina and Robert Durrant's boy. It would be all right; she could feel it in her bones.

Forewarned by the silken rustle of Lady Carey's petticoats, Bess put renewed effort into her polishing of an oak chest that stood at the end of the gallery, taking care to work the sweet cicely oil well into the linenfold panels. She had no wish to be the next object of Lady Katherine's rage. But, as she bobbed a hasty curtsy, she nearly sat down in astonishment. Lady Katherine appeared to be in the best of humours.

'Ah, Bess. Go to your mistress in a little while and tell her that I shall be most displeased if she does not complete her needlework this afternoon,' Lady Katherine said, thinking that, if she knew her daughter, the message would ensure Seraphina did the exact opposite. In fact she would wager that her daughter would be out in the park within the hour. Some fresh air would improve the girl's appetite and restore the colour to her face, she thought with satisfaction.

'Yes, m'lady,' Bess answered in amazement. And for a full minute Bess stood staring after Lady Katherine. She could not be certain, but she would have sworn that Lady Katherine was singing.

## Chapter Three

Two days later the Earl of Heywood halted his bay mare beneath the stand of oaks on a knoll that overlooked the estate of Mayfield. Below and to the left was a great wood, every tree a fiery mass in the autumn sunshine; to the right lay the well-tilled fields and pastures of Mayfield. Beyond that, circling the horizon, were the gentle, rolling Wiltshire downs. It was a view that had made many men wish for nothing more than to spend the rest of their lives in such a peaceful and pleasant spot, but the Earl took no pleasure in it. His dislike of the task ahead of him had waxed with every mile that brought him closer to Mayfield. Why the devil had he let Elizabeth Tudor and William Cecil talk him into this; surely there was another way to discover exactly what Sherard's widow was plotting without arousing her suspicions. Damnation! One wanton wife was more than enough for any man. His face twisted with the pain he always felt when he thought of Lettice; beguiling, beautiful and utterly treacherous. Sunk in unpleasant memories, he didn't even start as his companion pulled up his horse beside him.

'God's teeth, Richard!' the grey-haired man said a little breathlessly as he glanced at the Earl. 'Why the face? If it gets any longer your tailor could use it as his yardstick! Doesn't the prospect of inheriting a house hereabouts please you?'

'The country has great beauty, Tom.' He dragged his thoughts back to the present and forced his hawkish features into a smile.

'Not half as much as my niece.' Lord Musgrave grinned, slapping the Earl on the shoulder. 'When you marry her, Richard, you'll be the envy of every man in England.'

'Tom, the matter is not settled yet,' the Earl of Heywood said a little impatiently to prevent Lord Musgrave launching into another catalogue of his niece's virtues. During the last three weeks he had done some delving into Seraphina Carey's history and, if what he had heard was true, half the men in England had already sampled her delights.

'It will be when you see her,' Lord Musgrave laughed confidently.

'Perhaps.' The Earl was non-committal.

Seeing he was not to be drawn, Lord Musgrave changed the subject. 'I hear the Queen is dying and they do not give her until the end of the month? Is it true?'

'So Cecil told me.'

'I cannot think there will be many in England who will mourn her passing,' Lord Musgrave said, frowning. 'She's made one blunder after another, beginning with her marriage to that damned Spaniard.'

'Aye,' the Earl agreed. 'But we are to be spared the ultimate folly at least. Cecil has been assured that the Queen will recognise the Lady Elizabeth as her heir by right and law.'

'God be praised!' Lord Musgrave slapped his horse's neck in delight. 'I feared she would name the Stuart chit! That's the best news I've had in months!'

'Aye,' the Earl agreed sombrely. 'But we are not out of the wood yet. The French, the Spanish and the Pope would all give much to ensure Elizabeth is never crowned.'

'Please God she will be spared,' Lord Musgrave said fervently.

'Amen to that,' the Earl replied, wondering what Lord Musgrave would say if he knew his precious niece was plotting to assassinate Elizabeth so that the Queen of Scots might be offered the throne. He did not relish the prospect of breaking such a piece of news to a man who had been a loyal friend both to his father and himself. With an effort he forced a smile to his lips. 'Let us make haste, Tom; you have filled me with impatience to see this niece of yours.'

''Twill be nought to your impatience to wed her once you've set eyes on her,' Lord Musgrave boasted cheerfully as they set their horses into a fast canter.

The Earl gave a hollow laugh, unable to form a convincing answer in words. Then, before the older man could say any more, he urged his mare forward, down the steep, rutted, chalk track which led to the Mayfield estate.

'Gates of hell!' A few minutes later the Earl swore violently as his mare stumbled almost to her knees, nearly throwing him over her head. A man with slower physical reactions would almost certainly have been thrown, but somehow the Earl retained his balance as the mare lurched forward again. But he reined in immediately and swung down from the saddle.

'What is it, Richard?' Lord Musgrave asked, bringing his own horse to a halt and glancing back over his shoulder.

'She's cast a shoe,' the Earl answered, with some relief, as Pavanne was his favourite mount and he had feared worse damage. He lifted her forefoot and wrenched the flapping shoe free of the remaining nails. 'You'd best go on ahead; I'll walk her the rest of the way.'

''Twill be hours before our servants catch up with us; I'll send one of the grooms from the house with another horse,' Lord Musgrave called, and then urged his own horse forward again.

'Steady boy, steady!' Seraphina admonished her chestnut colt as she put him at the ditch that marked the edge of the wood. The gawkish colt cleared the ditch easily with a mighty but ungainly leap and landed awkwardly, skidding on the damp leaves which carpeted the ground. Instinctively she loosed the reins, giving him his head so that he could find his balance. She laughed carelessly as he took instant advantage, seizing the bit in his teeth and bounding forward in great ground-skimming strides. Her father's groom had been right; once he'd gained a few manners and a little sense there would not be a horse in the county to touch him. Exhilarated by his speed, she urged him on until grass, trees and sky merged into a blur of colour. Then ahead of her was the stone boundary-wall of the estate, tall and formidable. The wall her parents had expressly forbidden her ever to attempt again after she had come close to breaking her neck some years ago. But what if she did? she decided in a moment of recklessness. Death or marriage to Heywood! In her opinion, there was little to choose between them! The colt seemed to share her mood. Head high, ears pricked, snorting and snatching at the bit, he sped towards the wall. Too fast. Shortening the reins, she tried in vain to slow him. He had the bit clamped in his teeth and refused to respond. With all her attention fixed upon controlling the colt, she didn't see the man standing some fifty paces to her right.

'God's teeth!' The Earl swore aloud as he realised that, far from being bolted as he had first assumed when he had seen the horse and rider emerged from the woods, the woman meant to jump the wall. Something he would have thought twice about on Pavanne, let alone an unschooled and gawky colt. As he watched the slender, green-gowned figure struggle to control the mettlesome animal, he found himself caught between admiration for her skill and a presentiment of disaster. As he had half expected, the colt got far too close to the wall before its forefeet lifted to begin the leap. It twisted, slewing sideways, first one way, then the other. To his amazement, the woman had managed to stay in the saddle; though not for long, he thought grimly, starting to run as the horse reared up and almost toppled backwards, before plunging down and kicking its hindlegs up towards the sky.

No rider could survive that sort of buck and, even as the thought went through his head, the woman flew over the colt's shoulder and landed with a sickening thump at the base of the wall.

'Damnation!' He increased his pace, fearing he might already be too late.

Seraphina lay gasping for breath among a drift of fallen leaves which the wind had blown against the base of the wall. In the moment the colt had thrown her, she had discovered that she did care very much whether or not she lived to see the next day. And it was with deep relief that she realised that the leaves had saved her from anything worse than a few new bruises. She sat up slowly, furious with herself. To put such an inexperienced colt at the wall had been stupid and selfish…she could have broken Jupiter's legs as well as her own neck. The pheasant's feather in her cap had snapped and hung down drunkenly before her eyes. With an unladylike oath she threw off her gloves, plucked it out, and then rubbed at her right elbow and shoulder, which had taken the worse of the fall.

'I see you have come to little harm, through no effort of your own.' The voice was dry, amused and very male.

Startled, she twisted around and found herself confronted by a pair of long riding boots, made of the finest black spanish leather, as were the breeches that fitted the muscular thighs like a second skin. She looked up hastily and found her gaze arrested by mocking golden-brown eyes framed by lashes which were as black as his hair and close-cropped beard.

His eyes held hers for a moment and then dropped down to her lips that had parted in surprise, and on to the bodice of her habit.

Who was he to look at her in such a fashion? A mixture of fear and anger constricted her breathing as she endured his scrutiny. Her marriage to Edmund had taught her a bitter lesson about a man's superior physical strength. And, she thought, as she noted the muscled strength of his shoulders and arms, to compare this man to Edmund was like matching an oak tree against a willow wand. For the first time in years she found herself wishing she had obeyed her mother's instructions and had a groom accompany her. She also bitterly regretted the impulse that had made her select her oldest habit that morning. She had worn it out of contrariness, simply because her mother had insisted that, as a widow, she should wear mourning at all times. The faded and patched sage-green habit had been made for her when she was little more than a girl and Bess had found it difficult to make the laces meet across her breasts. For all it hid of her curves she might as well have been naked.

Yet she could not bring herself to avert her gaze. There was something naggingly familiar about his face which made her stare. No. She could not have met him before; this was not a face you would forget. It was strong, the jaw and cheekbones clearly defined and un-swept, the nose straight and fine, the mouth...there was something about the hawkish curve of his sensual mouth which sent a *frisson* of warning along her spine. This man was a predator, used to taking what he wanted, when he wanted.

The curve of the Earl's lips increased a little as he saw her shiver and guessed the direction of her thoughts.

'You need not be afraid. I mean you no harm.'

'I am not afraid of you,' she lied vehemently, dropping her lashes over her eyes.

'Perhaps not, since you seem to have no fear of death,' the Earl conceded, with the merest raise of his straight black brows. 'I trust you have good reason for wishing to break your neck.'

The indolent drawl and mocking brows erased her fear and replaced it with straightforward anger. She was in no mood for masculine condescension, even if he was dark and handsome as the devil himself.

'I am to be wed!' she snapped, her eyelids flashing upwards as she met his provoking tawny stare. 'Is that not reason enough for any woman of sense?'

'Or any man,' the Earl agreed, unruffled. He had meant simply to offer his assistance in catching her horse and to send her on her way. But now he found his curiosity aroused, and the task ahead of him momentarily forgotten. No lady would ride astride and alone, yet her speech was that of a gentlewoman. A steward's daughter in a hand-me-down gown, educated with the daughter of a great house? he mused. Or some noble-man's by-blow? Even sitting among the leaves with a smudge of mud on her cheeks she had an air that would not have disgraced a royal duchess. He found himself smiling at her. 'Had I known what was in store for me when I wed, I may have been equally careless of my neck.'

''Tis a pity you weren't,' she retorted, her temper more than rekindled by what she interpreted as more mockery. 'Then you would not have been here to laugh at my misfortune!'

'That would have been my loss,' the Earl returned smoothly, as his eyes made another lazy journey from her face to her slender waist.

'And my gain,' she said sarcastically, before pausing to wonder if it were wise to provoke a stranger when there was no help in shouting distance. But, to her relief, he showed no sign of anger, but merely flung back his head and laughed.

'I see you have a wit to match your beauty, maid.'

He grinned at her with a familiarity she found as disturbing as his compliment. It was a shock to realise that he had assumed she was of lesser rank. An understandable mistake, given her gown and lack of an escort, yet it irked her none the less.

'I am more often told I have a temper to match my hair,' she warned huffily, giving him a challenging look.

'Since it is hidden beneath your hood, I cannot be the judge of that. But no doubt it is the basest calumny.'

'Then your judgement is as poor as mine was in attempting that wall on Jupiter,' she retorted, further irritated by the mockery that lurked in the curve of his mouth and slant of his black brows.

'By God! I hope not!' the Earl replied with feeling.

'You don't have to agree with such alacrity!' She tried hard to cling to her anger, but somehow as his amused brown eyes caught hers again, she found her own lips curving upwards. 'All right!' she confessed with a smile. 'I was a little foolish.'

'A little?' His black brows lifted. 'I take it from your willingness to risk your life that your husband to be is not of your choosing.'

'He would not be of any woman's choosing,' she replied defensively, her smile fading as she thought of the marriage that lay ahead of her.

'They have found you some old dodderer with a house and a chest of plate, I suppose,' the Earl went on sympathetically, guessing from the state of her gown that such possessions would represent a fortune to her parents. It was a common enough fate for a beautiful girl with no dowry. And it would be a shameful waste he thought, appreciating the almond-shaped green eyes under the finely arched brows, vivid against her flawless ivory skin, and the generous mouth, with that tantalising provocative pout to the lower lip.

'He is near thirty and a widower,' Seraphina answered absently, having been distracted by his stare to the extent that she forgot he was a stranger and had no right to ask her such impertinent questions.

'A great age.' The Earl laughed wryly. That put him in his place; no doubt at twenty-eight he seemed impossibly old to a girl of what, he glanced at her face again, perhaps seventeen at the most. 'But a little experience may not make a man such a bad husband.'

'He has too much experience!' Seraphina said bitterly. 'They say that if he had a garter from each lady who has visited his bed he could garland Westminster Abbey.'

'If he has any wits he will eschew them all for you.'

Seraphina flushed scarlet and dropped her gaze hastily to the ground. She had received compliments before from several young men before her marriage, but never from a man whose eyes promised far greater pleasures than those given by his pretty words.

The Earl had to suppress a laugh. For all her outspokenness and defiance, it was obvious she was very inexperienced in the ways of the world. Having no wish to embarrass her further, he offered to catch the colt.

Hearing the undercurrent of laughter in his voice, Seraphina thanked him stiffly, without looking up. So, he thought her as green as her horse, did he? But she'd wager he'd not be quite so superior in a minute or two. The last time Jupiter had got loose, it had taken her father and half-a-dozen grooms three hours to catch him.

As he moved slowly towards the colt, she stood up and made a half-hearted effort to brush off some of the dry leaves that clung to her skirts. But her eyes were on the tall dark figure that stood a yard or two from the browsing colt; he was murmuring softly, his hand outstretched. She smiled as Jupiter's head came up and he blew suspiciously at the stranger. He had played this game before. But then the colt stepped forward, nuzzling at the man's fingers, and making no protest as he caught up its trailing reins. She was faintly disappointed, but somehow not surprised. There was a warmth in his voice, a seductiveness in his hands, as he caressed the colt's velvety muzzle, that would gentle the wildest creature…or woman. If Edmund had been such a man, if he had smiled at her like that, touched her with such gentleness…just once. But he hadn't. She had been a disappointment to Edmund in every sense…and if she had not pleased Edmund, how could she hope to please a sophisticate like Heywood, used to the company of witty and beautiful women?

'You are sure you can manage him?' the Earl asked, as he brought the colt to a standstill beside her. He was puzzled by the expression on her face. She looked desolate, defeated.

'No…' Seraphina answered absently, her thoughts still on Heywood. 'I doubt I ever will.'

The Earl's eyes softened as they dwelt on her face and saw the fear and uncertainty in her eyes. 'I was referring to the colt,' the Earl said quietly, as she stood staring into space, apparently having forgotten his presence.

'Oh…' She stared at him, startled by his perception. He was a stranger and yet he had read her thoughts so easily. 'Yes…' she answered belatedly, dropping her gaze to the safety of the ground as hot colour rose in her cheeks. 'The fall was my fault for overfacing him.' She went on too quickly, 'He is manageable enough most times.'

'Unlike the man they wish you to wed?'

'Yes…' she answered without thinking, again caught unawares by the ease with which he seemed to follow her thoughts. 'I don't know. I have not met him yet, but naught I have heard of him gives me much cheer...' She stopped, horrified by what she was confiding in a stranger. 'I had better be getting back.' She spoke too hastily again. 'Before Jupiter is missed...'

'You are not supposed to ride him!' the Earl guessed accurately.

'No, my father says he is too much like me in character.'

'Headstrong?' he teased. For no reason he could define, he wanted to drive the shadows from her green eyes, make her smile again.

'Ill-disciplined,' she corrected him ironically as she remembered Edmund's efforts to correct that particular fault in her character.

'Then I had better help you mount and get on your way, before your father discovers that he is correct.' The Earl laughed as he untwisted her stirrup leather and checked the saddle girth.

'Yes.' Her voice came out all wrong, as he turned to her, and put his hands on her waist. The sudden dizzying leap of her heart and flesh took her utterly unawares, as did the overwhelming, nagging sense of familiarity, that made her half expect him to take her in his arms, to hold her, protect her. But this was madness. He was married. A stranger. A moment ago she would have sworn she would have felt nothing but revulsion at any man's touch. And now...now a stranger had made her laugh, touched her, and it was as if a wellshaft had opened at her feet. One step more and she would be lost. She stared up at him helplessly, her silver-green eyes wide, utterly bewildered, and then the blood left her face, leaving her ashen.

He knew, just as he had seemed to know her thoughts before.

She heard his sharp intake of breath. The moment in which he should simply have lifted her into the saddle lingered and passed as his eyes held hers and darkened from amused amber to deep, knowing brown.

'Look at your betrothed but once in such a fashion and he will never leave your side.' His voice was low, husky, for once empty of mockery. Somehow, imperceptibly, the way his hands rested on her waist changed subtly. What had been a courteous gesture was now the beginnings of an embrace. Slowly, almost lazily, he drew her closer, until the space between them was no more than the breath of a piece of parchment. A heartbeat more and he would kiss her. Edmund had kissed her. *Once.* The memory tumbled her into instant, overwhelming panic. She jerked back, her eyes wide with fear.

The Earl released her at once, and made no comment, except for the silent, questioning lift of his straight black brows.

'You were helping me mount my horse, sir.' Feeling foolish, she blurted out the first thing that came into her head as her panic receded.

'So I was,' he answered drily as their eyes met again. 'I had forgotten.'

*And so had I;* the thought shocked her. But it was true. For a moment she had forgotten past and future, forgotten who she was and that he was a stranger.

Her mind had registered only the warmth in his lazy golden eyes, the curve of his mouth, the latent strength in his fingers as they tightened on her waist. She had wanted him to touch her—kiss her. The realisation sent her into deeper shock. She had been so sure that Edmund had killed such feelings, so sure that she would be immune to any man's blandishments or caresses, and now...she knew she was wrong. Aware suddenly that he was staring at her, she took a deep breath and did her best to appear cool. 'Then perhaps it is as well I reminded you,' she said without daring to meet his gaze.

'Yes,' he agreed, with a half-smile which did not reach his eyes. 'It is.' He held out his hands to her in an ironic invitation. 'With your permission?'

She inclined her head in a stiff nod of assent.

He picked her up easily and put her in the saddle, holding her no longer than was absolutely necessary. But it made no difference, her heart still skipped a beat as her body registered the contact.

Glancing up at her averted face, the Earl exhaled raggedly. What the devil had he been thinking of? Playing games with a virgin who had not made up her mind if she were willing or not! His mouth curved in sudden self-mockery. He hadn't been thinking. Touching her had been like taking a sip of heady wine; it left you craving for more. Not even Lettice had kindled such a swift, fierce desire in him. And putting her out of reach had done nothing to lessen his hunger. He laughed softly. He had evaded the snares of a dozen court beauties, but this green girl had almost caught him in her nets without trying.

For a moment Seraphina was aware of nothing but relief. He had let her go. And then, as she risked a look at his dark, amused face, she found herself utterly confused. She was angry. Humiliated. But for all the wrong reasons. Try as she might, she could not feel outraged at the way he had held her, whispered to her as if she were a tavern wench. Her anger was because he had put her aside so easily, because he could stand there smiling, at ease, when she had been shaken to the core.

Jerking her gaze away, she straightened the skirt of her habit and fished for the stirrups with her feet. She swore, half audibly as one of the leathers tangled in her petticoats.

'Here.' He reached out, caught her booted foot and guided it into the iron.

'Thank you.' She had meant to retrieve her pride, to sound cool, polite, but failed miserably as their eyes collided again. She wanted to cry out at the unfairness of it. Why must fate choose this moment to show her that it was possible for a man to set your flesh alight with a touch, or stop your heart with a smile? For the first time in her life she regretted being born a Carey, regretted being the heiress to Mayfield. Just for a day, an hour even, she wanted to be free from the duties and obligations of rank, of conscience.

'If I were free…' The regret in his voice mirrored her own thoughts, so exactly that she wondered for a moment if she had been insane enough to speak them aloud.

'But you are not.' She answered too quickly, betraying far more than she knew.

'No,' he agreed harshly. 'I am not. I have a duty…'
He could not prevent his mouth curling derisively on
the word, as he thought of how different Seraphina
Carey was likely to be from this transparent girl, who
had not even learnt to disguise her feelings. 'As do
you,' he added more gently.

'You think I could forget it?' She laughed a little
desperately.

'No, I suppose not,' the Earl said, looking away
from her green eyes. 'It may not be as bad as you
fear.' Without knowing why, he tried to cheer her.
'From what you say, he must be lusty enough, and I
can assure that to be near thirty does not quite put
you in your dotage.'

'His age does not matter. It is his vanity and con-
ceit,' Seraphina answered with a bitter smile. 'People
say he even had hopes of the Lady Eliza…'

She stilled her tongue just in time, remembering he
was a stranger. Nobles and commoners alike had gone
to the Tower for lesser slanders than that against the
house of Tudor. Seeing the sudden blankness on his
face, she felt acutely embarrassed. What a fool he
must think her! Falling from her horse, behaving one
moment like a lightskirt, the next a schoolroom
maiden and then prattling of a man she had never met.

'I have detained you too long, sir,' she said
abruptly, taking up the slack in her reins. 'Thank you
for your assistance.'

'Wait!' He caught the colt's head, halting it. 'I
could see that your husband does not have the opportunity to cause you too much misery. I could find
an office for him in my household? I have need of a

steward on one of my smaller estates. It would keep him busy enough to leave him little time for philandering.' And to leave yourself time to indulge in a little with a discontented wife, said a cynical voice inside his head. It was not a wholly unpleasant thought. He smiled at her. 'What say you?'

'It…it is most kind of you, sir,' Seraphina stammered in astonishment. As the Lady Seraphina Carey, she had never been in need of patronage in her entire life and she had been completely taken aback by his unexpected generosity. But then, as she imagined the reaction of the ambitious Earl of Heywood to such an offer, the humour of the situation struck her. 'But I doubt he would accept it.' Hard as she tried, she could not disguise her mirth.

'Why not!' asked the Earl, more than a little piqued by her reaction and change of mood.

'Because he is the Earl of Heywood,' she spluttered, her still-tender ribs aching with the effort of containing her laughter. That would teach him to judge by appearances, she thought, her eyes dancing with laughter. He looked as if he had been pole-axed.

'You are Seraphina Carey?' the Earl rasped. This was not the woman he had expected to find beneath that black veil. Damn it! All that wide-eyed innocence and pale vulnerability! She had pulled the wool over his eyes as easily as if he were as green as spring grass. He had come to deceive her, and had fallen at the first hurdle!

'Lady Seraphina,' she corrected him a little uneasily, her merriment dying as his eyes stabbed into hers like blades of polished jet.

'Then perhaps I had better introduce myself,' the Earl said tersely, furiously angry at his own stupidity. If nothing else, marriage to Lettice should have taught him never to judge by appearances. 'Though by your amusement, I suspect you already know my name.' He bowed with cold formality. 'Richard Durrant, Earl of Heywood, at your service, m'lady.'

'You…' For a fraction of a second her heart soared, and then as he continued to stare at her disdainfully, she felt the beginnings of panic as she recalled every word of their conversation. 'I…' she stammered, 'I was not making mock… I did not know who you were; you said you were married…'

'Was married; my wife died. As you must well know.' He was icy, contemptuous. 'So can we abandon this masque, *m'lady*.'

'It was no charade. How was I to recognise you? You…you are not what I expected…'

'Nor are you, m'lady,' he answered coldly, raking her with his eyes. 'I did not know it was the fashion for widows to ride out alone in pursuit of *sport.*'

His meaning was insultingly obvious, but she could find no answer to his barb. A mixture of misery and fear stilled her tongue. The look on his face, the contempt in his voice was all too familiar. He had judged her and found her lacking in everything a man wished for in a wife; just as Edmund had.

Disappointment, bitter as gall, put out the tiny flicker of hope she had felt on learning his identity. She *would* rather die than wed him! Her vision blurring with hot angry tears, she brought the reins down on Jupiter's neck.

'God's teeth!' The Earl leapt aside as the colt bounded forward, almost trampling him underfoot. 'Don't be such a damn fool!' he added, realising her intention a moment later. But it was too late. Horse and rider were no more than a stride from the wall. The Earl held his breath as the chestnut colt soared into the air, clearing the wall by a foot or more. It was only as they landed, and sped away across the park that he exhaled slowly. So that was Seraphina Carey! His mouth twisted into a sudden grim smile. He doubted that he would need to marry her to achieve his purpose. Whatever else had been a charade, the flare of physical attraction between them had been real enough? A week or two at the most should be enough to achieve what Cecil wanted. Few women could keep a secret in bed.

# Chapter Four

It was late afternoon before Seraphina let the colt amble across the park towards her home. It was a hotchpotch of a house, she thought, viewing it with increased clarity now she knew she would soon have to leave it again. The great façade of tall windows her grandfather had added in Henry VII's reign didn't quite match the style of the original fourteenth-century manor house, but in the late afternoon sunshine its silver-grey stone and gleaming glass gave it a serene, quiet beauty. She sighed, halting the colt as she watched a flight of her father's doves flutter down to roost among the chimneys. All through her marriage to Edmund she had clung to the idea of Mayfield as a haven, but not any longer. He was there. At this moment he was probably complaining of her outrageous behaviour in the park. But perhaps that was not such a bad thing; perhaps he would change his mind about wishing to wed her. That was it! The solution was so simple! Why had she not thought of it before? All she had to do was behave so badly that no sane man would contemplate taking her for a wife!

'M'lady! M'lady!'

She jolted at the shout. Looking in the direction from which it had come, she saw Dickon, the son of her father's steward, approaching as fast as his fat and sweating roan gelding would allow.

'I've been looking for you all over, m'lady!' Dickon said breathlessly as he reached her and pulled up his horse. 'Lady Katherine said you are to return to the house immediately.' He stopped abruptly as he noticed the mud and leaves that clung to the soft wool of Seraphina's habit. 'You've fallen, m'lady; are you hurt?'

'I hurt nought but my pride, Dickon,' Seraphina said wryly. 'Jupiter and I had a disagreement over the boundary wall.'

'The boundary wall! You could have been killed, m'lady,' Dickon scolded 'You should take more care.'

'I could see little reason to at the time,' Seraphina said half to herself.

'Not all men are as Lord Sherard, m'lady,' Dickon said sympathetically.

'Aren't they?' She laughed dully. 'What does my mother want of me?' she asked, though she already guessed the answer.

Dickon glanced at her pale face and then reddened and cleared his throat. 'M'lady,' he began tentatively. 'Your mother said not to tell you, lest you refused to come in.'

'I see.' She sighed. 'There was a time, Dickon, when you would never have taken my mother's part 'gainst me.'

Dickon went redder. 'We are not children any longer, m'lady; the days when you, me and Bess ran wild in the park are over. But if you must know, we have visitors from court—'

'The Earl of Heywood,' Seraphina broke in wryly.

'You know?' There was surprise on Dickon's ruddy face.

'Yes,' she answered distantly, realising that he could not have told her mother of their unorthodox meeting in the park. Perhaps he did not care for others to know when he had made a fool of himself. Vain as well as conceited, she decided, her mouth twisting with distaste.

'Lady Katherine said you are to make yourself presentable before coming to her,' Dickon added, with the expression of someone trying to step upon eggshells without breaking them.

'So she wishes to dangle me like a gilded doll in front of the prospective groom again does she?' Her voice cracked as anger welled up in her. 'Not a word of comfort or warning for me, or a thought for my feelings! But appearances must be maintained for the family's sake!'

Dickon looked uncomfortable but said nothing.

'I fear it is too late.' She gestured to her muddied habit. 'The Earl has already seen me in my finery! But then, it is best he becomes accustomed to my imperfections before he deigns to take me to wife, do you not think so, Dickon?'

'Yes…no…m'lady,' Dickon stammered warily, astonished by his mistress's statement 'But Lady Katherine said…'

'She may say all she likes.' Seraphina shrugged carelessly. 'She tells me often enough that I am not a child any longer, so surely I can choose my own gown and ornaments. In truth, I think I am a little overdressed for the occasion.' Tearing off her hat and hood, she threw them aside so that the heavy mane of her hair tumbled loose down her back and spilled on to Jupiter's quarters. 'There! Do you not think I look *presentable,* Dickon?'

'Yes, m'lady,' Dickon acquiesced with weary resignation, 'but there'll be fireworks, m'lady; you know your mother's temper is as hot as—'

'Mine,' Seraphina laughed humourlessly. 'Don't worry so; it'll not be you that gets singed. I'll tell my lady mother that you delivered her message faithfully enough. Now let us go; dutiful daughter that I am, I would not keep my *beloved* mother waiting!'

She slapped the reins down on the colt's neck, sending it flying across the turf towards the house, sitting straight and slim as an arrow in her saddle, with her fox-red hair streaming out behind her like a fiery banner in the November sunshine.

The great hall was gloomy, except for where shafts of autumn sunlight arrowed in from the three great arched windows in the outside wall. The Earl tensed as he watched Seraphina enter from his vantage point in the minstrel gallery. For one tortuous second, as she flitted through one of the pools of golden light, she reminded him unbearably of Lettice. Lettice had moved in the same way, bright and quick as a flame, so that even in a room full of beautiful women men's eyes were drawn towards her as if by a lodestone. Putting the unwelcome memory aside, the Earl allowed himself to study the slender form below again. He found his eyes lingering on the silken cloak of her hair that fell in soft shining waves almost to the level of her knees. A redhead. Lettice's hair had been red, but more orange, more flagrant, whereas this girl's hair was a blend of dark red, russet and cinnamon-brown. Rich and glossy as copper-beech leaves in the sun. He doubted many men would resist her. Such fiery, sensual beauty, combined with such seeming innocence, was a potent enough brew to turn any man's head—and to cause him to lose it. As he watched, she paused and glanced back over her shoulder, as if she felt herself observed. Silently, he shrank back into the concealing shadows, unseen by either of the women below.

'You sent for me, Mother?' Seraphina said, as she dropped the most perfunctory of curtsies to Lady Katherine, who was pacing up and down beside the stone fireplace that dominated the end wall of the great hall.

Lady Katherine turned on her heel so abruptly that the heavy hem of her silver-brocade and fox-fur overgown hissed like a scythe through the strewing herbs on the flagged floor, stirring up a scent of pennyroyal and rue.

'I sent for my daughter, the Lady Seraphina Carey,' she snapped furiously as her eyes travelled over her daughter. 'Not some ill-mannered hoyden with her hair hanging loose and wearing a gown that looks as if it's been trailed through the midden heap.'

'And does this ill-mannered hoyden have no greeting for her favourite uncle?'

'Uncle Tom!' Seraphina spun around with a radiant smile as her uncle stepped through a door that led from the great chamber into the hall. Lord Musgrave had always been her favourite uncle. During her early childhood, when her parents had been immersed in their grief for the children they had lost, he had brought affection and laughter into the hushed house. Never visiting without a gift for her: toys; gilded fairings; a new pony from time to time. At least in him she had an ally.

Watching from above, the Earl found himself momentarily incapable of any logical thought, except that she was nearly irresistible when she smiled in such a fashion.

'I did not know you were here!' Seraphina laughed as she flew to into her uncle's outstretched arms. 'You do not know how glad I am to see you!'

'Not half as glad as I am to see thee again, I'll wager,' said her uncle, engulfing her in a bear hug, and then frowning as he felt her wince.

'Still feeling your bruises, niece?' he said gruffly, having read of Sherard's treatment of her in a letter from Lady Katherine.

'Yes,' Seraphina said abruptly. The compassion in her uncle's eyes brought a lump to her throat. She could not even bring herself to talk to Uncle Tom about Edmund. It hurt too much. Swallowing hard, she added, as lightly as she could manage, 'And I fear I have gained a few more bruises since putting Jupiter at the wall this morning.'

Her uncle gave a quick smile of understanding. 'I told you he wouldn't grow into his hooves for a year or two yet.'

'This is no time to discuss horseflesh, Tom!' Lady Katherine interrupted, her voice brittle with rage.

Seraphina turned back to her mother in surprise. Lady Katherine was very fond of her brother and Seraphina had never heard her mother raise her voice to him before. She had intended to annoy her mother, but she had not expected to succeed to this degree. There was a coldness in her mother's pale green eyes which she had never seen before.

'Kate, 'tis probably all a misunderstanding. Just tittle-tattle, nothing more.' Lord Musgrave said sheepishly, fingering nervously at his lace-edged ruff. 'If I'd thought you'd countenance it for a moment, I'd never have told thee. But since Heywood may come to hear it, I thought you ought to know.'

'Misunderstanding or no; I will have the truth,' Lady Katharine hissed at her bewildered daughter 'Seraphina, I will have no more of your shilly-shallying about what happened between you and your husband. Answer me! Did you behave like a wanton at Sherard House?'

Seraphina stared at her mother in astonishment. How could she know what had happened on that night; she had told no one. 'What do you mean? I do not understand...' she began uncertainly, her hands lifting instinctively, as if to ward off a blow.

'I have heard a report that you were found in the straw with your husband's...groom.' Lady Carey's contempt knew no bounds.

'A groom, how terrible!' Seraphina answered with reckless relief, glad that the ridiculous accusation bore no resemblance to the truth. 'Would it have been better if it was a peer of the realm?'

The Earl's hawkish mouth tightened into a harsh line as he glanced down at her defiant face, which held not the slightest hint of apology or repentance. By heaven! He had thought Lettice shameless, but even she had never sunk quite as low.

Lady Katherine whitened, so shocked that she was unable to speak.

'Surely you do not believe such a tale, Mother?' Seraphina said hastily, as she saw Lady Katherine's expression. Belatedly she realised that her flippant remark had sounded like an admission.

'I do not know what to think, but I do know that you must have angered your husband and you will not tell how! Perhaps you are ashamed?'

It was Seraphina's turn to blanch and then colour with anger. She had long ago resigned herself to being a disappointment to her mother. But she had never thought Lady Katherine knew her so little as to believe such a tale.

'Kate...' Lord Musgrave began tentatively.

'Leave us, Tom; this is none of your affair!' Lady Katherine ordered peremptorily.

Knowing his sister's temper of old, Lord Musgrave risked one conspiratorial glance at his stricken niece and fled.

As mother and daughter glared at one another the Earl reflected that it was as well that women did not carry swords. If they had, he would have wagered on there being bloodshed. What made him decide to intervene he did not know, but a moment later he was descending the twisting stone staircase that led to the great hall.

'Ashamed?' The last shred of Seraphina's restraint broke under her mother's critical gaze. 'How could you? It is you that should be ashamed! You who would sell me to the highest bidder with no regard for my happiness. To my mind, there is less shame in lying with a groom who loves you than a prince of the blood who does not!'

'Seraphina!' Lady Katherine's hand rose and she would have slapped her daughter if it had not been for the abrupt entrance of one of the kitchen maids.

'What is it, girl?' Lady Katherine snapped, turning to the dishevelled and red-faced girl.

''Tis Cook, m'lady. He's scalded himself,' the girl stammered. ''Tis bad, m'lady,' she added apologetically, already backing towards the door.

'Sweet heaven! As if things were not bad enough! Well, don't stand there gawping, Jennet; run and fetch my ointments and some clean linen from the still room; take it to the kitchen. I'll be there directly.' She swung back to Seraphina as she moved to follow Jennet. 'Where are you going?'

'To help...' Seraphina began, 'I thought you would need...'

'I do not wish for your help, Daughter! You would be better employed on your knees in the chapel, praying for God's forgiveness and mine!'

Seraphina watched tight-lipped as her mother left.

Her mind was reeling from disbelief and pain. Edmund was dead and who else could have spread such a tale about her? And how could her mother even begin to believe it? In sudden despair she slumped against the wall, pressing her forehead against the cool stone.

'M'lady?' The soft enquiry came from the arched doorway to her right.

Seraphina jerked upright. Heywood. Her mother's accusation had driven him from her mind. Against all reason her heart lifted at the sight of him and then as quickly plummeted again. Unlike her uncle, she had no doubt that he had heard the rumours. Now she understood the contempt in his eyes when he had learnt her name, the edge in his voice when he had spoken so distastefully of his duty. That was the one thing they had in common. He must have no more enthusiasm for this match than she did. But no doubt the Carey fortune would make a useful addition to the Heywood coffers, she though bitterly, remembering that some of his family estates had been confiscated when he was sent to the Tower after Wyatt's rebellion.

Yet there was no hint of distaste in his face now. He was smiling at her as he stepped forward. A smile that turned her brain to wool, her knees to water. 'You...' Her voice was a whisper. 'My lord Heywood...' What was wrong with her; she could think of nothing except that clad as he now was, in black velvet doublet and hose, he reminded her of a great black cat: lazy, lean, and dangerous. She dragged her eyes from him and found herself staring at the pitcher of mulled wine set to warm upon the hearth. Feeling his eyes on her, she blurted out the first thing that came into her head. 'You must be fatigued after your journey; perhaps you would like some refreshment? Some mulled wine, perhaps?'

'That would indeed be welcome, m'lady,' he said formally. 'I expected to see your lady mother,' he added a moment later. 'I thought I heard her voice.'

'There was an accident in the kitchens,' she explained stiffly, wondering exactly what he had heard.

'Then it seems we are fated to be alone, m'lady.'

'Does it?' She mimicked his drawl. 'After our last meeting, I cannot imagine it a situation to give you much pleasure.'

'You are referring to the flattering description you gave me of my own character?' He threw his head back and laughed confidently. 'You need not apologise for that.'

'I am not,' she said bluntly. 'The truth needs no apology.'

And what do you know of truth? The Earl bit back the retort that came to his lips, reminding himself that he was supposed to be wooing her, not acting as judge and jury. He made himself smile. 'I see you are honest, if not kind. But tell me, what did you mean when you said I should find no pleasure in your company?'

'I meant the distaste with which you referred to your ''duty'' in the park. You seemed to think me very poor consolation for having to leave the *pleasures* of court.'

'Very true,' the Earl agreed drily.

'How...' she began, outraged, and then clamped

her mouth shut, realising she had just fallen into his trap.

'But that was before I knew who you were.' He added smoothly, 'though now I see your face again, I wonder I did not know you at once. Your uncle had warned me that you have a rare beauty.'

'Perhaps you were not looking at my face!' Seraphina retorted rudely, hating her own weakness for feeling pleased at his compliment. She glowered at him unrepentantly. Infuriatingly, he did not appear in the least put out, and she found herself looking away from his glittering eyes with undignified haste.

'It is difficult not to look at such a form as yours. It would make Venus herself jealous,' he replied easily, as his eyes raked her from head to toe. 'But I did not mean to offend you; none but a fool would seek your displeasure.'

'Then perhaps you are a fool, m'lord,' she snapped.

'Certainly, since I have angered the prettiest widow in the county,' the Earl countered with a deliberate smile, as he leant indolently against the stone chimney-breast.

She tensed, knowing suddenly that he was playing like a cat with a mouse, letting her score petty points, tossing her pretty compliments, while all the time he despised her. Well! She would not play his courtier's games! 'Why do you compliment me, m'lord? I have given you no reason to like me,' she asked baldly, lifting her chin to look him full in the face.

'That is not true,' the Earl responded instantly, caught off-guard by the change in her manner. No, he thought, she was not as like Lettice as he had imagined. There was no evasiveness in the green eyes, flecked with silver, which met his so directly. 'I find I like you exceeding well, m'lady, but then I have always preferred to trust my own judgement, rather than rely upon rumour. An example you would do well to imitate,' he added drily. 'Now you have made my acquaintance, are you still so opposed to my suit?'

'I do not wish to marry anyone,' she answered tersely.

'You find the prospect of a widow's life so attractive that you wish to eschew marriage?' he asked with a sardonic lift of his black brows.

'If you were a woman, you would not find it so surprising! Believe me, it is preferable to being a chattel with fewer rights than a servant!' Her bitterness spilled out. 'Or to being the possession of a man who neither likes nor cares for me! And you do not care for me, whatever pretty things you say now. I saw it in your face in the park when you learnt my name and I see it now in your eyes!' She turned from him, bending with a swift, angry movement to pick up the wine. 'You have no more desire to wed me than I you!'

'Don't I?' The Earl pounced, swift and lithe as a cat.

Her breath came in a ragged gasp as she found her hand caught by his a moment before it closed on the pewter handle of the pitcher. His touch sheared through her anger, numbing her mind, dissolving her flesh as he drew her unprotesting to her feet. They were so close she could smell the fresh, clean scent of the southern-wood and lavender that his servants used to sweeten his linen. She wanted to run, to hide from his mocking, knowing eyes. But she could not. He held her trapped in his golden gaze like a fly in amber.

The Earl smiled.

'Why do you regard yourself as having so little worth, m'lady?' he murmured. 'Beauty as well as fortune is a rare combination.'

'Does it give you pleasure to mock me?' She forced the words from her dry throat.

'Mock you?' His brows rose. 'Do you think I am unable to see beyond a shabby gown? You are beautiful, desirable to any man with eyes.'

'I wasn't to—' she began savagely, and then broke off. Why tell him of the humiliations she had suffered at Edmund's hands? She looked away, fixing her gaze upon a tapestry which hung on the wall.

'Why are you so afraid of the truth?' His soft question brought her eyes snapping back to his.

'The truth has never frightened me; 'tis posturings and deceit which make me uneasy!'

'Do you think I am trying to deceive when I say you are beautiful?' He smiled, and began to trace the delicate bones of her hand with his fingertips. 'I could convince you otherwise.'

'I do not need your sort of *convincing*,' she said breathlessly, wondering that the sudden pounding of her heart was not reverberating to the very beams of the hall. 'Kind as your offer is. And now, if you don't mind, m'lord; the wine is overheating...'

'It is not kindness which makes me want to kiss you,' he stated quietly. 'As you know.'

'I don't!' she snapped, her voice thin, brittle, as she saw his gaze drop to her lips and rest there. 'And I don't wish to! Now will you let me see to the wine?'

'The handle of the pitcher will be hot,' he said impassively, without releasing her hand. 'Take my kerchief.'

'It will spoil,' she protested with growing panic as he pushed the square of white silk and lace into her free hand. Her heart had slowed from a hectic race to the agonising beat of an execution drumroll. Why wouldn't he let go of her?

'It is of no consequence,' he said softly. 'I have others, whereas you have but two hands and I would not be the cause of harming them.' With deliberate slowness, he brought her imprisoned hand to his lips, turning it upwards and brushing her palm with his mouth.

It was the lightest of caresses, but it stopped her heart, her breath; she could do nothing but stare at him helplessly, seeking some sort of explanation. How could his touch do this to her body, when her mind told that this was naught but a courtier's game to him?

The Earl's breath caught in his throat as his eyes met hers, green and clear as glass. If he had not known, had not heard her admission with his own ears, he would have sworn this girl was an innocent. But why seek to mislead her own family?

Fool! His mouth curled as the answer came into his mind. What better excuse for clandestine meetings with men than to be believed a wanton? Reputations could be regained in time, heads could not.

'My hand; you are hurting!' she protested as he crushed her fingers in an iron grip.

'Your pardon,' he apologised hastily. Forcing a smile, he folded her fingers over her palm and placed her hand gently over her thudding heart.

His unexpected tenderness was utterly at odds with the emotions she had seen flickering through his eyes. Bewildered, she brought her furled fingers up to her lips in an entirely unthinking gesture.

'You see, m'lady, a peer of the realm would have been infinitely better,' he drawled derisively, holding her eyes with his.

She stared at him, the blood draining from her face. He *had* overheard her reckless, stupid remark. *And he had believed it.* She opened her mouth to defend herself and then stopped. She had sacrificed her pride before in an effort to please Edmund, to try and make herself the wife he had wanted. It had made no difference. If Heywood could not see for himself that the tales were false, then let him believe them!

'You think so?' With a huge effort she managed a disappearing smile. 'You value yourself too high, m'lord.'

'Do I?' His eyes moved to her hand which had dropped lifelessly to her side, still clenched, damning her as a liar.

'Yes,' she answered haughtily, straightening her reluctant fingers, her head high, unaware that her eyes had already told him just how much his remarks had hurt. 'Now, if you will excuse me—'

'Don't go! I'm sorry,' he added with genuine remorse. 'I was but teasing; I meant no insult. If my tongue is too sharp, it is because I am fatigued from the journey. Some wine would go a long way to sweetening it, m'lady.'

'Very well.' She gave in grudgingly, folding the square of silk he had given her. The duties of a hostess had been too well ingrained by her mother for her to ignore such a request. 'I should have served it sooner if you had let me.'

'Your pardon, m'lady.' He inclined his head in an ironic bow.

'There are goblets on the mantel; can you reach them down?' Seraphina asked curtly as she knelt to pick up the pitcher of wine.

He did as she asked, and she poured the steaming liquid into silver goblets, taking great care to avoid his gaze.

She stooped to set the pitcher down again, and the Earl's eyes darkened as they rested on her glossy red hair as it swung forward over her narrow shoulders, catching and reflecting the colour of the flames.

She straightened with unconscious grace and took her goblet from his hand, so scrupulously careful not to touch his fingers that the Earl had to bite back a smile.

'The wine is to your liking?' she asked tersely a few seconds later, as he stood sipping the cinnamon-and clove-scented wine in silence.

'It is excellent,' he said softly as his eyes met hers. 'It tastes of honey and spice, as I suspect would you, lady.'

His eyes dropped, drifting down over her slender figure, so clearly outlined in the tight habit.

Colour flooded her face, she felt as if he had stripped her naked and touched his lips to her flesh. How dared he speak to her, look at her as if she were…? But was that not what she wanted? Well! Since he had judged her so low, she would meet his expectations! Raising her goblet defiantly, she drained her wine in a manner that would have brought an instant reprisal from her mother. And then, with deliberate rudeness, bent and poured herself another measure without asking if he wished for more.

'It is not wise to drink so quickly, m'lady,' the Earl said a little censoriously, as he watched her raise her goblet to her lips again.

'I do not pretend to be wise, m'lord,' she retorted acidly, staring into the flames. 'If I were wise I should not have lain with a stable lad, should I?' She turned from him to stare into the flames.

She was so young, thought the Earl grimly. Young enough to care and be hurt by what others said and thought of her. Young and stupid enough to become embroiled in treason. Distaste for what he was doing turned the wine to vinegar in his mouth as he gazed at her slight figure, framed by the flames of the fire and cloaked by her glowing hair. *The burning one.* The name had a grim appropriateness. A traitress could go to the stake as easily as to the block. His mouth grew tauter as he saw her furtive sideways glance at him and the way she drew her goblet tight against her chest, like a shield, and wrapped her other arm across her body. She looked so defenceless, so frightened. Had she guessed the real reason for his presence? For one insane second, the Earl contemplated confronting her there and then. If she confessed all she knew now, before harm was done, there might be a chance of saving her slender white neck. Elizabeth Tudor owed him a favour or two. But a moment later he knew he dared not risk warning Elizabeth's enemies out of nothing more than a mixture of sentiment and lust. Seraphina Carey was steeped in treason, he reminded himself, and she must pay the penalty like any other traitor to the crown.

## Chapter Five

'I see Henry and Richard get on well enough,' Lord Musgrave observed that evening as he sat down beside his sister in the low-ceilinged parlour which the family used in preference to the great hall on cool evenings.

'Aye,' Lady Katherine answered after a swift glance at the other side of the room where her husband and the Earl were poring over one of the new illustrated maps. Her eyes flicked to the door and she frowned. 'Supper is going to be ruined if Seraphina does not make an appearance soon,' she muttered half to herself.

'Shall I send one of the servants to look for her?' Lord Musgrave offered.

'If you would. I'll have to go to the kitchen. With no cook, I dare not leave the pastries to the wenches—' Lady Katherine broke off with a gasp and went as white as her piecrust ruff. 'God's blood!' The oath hissed through her tight lips.

'Kate, what ails you?' Lord Musgrave began anxiously and then, as he followed the direction of his sister's gaze, he bit back a smile. Seraphina was standing in the doorway, her head high, a smile on her brightly painted lips, her green eyes huge and defiant, framed by blackened lashes.

'What is she playing at?' Lady Katherine almost choked as Seraphina sauntered across the room with a rustle of silk, to make a curtsy to her father and Heywood as etiquette demanded.

'Since you say she is so set against the match, I'd guess she seeks to convince Heywood that she is worse than she is painted to try and make him drop his suit,' Lord Musgrave said drily. 'You have to hand it to her, Kate; she's clever.'

'I'll give her more than a hand!' Lady Katherine hissed in a furious whisper. 'For a widow to dress in such a way!'

'She's wearing black; what more do you want?' Lord Musgrave observed mildly.

'Modesty!' Lady Katherine grated 'That gown was meant to be worn with a high-necked chemise; that crimson one is so low-necked it scarcely covers her! And she's painted and perfumed like a king's whore! I can smell the rose oil from here! When I get her back to her room, she will answer for this.'

'No, Kate.' Her brother put a restraining hand on her arm as she moved to leave her chair. 'Leave her be. She is not a child any longer, and Heywood will not be fooled by her borrowed colours.' His voice shook with smothered laughter as he glanced at the Earl. 'At least, not for long.'

'How you can find this situation amusing, Tom, is beyond me!' Lady Katherine shook off his hand angrily and sailed across the room, her skirts billowing around her like a galleon in full sail.

Lord Musgrave sighed. Then, settling more comfortably in his chair, he pulled the flaps of his black velvet house-cap down over his ears, and shut his eyes.

'Henry, will you tear yourself away from that map for a moment,' Lady Katherine murmured tersely to her husband after giving Seraphina a furious stare. 'I want you to speak to your daughter about her gown!'

Henry Carey blinked in surprise at his wife's uncustomary lack of manners. 'Of course, my dear.' He smiled kindly at his daughter, peering a little shortsightedly through his spectacles. 'It is a very pretty gown, Seraphina; very becoming indeed.'

Lady Katherine's mouth opened, but no sound came out.

'Thank you, Father.' Seraphina stepped forward and kissed him upon his cheek.

'She looks well in it,' Lord Carey continued cheerfully to his wife. 'And 'tis good to see some colour in her cheeks—'

'Colour? God's blood, Henry, don't you know paint when you see it?' Lady Katherine hissed in her husband's ear as she took his arm, and then, turning to Heywood, she smiled. 'You will excuse us for a moment, my lord?'

'Of course.' The Earl bowed.

'Thank you.' Lady Katherine inclined her head and then made a gesture towards the door. 'Seraphina—'

'Will entertain me admirably in your absence, lady,' the Earl cut in blandly.

For a moment Lady Katherine's mouth pursed and then she accepted her defeat with the slightest incline of her head. Turning to her bemused husband, she hauled him from the room.

Seraphina had to put a hand to her mouth hastily to stop herself from laughing; she had never seen her mother so neatly outmanoeuvred. Her eyes caught the Earl's and for a fraction of a second she found herself absolutely in tune with him, sharing silent laughter.

'Your father's right.' He smiled at her lazily, as his dark eyes travelled slowly over her oval face, severely framed by the gemstudded crescent which held her black silk French hood in place. 'You do look well. But then, there is nothing that would not become you, Lady Sherard.'

'If you seek to compliment me, I beg you not to use that name!' she retorted, the moment of rapport vanishing instantly. 'I hate it!'

'Your pardon m'lady,' he said sarcastically. 'I thought it was the custom for a widow to retain her husband's name until she remarries.'

'I care nought for customs. I detest the name and everything about it!'

'It would be easy enough to remedy the matter. If you remarried, the problem would no longer exist.'

'You already know my thoughts on marriage, m'lord!' Seraphina answered, furious with herself for stepping so easily into his trap. Then, remembering the part she was supposed to be playing, she forced herself to smile at him and give him what she hoped was an inviting glance from beneath her black lashes. 'But perhaps you could think of a way to change my mind, m'lord?'

'Certainly. It would be difficult not to,' the Earl drawled. He reached out idly to touch a puff of crimson silk which was pulled through the slashed upper sleeve of gown. 'Is this new plumage for my benefit, my lady! I am honoured.'

Seraphina gasped as his hand dropped away and grazed the bare white skin of her breasts. Heat flooded through her, turning her exposed skin pale rose. The contact had been insolent, deliberate. Her hand came up angrily, instinctively, and then stilled as his eyes met hers and his black brows tilted in a mocking question. She swallowed hard. 'Then I am happy if I have pleased you, m'lord.' Suppressed anger made her voice come out as a throaty whisper.

'I can think of ways you could please me more,' he murmured so that only she could bear, letting his eyes travel slowly upwards from her breasts to rest disturbingly on her mouth. 'No doubt you are familiar with them.'

'Familiar enough,' she lied, making herself smile up at him while she clenched the hands that longed to slap his face. 'But given your reputation,' she could not resist adding, 'I do not doubt there is much you could teach me, m'lord.'

'My reputation palls beside yours, m'lady.' He returned her thrust coolly. 'I shall be happy to bow to a master, or should I say mistress, of the art.'

'Then at least your head will be as low as your mind, m'lord!' she snapped.

There was a moment's silence as their eyes clashed

and held, emerald striking glittering jet sparks from brown.

'That's better, m'lady, I ever did prefer a well-spiced dish to the sickly sweet.'

'Then you had best be careful you do not burn your mouth, m'lord,' she answered tartly.

'I would say it was you that was in danger of burning,' he drawled as his eyes travelled insolently down and rested upon her breasts. 'You have the sort of skin which turns to fire so easily.'

She did not respond to his provocation. His words had conjured up a nightmare image in her mind. A girl, wrapped in flame, screaming.

'M'lady?' He was looking at her with narrowed eyes. 'Are you unwell? You look pale.'

'No,' she answered abruptly. 'You made me think of something I wish I could forget.'

'What?' he prompted softly.

'A girl they burnt upon my husband's estate. My husband made me watch. My punishment for pleading for the heretic's life.' Her voice grew hoarse with an anger that would never fade. 'She was no older than myself. I'd often given her food and clothes, since her family had died of the plague and she was not like to get a husband because she was a little simple. She could not even reck her own age or read her name, and they burnt her for not being able to tell what a sacrament is or how many there are! When they lit the fires, she kept screaming to me to help her, and there was nothing I could do except pray the smoke would smother her before the flames reached her.'

'You do not believe that heretics should burn?'

'What is a heretic, but someone who chooses to worship God in a different way from those who rule?' The surprise in his voice stung her into a reckless reply.

'A dangerous philosophy, given the beliefs of our Queen,' he said slowly, watching her angry face intently.

'But hardly an unusual one among my contemporaries, I suspect,' she retorted. 'First, we had King Henry's reforms, then King Edward's Protestan tism and now—' she paused '—Queen Mary demands that we all become Papists again. It is a wonder to me that anyone can be certain enough in their beliefs to burn men alive for no crime but using one prayer book rather than another.' She broke off as she realised that he was staring at her oddly. Edmund had told her often enough that it was not a woman's place to voice opinions on such matters and no doubt he thought the same.

'And to me,' he startled by her agreeing softly. 'I've always thought burning a barbarous punishment, even for treason.'

'Treason.' She looked at him with puzzled eyes; how had they come to be talking of treason? It was a topic which the wise always avoided. 'I think the axe or rope is punishment enough,' she blurted, 'after fair trial, which is too often not the case.'

'Aye, fairness is not a trait I should rely upon in a Tudor.' His voice dropped 'Nor mercy. Something you might do well to remember.'

Unease slid like ice along her spine. It was almost,

almost, as if he were warning her. But what had she to do with treason?

'Ye gods, Richard!' Her uncle's voice came as a welcome interruption as he joined them. 'Since when did a man woo a girl with talk of treason and religion? If you can think of naught better to say, come and have a game of dice with me.'

'I will, Tom,' the Earl agreed easily. 'And I ask your pardon, lady, if my conversation has distressed you.'

'Why should it?' she answered, and then, looking at her uncle, she added, 'The Earl is our guest; you will not use the dice Ralph made, will you?'

'Ralph Fenton? Then we'll be well matched.' The Earl laughed. 'He also supplied mine.'

'You as well?' Seraphina exclaimed. 'But then, no one at court is honest.'

'Stop looking so shocked, girl,' her uncle grinned, 'and fetch us more of your mother's pastries.

Seraphina sighed and she lounged among a heap of tapestry and jewel-bright silk cushions beside the parlour fire. Her eyes prickled from the black she had put on her lashes, and her skin felt dry and stiff. She hated wearing paint and wished she could go and wash it off. How much longer must she keep up this masque? she wondered gloomily. It was now the eighteenth of November; the Earl had been here for two weeks and showed no inclination to leave.

Absently, she stroked the silky ears of the hound

puppy, which lay snoring happily beside her, utterly content, its belly round and full with milk.

'You're a lucky creature,' she said, half to herself.

'And you are an ungrateful one!' Lady Katherine snapped as she swept in and seated herself in her favourite chair. 'Can you think of another man who would have spent hours digging a foolish puppy out of a rabbit burrow with his own hands, simply to please you?'

'No, I suppose not,' Seraphina said reluctantly. She had heard the puppy whining while riding in the woods that morning. She had been horrified when her father and uncle had said there was nothing they could do. The Earl had said nothing, and she had thought him uncaring. But several hours later he had come to her bedecked in chalky soil from head to foot, with a squirming bundle in his arms and a broad grin on his face. With his hair tousled and stripped of his usual veneer of elegance, he had looked almost vulnerable as he waited for her praise. And she had hated him for it. Hated him for making her heart turn over, hated him for making her care what he thought of her.

'After the storm you made about that stray this morning, you might have least have thanked him with a little warmth,' Lady Katherine continued. 'He deserved more than that cool little thank-you. 'Tis a mystery to me why he has stayed so long here. These last few days, the greater courtesy he shows you, the ruder you have been to him. Ignoring him one moment, the next flaunting yourself like a courtesan!' Lady Katherine grimaced. 'Even your father has begun to notice! Do you wish to disgrace our family, your name?'

'No, of course not—' Seraphina began tersely.

'So, I have your word that you will abandon this masquerade?' Lady Katherine seized the advantage mercilessly.

'What masquerade?' Seraphina answered after a fractional hesitation in which she pretended to brush a speck of dust from her black silk sleeve.

'Do you think I am a halfwit?' Lady Katherine said exasperatedly. 'You know as well as I that I am speaking of your dress and your manners this last fortnight. You like Heywood, so why behave like this? Why treat him so—?'

'I don't like him!' Her own vehemence surprised her as well as the sleeping puppy, which jolted awake and looked at her anxiously. Avoiding her mother's gaze, she stroked it mechanically with her hand until it settled again.

'God grant me patience!' Her mother uttered the supplication with a distinct lack of the quality mentioned. 'I might be your mother, and you may think me a tyrant, but I am a woman. Do you think I have not seen how you look at him when you think yourself unobserved, or how you start like a scalded cat if his sleeve as much as brushes your shoulder when we are at table. And when you forget your ridiculous determination to dislike him, I have seen how he makes you laugh and smile as you used to, before Sherard—' She broke off as the door swung open and her husband, brother and the Earl entered.

'My lords…' Lady Katherine smiled as she curtsied

and then bustled forward. 'Come and be seated by the fire; you take that chair, Tom; Henry can have the couch. Since the Earl has the youngest bones, I am sure he will not mind sharing the cushions with Seraphina.'

'Of course not.' The corners of the Earl's mouth flicked upwards as he intercepted the glare Seraphina gave her mother as she too stood up and made her obeisance. Blood rose to her cheeks, as hot as the fire on her back. She could not bear to be so close to him; not now, when her feelings were so confused.

'You may have them all,' she said, stooping to the drowsy puppy. ''Tis time Thorn had more milk.'

'I would not advise it yet,' the Earl said easily. 'After so little for two days, if you give him more now he will certainly be ill.'

'Heywood's right; what are you thinking of, girl?' her uncle chafed her from the opposite side of the fire. 'Not the dog, I'll warrant.' He grinned as she scowled at him, before he made a point of engaging both her parents in conversation.

Her attempt at escape defeated, she sat down again, drawing her skirts close so as to make room for the Earl. The cushion behind her back sank as he rested his arm upon it. She shrank away, unbearably aware of how small a movement it would take for them to touch. Not since the day of his arrival had he touched her in anything but the most formal way. But she could have listed every fleeting, accidental contact from the brush of her skirts against him in a narrow doorway to the collision of their fingers when they both reached to take a sweetmeat from a dish.

'I have been wanting to speak to you.' He spoke quietly, so close to her ear that she shivered as she felt the warmth of his breath on her skin.

'About what?'

'Your *future*.'

'My future?' Her heartbeat slowed. 'What has it to do with you?'

'Everything.' His eyes met hers as she turned her head. 'You have made it plain enough you do not want my suit, but you must reconsider. I am offering you my protection as well as my name.'

'The fetters and chains of marriage! Why should I want either?' she answered acidly, dropping her gaze to her fingers as she pleated and smoothed the emerald silk of her kirtle, over and over.

'I think you know; surely you have guessed—'

'Guessed what?' She lifted her chin to look him directly in the face.

He gave an exasperated sigh. 'If you refuse me, do you think it will end there? There will be others whose *wooing* may not be so gentle as mine.'

'Then they will be easier to refuse than you—' She broke off, horrified at her own admission. 'I didn't mean—'

'Jesu!' he interrupted her roughly. 'You will not be able to refuse *those* suitors, and you know it.'

'I don't know what you are talking about.' Her voice was husky with relief. Thank God! He had not noticed her slip of the tongue.

'You must know—' he began urgently and then stopped abruptly as he saw the total bafflement on her face. 'If you don't, then—'

'Then what?' she prompted him in an impatient whisper, her bewilderment increasing.

'Then I begin to think I have been the greatest fool in Christendom,' he said softly.

She stilled, her confusion forgotten as he met her gaze. There was a gentleness in his eyes and voice which was new to her. A gentleness which slowed her heart and brought the sudden, unexpected prick of tears to her eyes as she found herself wishing that they might begin again, wishing—what? That she might be his wife! She jerked her eyes away, shocked by her own weakness and stupidity. He thought her a wanton and despised her for it! Despised her, just as Edmund had—she must remember that at all costs.

'Seraphina.' Her mother's impatient tone made her aware that the others in the room had fallen silent and were looking at her expectantly. 'You haven't played once since the Earl came. Take up your lute; I have a mind to hear a tune.'

'Must I?' she answered with ill grace, feeling drained and shaky inside. 'I always play badly before—strangers.' She used the last word deliberately.

'Nonsense!' Lady Katherine snapped. 'And you can scarce count my Lord Heywood as a stranger.'

'I should hope not,' the Earl responded smoothly. 'Will you not indulge us, lady? I can think of few things I should like better than to hear you sing.'

'Can't you?' She regretted her acid retort the moment it left her lips.

'Of course—' the corners of his mouth flicked up in a humourless smile '—but this is scarce the time or place to list them.'

See! she told herself angrily; he speaks to you as if you were a courtesan! And you would think of wedding him? Scarlet-cheeked and angry, she turned away hastily and reached behind her for her lute. 'I cannot find the plectrum,' she said tersely, a moment or two later after a desultory search amongst the cushions. 'Perhaps the Earl would prefer to play cards or dice—'

''Twill be inside,' Lady Katherine broke in firmly. 'I recall seeing young Master Waldegrave playing with it when he visited with his mother last week.'

Resignedly, Seraphina turned the instrument upside down and shook it. It rattled and a moment later the small piece of carved bone tumbled out, falling through her nervous fingers into the rushes.

The Earl leant forward to retrieve it and then, to her surprise, took the lute from her. 'You seem tired. Let me play while you sing?'

'As you like,' she said coldly, caught off balance by his unexpected kindness. 'No doubt my skills would not match those you are used to at court.'

His brows lifted a fraction at her rudeness, and suddenly she wanted to apologise, to explain how Edmund had always criticised her playing while he had naught but praise for Grace, but the words would not come. She watched bleakly as he turned the turning pegs of the lute and began to try out the strings. If only, if only it had been him she had wed a year ago. A year ago when she had still believed that a good marriage could be built if there was will enough on the woman's part, believed that if you tried hard enough, you could make your husband come to love you—if only; the intensity of her own longing shocked her and, when he lifted his head without warning, she had no time to hide her thoughts or look away. She was lost in the gold-flecked darkness of his eyes. His fingers fumbled a chord and then stilled as he returned her stare.

'Well, are you two going to sing or sit looking at each other all night?' Lord Musgrave growled several seconds later, rousing himself from his apparent doze beside the fire.

'Uncle!' Seraphina began exasperatedly.

'Patience, Tom.' The impassive mask of the Earl's face turned to a smile. 'You may wish we had when you hear us.' He turned to Lady Katherine. 'What was it you wished to hear?'

'"Greensleeves"—if you know it, m'lord?'

'But I thought you hated that tune,' Seraphina said, her eyebrows winging upwards.

'So did I,' said Lord Carey mildly, looking up from one of the new printed books. 'You said it always makes you think of her—'

'It does indeed remind me of Anne Boleyn,' Lady Katherine interrupted abruptly. 'But I had many happy times in her company before she fell out of favour with the King.'

'I know it well, Lady Katherine. It was ever a favourite of my father's.' The Earl gave Lady Katherine a slanting grin. 'But no doubt you know that?'

'I do recall something of the sort.' To Seraphina's surprise, her mother laughed. 'You are very like your father, my lord, in looks and in impertinence. Now play, before I crown you with the lute as I once did your father.'

Seraphina's eyes widened, but she was prevented from saying anything as the Earl struck the first plaintive chord and she began to sing, nervously at first, and then with more confidence as his voice joined hers in the refrain.

'Your voice is, in truth, very fine,' the Earl said, as he let the last evocative note die away. 'What other talents do you seek to hide, m'lady?'

'Not many of the domestic variety,' she confessed.

He discarded the lute and laughed, leaning forward on the cushions. 'Those were not the ones I had in mind.'

Colour ebbed from her face as his eyes met hers and told her exactly what he did have in mind. She inhaled raggedly; what was wrong with her? She had set out to make him think her a lightskirt and, when he treated her as one, she hated it.

'I'm sorry, m'lord. I did not catch that,' Lady Katherine said, hiding a yawn behind her hand. They were all in need of their beds, she thought, especially Seraphina, judging by her sudden pallor.

'I said your daughter has many unexpected talents,' the Earl lied smoothly. 'Her tutor must have been a very able man.'

Seraphina's pallor gave way to hot, angry colour as she caught the insulting nuance in his words.

'Brother Francis was very competent,' Lady Katherine answered, blithely ignoring the undercurrent of tension between the Earl and her daughter. 'And Seraphina was an able student when she applied herself.'

'I do not doubt it,' he drawled, smiling at Seraphina in a way which made her want to strike him, hard. 'So, he was a monk...' he added, watching her face carefully.

'Yes! A monk and, what is more, one who respected his vows!' she hissed in a furious whisper.

'How did he come to be your tutor?' he enquired mildly, apparently oblivious to her anger.

'My father found him near dead from starvation by the roadside after King Henry dissolved his monastery; he had lived there since he was a child and knew no other life.'

The Earl glanced at Lord Carey. 'So, you gave him a place in your household out of pity?'

'And respect,' Henry Carey added firmly, raising his head from his book. 'He was a very learned man and a superb illuminator.'

'You always were a soft touch, Henry; the man was an abbey lubber,' Lord Musgrave growled, rousing himself from his doze beside the fire.

'Perhaps. But the books he created for me will be treasured long after you and I are nought but dust, Tom,' Henry Carey replied, unperturbed by his brother-in-law's judgement of his character.

'Books! Pah! It's not books you want to be remembered by! It's grandchildren. Do you hear that, Seraphina? It's time you found a man to take to your bed rather than a milksop like Sherard!'

'Yes, Uncle,' Seraphina grated, all too aware of the appraising glance the Earl had given her. She was exceptionally glad that the moment was lost as David Hart, her father's steward, strode into the chamber without waiting for the answer to his knock on the door.

'Lord Carey!'

'What is it, Davey?' Henry Carey got to his feet, his eyes anxious as he looked at his steward's face.

'There is a messenger from Hatfield, m'lord—Sir Edward Grey.'

'From Hatfield?' The Earl rose to his feet abruptly. 'Send him in at once, man!' Then, remembering his manners, he turned to Henry Carey. 'I'm sorry, m'lord; I forgot myself.'

'It is forgotten, Lord Heywood. You share my thoughts, I think.'

The man that stumbled into the circle of firelight was caked with dust and mud from the roads. 'My lords.' He inclined his head to the three men who were all staring at him expectantly.

'The Queen is dead, m'lords, long live the Queen. The Lady Elizabeth— I mean, the Queen,' he corrected himself hastily, 'asked that I should bring this to you at once, m'lord Heywood.' He reached into the leather pouch that hung on his belt and pulled out a piece of folded parchment. 'And tell you to come to Hatfield with all haste.'

The Earl broke the seal and scanned the parchment, frowning as he decoded the cyphered message. He lifted his head abruptly and looked toward Lady Katherine. 'I apologise for the inconvenience, lady, but I must leave tonight.'

'Of course; Davey, tell the servants to make ready for the Earl's departure, and be sure food is made ready for his journey.'

Lady Katherine was gracious and smiling; only Seraphina saw and understood the disappointment in her eyes. There had been no formal talk of a betrothal, and now it seemed unlikely there ever would be. Now that Elizabeth Tudor was Queen, half the marriage-able heiresses in the land would be cast in the Earl's path, so why would he waste further effort on a girl who was apparently wanton and unwilling to boot? The thought should have pleased her; it was exactly what she had intended, so why, when she glanced at his dark, hawkish face, did she feel such a sick hollowness at the prospect of his being someone else's husband? After what Edmund had done to her, she knew that marriage was nothing to be envied. And, once he had gone, and she no longer had to suffer his disturbing physical presence, this numbness would disappear and she would be glad and thank God for her escape from another loveless match.

The Earl's frown deepened as he refolded the parchment. Cecil's instructions were brief and clear enough. And there was only one way he could demand that Seraphina follow him to court within the week without giving rise to awkward questions, and that was to insist on a short betrothal and speedy marriage.

'M'lord?' He turned slowly to Henry Carey. 'You will appreciate that there is no time for formalities. It is no secret that I came here to seek your daughter's hand. Within reason, I will agree to whatever terms your lawyers ask. So, do I have your consent?'

Lord Carey looked hesitantly towards his daughter, who seemed to have turned to marble.

'I already have the Queen's approval,' the Earl added.

'Well, in that case…' Lord Carey looked helplessly at his daughter and then jolted as his wife nudged him with her elbow, none too gently. 'You have my approval, m'lord.'

'And mine,' Lady Katherine said warmly.

'The Queen will be delighted; she always takes an interest in her kinswomen.' The Earl smiled, but there was a question in his eyes as he glanced towards Seraphina's rigid form. 'I can take it the matter is settled, then?'

'You cannot!' The words tore from her throat as she looked wildly from him to her father and scrambled to her feet. 'I won't marry him, I can't. You don't understand. None of you understands…'

'You'll do as you are bid or leave this house tonight, since it seems you have neither respect for your prince, nor loyalty to your family!' Lady Katherine snapped.

'Uncle Tom…' She turned to her uncle, begging him with her eyes to intervene, but he gave her an apologetic smile and shook his head.

'M'lady…' The Earl took a step towards her, his hand outstretched.

'No!' She backed away from him as if he were death itself, and then, snatching up her skirts, she turned and ran.

# *Chapter Six*

She ran blindly from the parlour, skidding down the shallow stone steps into the shadowy great hall and then out into the screen passage, where she collided with Jennet, who was bringing ale for the messenger. The pitcher of ale went flying from Jennet's hands to shatter upon the flagged floor. Babbling an apology, she side-stepped the startled maid and flung open the door which led to the stairs. Her skirts in her hands, she began to climb the twisting flight, stumbling in her haste, and cursing her cumbersome skirts, and high-heeled silk slippers. She did not know where she was going. She knew only that she could not face another marriage like her first, and that she had to get away, hide, until he had gone and she was safe.

'M'lady! Wait!' She jolted and looked back as his voice echoed after her, and then fell headlong over the edge of the uppermost step on to the landing. Blind panic brought her scrambling back to her feet in seconds as she heard him bark a question at Jennet, followed by the sound of his feet on the stairs. The bends in the stairs hid him from her sight, but in a moment or two he would reach her—and she had not a hope of outrunning him. She had to hide until he gave up and went away. But where? She looked about her wildly, conscious all the time of his footsteps coming ever closer.

The gallery. The east entrance was only a few steps away; with luck he would go straight past, expecting her to head for her chamber.

Moving on tiptoe, she crept the few paces to the gallery and breathed a prayer of relief as its heavy oaken door swung easily and almost silently on its well-oiled hinges. She shut it with extreme care, easing the latch into place with her fingertips so that it did not drop and make a noise. A moment later she heard the familiar creak of the topmost stair. She froze, her fingers still lifted to the latch and her cheek pressed against the cool, silky wood. He halted and there was a silence which seemed to be filled with the sound of her own heart, thumping against her ribs in rapid, jerking beats. She held her breath as the sound of his footsteps began again—one, two, three. She counted inside her head—one more and he would be outside the door. Her fingers touched the bolt above the latch; instinctively, without thinking, she slid it home. The click it made was soft, but seemed to her like the crack of a whip. She should have left well alone; supposing he had heard?

'M'lady?' He halted and his quiet enquiry answered her unspoken question. She remained rooted to the spot, unable to move or even breathe as the latch, a scarce inch from her fingers, began to lift.

'Gates of Hell!' He swore exasperatedly as the door

refused to give and then sighed audibly. 'Open the door. We have to talk.'

She made no answer. He could not be sure she was there. The silence stretched; she could hear nothing except his breathing, a little uneven like her own, and the splutter and hiss of the torches, which provided little islands of light in the gloomy gallery.

'Open this damned door!' He struck the door in frustration, and she jerked back a pace as it shook. 'You must know what is at stake here! The Queen ordered me to seek your hand!'

Still she said nothing. She heard him inhale raggedly and half expected him to hit the door again. But there was another silence which seemed to last forever.

'On your head be it,' he said at last, the anger in his voice replaced with a flat weariness, almost hopelessness. 'I am not accustomed to begging, lady, and I will not waste more of my time.'

For several minutes after his footsteps had died away, she remained motionless, her mind and body numb at the enormity of what she had done. She had defied her family and made a fool of one who was likely to become the most powerful man in the kingdom, and defied the Queen's wishes. And none of that seemed to matter as much as the thought that she would most like never see him again, laugh with him again, be touched by him again. And all because she was afraid that Edmund had been right about her inadequacies as a wife. Afraid that Richard Durrant would have good reason to despise her, afraid that he only wanted her for her name and fortune.

Shivering, she wrapped her arms about herself, part for comfort, part because of the cold. With neither of the fires at each end lit and its long wall of windows, the gallery was freezing as it always was, except in high summer. She had best go to her chamber, she thought dully; no doubt her mother would be looking for her and she would rather face her there than here in the cold and dark. Slowly, head bowed, she began to walk along the gloomy gallery.

She did not see the tall, silent figure standing in the shadowed doorway until she almost walked into him.

'I thought you had gone…' she said shakily, halting and then retreating a step. 'Why will you not leave me alone?'

'I don't know.' He gave a humourless laugh. 'Perhaps it is just that I cannot bring myself to abandon you to your own stupidity.'

'I fear you must,' she said thickly. 'Now let me pass!'

He moved as she stepped forward, blocking her path with his body, filling her vision with the black velvet wall of his chest. Her heart, breath and mind all seemed to stop as her body prickled into acute awareness. They were too close, dangerously close. She could feel the warmth of his body, see the clouds of his breath as they met and merged with hers in the freezing air.

It should have been the easiest thing in the world to push past him or to turn and go back the way she had come. He would not detain her by force; she knew that instinctively. But then he did not need to resort to such measures. Her own body held her prisoner, refusing to obey the commands of her brain. The seconds in which she should have moved spun out like an over-stretched thread.

Slowly, delicately, as if half expecting her to break, he touched his fingertips to her pointed chin, tilting up her face.

'You're trembling.' His voice was almost accusatory as his eyes travelled over her face.

'It is cold,' she blurted, dragging in a breath.

'Cold? Is it?' His mouth curved suddenly. 'I had not noticed. But then, I do not notice much when you are near, except that your skin turns to fire, wherever, whenever I touch you...'

She gave a tiny gasp as he ran the pad of his thumb across her lips, then along her jaw. It was a tiny, faintly abrasive caress, but it tumbled her into a new, startling sensual awareness. Suddenly everything was a caress, from the silken brush of her petticoats against her thighs to the abrasive rasp of her linen bodice against her hardening breasts as she inhaled. It was tantalising, unbearable; she wanted it to stop...or...her mind could not take her further. It was outside her experience. But her body was moving instinctively, swaying towards him, or was he pulling her closer? She did not know...nor care.

'Trust me...marry me...' His whispered words shattered the spell.'

'I can't!' She recoiled, putting a space between them again. 'I am not the wife for you. You waste your time...and expertise!'

'Obviously!' He was coldly derisive as he stared at

her. 'The only waste will be if you do not listen! Do you really think that you will be allowed to remain here, buried in the country, free to do as you choose? Refuse me and there will be others.'

'Whom I shall also refuse.'

'You may not have that choice,' he rasped.

'Why not?' she asked uneasily, jarred by something in his tone.

He studied her face for a moment and then gave an exasperated sigh. 'Being an heiress and kin to the Queen would be reason enough. How long do you think you'll be allowed to remain unwed?' he said tersely. 'Your mother is already threatening to turn you out in your petticoat.'

'My mother spoke in anger; my family would not force me to a match I did not want,' she replied desperately, trying to convince herself as much as him.

'Wouldn't they? Not even for a Queen's favour?' He was dismissive. 'Was Sherard your choice?'

She bowed her head, unable to answer him. She had wed Edmund Sherard because her father had told her it was necessary to protect her mother from Mary Tudor's wrath. Lady Katherine had never troubled to hide her liking for the Protestant faith nor her dislike for the old.

'I thought so…' he sighed, as he watched her face. 'So, use your wits and think who your next suitor might be if you succeed in refusing me. Old Westliffe is looking for a new duchess; the last died of the pox he gave her; or there is Mortimer. I heard him express an interest in you.'

'Mortimer!' Her head came up abruptly.

'Yes, Mortimer.' His mouth twisted as he read her expression. 'Whose last wife took her own life rather than remain wed to him. They say he cannot get his pleasure without inflicting pain.' He smiled insultingly. 'But then, perhaps it is a prospect you would find exciting, since it seems you found Sherard's bed so dull you took to the stable—'

'You believe that of me?' Her voice splintered. 'And yet you seek my hand! Who do you despise the most! Yourself or me?'

'Oh, myself, lady.' He laughed raggedly. 'Don't ever doubt that.'

Her eyes flashed up to his, startled by the depth of his bitterness.

'Then why?' she began.

'Because I have no more choice than you,' he grated. 'The Queen has ordered me to wed you. As your family has ordered you to wed me.'

'The Queen…'

'Yes, the Queen,' he replied drily, watching her face, 'whose wishes you would do well to obey.'

'Is it treason to refuse to wed? What will she do to me for refusing you?' she flared. 'Cut my head off? I should not care if she did. Marriage is for a lifetime, at least beheading is quick!'

'Only if the axe be sharp,' he grated, his face very white. 'And you should not jest about such matters; do not forget who fathered her. The Tudors are a dangerous brood when crossed.'

'I know.' She swallowed, her mouth suddenly dry. It was one thing to defy her parents, but the Queen… 'Please.' She lifted pleading eyes to his. 'Could you not tell her that you did not find me pleasing enough to wed?'

'It would not be true, and only a fool tries to lie to Elizabeth Tudor.' He was implacable.

'But…but you think me a wanton…' she protested as she felt colour rise in her cheeks.

'Wanton or innocent, it matters not much when the bride is kin to the Queen and brings a fortune with her,' he answered cynically.

She bit her lip as a lump rose in her throat. She knew that was what had brought him here, knew what he thought of her; so why did it hurt her to hear him say it so bluntly? She scrubbed impatiently at her pricking eyes with her hand. Her wrist caught the corner of the gilded crescent which held her French hood in place. It tumbled on to the rushes with a soft thud, like the noise they said a severed head made when it fell, only not so loud. She stared at the pool of black silk, gleaming dully like fresh blood in the reddish glow of the torch above their heads. If the queen bid you wed, was it treason to refuse? Feeling sick and afraid, she slumped against the doorjamb, her face whiter than sun-bleached linen as she tried to blot out the images of the scaffold which had risen in her mind. Such thoughts were foolish…but were they? If a King could cut off the head of women he had lain with, professed to love, would his daughter hesitate to punish a distant kinswoman for disobedience, with the Tower…or even the axe?

'M'lady, are you faint?'

'Don't!' she almost screamed, recoiling from him as if from an executioner as he touched her shoulder.

He dropped his hand immediately, his mouth setting into a thin line as he scanned her face. 'I had not realised you find me so distasteful, lady,' he said slowly. 'I had thought—' He broke off and gave a humourless laugh. 'It does not matter what I thought; 'tis obvious I was mistaken. I will not importune you further.'

'Don't go! Please!' Her voice was ragged, desperate even to her own ears.

He swung around, his face harsh, unforgiving. 'I see little reason to stay.'

'Please…' she choked on the word, trying to stop the tears which blurred her vision and wondering why she had called him back.

'Well?' He was impatient.

'Elizabeth…' she blurted out her fear like a child. '…the Queen…she would not really cut off my head, would she?'

'Who knows what a Tudor will do when angered,' he answered grimly.

'Surely…' Her voice faltered as she put an instinctive hand to her throat, and then, as he continued to stare at her coldly, her face crumpled and she began to turn away.

'Come here!' He caught her shoulders, pulling her around to face him again. 'If you are so afraid, let me help you—' He stopped, the angry line of his mouth softening as he saw the tears which rolled silently over her blackened lashes, leaving sooty trails on her cheeks. He sighed. 'Don't you understand? The Queen has ordered us to wed. If you please her in this, perhaps I can—'

'I understand pleasing the Queen is all you care about.' The heavy twist of her hair tumbled loose down her back as she threw back her head to meet his gaze with angry, frightened eyes. 'That and my fortune is all that drives you to seek a wanton's hand! All that brought you here! All that keeps you here!'

'No!' He jerked her forward, wrapping his arms about her, crushing her, so that her hands and arms were trapped between them. 'You are what keeps me here.'

'Don't lie!' she choked, twisting her face aside as his head dipped. But it was too late. She gasped as she felt the sudden warmth of his mouth, grazing her lips, burning through the obscuring silky veil of her hair. She went still, knowing now with absolute clarity why she had been so afraid of him. She knew what he was, an ambitious philanderer with neither conscience nor heart—but a touch, a kiss and she was his, for the moment, forever.

'No...' Her protest was despairing as his mouth touched hers again. He raised his head, and slackened his hold on her until she was only loosely bound by his arms.

'Do you hate me so much?' he asked wearily, as his hands lifted to cup her averted face, turning it back to his.

Hate him...if only she could! But it was impossible when he looked at her like this, his eyes blacker, darker than coal. Impossible when his fingers stroked back the silky skeins of hair from her face with such gentleness. Slowly, mutely, she shook her head.

'You should do.' His fingers tightened suddenly in her hair. 'It would be better for us both.'

She stared up at him, not understanding the barely audible words, the bleakness in his voice or the bitter curve of his mouth. Not understanding anything except that against everything experience and sense told her, she wanted, needed, this man to hold her, touch her, kiss her.

'Jesu...' He swore softly, as slowly, almost unwillingly, he bent his head and kissed her. Once, twice...gentle, almost reluctant kisses...and when her lips softened beneath his he jolted as if burned, and lifted his head, staring at her as if he had never seen her before. It was pure instinct which made her lift her hands, slide them into his soft, dark hair, holding him, inviting him in the only way she knew. All constraint left him in that moment. She saw desire, raw, fierce, flare in his eyes, felt it as his hands dropped from her hair to her waist and pulled her against him.

She shut her eyes, her hands falling back to his shoulders as he kissed her again. Hard, hungry kisses, crushing her lips until they parted to his tongue and allowed him possession of her mouth. And then she was melting in his arms like sealing wax over a flame as his kiss deepened, melting, burning inside, as his hands moved as hungrily as his mouth, smoothing over the tight silk of her bodice, tracing her spine, her ribs, the soft undercurve of her breasts, and then their aching, taut tips. Circling, rolling, until she could bear no more of this delicious, tantalising pleasure and instinctively pressed against him, silently begging him to stop or somehow release the new, almost painful tension in her body.

He groaned, and swung her round, crushing her against the panelled wall with the weight of his body as his mouth moved from her lips, down her throat, kissing, nipping softly, nuzzling aside her chain of rubies to find the beating pulse at the base of her neck, and then down further, over the slope of her breasts, to suck on the hard bud of her nipple below its covering of silk until she was unable to bear the spiralling pleasure and caught his head between her hands and lifted it from her breasts with an incoherent plea for him to stop or—she didn't know what she wanted or how to ask for it.

He laughed softly as he kissed her again with a new, dangerous gentleness, moving his lips against hers in a way which made her feel yielding, boneless. Her fingers slid from his hair and curled on to his shoulders and then down, with a boldness she had never dreamt she would possess. Touching, learning the strength and leanness of his whip-hard body beneath its covering of silken velvet. His mouth stilled on hers as her hands moved hungrily over his chest.

'No...' The word crawled from his mouth as he pulled away from her, putting his hands on her waist, holding her at arm's length.

Swaying between his hands, she opened her eyes slowly, feeling bereft and spun-out and as fragile as Venetian glass. There was an aching void inside her, a void which filled with misery. Had Edmund been right—was the fault in her? Didn't he want her either?

She looked at him helplessly with blurred green eyes.

'I don't understand…' He spoke raggedly, echoing her own thought. 'You will not wed me, yet you would be my mistress?'

'Mistress!' She swallowed, her mouth and throat dry. 'I am a Carey; I will be no man's mistress.'

'I could make you mine.' His fingers circled slowly on the small of her back, sending a tremor through her body. A wicked, shocking joy sheared through her. He did want her. And he was right; he could make her his mistress if she so desired. He had but to kiss her and she forgot all pride, all sense of right and wrong. The thought sobered her. She dropped her lashes over her eyes, unable for a moment to meet his gaze.

'Now, if need be…' His voice thickened and slurred as she touched the tip of her tongue to her dry and bruised lips.

'Here!' Her eyes flew up, wide with shock and disbelief. 'Do you think me a—'

'Wanton?' His brows lifted as their gazes met. 'That is what you intended, is it not?'

'Oh…' She coloured. 'You have known all the time that I…'

'Almost,' he said drily. 'If you would play the sophisticate and the wanton you should learn to pretend with your eyes as well as words, or else the performance lacks conviction—' his face softened as he lifted a fingertip to her cheek '—especially when your paint is washed half off with your tears and…nor should you close your eyes when you're being ·kissed.'

'Shouldn't you?' she stammered.

He shook his head. 'Sherard did not teach you much of lovemaking, did he?'

'No,' she admitted, her eyes darkening to the colour of pine needles as she recalled the two occasions on which she had gone to Edmund's bed; the first as a nervous bride, the second as a desperate and humiliated wife. 'He...I did not please him. That is why...why I was so afraid of wedding you—'

'Was?' His breath caught audibly and his eyes lit in a way which sent her heart leaping against her ribs. 'You have changed your mind? You will marry me?'

'Yes.' A weight seemed to lift from her as her lips framed the word. 'If you are sure it is me you want, not my fortune alone.'

'Fool...' He lifted her to him and kissed her. 'Keep your fortune; it is you I want—in my house, at my board and in my bed.'

'More than any other lady?' she asked in a rush, her stomach knotting. 'I know at court it is customary to...have mistresses, but I...could not share you...'

'Nor I you.' He smiled at her. 'I shall want none but you for as long as we—' He broke off, the colour draining from his face as she shut her eyes and let her head rest against his chest, a soft smile on her lips.

'For as long as you live—' The last word died on his lips. In the last few minutes he had forgotten what had brought him here, forgotten he was holding a trai-

tor to the crown in his arms, forgotten what his purpose was.

'I should like us to be wed before New Year,' he
said abruptly a few seconds later, trying to keep the
bleakness he felt out of his voice. 'It would mean your
following me to court as soon as is possible. There
will be talk, of course, since you are so newly wid-
owed.'

'I shall not complain at that.' She lifted her head
and smiled at him, her face incandescent and glowing,
with the sweet, new knowledge that he wanted her.
Wanted her for his wife so much that he was prepared
to flout convention. He was going to be her husband,
and it was going to be all right. He was kind, he made
her laugh, he desired her…and perhaps, in time, he
would come to love her.

The Earl shut his eyes, momentarily unable to face
what was written so clearly in her shining eyes. Traitress she might be, but she was offering him her heart
as well as her body…and no doubt the secrets Cecil
had instructed him to prise out of her along with it.
He had but to take her to his bed, whisper some lie
about loving her and there would be naught she would
not tell him. But he could not do it. There were some
depths to which he would not stoop, not even for
Elizabeth Tudor's sake. Some lies he would not and
could not tell. Dragging his hands from her waist, he
cleared his throat. 'I am grateful to you, m'lady, for
your cooperation. In different circumstances, I should
not wish for such haste. But I hope to spend much
time privy to the Queen; my being wed will prevent
much malicious gossip and damage to her reputation.'

'I see.' She struggled to keep her voice steady as disappointment, sharp and bitter as gall, made her insides contract. 'You hope to be given office?'

'It is a rare courtier who does not,' he answered tightly.

'As rare as one who weds for love rather than gain.' She gave a laugh which was a shade too bright to be convincing.

'I fear so.' His eyes held hers for a moment, and then he looked away. 'It is getting late; we should return to the others.'

'Yes,' she agreed stiffly, placing her fingertips on the arm he offered with formal politeness, her half-formed dreams disintegrating. Had she really thought that *she* had melted the Earl of Heywood's heart where so many had tried and failed? He wanted her for his wife; that was true enough. But the only reason was ambition…and she should never, ever have been foolish enough to doubt it. But it was too late now; there was a part of her which would have wedded him if she had known him to be the devil himself.

The Earl's breath caught as she glanced up at him, her eyes huge and dark in her thin face. God! She looked as if he were leading her to the scaffold. And perhaps he was. The thought disturbed him more than he had thought possible. Set-faced, he led her along the gallery, cursing Cecil, Catholic conspirators and his own sentimentality with every step.

'Well, it seems the Earl will have to wait for your company at court,' Lady Katherine announced briskly the following morning as she removed her hand from her daughter's forehead. 'Bess is right; you have a slight fever. You'd better keep to your bed until it is gone.'

'But I can't!' Seraphina jerked upright in her bed and then grimaced at the jolt to her aching head. 'He said I was to follow at once—he'll be angry with me, like Edmund.'

'Nonsense!' Lady Katherine said firmly. 'He would not wish you to risk your health. I shall write and explain that you are not fit to travel—'

'But the Queen—' Seraphina began exasperatedly.

'Enough.' Lady Katherine held up a shushing finger. 'I will not endanger my daughter's health for anyone's whim, be they Earl or Queen. So stop fretting; a week or two's absence will make him appreciate your company all the more. Now rest, while I fetch something for your headache.'

'Your mother's right,' Bess said as the door shut behind Lady Katherine. 'Besides, you don't want to arrive at court looking less than your best, do you?'

'No,' Seraphina conceded grudgingly, slumping back against her linen pillows. When the Earl next saw her, she wanted him to be helpless with admiration, as helpless as she had been when he touched her.

'And,' Bess went on as she smoothed the coverlet, 'at least there will be time to make a new gown or two. I'll wager your mother will not say the green velvet is too costly this time.'

'True...' A faint smile curved Seraphina's lips as she shut her eyes and let herself drift back into sleep.

\* \* \*

'So, my lord, your betrothed has recovered from her *illness* at last and deigns to join us later today.'

The Earl started as the Queen spoke suddenly. It was nearly three o'clock in the morning and he had almost fallen into a doze in his chair as he waited for the Queen and Cecil to finish poring over the papers which littered the table at which they sat.

'The illness was genuine—' he began hastily. 'I sent my own physician and he assured me—'

'I do not care about the state of her health; I want to know if you are certain that she is the woman we are looking for,' the Queen said impatiently.

'I don't know. The more I think on it, the less sense it makes.' The Earl frowned as he gathered his wits. He had been thinking of Seraphina, but not of treason. 'I would swear she is no more a fanatic than she is a wanton. If I had not followed her from the cottage myself, I would swear we are barking up the wrong tree…'

'Then perhaps you should see this, m'lord; it was pushed beneath my door some time last night,' Cecil said coldly, holding out a piece of parchment to the Earl.

With instinctive reluctance, the Earl took the document. He could see from Cecil's face that he was not going to like what he was about to read.

The letter was ill-written and misspelt, with more blots and crossings out than words. But its message was clear enough and utterly damning. It began with a reiteration of the slanders about Seraphina's virtue and then went on to accuse her of plotting against the Queen's life, and of murdering her husband when he had refused to participate in her schemes. He bit his lip as he read to the end of the letter. Had she duped him utterly? Were these the secrets she was hiding, the reason for her so evident fear?

'Well, my lord, what say you?' Cecil asked impatiently.

'She detested her late husband, that is true enough.' The Earl grimaced. 'But she makes no secret of it, and she seems no devotee of the old faith. If anything I would say she leant towards the new, like her dam...' He stared again at the parchment in his hand. 'And as for this...its author does not even dare put his name to it. It has been made to look as if it is written by someone of little education, but the paper is the finest quality, as is the ink; the pen was sharp, the letters well formed—'

'Spare us the details, m'lord. All of this we can see for ourselves,' Elizabeth interrupted peremptorily. 'Tis obvious you don't wish to believe the girl a traitor.'

'No. I don't, Your Grace,' the Earl said resignedly, wondering if there was anything Elizabeth Tudor's sharp eyes did not see. 'If she is involved, I would wager my life it is not by choice.'

''Tis not your life that is at stake, m'lord,' the Queen retorted. 'Now, tell me why you are so doubtful of her guilt?'

'Instinct, Your Grace,' the Earl said, meeting her eyes.

'Instinct?' Elizabeth's plucked brows lifted again. Then she gave a half-smile. 'I can scarcely argue with that; my own has saved my neck often enough. But have you any proof to substantiate it? Both evidence and rumour count against her so far.'

'No,' the Earl admitted tersely, aware of the disapproval on Cecil's face. Cecil was a man who dealt in facts, not feelings. 'As yet I have no proof either way.'

'Then I wish you would hurry up and find some,' Elizabeth said flippantly. 'Cecil here looks as if he is about to have apoplexy every time I as much as eat a sweetmeat that has not been tasted. I am half tempted to arrest the girl and get a confession from her and be done with it.'

'That might not be wise,' Cecil began thoughtfully, 'but perhaps we could take the risk.'

'No!' The protest burst quite involuntarily from the Earl's lips. He had been in the Tower; he knew what getting a confession meant. He had heard the screams, seen the broken and bloodied bodies, heard innocent men and women confess to any crime, simply to make the torturers stop. 'You mustn't do that—'

'Must not?' the Queen enquired with a mildness which did not match the steely glint in her dark eyes. 'Pray tell me why not?'

'Your pardon, madam; I meant no disrespect,' the Earl apologised hastily. 'I merely meant that to arrest her and extract a confession by forcible means will only do you harm in the eyes of your supporters as well as your enemies. And you need all your friends until you are crowned and your government secure. Give me a little more time; I shall discover the truth soon enough, without cost to you.'

''Tis good of you to defend *my* interests, Richard.'

The Queen eyed him coolly. 'I am flattered. I expected you to leap at any chance to avoid taking the Carey girl to the altar.'

'Not at the expense of justice and your reputation as a wise and merciful prince, madam.'

'How very noble of you to make such a sacrifice for my sake,' the Queen said lazily, clicking her long rope of pearls through her fingers. 'To marry a girl so like your late wife must be exceedingly distasteful.'

'She is not in the least like Lettice, madam,' the Earl replied decisively. 'Except for the colour of her hair, there is no resemblance.

'I do not doubt it.' Elizabeth smiled triumphantly and let her pearls drop back into place with a clatter. 'If she were, you would not refute the comparison so violently nor defend *her* so stoutly.' Then, seeing the Earl was momentarily at a loss, she laughed. 'You look in need of your bed, m'lord. Since your betrothed will be with us in a few hours, you had best get some sleep and sharpen your wits. We will discuss this further in a day or so.'

'Yes, Your Grace.' The Earl rose and bowed.

'Richard!' The Queen called after him as he reached the door. 'Be careful that you do not throw your head away with your heart!'

The Earl halted. It was on the tip of his tongue to ask her what the devil she meant by that, but he swallowed his anger. The woman who stared at him so imperiously was no longer the Lady Elizabeth whose imprisonment he had shared, but his sovereign, Henry VIII's daughter, and God help the man who forgot it.

'My head, like my heart, is in your hands, madam.'

Elizabeth smiled her close-lipped smile. 'And my life will be in yours, and probably has been already if the girl is as pretty as they say.'

'Prettier, madam,' the Earl said drily. 'But be assured, your life will always be safe in my hands, even if the girl is not.'

'You don't really think his loyalty might be swayed by this girl, do you, Your Grace?' Cecil asked as the door shut behind the Earl and there was the clash of the guards' halberds as they came to attention again.

'Of course not,' Elizabeth answered complacently, idly tracing the embroidery on one of her white satin sleeves with a slender finger. 'Perhaps you should give up affairs of state for matchmaking, Cecil. It seems the girl has ruffled my hawk's feathers. 'Tis high time someone removed his hood and made him see not all women are brainless lightskirts like that creature he married.'

'He only has to look at you to know that, Your Grace,' Cecil said dutifully.

'Flattery doesn't suit you, Cecil.' Elizabeth laughed. 'So let us get back to business. Tell me, have you found a Bishop with a conscience that will stretch to crowning the daughter of a witch yet? Or shall I have to start roasting a few as my sister did?'

'Madam!' Cecil was shocked.

Elizabeth sighed, frowning at a chip in one of her talon-like nails. 'It was a jest, Cecil—remember those?'

## Chapter Seven

Some nine hours later, Seraphina grimaced as she looked about the small panelled chamber she had been allocated in Somerset House. The court was overcrowded, and she knew she was very privileged to have been given a room to herself, no matter how small, but she could not help wishing it a little larger. There were not half her possessions unloaded and already there was scarcely an inch of floor left showing. With a sigh she picked up a bundle of sheets and squashed them into an already overfull linen chest.

'M'lady!' Bess's voice came from the open doorway, breathless and a little desperate from behind a precarious stack of bundles and boxes, the uppermost of which were wobbling dangerously.

'Hold still; I'm coming!' Seraphina dropped the lid of the linen chest and picked her way through the chests, bundles and caskets as quickly as she was able. In her haste she stubbed her stockinged toes on an ironbound chest.

'God's teeth!' she gasped as she grabbed a teetering box of Venetian glasses from Bess. 'Have you found the box with my shoes yet?'

'No, m'lady.' Bess dumped her burden upon the floor with a sigh. 'I'll go and have another look; it must be in the wagon somewhere.'

'Leave it,' Seraphina said as she looked at Bess's flushed and rosy face. 'You and Dickon must be in need of rest and sustenance. Go and see if you can find the kitchens and get us all some refreshment; we'll finish unpacking after we have eaten.'

'Yes, m'lady,' Bess agreed with a broad smile and turned to go, then she glanced back over her shoulder at her dishevelled mistress. 'Shall I not at least dress your hair first, m'lady? All the pins have come out, and as for that gown, there's more dust on it than you'd find in a flour mill. 'Tis me your mother will blame if she sees you in this state. You know what she'll say.'

'Naught she has not said to me a thousand times before,' Seraphina muttered. 'Don't fret; I can see to my hair. Now, please find us some food. And see if you can lay your hands on some mulled wine or ale,' she added with a dubious glance at the sullenly smoking fire in the small fireplace. 'I fear we'll get precious little warmth from that.'

'Aye,' Bess sniffed. 'Here we are among the greatest in the land, and it seems they have not even taught the skivvies that you cannot lay a fire with damp wood. I'll get Dickon to look for some dry kindling.'

'Fiddlesticks!' Ten minutes after Bess had left, Seraphina swore loudly, as a heavy wing of her red hair tumbled down over her face for the third time. After wrestling with the pins in vain, she had given up trying to put her hair up and settled for simply taking back the sides with combs. It would only have taken Bess a matter of seconds to secure them neatly, so why wouldn't the stupid combs stay in? Angrily, she seized two handfuls of her thick, silky hair and stabbed the combs into place. They held for a moment and then as she turned her head to the mirror began to slip. 'God's blood!' she swore ferociously, and then froze as she glimpsed a blurred figure in her metal mirror.

'You would seem to require some assistance, m'lady.'

The voice confirmed what she knew already. Heywood. She spun around, her black skirt belling about her narrow waist, her hands still raised to her head.

The Earl was leaning indolently against the doorjamb, watching her with eyes which glittered with ill-concealed amusement.

'Not from you,' she retorted, returning his scrutiny with as much dignity as she could muster. He was dressed with expensive simplicity in tawny velvet, his only ornaments a single gold earring and a border of lace on the deep collar of his cream silk shirt, which lay open. She lifted her eyes hastily from the V of flesh with its sprinkling of black hair. Jesu! She had forgotten how tall he was, how muscled and lean, how very *dangerous*.

'I see your malady has not altered your sweet temperament,' he drawled. 'I trust you are quite recovered? Lady Katherine would have preferred to keep you at Mayfield another week, I understand.'

'My mother always fusses overmuch; I am quite well.'

'Very well, I would say, but then you always look well to me, lady.' He smiled mockingly.

She flushed, suddenly furious with him. Why did he have to come now, when her hair was hanging down her back and she was wearing the plaintest, dustiest of gowns? In the twenty-eight days since she had seen him last she had imagined this meeting a thousand times. Imagined herself elegantly dressed, poised, sweeping into a room full of courtiers and dazzling them all with her wit and beauty while he looked on admiringly. And then when they were alone he would confess how he had been bewitched by her from the first, and swear to eschew even his ambition for her sake...while she regarded him with cool disdain. So much for stupid, childish dreams, she thought crossly. Here she was, moonstruck as the greenest country girl, while he laughed at her.

'What do you want?' she asked ungraciously, trying to push the combs more firmly into her hair.

'And good day to you, m'lady.' He laughed and made her an insolent bow.

'Is it?' she snapped. She did not need him to teach her manners!

'How could it not be when I am looking at you?' His eyes dropped blatantly to the jut of her breasts beneath her gown.

She dropped her arms with undignified haste, and wrapped them instinctively across her body. With so much unpacking to do she had taken off her boned corset because the ends of the bones dug into her flesh every time she bent to take something from a box, but now she wished that there were more than a layer of soft wool and fine linen between her flesh and his rapier-sharp gaze. Well, she was wiser now to his lecherous looks; she knew they meant nothing. 'Save your flattery for those that want it,' she said with what dignity she could muster, uncomfortably aware that one of the combs had slipped again and was now hanging drunkenly over one ear. Keeping one arm clamped in place, she wrenched it free with an angry gesture. 'I do not need your compliments.'

'I disagree, m'lady.' His voice was suspiciously muted as he played idly with one of the tasselled gold cords that should have held his collar closed. 'You respond to them like a flower to the sun. I think Sherard must have starved you of warmth.'

'And do not you intend to do the same?' she seared, furious at the way he was mocking her. 'One marriage of convenience is much like another.'

'Not when the bride is as beautiful as you,' he drawled, raking her with his eyes.

'Oh, stop it!' She turned away from him furiously. 'Go and play your courtier's games elsewhere!'

'I am sorry,' he apologised sincerely. 'At court such things become second nature. If I promise not to compliment you again, may I come in?'

'No, you cannot,' she began, swivelling back to face him again. 'My maid is not here and there is no room.'

'There is space here beside you, m'lady,' said the

Earl, all innocence as he stepped over a bundle. 'And, as for chaperons, I shall not tell if you won't.'

'You are…' She started to tell him what she thought.

'Welcome!' He grinned at her, a wide, boyish grin. 'How kind of you to say so, m'lady.'

Seraphina could not think of a suitable reply and even if she had, she would not have been able to utter it. There was scarce an inch of space between them, and her mouth and throat had dried as her body had registered his closeness. Southernwood. The clean, spicy scent of his skin set off a wave of unwelcome, searingly vivid recollection. It was all too easy to re-member what it had been like to be in his arms, to be kissed by him. His brows rose as he caught her gaze, and she took a hasty step back. A moment later she was tumbling ignominiously backwards as the low arm of the chair caught her behind the knees. She went down in a welter of petticoats, dropping the brush and comb.

'God's teeth!' She swore ferociously as she found herself trapped sideways in the chair by the weight of her skirts. She could not get her feet to the ground or get any leverage with her hands. Why, oh, why did she have to make a fool of herself again? First the fall from her horse, next her stupid charade at May-field, and now this!

'I see your mourning is only skin-deep.' His voice shook with ill-concealed laughter as his eyes skimmed over her shapely legs sheathed in fine scarlet wool stockings.

'It is you who will be mourning if you do not help

me out of this chair!' she threatened, tugging in vain
at her skirts in an attempt to restore some semblance
of modesty. 'For I swear I will box your ears!'

'Temper, temper,' admonished the Earl, with a
mildness which made her think of murder. 'Is that any
way to address your betrothed?'

'I'll address you with that broom over there if you
do not stop laughing at me and help me up!' Seraphina grated. 'This is all your fault; I said there was
not room enough.'

'Such a sweet request requires much thought,' he
drawled, standing with his arms folded. 'Especially
when it was so gently made.'

'Oh, you…' Her insult was lost as he bent without
warning and caught her wrists, hauling her to her feet
so abruptly that she was catapulted against his chest.

Her breath ceased and her heart stopped as his arms
closed around her, steadying her. Her anger vanished,
replaced by a sense of wonder that all he had to do
was touch her. Her heart thudded back into life, so
loud, so clamourous, she thought he must feel it beating against his ribs. She looked up as she heard him
exhale softly and felt his arms tighten about her. His
eyes were dark, burning as they dropped from her
clear, green eyes to her fractionally parted lips, and
then flicked up, over her shoulder. She half turned her
head to follow his gaze, and then hastily turned it
back again as she found her vision filled by the tester
bed. The blood left her face as she knew with sudden,
instinctive knowledge that he could take her here and
now, and she would not gainsay him. When he
touched her, she lost all reason, all pride. And he

knew it. His expression had changed to one of cold contempt as he met her transparent green eyes, and he released her abruptly.

She sat down stiff-backed upon the chair, half relieved, half annoyed that now she had agreed to wed him he did not seem to think her worthy of seducing further.

'You look a trifle wan, m'lady,' he said tersely. 'Did you hurt yourself when you fell?'

'No.' It was a half-truth. The fall had not hurt her physically, but her pride was in tatters. Savagely angry with herself and him, she kicked a fold of her gown into place over her stockinged toes and glared at him.

'Receiving a guest while not fully dressed.' His hawkish mouth flicked up at the corners. 'I doubt your lady mother would approve.'

Her eyes flashed, emerald with anger, as she crossed her hands over her breasts again.

'Your shoes?' he asked drily.

'Oh.' She crimsoned, feeling a fool again. 'I cannot find the box my shoes are in. And the boots I travelled in are damp.'

'I trust you will find them in due course,' he answered lightly, seating himself on the linen chest and resting one elbow on a spice casket. 'Or do you intend to wed me barefoot in your smock?'

'I doubt I should find you at the altar if that were the extent of my dowry.'

'You undervalue your worth.' He sounded almost sincere as his tawny eyes drifted over her slight figure. 'Even penniless in your shift you would have much to recommend you.'

'Do you break all your promises so easily?' She glared at him. 'You said you would not invent any more compliments!'

'They are not invention.'

'Now you're doing it again!' she exploded. 'I haven't the time to listen to a courtier's idle chatter. I should be grateful if you would leave me to my tasks.'

'I should not bother to unpack further if I were you,' he answered easily, making no effort to move.

'Why not?'

'The Queen moves to the palace of Whitehall on Friday; I only found out myself an hour ago.'

There was an audible groan from Bess who appeared at that moment in the doorway, her eyes widening as she saw the Earl.

'If this is what court life is like then they can keep it,' she announced, slumping against the doorjamb. 'Moving from pillar to post, and not a scrap of food to be had before dinnertime. You would not credit it, m'lady! Two kitchens the size of barns, yet to get a loaf of bread you have to send out to the public ovens.'

'I would credit it,' laughed the Earl. 'God knows, even the Queen has difficulty in getting a meal served on time. I take it neither of you has broken your fast as yet?'

'No,' Seraphina admitted.

'Then you are both invited to my apartment. I have bread, meat, cheese and ale,' the Earl said, in a tone that brooked no argument as he held out a hand to Seraphina.

'But...' she began, bemused by the change in his manner. 'My gown is not fit to be seen, and I have no shoes.'

'I know a passage no one uses but the servants. He reached out and caught her hand, pulling her on to her feet. 'Now, come along before you grow faint from hunger. You have little enough flesh on your bones as it is.'

So he thought her scrawny, did he? She opened her mouth to refuse his offer, but closed it again as she saw Bess's pleading expression, and allowed him to take her arm and lead her from the room.

Seraphina looked about his apartment curiously as he gave instructions to his manservant to set out some food and fill a basket with provisions for Bess to take to Dickon. Like his clothes, the furniture he favoured was plain, but of the highest quality; polished oak and yew gleamed in the sunshine that streamed in through the pair of narrow windows in each wall. There were rich Turkey carpets on the floor instead of rushes, tapestries on the walls, and well-cushioned chairs beside the blazing fire. Papers and books bound in tooled leather lay neatly on a chest, with sharpened quills and ink lying ready to be used. A lute hung on a hook on the wall, near a painted harpsichord, on which some sheets of half-written music lay and in a corner was a rapier of damascene steel, lying carelessly propped against the wall.

Bess followed her gaze. 'They told me in the kitchens that he's as good a swordsman as he is a lover,' she muttered.

'Hush,' Seraphina hissed at her, scarlet-cheeked, as the Earl lifted his head and caught her gaze. 'You had better take the basket to Dickon,' she added more loudly.

'John will carry it for you.' The Earl gestured to his servant to follow Bess, who gave the Earl a meaningful look.

'I shan't be long, m'lady,' she said.

The Earl laughed as the door shut behind them. 'Is she always so protective?'

'Always.' Seraphina found herself suddenly shy at being alone with him in his rooms and turned away and picked out the beginning of a madrigal upon the harpsichord. For the first time she noticed a toy horse lying on the floor beside it, and its tail a little distance away. It looked utterly incongruous in the well-ordered room.

'My son's.' She started as the Earl spoke from behind her and then stepped forward to pick up the toy and place it on the mantelshelf. 'I promised I should mend it before he comes again.'

'Your son? My uncle said your wife died in child-bed...'

'She did, but the child survived.'

'I didn't know,' she said awkwardly, trying to take in the fact that she was to gain a stepson as well as a husband and in the next few weeks. 'How old is he?'

'Robert? He will be three years old next summer,

God willing...' His hand lingered on the little horse as he spoke, as if he was reluctant to put it down.

'I will do my best to be a good mother to him,' she said softly, as she saw the expression on his face. 'Shall I meet him soon?'

'No.' There was something in his tone which froze the rest of her questions in her throat. 'He spends most of the time in the country in the care of his nurse. It will not be necessary for you to have much to do with him.'

'Why?' She was aghast. 'If I am fit to be your wife, surely I am fit to care for your son? I swear I will be kind to him.'

'I don't doubt that for a moment.'

'Then why, in heaven's name?'

'Because I will not cause him unnecessary hurt. He will become fond of you and when—' And when your marriage is over... He choked back the words which had risen to his lips. 'He will be upset when he must remain in the country and you come to court with me. It is better he does not become too attached in the first place.'

'You think so?'

'I do not wish to discuss it further,' he said, an unmistakable warning in his voice.

But I do. She bit back the retort that came to her lips. The child was his son, not hers; she had no right to interfere in his upbringing but...she had no intention of letting a little boy think that his stepmother cared nothing for him, even if his father gave more attention to his ambition than to his child. One way or another, she would persuade him to let the child come under her care. Aware that he was regarding her speculatively, she lowered her lashes over her eyes. 'As you like, m'lord; he is your son and no doubt you know best.'

He laughed suddenly and shook his head.

She looked at him, puzzled.

'Your meekness, lady, is about as convincing as your attempt to play the wanton,' he answered the question in her eyes with a wry smile. 'I do not care if you obey in naught else, but in this I insist you do as I ask.'

'And if I rebel?' She met his gaze steadily.

'Rebellion is always a dangerous game, lady; you—' He broke off as there was a light tap upon the door and he crossed the room to answer it.

She frowned, wondering how she was going to get him to change his mind about his son.

'I'm sorry, I thought you were alone, my lord…'

She could not help catching a fragment of the murmured conversation between the Earl and whoever was at the door. There was something familiar about the voice, but she had to be mistaken; Grace was not at court. Curious, she moved a step so that she could see who it was that he was talking to.

'Seraphina!' It was Grace who recovered from the surprise first. Her finely plucked brows rose as her gaze flicked from Seraphina to the otherwise empty room. 'I did not know you were at court.'

'I arrived this morning. We had no food; the Earl was kind enough to invite us to dine… My mother and father are delayed…the wheel of their carriage broke….' She found herself babbling an explanation.

She knew Grace well enough to catch the nuance of deep disapproval. 'Bess was here but a moment ago…'

'I am not your confessor, Seraphina,' Grace said softly, her fair brows lifting. 'But don't worry, I will not prattle. But you, my lord—' she gave the Earl a disapproving glance '—you should know better than to so risk a lady's reputation, even if you care so little for your own. I will not have my friend disgraced.'

'I stand corrected, Mistress Morrison,' the Earl answered coolly, meeting Grace's gaze. 'I did not know you and Lady Sherard were so well acquainted.'

'We are kin by marriage,' Grace answered before Seraphina could speak. 'Lord Sherard was my cousin; I stayed often at Sherard House, Seraphina and I are like sisters, are we not?'

'Yes…' Seraphina found herself agreeing, a little surprised that Grace was so effusive.

'*Your* cousin—' The Earl was staring at Grace in a way which made her feel distinctly uneasy. 'You did not tell me that when we last met at Queen Mary's court. I had no idea you were so well connected.'

'I did not think it would be of interest,' Grace said stiffly.

The Earl's mouth curved into a slow, dangerous smile. 'But you always interest me, lady; did I not tell you that when—'

'I am sure Lady Sherard has no wish to be bored by reminiscences she cannot share.'

The ice in Grace's tone was unmistakable and there was a sudden silence in which the tension was almost tangible.

'I don't mind,' Seraphina said belatedly, as the Earl and Grace stared at each other.

'But I do,' Grace said briskly. 'I only came to collect the music the Earl had promised me.'

'Of course,' the Earl said smoothly. 'But first, since you are so well acquainted with my betrothed, come and take a cup of wine.'

'Your betrothed!' Grace's eyes went very pale, almost grey rather than blue as they met the Earl's gaze. 'You jest…'

'If you will not believe me, ask your friend.'

'Jesu.' The blood drained from Grace's face as she shifted her gaze to Seraphina. 'Is this true…?'

'Yes,' she answered, bewildered by Grace's uncustomary lack of composure. 'I can see you are surprised; will you not come and sit down?'

Grace followed her into the room and sank into a chair with a rustle of her grey satin petticoats.

'So…' Grace inhaled and then lifted her chin to look at first the Earl and then Seraphina. 'When are you to be wed?'

'At the end of December,' the Earl replied as he handed each of them a cup of mead.

'So soon!' Grace went very white. 'You can't—'

'Why not?' he drawled lazily.

'Because—' Grace began passionately and then stopped. 'Because it is unseemly. Lord Sherard is scarce cold in his grave…' Her blue eyes filled with sudden tears. 'And Seraphina, what will people say of you?'

'The haste was not my choice…' she found herself apologising.

'Nor would it have been mine,' the Earl said drily, 'if not for political necessity. Now will you excuse me while I find the music you wanted?' He bowed to them both and disappeared into an antechamber.

Seraphina took a swallow of her mead, but its sweet, fiery taste did naught to dull her anger. Political necessity! It was one thing to know his reason for wedding her, but another to have it paraded before others!

Some of the colour had come back to Grace's cheeks and she drank a little of her mead. 'I am surprised you agreed to such a match. After Edmund died you swore you would never wed again—and to wed him of all people. He has neither principles nor heart when it comes to women…or faith.'

'It was wed him or be thrown out of doors by my family and incur the Queen's wrath besides. You do not think I have any affection for him, do you?' Seraphina spoke with deliberate loudness, wanting him to hear, wanting to pay him back in his own coin.

'I'm sorry.' Grace's face softened suddenly. 'I forget that heiresses often have even less choice than a poor relation. If you have need of a friend when you are wed, you may rely on me.'

'Thank you. But enough of me; tell me how you come to be at court? I thought you would prefer to remain quietly at Sherard House now that…things have changed.'

'You mean now that we have a Queen who does not favour the true faith…?' Grace smiled ruefully. 'I should have preferred to remain at Sherard House, but it was not possible.'

'Surely Edmund's heir did not turn you out?' Seraphina asked as she looked at Grace and gloomily noted the difference in their apparel. Grace, as ever, was immaculate from her fragile lace cap to the unscuffed silk toes of her shoes. There was not even one silver-gold hair out of place. She wondered with a sinking heart if the Earl had made the same unfavourable comparison.

'No,' Grace answered after a moment. 'But his lady wife did; the new Lord Sherard had a roving eye which wandered in my direction once too often.'

'No man could blame him for that,' the Earl drawled, as he came back with a sheaf of music. 'You may keep this copy, mistress; it would be a shame to see such pretty fingers stained with ink.'

'Thank you, but I would not wish to be in *your* debt.' Grace put down her mead and got up, clutching the music to her like a shield. Seraphina stared at her, startled by the acidity in her tone. A fleeting, half-formed suspicion slid into her mind. Then she almost laughed. Pious Grace and the Earl! That was ridiculous, wasn't it? She glanced from Grace to the smiling Earl, who seemed not in the least put out by Grace's sharpness.

'As you like, mistress.' The Earl shrugged. 'But please, don't go before you have finished your wine.'

'I must.' Grace was terse as she turned towards the door. 'Lady Lennox will be waiting for me.'

'Wait!' the Earl commanded. 'How do you plan to go to Whitehall on Friday?'

'By wagon, with Lady Lennox's luggage. She is to use her litter and the carriage is full.'

'Then you must travel on my barge, as I hope you will, m'lady,' he glanced at Seraphina.

'Yes, of course,' she answered without hesitation. After three days of bone-jarring travel on rutted and potholed roads, she would have accepted the invitation at any price.

'Then it is settled?'

'If you insist,' Grace answered the Earl coldly, before smiling at Seraphina. 'I shall see you before then, of course? Perhaps at the masque tonight, if you have need of a chaperon?'

'Yes, thank you.' Seraphina tried hard to sound eager. She knew she could not attend the masque or travel on the barge without a chaperon, but she would rather it was her mother. How could she hope to dazzle the Earl when Grace was standing beside her? Polished, beautiful Grace, who possessed all the womanly virtues which Edmund had accused her of lacking.

'If I had known you disliked her so much, I should not have suggested she travel with us,' the Earl said when Grace had left and they were alone again.

'Dislike her? How could I?' She jolted, hating the way he read her face so easily. 'If it were not for her—' she stopped. There were some humiliations which went too deep to speak of, particularly to him. 'Besides, no one could dislike Grace. She is pious, modest, virtuous and very kind.'

'A veritable paragon,' he laughed drily. 'Perhaps I should have sought her hand instead of yours.'

'Then why don't you?' She had meant to sound

light, not bitter, but the words came out all wrong as a lump rose in her throat.

'I was jesting, lady.' He looked at her quizzically. 'You cannot really think yourself Grace Morrison's inferior, can you?'

'Why not?' She laughed jerkily. 'My late husband did and made no secret of it!'

'Then he was a man of little taste and less judgement,' he said emphatically, catching her hand and pulling her to her feet. 'Whereas I—' he grinned at her '—have always preferred the company of sinners to that of saints.'

'Thank you, my lord,' she answered acidly. 'But I doubt it will stop you complaining of my sins once we are wed.'

'Are they so very great?'

There was an odd edge to his mockery which fuelled her anger. 'Yes,' she snapped. 'So don't say you were not warned.'

He looked at her with peculiar intentness for a moment and then laughed a little brittlely. 'I find that difficult to believe, so say I am forgiven, then come and eat.'

'Very well.' Still angry, she let him lead her to the table, where she sat in near silence, responding in monosyllables to his attempts at conversation.

'Is the food not to your liking?' he asked after a particularly lengthy silence. 'I will send John for something else when he returns…' he offered as she picked at the crusty warm bread, cheese, ham and sweet apples.

'No. It is excellent.' She answered guiltily, aware

that she scarcely deserved his hospitality. She had overreacted, she admitted to herself, simply because he had teased her about Grace. Grace, who had been held up as an example of all that she should have been, and was not.

'I'm sorry—' They both spoke at the same moment.

'No, the apology should be mine.' His eyes sought hers across the table as he spoke. 'I forgot that you are new to court and do not know that people often say what they do not mean. I did not mean to distress you.'

'You didn't,' she lied hastily. His dark brows lifted and she dropped her gaze to the table. 'It is just—just that Edmund could see no fault in Grace and so many in me—' She laughed nervously. 'And he was probably right.'

'I see.' His mouth twisted. 'Yet you say you do not dislike her.'

'It was not her fault. It was natural he should be fond of her and she him. If Edmund had not taken her in after her parents' died, she would have been a pauper. They left her naught but debts.'

'And was she suitably grateful?' he asked cynically.

'No! It was not like that—' she said shocked. 'It was just that they were more like twins than cousins. They were alike in looks, tastes, their faith; if they had swapped clothes, except for their height, you would have been hard put to it to tell the difference!'

'Twins! God's breath! I have been addle-pated!' She stared at him in bewilderment as he leapt to his feet, so suddenly that he sent his chair toppling backwards. 'You will not mind if I take you back to your chamber now? I have just remembered an appointment...'

'Of course not...' she said, bemused as he took her hand, brought her to her feet and almost pulled her from the room into the corridor. 'Thank you for the meal.'

'It is I who should thank you for your company.' He smiled at her, a wide, almost carefree grin that made him look no older than herself.

'Oh, n-no...' she stammered, wondering if she would ever become indifferent to his smile, his touch, his voice. 'It is not necessary.'

'It is.' He laughed exuberantly, seizing her around her narrow waist and swinging her round and round until she was laughing helplessly, without the slightest idea why. She only knew that something had changed between them, and changed for the better. And if he was happy, then so was she. She was still laughing when he caught her against him and let her slide down his chest until her toes just graced the ground and her face was exactly level with his. Her laughter died instantly as his eyes found hers. It was like drowning in warm, dark honey, and it was so natural to lift her hands from his shoulders, cup his face and touch her lips to his warm, velvety mouth.

She felt him go rigid, heard his shocked intake of breath and then almost roughly he set her down, holding her at arm's length.

'I'm sorry,' he said stiffly. A man might kiss a woman, but a respectable woman must never seek such favours. 'I did not mean to do that. You must think me immodest.'

He stared at her for several seconds, his eyes shuttered, unreadable. 'I think only that you deserve better than—'

'Better than you. I could not agree more, Richard,' an amused masculine voice drawled from behind them. 'So you had best introduce me at once, lest I decide to tell your betrothed.'

Leaving one hand on Seraphina's waist, the Earl turned to greet the tall, dark-haired man lolling against the wall and regarding them with sardonic eyes. 'I said better, Robin,' he returned lazily. 'And this *is* my betrothed, Lady Sherard.'

'Your pardon, m'lady.' The man recovered himself well and made a sweeping bow to her. 'Lord Dudley, at your service.'

'I am pleased to make your acquaintance, m'lord,' Seraphina answered, astonished that her voice could sound so cool, when her cheeks were on fire. Given her dusty dress and dishevelled hair, it was not surprising that he had obviously taken her for a serving wench and he must have seen her kiss the Earl... She groaned inwardly.

'And I yours, m'lady.' He raked her with a frankly admiring glance. 'I wondered what had brought about Richard's sudden change in heart towards the state of matrimony. Until a week or two ago, he swore he would not wed again—'

'Robin,' the Earl broke in, pulling Seraphina closer to him and exchanging a significant glance with the other man. 'If you will excuse us, we are in a hurry...'

'So I saw.' Robin Dudley smiled and Seraphina's embarrassment increased a thousandfold. It was obvious that he thought they were in haste to reach a bedchamber. 'Lady Sherard.' He nodded to her. 'I hope we shall meet again soon.'

'Yes.' She managed a smile and then, as Robin Dudley disappeared around a corner in the panelled corridor, she glared up at the Earl. 'He thought...'

'It does not matter,' he reassured her. 'Robin is a friend; he will not blab, because he knows he will feel my fist if he does.'

'I thought you said he was a friend.'

The Earl grinned. 'He is, but we have occasionally fallen out...over women.'

'But he is married, is he not?'

The Earl laughed cynically. 'What difference do you think that makes? Men take a wife for gain; they look elsewhere for pleasure.'

'Thank you for reminding me,' she answered tersely. 'I was in danger of forgetting.'

His face softened suddenly as he glanced down at her. 'If it's any consolation, so was I for a moment. Now come, I have little time as it is.'

*A moment.* She did not know whether to be pleased or furious as he took her hand and almost pulled her along the corridor in his wake.

## Chapter Eight

Seven days later the Earl of Heywood leant idly against the sunwarmed bricks of a wall that made up one side of a small courtyard. Out of the wind, it was almost as warm as spring. It was difficult to believe that it was Christmas Eve. His mouth curled up at the corners in a wry smile. It seemed even the weather was anxious to please Elizabeth Tudor. He shifted his weight on to his other foot and glanced up at the bright sun. It was nearly noon; where the devil was Cecil? He could not wait any longer or he would miss the opportunity to further his acquaintance with Grace Morrison. He straightened and began to walk slowly towards a half-open door on the opposite side of the courtyard.

Seraphina flung open a heavy oak door and swore beneath her breath as she found herself confronted with a flight of stone steps leading down into a small enclosed courtyard. The buildings that made up the palace of Whitehall sprawled over twenty-three acres and she would swear she had covered most of them in the last half-hour. She was hopelessly lost. At this

rate, it would be afternoon before she found her way
to the stableyard. She hesitated, uncertain whether to
retrace her steps or go on, then the figure disappearing
into the building on the far side of the courtyard
caught her attention. The Earl! Even with his back to
her, she knew him instantly.

Bundling up the flowing black skirts of her habit
over one arm, she started down the steps, taking two
at a time.

Some instinct made the Earl turn in the doorway
and glance back over his shoulder. He froze for a
moment as he saw the figure hurtling down the steep
stone steps, her slender silk-stockinged legs flashing
pale against her black skirts. Then with an oath he
began to run.

He reached the foot of the steps at the same moment as she did. She flew off the last step, tried to
stop and failed ignominiously as the leather soles of
her soft boots slid on the brick paving. Instinctively
she released her skirts and stretched out her hands to
him.

'Gates of Hell!' he swore, as he caught her hands
and steadied her. 'Isn't breaking your neck by falling
off horses good enough any more? What possessed
you to come down the steps like that?'

'I was but following fashion,' she replied breathlessly. 'So many of the ladies hereabouts throw themselves at your feet; I thought it was the way to greet
you!'

'It is not funny; you could have broken your neck!'
His grip tightened on her fingers, almost crushing
them. 'An infant would have had more sense!'

She wrenched her hands free and glared back at him.

'Perhaps I should show more sense if you stopped treating me like a child!' she snapped, the resentment which had been growing in her for days surfacing suddenly. 'One moment you almost ignore me, the next you tell me to whom I may speak, where I may go, and even at what time I must retire for the night!'

'I am simply trying to protect you—' he sighed wearily '—there can be unexpected dangers at court—'

'I'm quite capable of defending my honour from importuning rakes, if that is what you mean!' she cut in fiercely. 'I'm eighteen years old; I know how to conduct myself as a lady!'

'Really?' he drawled as his brown eyes drifted over her. 'Have you looked in your mirror of late?'

Instinctively, she put a hand to her fiery hair. As she had feared, much of it had escaped from her black and silver snood. Cursing silently she groped at the back of her head for the pins which should have anchored the net.

He watched her struggle for a moment, his face unreadable. 'Here, let me try.' He sounded half exasperated, half amused.

Her own hands dropped back to her side as his hand smoothed her hair back from her brow. She stood very still, all too aware of his nearness. It was the first time in days they had been alone. There was nothing to stop him holding her, kissing her, as he had at Mayfield. She swallowed, trying to ease the sudden dryness of her mouth and throat, shocked by the wanton nature of her thoughts. She shut her eyes, thinking to blot out the image of his wide, hawkish mouth that was so close to hers. But that was worse, because other infinitely more disturbing images tumbled through her mind as the featherlight caress of his fingers on her hair wound her body into ever tighter tension. She could not stop herself from flinching, as his palm, roughened and hard from years of practice in the tiltyard, grazed her cheek.

'Did I hurt you?' he asked, his hands stilling. 'I did not mean to pull.'

'Yes,' she lied, keeping her eyelids lowered. If she looked at him, he would know. And she was not going to make a fool of herself a second time by offering him what he did not want. 'I'd rather the pot boy dressed my hair than you!'

'Liar.'

Her eyes flew open, green and transparent as glass. 'What do you mean by that?'

He smiled at her lazily. 'You know. Now turn round and keep still.'

Furious, she did as he said. He knew, damn him, he knew, and he was laughing at her, treating her as if she were a child again. Her head jerked as he touched the nape of her neck, while he folded her hair back into the net.

'Gates of Hell!' he swore. 'I said keep still. It would be easier to pin down a cloud than this stuff, and I've just skewered my finger with a pin.'

'Good!' she replied with great satisfaction. 'I'm sorry my hair does not please you. Since I cannot change it, perhaps you had better take another wife!'

'I don't want—' he paused to suck his finger '—another wife.'

'Don't you?' The doubts which had plagued her for days came spilling out. 'You have not shown overmuch pleasure in my company these last few days.'

'Haven't I?' he said, after a fractional hesitation, as he pushed the last pin into place. 'It was not my intention. Have the entertainments I have arranged not pleased you?'

'They would have pleased me more if you had shown me as much attention as you have Mistress Morrison,' she persisted, swinging round to face him. 'I begin to wonder if you indeed wish it were her you were to wed!'

'Don't talk nonsense.' He frowned as he met her angry emerald eyes. 'I thought you would be glad to have her company among so many strangers, that is why I have taken pains to be pleasant to her.' He gave an odd smile as he saw the lingering doubt in her eyes. 'She is your friend, is she not? You were singing her praises but a few days ago. Don't you trust her?'

'Of course I do!'

'But not me,' he stated drily.

'How can I when you flirt with her all the time?'

He put a hand to his close-cut beard and rubbed his face. Then he sighed. 'You are at court now, not in the wilds of Wiltshire. As I have tried to explain to you before, flirting with a pretty woman is as common as breathing here and it means nothing.'

'And nor does a betrothal, it seems!'

'There is no call for you to be jealous.'

'Isn't there? I have been at court seven days and you have not once as much as—' she broke off, her cheeks scarlet at the thought of the accusation she had so nearly made.

'What? Danced attendance, showered you with kisses?' He gave a self-mocking laugh. 'I leave that to the loons; I have my reputation to think of. I'd be the laughing stock of the court if it was thought that I was in love with my betrothed!'

'I see,' she said stiltedly.

'No…you don't.' The mockery left his eyes abruptly as he scanned her face. 'If you did…you would not care so much what I do or say, and that would be for the best.'

'What do you mean?' she asked, bewildered.

'Nothing, I was but thinking aloud.' He looked away. 'Now, if you will excuse me, I must leave you. I have an appointment.'

'I know; I was looking for you,' she admitted awkwardly. 'Bess said your man had told her you were to ride out to supervise the gathering of the greenery for the Yule celebrations. I wondered if I might come with you…' Her voice tailed off; she knew from his frozen face that it had been a mistake to ask.

'You will find it tedious; that is why I did not suggest it…' the Earl began tersely.

'Oh, no,' she contradicted him eagerly. 'I always loved fetching the greenery to deck the hall at Mayfield. Everything at court is so strange, it would be pleasant to do something so familiar.'

'But Crecy, your grey, he's lame, isn't he?' he protested.

'My father says I can take Jupiter if I am with you…'

'No!' He was curt. 'I will not be responsible for you upon that beast.'

'There is Dickon's gelding…'

'That would not keep up with the cart, it would be blown after a mile—'

It was the hint of desperation in his voice that made her see what she should have realised at once. He did not want her to come. Foolishly, she had clung to the hope that he might welcome the opportunity to be with her outside the formality of the court.

'Then I will not detain you longer.' She gave him her brightest smile, determined that she would not humiliate herself more than she had done so already. 'Good day, m'lord.'

She turned away abruptly and began to walk back towards the steps.

The Earl watched her with bleak eyes, hating himself. Against the great rosy brick walls of the palace, her straight-backed, black-clad figure looked very young, very alone. He bit his lip as he saw her wrap her arms about herself, a gesture which was beginning to become familiar to him.

'Wait!' His voice echoed around the courtyard and one or two curious faces peered out from windows.

She halted and turned with slow dignity to face him, her head high, and her eyes dry and very bright in her white face.

'I'm sorry,' he said simply, as he walked towards

her. 'I did not mean to be so unkind. I have much on my mind at present. If you still wish to come, I have a horse you may ride.'

'I have changed—'

'It would give me pleasure to have your company...' he cut in before she could finish her refusal. 'Come. As a favour to me...please?'

It was the last barely audible word which melted her pride to nothing. Just for a second she had glimpsed a vulnerability in his face which caught at her heart. He looked tired, almost hunted. She felt a sudden flare of resentment for the new Queen who danced half the night and worked the rest, and expected her favourites to do the same.

'Very well.' She gave him a tentative smile. 'As a favour to you.'

He smiled back, but did not meet her eyes. 'Then come on; we are late already.' Catching her arm, he pulled her along in his wake, through the maze of courtyards and corridors, until they reached the stableyard.

One of his stablehands came hurrying to meet him. 'The others are already at the west gate, m'lord. Lord Dudley said—'

'I can guess,' the Earl cut in. 'Put the new lady's harness on Madrigal and be quick about it, Jem.'

'Yes, m'lord.' The groom looked faintly surprised, but hurried to do his master's bidding.

'Thank you, Jem. Now, see that Pavanne is ready, will you?' the Earl said a few minutes later, as he stepped forward and took the reins of a milk-white mare from Jem.

'This is the horse you are loaning me?' Seraphina asked breathlessly.

He laughed. 'You look like a child who has had a gilded fairing dangled before her nose.'

'I feel like one,' she replied absently as her eyes travelled over the mare, taking in the alert head, with its broad brow tapering to a delicate muzzle, the powerful quarters and shoulders, the slender legs and dainty hooves. 'I can scarce believe I am to ride her! She is beautiful…'

'Aye, she has intelligence, strength and courage; the perfect combination of qualities for a horse,' the Earl agreed.

And for a man, the thought flashed through her mind as she glanced at him.

'She is spirited, though. If you have any doubts about handling her, I can send Jem to fetch another?'

'Do and I'll…' She stopped, realising from the tilt of his brows that he was teasing her. Glowering at him, she stepped forward slowly and stood very still as the mare blew warily at her. Only when it nudged at her with its velvet-soft nose did she lift her hand carefully to stroke its satiny neck. 'Where did you get her? I've never seen her like, except your mare, Pavanne.'

'They're half-sisters. I bred them both from stock my father bought from a Turk when he was in Venice as an envoy. The Turk swore that they were from the Sultan's own stables.'

'I can believe it; she's fit for a queen.'

'Yes,' he said wryly. 'Or for my betrothed. She is yours, if you want her?'

'Mine? Want her?' Her face lit with joy. 'Only a fool would not!'

'Aye…' he said distantly. 'And perhaps only a fool would think of parting with her.'

'I'll understand if you have changed your mind—' she began, unaware that her fingers had meshed possessively in the mare's mane.

'No.' His dark eyes skated from her face to the betrothal ring on her hand, glittering amid the mare's snowy mane. 'Don't worry; I was thinking of something else. The mare is yours to keep, whatever happens between us—'

She stared at him, her joy in the mare tainted now by the sense of unease that had grown in her all week. 'Is she to be my consolation for banishing me to the country once we are wed, like poor Amy Dudley?' she asked raggedly, summoning up her courage. The fear that he would not want her with him had been growing in her mind for days.

'No.' He shook his head. 'I will not send you away from court.' He sighed as he saw the doubt in her eyes. 'You don't believe me, do you?'

'Do you blame me?' she asked quietly, as their eyes locked. 'First you court me, then almost ignore me. Now you give me a horse worth a king's ransom, but speak as if there is no prospect of happiness for us. I don't know what to believe…' Her voice tailed off as the clatter and scrape of metal-shod hooves on the cobbles made her realise they had company.

'Believe nothing he says,' Robin Dudley's cynical voice advised her, as he reined his black to a halt a yard away from them. 'He's as unreliable as a weathervane. We've been waiting for him this last half-hour. These days he is never where he says he's going to be. He's harder to track down than a man bent on deceiving his wife—'

'Well, you've found me now,' the Earl broke in smoothly. 'And since you're in such a hurry, move that hulking great beast of yours back a pace; there is no room for Lady Sherard to mount.'

'Lady Sherard is coming with us?' Robin Dudley's dark brows rose as he reined back the black.

'Yes,' the Earl replied coolly, as he met Dudley's gaze. 'She is eager to try out her new horse.'

'*Her* new horse?' Dudley's eyes flicked to Madrigal. 'You've given her the mare?'

The Earl inclined his head.

'Jesu!' The other man's breath whistled through his teeth. 'Then it seems you truly have a price higher than rubies, m'lady.'

'What do you—?'

'Why don't you go back to the others and tell them to set off, Robin?' the Earl spoke over her question. 'If you're riding that carthorse, we'll catch you soon enough.'

'I doubt it.' Robin Dudley grinned back at them over his shoulder as he turned his horse. 'Shall we say ten angels to whoever reaches the split oak first?'

'You're always so eager to part with your money.' The Earl shook his head in mock despair.

'At least I haven't parted with my senses,' Dudley returned, his eyes flicking from Madrigal to Seraphina. 'Not that I blame you...'

'What was he talking about?' Seraphina asked as

soon as he was out of earshot. 'What is so strange about your giving me Madrigal?'

'Nothing,' the Earl replied tersely. 'Come here, I'll help you mount.'

He put his hands on her waist and for a moment as their eyes collided it was as if time had run backwards to the moment he had first touched her in the woods at Mayfield. There was the same sense of recognition and inevitability. She belonged to this man, whether she wished to or not; it was something beyond her control. And he knew; she saw it in the blackness of his gaze, felt it in his hands as they tightened on her waist, heard it in the catch of his breath. She swayed slightly between his hands, her legs going suddenly weak as he bent his head. She shut her eyes, dazzled, and a little afraid of the desire in his eyes. And then abruptly the contact was broken as he swung her up on to Madrigal's back so swiftly that she almost went over the other side and had to scramble for her balance, causing the mare to dance in protest.

'Your pardon,' he said drily as he watched her take up the reins and expertly settle the mare. 'I did not expect to lift you so easily; you're too thin—you need to eat more.'

'God's breath!' she exploded, her nerves ragged and her body aching with disappointment. 'First my hair, now my figure. Is there nothing about me that pleases you?'

'Of course,' he drawled as his eyes made a lazy appraisal of her.

'What?' she snapped, made suspicious by the way the corners of his mouth had lifted.

'Why, your sweet and gentle temperament, m'lady.' He laughed, ducking, as she drew one of her riding gloves from where it was tucked into her waistband and hurled it at his head. 'Now, where the devil is Jem? If he doesn't hurry, I may end up owing Robin money after all.'

'They must be at least a quarter-mile ahead,' Seraphina said as they left the sprawl of palace buildings behind them and reached the edge of open countryside.

The Earl smiled. 'We had to give them a chance. These horses are faster than any in England. Give Madrigal her head and you'll see what I mean.'

She did as he said, touching her heels to the mare's side. Madrigal flew forward into a floating, effortless gallop, so smooth it was almost as if her hooves didn't touch the ground. The distance between them and the rest of the party closed faster than she had imagined possible. She glanced sideways; the Earl was beside her, Pavanne matching her mare stride for stride. He caught her gaze and grinned, sharing her elation.

They were within twenty yards of the main party when Robin Dudley looked back over his shoulder and immediately kicked his black into a faster pace. She heard the Earl laugh beside her and then Pavanne passed her, and began to close on the larger black. Madrigal was pulling on the bit, demanding to join her stable companion. She let the mare have her head, and they sped past the group of richly clad courtiers. Ahead of her the Earl and Robin Dudley were riding stirrup to stirrup, hurling good-natured insults at each other as they vied for the lead. She glanced ahead and saw the split oak, standing on the edge of the wood. She bent low on Madrigal's neck, and found herself gaining on Dudley and the Earl. Fast as their horses were, Madrigal was bearing a much lighter weight, which was all the advantage the mare needed.

'Ten angels apiece, gentlemen?' she taunted them, as she came level and then swept past, laughing as she heard them both cursing in her wake.

She reached the oak four lengths ahead of them. She reined in, her face glowing with the exhilaration of the ride.

'I should have known giving you Madrigal was a mistake.' The Earl laughed as he pulled Pavanne up beside her. 'I shall end up a poor man.'

'So shall I; so how about letting me recoup my losses?' Robin Dudley said to the Earl as he glanced up to the top of the oak. 'Shall we say another ten angels to whosoever cuts the first piece of mistletoe from the crown?'

'Taking money from you, Robin, is easier than taking sweetmeats from an infant,' the Earl laughed, vaulting down from his saddle.

Seraphina's heart contracted as she too glanced up at the top of the tree. It was near a hundred feet to the crown. And the branches near the top looked dangerously frail. If he were to fall…her heart stopped.

'Please…' she appealed to both men as they began to strip off their riding boots and gauntlets. 'There are some other oaks over there where the mistletoe is on lower boughs.'

'Don't fret, sweeting.' The Earl gave her a smile which made her feel warm from head to toe. 'I've no intention of dying yet. Robin, are you ready?' He turned away, leaving her caught between fear and joy. Sweeting. He had called her sweeting. It was the first time he used such an endearment, and she prayed it would not be the last as she watched the two men begin the climb, one either side of the great oak's trunk.

'Let's take a rest, Richard,' Dudley said breathlessly, as they both reached a fork about fifty feet off the ground.

'Too much wine last night, or is it that new maid of honour?' The Earl laughed as he leant against the trunk of the great oak, one hand resting upon another branch for balance. 'You're losing your edge, Robin.'

'At least I'm not losing my wits,' the other man returned. 'You aren't serious about giving her the mare, are you?'

'Why not?' the Earl asked impassively.

'You know damn well why not! The Queen is expecting that mare to be your New Year's gift to her; she's dropped enough hints.'

'Then she'll have to be disappointed,' the Earl replied drily. 'And just think of the opportunity it will give you to console her, Robin, and how grateful she might be. The manor of Rafton is going begging, is it not?'

'It would make a welcome addition to my coffers,'

Dudley conceded with a grin. 'But why give me the advantage?'

The Earl smiled sardonically. 'Perhaps, unlike you, Robin, I value my future wife's happiness above ambition.'

Dudley threw back his head and laughed, his teeth wolfish against his reddish beard. 'You'll be asking me to believe you're in love next. What's the real reason, Richard—guilt? From what I've seen of Lady Sherard, I wouldn't count on placating her with gifts when she finds out; she doesn't look the sort to be bought—'

'When she finds out what?' The Earl's eyes lost all trace of amusement.

'About your seige upon Mistress Morrison's honour. Neglecting your betrothed to seduce her kinswoman a week before you wed is a little near the bone, even for you, Richard,' Dudley drawled lazily. 'I had not realised we were so alike. Until now, I thought you still had a remnant of conscience left. Still, one man's wastefulness is another man's gain. I'll be more than pleased to compensate Lady Sherard for your lack of interest.'

The Earl's eyes narrowed as they met Dudley's mocking gaze. 'If I thought you meant that, I would push you off that branch now. Touch her and I will kill you.'

'Pax!' Dudley held up a hand in a staying gesture. 'I see you have lost your sense of humour as well as your conscience. I was jesting.' But then he frowned. 'Damned if I see why you have to look further than your betrothed. She's young, beautiful, and by the

way she was looking at you just now, more than halfway to being in love with you, and an heiress to boot.
What more do you want, Richard?'

'For my friends to keep their noses out of my affairs,' the Earl growled, reaching for a hold on the
next branch. 'Now, shall we go?'

'Oh, what are they doing now?' A pretty, dark-
haired young woman groaned, as she brought her
horse to a halt beside Seraphina and stared upwards
into the oak. 'Why can't they leave it to the servants;
there are ladders and ropes on the wagon!'

'They have a wager as to who shall cut the mistletoe first,' Seraphina answered, without taking her eyes
off the Earl. She was mesmerized by the rhythmic
movements of his arms and shoulders beneath his billowing silk shirt as he climbed from branch to branch
with the supple agility of a cat.

'They wou…ld!' The young woman's voice rose
and fell as Robin Dudley slipped and had to catch at
a branch. 'Mother of God, I cannot watch. They were
ever the same as children; it was always who could
ride fastest or climb highest. How either of them has
survived this long, the Lord alone must know.'

'You know them both well?' Seraphina said hesitantly, wondering suddenly if this pretty and pleasant
young woman was one of the Earl's reputed con-
quests.

'Yes.' She smiled 'Richard was sent to be brought
up in our house when he was a child, and whenever
we came to court, he came with us, of course. Oh!'
She put a daintily gloved hand to her mouth. 'I'm

sorry; I have not introduced myself. I'm Lady Sidney, Robin's sister, and you must be Lady Sherard.'

'Yes,' Seraphina answered, slightly startled to be recognised and more than a little relieved.

'I thought so.' The woman smiled. 'You are exactly as my brother described you.

'Oh.' Seraphina felt herself blush as she remembered in exactly what circumstances Robin Dudley had first seen her.

Mary Sidney laughed. 'Don't look so alarmed. He said naught but good of you and that he had not seen Richard look so happy in years as he did in your company, which makes you a friend of mine, because I am mighty fond of Richard. He deserves some happiness after Lettice—' She stopped suddenly. 'I am talking too much as ever; it is nerves. Tell me, have they reached the mistletoe yet?'

'Yes,' Seraphina answered in a choked voice as she watched the Earl inch along a dipping and swaying branch and snatch a handful of mistletoe and push it into his belt.

Mary looked up, shading her eyes against the sun with her hand. 'Neck and neck as ever...' she sighed. 'Please God, they do not break them.'

'Amen to that,' Seraphina muttered. 'I have been praying since they set foot on the first branch.'

'I am afraid you will spend much of your married life in such activity,' Mary Sidney said sympathetically. 'Danger is bread and meat to Richard, as it is to Robin—but there are compensations, of course...' she added, with a grin which made her very like her brother. 'I'd rather have the company of men who have a little of the devil in them than too much of the saint.'

'So would I,' Seraphina answered with feeling, thinking of Edmund's cold, compassionless piety. Then she gasped as there was a noise like a pistol shot and the branch that the Earl was standing on broke and fell away beneath his feet. She shut her eyes. He was going to die and she could not look. As if from a great distance, she heard a woman scream and the sickening thuds as something heavy fell, crashing from branch to branch, for what seemed like forever. She was falling with him into a dark, bottom-less void. She felt twigs showering down on her head and face, but still she could not open her eyes. If she could not see, it would not be real. She jolted at the final sickening thud of impact with the ground.

Then someone had caught her hand and squeezed it tightly. 'It's all right. It was just the branch.'

Mary Sidney's shaken voice penetrated the dark-ness in her mind. 'He has not fallen. Robin is going to help him.'

Slowly she opened her eyes and looked up. The Earl had not fallen. Yet. He was hanging from the bough which had been directly above his head, all his weight on his hands. The branch was bending, slowly, inevi-tably, into an arc. The courtiers had been shocked into absolute silence and she could hear it creaking. It was too thin. It was going to break. She looked wildly for Robin Dudley. He was still several feet away, easing his way around the girth of the trunk. The Earl was inching towards the thicker part of bough, hand over hand, and it creaked louder with every shift of his weight.

Mary Sidney's hand tightened on hers and Seraphina knew she was thinking the same as she was. Robin Dudley would never reach him in time. Either the branch would break, or his grip would give out. She stared at the other dark-haired man. Why was he standing still, braced against the trunk? Why wasn't he moving quicker—and then suddenly she understood as she saw him stretch out a hand high above his head for the Earl's foot, taking all his weight as the Earl let go of the bough with one hand and reached for another slightly lower handhold above Robin's head. With what seemed like agonising slowness to the watchers below, he managed to move his other foot to Dudley's head, then from his hand to his shoulder, using him like a human ladder, until he was standing safely beside him in the fork of one of the greater limbs of the tree. A moment or two later they both began the descent, climbing down with the same confident ease as they had gone up.

There was a sudden outburst of chatter and laughter from the courtiers as the tension of the last few seconds was released. Many of them hurried to wait beneath the tree to greet the two men.

Mary Sidney released Seraphina's hand and crossed herself in the old way. 'I could box their ears!' she muttered furiously. 'They are too old for such stupid games.'

Seraphina nodded; she was still numb with fear. A fear which did not leave her until she saw the Earl drop lightly from the last branch to the ground, closely followed by Robin Dudley. The two men were immediately surrounded by the crowd of eager courtiers and she could see naught of the Earl but his dark head.

'Seraphina! I thought it was you that passed us. Did you not see me? Or are you avoiding me? I have begun to think so.' She swivelled in her saddle at the familiar tones and saw Grace trotting towards her on an elderly, mild-looking brown gelding. Dressed in pristine grey velvet with the sun turning her neatly netted hair to silvergilt, she looked demure and ethereally beautiful.

'Avoiding you? Of course I have not.' She returned Grace's smile awkwardly as she lied. She had avoided Grace for the last day or so, because she could not bear to watch the Earl flirt with her. Anyone else— but not her.

'Are you sure?' Grace asked anxiously as she halted her horse with a clumsy jerk upon its reins. 'I was afraid I had offended you in some way.'

'No, of course not.' Seraphina coloured, her sense of guilt increasing. It was not Grace's fault.

'I am so glad.' Grace gave a sigh of relief. 'The other night I thought you might think I was encouraging the Earl to partner me in the dancing overlong. It was not my doing, I swear.'

'I…I know,' Seraphina answered raggedly.

'I told him he was neglectful of you,' Grace went on. 'But he became so angry I was afraid to protest further. He can be so insistent.'

'Yes,' Seraphina said woodenly, as all the pleasure she had felt at being given Madrigal drained away.

'And, of course, you never neglect your duty as a friend, do you?' Mary Sidney said coolly. 'Your virtues are an example to us all, Mistress Morrison.'

'You are too kind, Lady Sidney.' A faint colour stained Grace's cheeks as she met Mary Sidney's eyes. 'Now, if you will excuse me, I see Lord Denleigh desires my company. I will see you this evening, Seraphina. I have some lace which will be perfect for your new gown; I will bring it to your chamber.'

'Thank you.' Seraphina forced another smile, and then sighed with relief as Grace rode away.

'I do not care for her style of friendship,' Mary Sidney said thoughtfully when Grace was out of earshot.

'She has always been kind to me,' Seraphina said loyally.

'Has she?' Mary Sidney's dark brows rose a fraction. 'I am not—' She stopped, her face softening. 'Look at them,' she sighed. 'Grinning as if they had just won a tourney, not near broken their necks.'

Seraphina followed the direction of her gaze, and saw the Earl and Robin Dudley remounting their horses. As if feeling her stare, the Earl turned in his saddle and smiled at her. A wide, wicked grin that lifted her heart. Momentarily nothing seemed to matter except that he was alive, safe and he was smiling at her.

'He does not look as if he needs reminders about duty,' Mary Sidney teased gently as she glanced from the Earl's face to Seraphina's. 'I'd say he was smitten.'

'Do you really think—' Seraphina began, blushing,

and then broke off as the Earl reined in beside Grace. Feeling sick, she watched as he held up a piece of mistletoe and leant across to silence Grace's laughing squeal of protest with a swift kiss.

She dragged her eyes away. Flirtation at court might mean nothing, but it did not stop it hurting so much that she wanted to hit him. If he must flirt, why Grace? Why not her?

'It is only harmless fun…' Mary Sidney said uncertainly, her hazel gaze darkening as it rested upon the Earl.'

'Yes…' Seraphina answered thickly. 'If you will excuse me. I am not feeling well, perhaps you will give the Earl my apologies.'

'No!' Mary said urgently, catching her rein and halting Madrigal as she began to turn her away. 'It will only be grist to the gossips' mill. You do better to pretend you had not noticed.'

'Better still to pay him in his own coin,' Robin Dudley said, as he came up and flourished a piece of mistletoe and leant across and kissed her lightly upon the cheek before she could prevent it. 'He must have lost his wits to waste a berry on her when he might have your kisses.'

'Robin…' There was a warning note in his sister's voice. 'Richard is on his way over here; was that wise?'

'No, but 'twas very sweet,' Dudley interrupted his sister and grinned at Seraphina. 'Since it may well cost me my life, will you not grant me another, lady?'

'I think not,' she said, and managed to dredge up a smile which did not reach her eyes as the Earl can-tered towards them. Robin Dudley had kissed her and it had not moved her as much as one glance from Richard Durrant's brown eyes. Was this how it was to be? She in hopeless thrall to him, while he dallied as he pleased. Never! Not while she had breath!

'Nor do I.' The Earl's voice was low, dangerous, as he halted Pavanne beside them. 'I trust you have not forgotten Lady Sherard is to be my wife, Robin?'

'I rather thought it was you who had forgotten,' Seraphina said with acid sweetness, before Dudley could reply.

'That is different—' he said roughly.

'How so? Because you are a man?'

The Earl sighed heavily, and then glanced from Dudley to his sister. 'Perhaps you would leave us for a moment?'

'Of course.' Mary gave Seraphina a swift, sympathetic smile and then glared at her brother. 'Come along, Robin, before you cause more trouble. It was none of your betrothed's doing, Richard,' she added, as she rode away.

After the pair had ridden off, he looked at her, almost warily. 'Well? Have you naught to say?'

'Have you?' she retorted.

'Only that I am sorry. I did not mean to distress you.'

'Then why—'

'Tomfoolery,' he said abruptly. 'It meant no more to me than this did to you.'

She jolted, colouring as he leant across and briefly touched the place on her cheek where Robin Dudley had kissed her.

'How do you know that that meant so little?' she said, piqued that he was so certain.

'I saw your face—' he shrugged '—fortunately for Robin...'

'Oh.' She dropped her eyes, wishing that he did not find her so transparent.

'Do you forgive me, then?'

'I suppose so,' she said slowly, raising her eyes to meet his. 'But I insist on one condition.'

'What?' He met her gaze warily.

'That you do not go climbing trees again. I thought you were going to die.' It was not what she had intended to say and her voice shook on the last word.

'So did I.' He laughed suddenly, his eyes warm and golden. 'You have my word on that if naught else. And—' he paused, his expression growing serious. '—I thank you for your concern; it is more than I deserve.'

'True.' She smiled wryly.

'You didn't have to agree!' He laughed again. 'But I fear you're right.'

'And I know you're right,' Mary Sidney said, as she brought her chestnut gelding back alongside them. 'Now you've made your peace, will you come and help us find the holly bushes? Rob never can see the wood for trees.'

'Nor can I at times,' the Earl said beneath his breath as they sent their horses into the woods. 'Nor can I...'

# Chapter Nine

Seraphina yawned behind her hand as Bess made the final adjustments to her gown of russet velvet and cinnamon silk. Elizabeth Tudor seemed to exist on a minimum of sleep and expected her courtiers to do likewise. The last nine days had become a hectic procession of banquets, masques, and hunts as the Yule celebrations had reached an almost feverish pitch. She yawned again, wondering where the Queen found the energy to hunt, dance half the night, and attend to matters of state.

'I told you to retire as soon as the Queen did last night,' Bess said. 'What possessed you to sit up at cards?'

'I felt like it,' Seraphina lied. She had been bone-tired, but the Earl had invited Grace and herself to play cards and she had not wanted to leave him alone in Grace's company. Not that it had made much difference, she thought bleakly. For all the attention he had paid her, she might as well have been invisible.

Bess made a disapproving noise in her throat. 'Just because the Queen must live every moment as if it were her last, you don't have to. I swear you've lost what flesh you had this last week. She'll have no courtiers left by Twelfth Night, if she carries on at this rate!'

'After spending so much of her youth with the threat of the axe over her head, you can scarce blame her for being so greedy for pleasure,' Seraphina said, grimacing at her reflection in the mirror and deciding Bess was probably right. Her face was all eyes and mouth, and as for the rest of her—she sighed, wishing she were as well endowed as Grace. If she were, then perhaps the Earl's eyes would follow her instead of Grace, and perhaps he might look at her as he had done at Mayfield when they had first met.

'That's better,' Bess smiled, as she made a last tuck about Seraphina's tiny waist and pinned it in place. 'These colours suit you wonderfully well.'

Seraphina forced her attention back to her reflection in the mirror. Since the fabrics were so luxurious, she had chosen a simple style: a low square neck, the tiny waist shaped to a point, from which the overskirt divided to show the cinnamon silk kirtle beneath. Only the sleeves were elaborate, the outer wing sleeve, lined with silk and trimmed with fox, fell to the hem, the undersleeve of russet velvet was slashed and pinked to let tiny puffs of her cinnamon silk chemise be pulled through. Bess was right; the autumnal colours of the gown did suit her, reminded suddenly of the day she had first met the Earl in the woods at Mayfield. Had he thought of it when he had chosen these materials as a gift for her? No. She was a fool to even let the thought cross her mind.

'The silk alone must have cost a fortune. The Earl is very generous,' Bess said approvingly as she twitched out a fold of the skirt and stood back to admire her handiwork.

'Or very guilty.' Seraphina's mouth twisted. 'Does he really think this profusion of gifts will console me for the fact that he cannot take his eyes off Mistress Morrison whenever she is within sight!'

'I'm sure he cannot prefer her to you,' Bess said, frowning. 'He's stuck to you closer than pitch to a plank these last few days.'

'Yes…' she answered slowly. 'But he takes care never to be alone with me, never to touch me. And he treats me like a child. He even tells me who I may or may not speak to. I danced a measure with Sir John Malgreave last night and he behaved as if I'd danced with the devil. And you cannot think of anyone more harmless than Sir John.'

'He is simply taking care of your reputation. Don't fret so; you are going to be his wife.'

'Wife! What consolation is that if he never touches me except when etiquette demands it? I'd rather be his mistress if—' She bit back the shocking admission that she longed for him to take her in his arms, longed for him to kiss her, to touch her as he had at Mayfield; Bess looked shocked enough already '—if his eyes would follow me about a room as they do her. I am so afraid, Bess, so afraid that it will be like Edmund all over again, that he will not want me…'

'You! Afraid?' Bess snorted. 'Since when have Careys been afraid, and for that matter, when have they ever given up something they wanted without a fight?

Are you saying you cannot take his attention from that whey-faced icicle!'

'It is not just the way he looks at her, it is the way he is with me. He is so remote.'

'Then it is her doing!' Bess was indignant. 'She'll be trying to snare him to spite you!'

''Tis not her fault; she has told me how embarrassing she finds his attentions—'

'And you believed her?' Bess snorted derisively. 'You're letting your gratitude to her sway your judgement.'

'How can I not be grateful? If it were not for her, Edmund would have killed me...'

'If it were not for her, things might not have come to such a pass!' Bess snorted. 'I can hear her now, dripping her poison day after day, sweet as honey and mild as milk! ''Poor Seraphina, she cannot help her frivolous nature...'twas not her fault she was raised a heretic...the young cannot help a little vanity...'''

'She was trying to protect me from his anger.'

'Trying to provoke it, more like!'

'Don't be ridiculous!' She strove to sound dismissive, to put aside the host of doubts that had arisen so suddenly in her mind as memories from Sherard House came flooding back. 'Why should she wish me harm?'

'Because she was afraid her cousin might come to love you more than he did her. She was jealous! I swear she was determined that since she could not share his bed, no other woman would!'

'Bess! That is ridiculous! They were cousins.' She

protested instinctively, because she could not bear to believe it true.

'I saw her kiss him the day you were wed and it was not a cousinly kiss!'

'That is enough! She was my friend. I owe her my life. I will hear no more of this! Now get me out of this gown; I cannot put off my black until tomorrow.'

'As you like, m'lady.' Bess obeyed sullenly.

Her frown deepened as Bess helped her into her petticoats and black velvet gown. Dear God, she was tired of dowdy black, even if it did lend her skin a translucent whiteness and emphasise the redness of her hair. She wanted to dazzle him, make him look at her and no one else. At least she would be able to put off her mourning from tomorrow. Tomorrow. To-morrow she would be his wife, share his bed...if he wanted her. Last night, when she had stumbled against him accidentally in the dancing, he had put her from him as if she had the plague, almost as if he could not bear to have contact with her. Just like Edmund. If her second wedding-night was like her first...

'No...' Fear overwhelmed her suddenly. She turned from the mirror and sank down upon the bed, her face in her hands.

The linen sheets of the great bed had been cold against her flesh as the laughing women had hustled her between them. In all the excitement of the wed-ding, no one had thought to warm them. She had sat propped against the embroidered pillows, managing to smile at their jokes and reassurances as she stared straight ahead, far too embarrassed to look at her new husband as he was also stripped and bundled in beside her amid a barrage of male laughter and lewd comments. It wasn't until they were alone that she had dared turn her head and smile shyly at Edmund. He had not responded but had simply stared at her. The silence had become awkward. She had swallowed, wishing he would say something, do something before her courage failed her utterly.

'The perfume you are wearing—' He had spoken suddenly, abruptly. 'Where did you get it?'

'Your cousin gave it to me, m'lord,' she had replied nervously. 'She said it was a favourite of yours; I wore it to please you.'

'Well, it does not! Wash it off!'

'M'lord?' For a moment, before she had seen the coldness in his blue eyes she had thought he must be jesting.

'I said wash it off! Are you addle-brained? There's a jug and basin upon the chest.'

He had flung back the sheets and pushed her from the bed so violently she had gone sprawling painfully on the rushes.

'Why…' She had been utterly bewildered as she had scrambled to her feet, clasping her hair about her like a cloak.

'Because…it does not suit you as it does her! Now wash!'

The water had been icy, the linen rough, but she had scrubbed obediently at her skin, shivering. When she had finished, she had gone shyly back to the bed, glad to cover herself with the sheet. He had lain so still, his eyes closed, that she had wondered if he had fallen asleep.

'M'lord…' Very tentatively she had touched his shoulder with her fingertips. 'I have done as you wished—'

'Don't touch me!' He had lashed out, catching her lip with his ring and splitting it.

She had put her hand to her face, disbelieving. 'M'lord…what have I done to anger you? What is wrong…?' she had asked in bewilderment.

'Wrong?' He had laughed harshly as he flung himself from the bed and snatched up his robe. 'You are what is wrong, with your devil's hair and whorish, heretic ways! I shall spend this night in the chapel, praying for your soul and mine.'

'Seraphina, are you not ready for the joust yet?' Lady Katherine's voice brought her jolting back to the present. 'I have brought you—' She stopped as she saw Seraphina's pale face. 'What ails you? Are you ill?' she asked sharply.

'No, it is nothing, Mother. I am a little tired, that is all.'

'Mmm…' Lady Katherine looked at her daughter critically. 'You should have gone earlier to your bed. Perhaps once you are wed you will not be afraid to let the Earl out of your sight.'

'Mother!' Seraphina said exasperatedly. 'It had naught to do with him; I simply wished to play cards.'

'If you say so.' Lady Katherine smiled. 'But be sure to retire early tonight; you will want to look your best tomorrow, which is why I have brought you this—' She shook out the bundle of shining cloth of silver fabric in her arms. 'Well? Would you like it?' Lady Katherine demanded. "Tis a gown that belonged to Anne Boleyn.' She sighed, her eyes suddenly far away. 'I still half expect to see her here; she was so full of life. I remember her dancing before the king in this. Like a silver swan...'

'This gown was hers?' Seraphina asked, shivering slightly as she touched the costly fabric, heavy with silver thread. 'But it is like new!'

'She wore it but once, then gave it to me for my wedding-gown. She was always generous to her friends.'

'But, do you not wish to keep it?' Seraphina asked, knowing that her mother had been fond of Anne Boleyn.

'No, but I should like to see you wed in it before her daughter. It should fit you well enough. I was like you at your age, thin as a rake...as was she, of course.' Lady Katherine's voice had become a little husky, and Seraphina was surprised to see her mother's eyes were glistening with tears. 'Learn from what happened to her, Seraphina; you must learn to guard your tongue at court. Always think before you speak and stay silent if you are not sure. For all her youth and high spirits, never forget Elizabeth is King Henry's daughter.'

'I shall do my best, with your help,' Seraphina smiled wryly.

'You must learn to survive on your own. Your father and I will be returning to Mayfield after the ceremony tomorrow.'

'Must you?' She felt panicky. Although in the whirl of entertainments she had not seen much of them, her parents' presence had been reassuring. No one had dared mention the rumours about her first marriage before the Earl, but when he was absent more than one courtier had made snide comments, until they had felt the edge of Lady Katherine's tongue, ruthlessly exposing their own shortcomings.

'Your father is not well.'

'What ails him?' Seraphina asked in alarm. She had been so wrapped in her own fears about the future that she had not given much thought to her ageing father's health.

'Nought that is serious,' Lady Carey replied calmly. 'A touch of rheumatism. But he is not a young man. He cannot dance from dawn till dusk every day. He will be more comfortable in his own home rather than in this overcrowded rabbit warren. Do not look so alarmed. You will have your husband to look after you.'

'If he even remembers that I exist after we are wed,' Seraphina murmured. Now the marriage was so close, her fears that it would be like her first had grown ever greater, and if it was, she could not bear it...

'Seraphina, are you listening to me?' Lady Carey said impatiently, tapping her daughter on the shoulder.

'Your pardon, Mother,' Seraphina said apologetically, realising that she had not the slightest idea what her mother had been saying for the last few seconds.

'I should think so!' Lady Carey said with affectionate disapproval. 'The way you moon around these days, anyone would think you were lovesick! I was saying that it was time Bess saw to your hair or you'll be late for the joust and it's inexcusable to arrive after the Queen.'

'She is right, m'lady,' Bess agreed, hovering by the looking-glass with a brush and comb in her hands.'

'Just put it in the gold net, Bess,' Seraphina said as she shook out her satin skirts. 'And, as for being lovesick, Mother, I have more sense than to choose to love a man who patently does not love me!'

'If you think love is a matter of choice, you have much to learn,' Lady Katherine sighed.

'I am not in love with Rich—Heywood,' she answered crossly. 'He's a philanderer and a cynic. He cares for naught but ambition and his own pleasure.'

'If you say so,' Lady Katherine agreed, with a mildness that made her daughter glower. 'Shall I tell your father that you are having second thoughts? I saw that Towton was much taken with you at the masque; he would be as suitable a match. It would cause a scandal, of course, but if you would prefer—'

'No!' The exclamation left her lips far more emphatically than she had intended.

Bess gave a muffled cough which sounded suspiciously like a laugh. But Lady Katherine simply looked at her daughter, her well-groomed brows tilted up at the corners.

'It would disgrace the family to break the betrothal now...' Seraphina added lamely, hoping that she sounded more convincing to her mother than she did to herself.

'I am touched by your sense of family duty.' Lady Katherine's voice shook very faintly and the corners of her mouth twitched. 'Now, if you will excuse me, I must get back to your father…and you had best get to the joust.'

'Seraphina!' Mary Sidney beckoned to her from a bench beside the rails that held the crowd back from the lists. Somehow she managed to squeeze through the milling, chattering crowd until she reached the petite figure.

'Richard told me this is your first joust and asked me to look out for you. I have saved you a place so you have a good view,' she said, smiling and gathering her blue velvet and marten-fur gown about her, so that there was room for Seraphina to squeeze in. 'Richard is favourite to win, although Robin will do his best to prevent it.'

'I don't doubt it,' Seraphina laughed in response to Mary's smile and then sobered. 'They will not get hurt?'

'Those two?' Mary shook her head. 'Never, they're both strong as oxes and skilled, which is the most important thing, so don't look so worried. Richard will be hale enough tomorrow.'

'Yes,' Seraphina agreed without enthusiasm, earning a searching glance from Mary.

'You are not still fretting over that business with Mistress Morrison?' she asked compassionately. 'It was nothing…I am certain.'

'I wish I could be.'

'But he has been like your shadow all week and he

was most insistent you should be well looked after while he is engaged in the joust.'

'Well looked after or kept out of the way?'

'I am sure that is not the case.' Mary protested a little too vehemently to be absolutely convincing. 'Now, stop worrying and enjoy the joust.'

Seraphina looked along the length of the lists where Mary had pointed. At each end a fully armoured knight was already in place. Their richly caparisoned mounts were stamping their feet impatiently and tossing their heads, almost lifting the young squires that held them off their feet.

'They are a little frightening, are they not?' Mary Sidney said, following Seraphina's gaze to the heavy horses and their metalled riders. 'I should not care to be in their path on the battlefield!'

'Nor I,' Seraphina agreed with feeling. 'Who are the riders?'

'My lords Ashton and Knollys—I think...' Mary said shading her eyes against the winter sunshine to make out the devices on the red and blue pennants.

But Seraphina's attention had been caught by the familiar figures leaning on the opposite rail. One tall and dark, the other slight and silvery fair. As she watched, she saw Grace laugh, turn, reach up, and touch his face...and he bend his head to hers and kiss her upon the mouth. It was done so easily, so lightly, so very familiarly...

She jerked her gaze away, feeling numb. Until this moment she had not realised how desperately she had clung to the hope that her suspicions were wrong.

How long had they been lovers? she wondered miserably. A week, a month…longer? Perhaps at Queen Mary's court. Sweet heaven, how easily they had duped her. He with his compliments and gifts, and Grace with her talk of friendship and pretended hostility towards him. Or perhaps it had not been pretended at first, she thought, remembering Grace's reaction to the news of their betrothal. Had she feared she would be discarded?

She drew herself up straight, twisting the ornate ruby and diamond betrothal ring he had given her on her finger. His ring, which she had taken such secret pride in wearing. Dear God! How could she have been so naïve, so full of foolish, stupid dreams.

'Seraphina? Is there something wrong?' Mary touched her arm, her brown eyes anxious as she scanned her face. 'You look very pale…'

'It is nothing,' she lied, pinning a bright smile on her face. 'I am not accustomed to so many late nights, or so many entertainments all day and every day.'

'You're sure?' Mary looked unconvinced. 'You would not like me to take you back to your chamber?'

'No, thank you.' Seraphina shook her head. 'Is that the Queen coming?' She changed the subject hastily as scarlet- and gold-liveried heralds blew a fanfare. And, for a moment, she found herself forgetting everything as Elizabeth Tudor glided along the blue carpet, laid from the palace to her dais. She was gowned in glistening white brocade, and gems were woven into her golden-red hair that streamed to her waist, glowing and glinting in the winter sunshine. It was as if a Queen had stepped from one of the old legends. Even the most seasoned and cynical of courtiers seemed awed as they bowed like corn before the scythe as she passed, smiling and nodding to her favourites.

'She looks so regal; you would think she had been Queen all her life,' Seraphina said, as she and Mary straightened from their curtsies.

'I think in her mind she has,' Mary answered softly. 'They say Tom Seymour was the only man that came close to making her forget her destiny.'

'I cannot imagine her being fool enough to fall in love,' Seraphina said slowly.

'No, nor I.' Mary's eyes were sombre as they rested on the shining figure of the Queen. 'Though I fear there will always be men who will hope to touch her heart. I keep telling Rob to remember she is her father's daughter, but I fear he does not listen—'

A second fanfare blotted out the rest of her words as the Queen stepped on to a dais hung with cloth-of-gold and held up a white and silver gauze scarf. With a graceful gesture she let it fall, and the herald blew a single flourish of notes—the signal for the tournament to begin.

'It will begin now,' Mary said, after the Queen had seated herself on a couch covered with purple velvet cushions. 'Keep a good watch on the ends of the lists; you should see your betrothed soon.'

My betrothed, but Mistress Morrison's lover. Seraphina bit back the bitter retort that came to her lips. No one would know how much he had hurt her...no one. Tight-lipped, she stared at the first combatants.

The horses surged forward as the squires released their heads, lumbering into an inexorable canter. The knights lowered and levelled their lances. And then, behind Lord Knolly's end of the lists, she glimpsed the Earl emerging from a red and gold pavilion with Robin Dudley. At this distance they looked almost like twins, matching each other inch for inch in height and both dressed in quilted buff jerkins and breeches, over which each had begun to fasten his armour. But she knew which was the Earl instantly, though it was too far to discern features. Robin Dudley moved with conscious elegance and purpose, but the Earl had the effortless, fluid grace of a cat. They were laughing, clowning, striking each other mock blows upon their cuirasses with their fists.

'I have not seen Richard so light-hearted in years.' Mary Sidney smiled, as she too glanced at that end of the lists. 'I would almost think him in love.'

'Yes,' Seraphina agreed flatly, tearing her eyes from the Earl. He was in love. But not with her. The pain she felt was physical. She leant against the rail, staring unseeingly at the other side of the lists, not daring to look at Mary for fear of disgracing herself and breaking down in tears. A scrap of moving colour, a wicker ball, bright and gaudy against the scuffed grass of the lists half caught her downcast gaze as it rolled from beneath the rails and into the red knight's path. Then her heart stopped as a child toddled after it. A boy, still in petticoats and bonnet, with a toy wooden sword clasped in one chubby fist. Dear God! Had no one else seen him! No. The spectators were watching the knights, and the combatants' vision was severely limited by their visors. A shouted warning would be lost among the hubbub of chatter and cheering.

'What is it?' Mary Sidney asked, hearing the gasp of horror.

But Seraphina did not answer. She had already kicked off her high-heeled silk slippers, and was bending beneath the rail. Snatching up her skirts, she ran as she had not run since she, Dickon and Bess had played chase in the park at Mayfield.

'Seraphina!' Mary's frightened voice floated after her. But she dared not pause. The horses were close. The ground beneath her stockinged feet was shaking. Others had noticed now. She heard shouts, screams, but they seemed remote and far off amid the drumming thunder of the hooves, the creaking leather and clank of armour. Sobbing for breath, she lengthened her stride. She could smell the sweat that foamed upon the necks of the snorting horses as they closed. If the child kept walking...no, don't! If she had had the breath she would have screamed as he stooped to pick up the ball and then dropped it again so it rolled further beneath the centre rail and into the path of the blue knight. Doggedly, oblivious to his danger, he followed it. God! She would never reach him in time. In desperation she threw herself forward. The ground was hard, the impact jarring, driving the air from her lungs, but she caught the boy's petticoats and dragged him down with her, rolling so that he was protected by her curled body.

'Levee!'

She heard the frantic command of the knight with a peculiar sense of detachment, wondering if she was already dying as the pain in her chest became unbearable. The horse grunted as it heaved its body into the air, it seemed to hang above her for an eternity, and inevitably began to drop. She shut her eyes as she felt its iron-shod forefeet strike the earth close to her head; its back feet would never—the blow to her shoulder was swift, stinging, but nothing compared to the suffocating, knife-sharp agony in her chest. She opened her eyes to the dazzling sun. The horse had passed. She was alive. The child!

She tried to sit up, but could do no more than drag herself on to one elbow as she tried to gulp air into her empty lungs. The boy was unhurt. Wriggling out from beneath her skirts, he looked at her in bemusement. For a moment he looked as if he might burst into tears. Then his face lit up and he pointed at the group of courtiers running across the grass towards them.

Ahead of them all was the Earl of Heywood, running at full pace despite being half-armoured, with Grace Morrison and Mary Sidney close behind him.

The expression on his face drove even the tearing pain of breathing out of her mind. Had he come to care a little for her? But then, as she looked again at the child, the truth destroyed her fleeting hope. The boy was *his* son; she wondered that she had not seen it at once as she watched him drop to his knees and scoop the little boy up into his arms.

'Are you hurt, Robert?' The love and fear in his face as he swept up the child and kissed the small round face twisted at Seraphina's heart.

'Please say he is not!' She heard Grace's voice, 'It

is all my fault; I only took my eyes off him for a moment.'

'He's all right.' The Earl was brusque as his eyes went over the boy's shoulder to Seraphina. 'But I fear Lady Sherard is injured. Mary, will you take Robert back to his nurse? Mistress Morrison will show you where to find her.'

'Of course.' Mary hastened to take the boy from his arms.

'But I cannot leave Seraphina,' Grace protested, her blue eyes sparkling with tears. 'She is as dear to me as a sister.'

'I will look after Lady Sherard.' The Earl silenced her with a single look. 'Lady Sidney is waiting.'

Grace looked at Seraphina and made a helpless gesture. 'I shall see you later, as soon as I can.'

Hypocrite! Seraphina wanted to shout.

'Lady play again?' Robert asked a little wistfully, leaning away from Mary to point at Seraphina as he was carried away.

'Don't be silly! This wasn't a game, you stupid child!' Grace said stiffly. 'You nearly got yourself and Lady Sherard killed!'

Robert's bottom lip wavered.

'Play…soon…' Somehow she managed to gasp out the words and force her mouth into the semblance of a smile.

'Yesh. Bye bye, lady,' Robert said more happily, as he was borne away.

'That was kind,' the Earl said softly as he knelt beside her. 'But you must not talk except to tell me where you are hurt.'

She stared at his dark, chiselled face. Hurt. Oh, yes, she was hurt! But not in the way he meant. Why hadn't he told her his son was at court? Because he would rather entrust him to Grace's care than hers.

'Seraphina. Where are you injured, tell me?' His voice was sharp, almost she thought, impatient.

'Not…hurt…little…winded…' She choked out the words, as she struggled to sit upright. She blinked, trying to focus; the Earl had become blurred, and the lists seemed to be spinning faster than one did in a galliard.

'More than a little, I think.' He sighed, lifting her into his arms and standing up.

She let her head fall against his shoulder with relief. He'd held her like this before, but when? Her mind was too hazy with shock, too occupied with the struggle to breath to let her remember. She only knew that when he held her, she was safe, she belonged. Except that she didn't. He didn't want her; he wanted Grace. Did Grace feel like this when he held her? The thought sliced through her, twice as sharp as her searing breaths.

'Sorry, did I hurt you?' The Earl frowned as he felt her flinch and recoil in his arms.

'Shall I send for the physician?' She heard Robin Dudley's voice from close beside them. 'She's white as snow, Heywood—'

'No…' She gasped a protest. 'No…hate…physicians…leeches…'

'No physicians, I promise you,' the Earl soothed. 'But perhaps you will tell the Queen what has occurred, Robin; she will wish to know.'

'Of course. I wish you a speedy recovery, m'lady.'

'Now, m'lady.' The Earl smiled down at her. 'A minute or two and we will be at my pavilion; you will be able to rest there. The pain will soon go.'

It won't. It won't. She wanted to shout at him. Her breath was easier already, but nothing would numb the pain of knowing that the one man she wanted loved another woman. For days she had dreamed of being so close to him, dreamed of him looking at her so tenderly, but, now she knew about Grace, it was unbearable to be in his arms. 'Put...me...down.' she begged breathlessly. 'I...can...walk...'

'Perhaps.' He shook his head and gave her an odd smile that made her heart stop. 'But tomorrow you will be my wife, so you might as well begin to practise obedience to my wishes now, m'lady, and I say you will be carried.'

Defeated, she let her head fall back against his shoulder as he carried her through the crowd of anxious onlookers.

'God's breath...' He halted in mid-stride. His arms contracted, holding her so tightly she almost cried out in protest. But something in his face silenced her. He was ashen beneath the weathered veneer of his skin, white-lipped. And then she understood why as her eyes followed the direction of his gaze to where the wreckage of Robert's wicker ball lay smashed into the turf by the horses' hooves.

'When I think of what might have happened. It could have been his skull...' He echoed her thought in a whisper. 'And I have not even thanked you yet. If aught had happened to Robert—'

'Anyone…would…have…done…same…' she broke in. Gratitude was the last thing she wanted from him.

'I don't think so.' He bent his head and dropped the lightest of kisses on her hair. 'You saved my son's life,' he said softly, scarcely aware he was speaking aloud. 'If there is any reward I can give you, ask.'

'Your son's safety is…reward enough. There is nothing…I want…from…you.'

'Nothing.' His eyes darkened as they studied her face.

Except your love. The words were on the tip of her tongue. But she was not brave enough to utter them, not brave enough to hear his answer.

Nothing. The Earl's mouth tightened as she buried her face against his chest. Perhaps it was as well. What did he have to give her but lies and deceit? Grim-mouthed, he walked on in silence until they reached the privacy of his red and gold silk pavilion.

'M'lord!' His freckle-faced squire dropped the piece of armour he had been polishing and stared wide-eyed at his master's burden. 'Can I help, m'lord?'

'Yes, by seeing my horse is not left standing shivering in the wind. Walk it until I am ready or else it'll go lame on the first tilt!'

'Yes, m'lord!' The squire sped from the tent, his face as red as his bright copper hair.

'Can you stand?' His voice was gentle again as he spoke to Seraphina.

'Yes…' she answered uncertainly. Her breath was easier, but her legs were like water.

Set faced, he kept an arm about her waist, steadying her as he swept a pile of armour off a low, cushioned couch with one impatient gesture.

She sank down gratefully, clutching instinctively at the gaping sleeve of her gown.

'Gates of Hell! You are hurt! Let me see.'

'It is naught…' Her breath caught as he bent to part the torn edges of fabric and his fingers brushed against her skin. 'Just a graze…'

'Let me be the judge of that—' he touched the mark the horse's shoe had left on her skin with gentle fingers '—it should be cleaned.'

Too weak to argue, she slumped back and watched as he stripped off his cumbersome breastplate and the stiff, quilted under-jerkin. The exertion of running in the armour had made him sweat, and his fine linen shirt clung to his torso, emphasising the strength in his shoulders, the flatness of his stomach. Her mouth went dry as she felt a weakness in the pit of her stomach that had nothing to do with her injury or shock. Her eyes followed him of their own volition as he went to a table and poured some aqua vitae from a flagon into a silver basin and tore a strip of linen from another shirt that was flung carelessly over a trestle on which his saddle rested.

'It will hurt a little,' he warned as he came back and sat beside her. 'I'll have to loosen your gown if I am not to tear the sleeve more; do you mind?'

'No.' She tried to sound cool and composed as she sat up and half turned from him.

His fingers were deft and quick as he unthreaded the uppermost laces.

'You seem well practised,' she could not help observing, the prickling tension in her body making her irritable.

His hand stilled for a second. 'Practised enough; would you have expected different?'

She could hear the smile in his voice, though she could not see his face.

'No, I wouldn't,' she said raggedly, as he eased the loosened gown from her shoulders.

'God's teeth!'

His shocked oath startled her; only then did she remember the other, still visible bruises and whip marks on her back.

'Who did this?' His voice was honed, sharper, colder than an apothecary's knife.

'My late husband,' she answered flatly, feeling ugly, ashamed.

'I see.'

From the corner of her eyes she saw him bend and dip the linen in the basin which he had placed on the floor. Did he see? Or did he assume that Edmund had had good reason to beat her. She had to know. 'Aren't you—' she winced as he dabbed at the graze with the stinging liquid '—going to ask why?'

'Only if you wish to tell me…' He went on cleaning the graze. 'There can never be sufficient excuse for this; no decent man would use a woman in such a way, whatever her supposed offence. There were times with Lettice when I came close to striking her, but I never did. And nor will I ever strike you.'

'There are other ways of hurting than with the hands.' She spoke her thought aloud.

'You do not need to tell me that!' He laughed bitterly. 'Lettice knew them all.'

'Is that where you learnt the art?' She returned huskily.

'I have never wished to hurt you, believe me.' His hand stilled on her shoulder. It was warm, heavy, almost caressing.

'Then why keep your son from me?' She twisted to face him, oblivious to the fact that her gown was hanging loose almost to her waist and that the round-necked shift of sheer silk she wore beneath did nothing to disguise her breasts. 'You did not even tell me he was at court!'

His lashes dropped, veiling his eyes. 'I told you. It is best if he does not become too attached to you.'

'Too attached!' She stared at him in disbelief. 'I will be his stepmother! Yet you entrust him to *her* rather than me!'

'I didn't,' he grated. 'Mistress Morrison met Robert and his nurse and offered to take him to where he would have a better view. She is the last person I would entrust with Robert.'

'But the first to get your kisses!' Her voice cracked and she jerked her head away, so he would not see how close she was to tears. 'Do not trouble to deny it; I saw you.'

'It is not as you think.' He sighed heavily. 'You don't understand.'

'No, I don't! At Mayfield when you wooed me, and sometimes when we are together here and you are kind, I begin to think—' She broke off, choking back a sob. 'What is the use? It was all lies, was it not?'

'No…not all,' he said, almost inaudibly as his eyes travelled over her face and then dropped to her grazed shoulder. 'Though it has taken me long enough to realise it. When I saw you lying there on the lists…if you had been killed…'

'Then you could have wed her instead!' she said thickly. She tried to get up and stumbled as she trod on the hem of her gown. Scarlet-faced, she wrestled to free her heel from its folds.

'The only woman I wish to wed is you!' He reached out and grabbed her shoulders, pulling her down again, so that their faces were no more than a handspan apart. 'What must I say to make you believe it?'

'Will you swear to have no more to do with her?'

'I can't. Not yet.' The words were dragged from his throat.

'Why? What has she that I do not? Tell me!' She turned angry eyes to his face. 'Am I so displeasing to you?'

'Jesu! Is that what you think!' he groaned.

'I think that since we are to be wed you would be better kissing me than her!' She blurted out her resentment and hurt. 'You have scarce touched me since Mayfield.'

'You think I have not wanted to! I have thought of little else, day or night.'

'Haven't you?' Her voice dwindled to a shocked whisper as she met his gaze and saw the raw desire in his eyes. 'Nor have I—' Her admission was stopped by his mouth on hers as he pulled her to him. She knew as his mouth took hers that there would be no going back from this, no escape. His lips, his hands were relentless, melting her, burning her until she was drunk with desire, returning kiss for kiss, touch for touch without thought or inhibition. It was easy, so easy to slide her hands beneath his loose linen shirt, to feel his skin, satin-smooth or rough with hair against her palms. He groaned as she found places where he was as sensitive to her touch as she to his. Emboldened, she let her lips leave his and touched them to his throat. He tasted salty, male. He made a low noise in his throat and lifted his head to look down at her, and it was only then that she realised they were now lying amid the tumble of silken cushions.

'Don't...' she protested instinctively, linking her hands behind his head and trying to pull him back to her, and then, as his absolute stillness penetrated, she opened her eyes. He was beside her, leaning on one elbow, staring down at her.

'What is it?' Her hands dropped to her sides.

'Nothing...' His voice was velvety, like a caress. 'It is just...I had not realised how beautiful you are, or how much I want you, will always want you...' His free hand began to move as he spoke, sliding over the gossamer silk of her shift, stroking her almost lazily as he held her gaze, watching her reaction to his touch.

She lay helpless, floating in delicious, tantalising pleasure, with no desire to do anything but submit to his caresses. Somewhere in the back of her mind was the knowledge that she was behaving shamelessly, wantonly, that they might be disturbed at any moment. And she did not care at all, not while he looked at her as he was doing now, touched her so. She gasped and jolted as his thumb circled her nipple, slowly, unbearably slowly, winding her body tighter and tighter, until she could not bear it and reached for him, burying her hands in his hair and dragging him down, seeking his mouth hungrily, arching against him in blind, instinctive need.

There was a new urgency in them both. Her sense of frustration was as great as his as the cumbersome folds of her skirts prevented the downward exploration of his hands. With an ease that made her feel weightless, he lifted her to a sitting position, and slipped from the couch to kneel before her while his hands travelled down her spine, freeing the remaining laces of her gown and petticoats, while his mouth closed on the hard tip of her breast, making her so dizzy with pleasure she almost fell as he brought her to her feet. He held her, swearing softly as the tight lower sleeves prevented the gown falling to the floor. For a moment he fumbled with the buttons at her wrists, and then simply wrenched until the threads broke. She felt featherlight, fragile, vulnerable as the velvet gown and petticoats pooled around her feet leaving her naked but for her silk shift. And then she was aware of nothing but his hardness and weight, pressing her into the couch as he laid her down beneath him. She shut her eyes again, overawed, a little afraid of the unmistakable evidence of his desire against her flesh.

'What's wrong?' He lifted his head from her throat and kissed her mouth lightly as he felt her tense.

She lifted her lashes to meet his gaze. He was pale, taut with desire.

'You really want me?' There was a note of wonder in her voice.

'Can you doubt it?' He gave a husky laugh and stopped her response with a kiss.

She pushed against his chest to make him relinquish her mouth. 'But Grace?' she began, and then found herself distracted as her hands slid beneath his loose linen shirt, and her fingertips registered the satiny texture of his skin, the silky crispness of the scattering of black hairs across his chest.

'Do you—' he jolted and trapped her hands beneath his as she found his nipples '—have to ask about that now?'

'Yes,' she said simply. His eyes were dark, pools of molten gold in his chiselled face. She could feel the uneven thud of his heart beneath her palm, as erratic as the beat of her own pulse.

'She means nothing. I seek her company out of necessity...' His voice trailed off; he had said far too much already. Cecil would never forgive him, and he didn't give a damn.

'Necessity?' She was bewildered. 'How can you say she means nothing, and then confess your need of her is so great you cannot stay away from her?'

'Fool.' He silenced her with a kiss. 'I have the only woman I need here, in my arms.'

'I don't understand...' she began slowly, her mind

and body too blurred with desire to make sense of his words. 'If you want me, not her, why did—'

'I don't understand either…' he interrupted almost tenderly, bending his head to kiss her. 'This was not supposed to happen.'

'Indeed not,' said a cool female voice from the entrance of the pavilion. 'I understand you are not to be wed until the morrow… No!' The voice was raised. 'Mary, stay at the door, but the rest remain outside. It would seem Lady Sherard is a little *faint* and needs air.'

'Yes, Your Grace.' Mary Sidney's voice was clearly audible, a little too loud to be quite natural.

Your Grace! The Queen! Seraphina went rigid. This could not be happening! The Earl moved faster than she had thought possible, snatching up a cloak from the end of the couch and throwing it over her, before bowing to Elizabeth.

'Lady Sherard is indeed faint, Your Grace; you will excuse her if she does not stand?'

'You do look very *pale*, Lady Sherard,' Elizabeth observed drily, as she held out her long white hand for the Earl to kiss. 'No doubt it is the shock.' Her dark eyes were unreadable as they rested assessingly on Seraphina's face. 'Perhaps it would be wisest for you to stay there.'

'Thank you, Your Grace.' Seraphina managed to choke the words out, knowing that her cheeks were now a burning scarlet. She snatched a frantic glance at the Earl. Jesu! How could he be so unconcerned! So cool. It was obvious the Queen knew exactly what she had interrupted. Elizabeth was renowned for her high moral standards. Could she put them in the Tower for this? Perhaps she would judge her immoral, forbid the match; the Earl was one of her favourites. She let her eyes come back to the slender, auburn-haired young woman and braced herself for the worst.

To her astonishment, Elizabeth seated herself on the end of the couch and smiled at her.

'I was concerned for your health after such a brave act, Lady Sherard,' she purred, 'but I can see that the Earl's expert care is speeding your recovery...' She let the words hang in the air before turning to the Earl. 'Your talents never cease to amaze, Richard.'

'It is good to know I can still surprise you, Your Grace,' the Earl returned smoothly, without a trace of embarrassment.

Was he mad? Seraphina wondered, or was this whole nightmare just a bad dream? Whatever it was, she was out of her depth.

'Not half so much as I have just surprised you, I'll warrant!' Elizabeth flung back her head and laughed wickedly. Then turning back to Seraphina she spoke more soberly. 'I am truly glad you were not much harmed. I should be pleased to have you among my ladies after you are wed. Would you be happy to wait on me, Lady Sherard?'

'Yes, of course. I mean, thank you, Your Grace,' Seraphina found herself stammering. She could hardly believe it. Instead of being punished, she was to be rewarded with the honour of waiting on the Queen. Joyously she looked up at the Earl. Surely this would please him?

But the Earl avoided her gaze. His heart had turned

to stone. He didn't want her so close to the Queen. It was too dangerous; the risks were too great. If any attempt were made on the Queen, Cecil would not wait for evidence of guilt one way or the other and as yet he had not the proof which would protect her. 'I do not like to disappoint you, Your Grace,' he invented quickly. 'But I had intended to send my wife to my estates once we are wed. She is used to the country air; I fear that court life will not agree with her. With your permission, of course, Your Grace.'

He wanted to be rid of her after what had just happened. Seraphina felt numb. She couldn't believe it. She didn't want to believe it...

'Well, you don't have it,' Elizabeth answered sharply. 'Having just become acquainted, I wish to know Lady Sherard better, as I should have thought you would.'

'Then, of course, she must stay,' the Earl conceded through gritted teeth.

'God's blood, Richard!' Elizabeth laughed. 'You look like a falcon who has just had one of its brood snatched by an eagle. Serving me is not a death sentence!'

It could be, the Earl wanted to shout, but he held his tongue.

Elizabeth got up and nodded to Seraphina. 'The matter is settled, then. Lady Sidney will acquaint you with your duties—' she smiled '—and help you with your gown. As accomplished a nurse as he appears to be, I suspect the Earl is more used to the removal of ladies' apparel than its replacement.' She turned to the Earl with a glittering smile. 'You are to be congratulated on your choice of bride, m'lord. Such courage is rare and should be treasured closely.'

'It will be, Your Grace. Once we are married, I shall not let her out of my sight,' the Earl answered, bowing low. 'You have my word on it.'

Seraphina stared at him as the Queen left. Minutes ago his reply would have made her heart leap with joy. But his face was cold, as distant as when he had first learnt her name. Unease rippled along her spine. 'Why didn't you want me to wait on the Queen?' she asked slowly. 'Do you think I will be an embarrassment to you at court? I know I have much to learn—'

'It is nothing like that; I had only your good in mind.'

'Then it is because of Grace,' she guessed bleakly.

'No!' He turned away and began to put on his armour with sharp, angry movements. 'Can't you forget Grace Morrison for a moment?'

'Can you?' She taunted him bitterly, her own temper rising.

'No!' He swore viciously as a buckle on his breastplate jammed, then flung the piece of armour aside as he spun to face her again. 'God's blood! What chance of that is there when you speak of naught else—'

'So it is my fault you cannot put her out of mind?' she seared back at him. 'Don't my kisses match hers, m'lord? You seemed well enough pleased, but then perhaps you were thinking of her!'

'Jesu! You go too near the mark, lady—'

'Too near the truth, you mean!' she retorted.

'The truth!' He gave a choked laugh. 'You know about as much of that as you do of lovemaking—'

He stopped abruptly as he saw her expression and heard her snatch a breath as if he had punched her. 'I simply meant that if you could not tell—'

'There is no call for apology,' she hissed as her hurt gave way to blinding, incandescent anger. 'The disappointment, *my lord,* was mutual!'

'God's blood!' His fury rose to match hers as he lunged forward, caught her shoulders and lifted her to her feet. 'What must I do to make you see—' He broke off as she twisted out of his grasp and snatched up his dagger from a chest and waved it at him.

'Touch me again and I will—' She wrestled to free the blade from its scabbard, and then swore as it came out suddenly, skimming her fingertip with its razor edge.

'What?' he mocked, as she dropped the dagger and put her finger to her mouth to suck at the bright scarlet bead of blood. 'Cut your hand off? Here,' he added roughly, reaching out, 'let me see—'

'I said don't touch me!' Her ferocity shocked even herself as he reached out. 'I hate you! And I always will! Always! So leave me alone!'

He froze and then his hand fell away and he exhaled slowly. 'Perhaps that would be best. I am going to take some ale with Dudley; I'll tell my squire to bring my armour to me there. Consider my pavilion yours for as long as you require it. Good day, my lady.' He bowed and strode out, almost knocking over Lady Sidney and Bess who arrived at that moment.

'What was his hurry?' Mary asked brightly. 'You'd think the place was afire—' She fell silent as she looked at Seraphina. Then she hurried forward at the same moment as Bess. 'Come, sit down; you're shaking like a leaf—your hands are like ice. This one is bleeding! Whatever happened?'

'We—we—quarreled,' Seraphina stammered, grateful for the cloak Bess wrapped about her shoulders.

'Oh…' Mary subsided into an embarrassed silence.

'Quarrelled!' Bess muttered as she dabbed at Seraphina's hand with a handkerchief. 'I'll give him quarrel, to leave you in a state like this after what you did for his son. Did he hurt you?'

'No.' She almost managed a smile at Bess's furious loyalty. 'I hurt myself—' her voice splintered '—in more ways than one.' She gave a shaky, bitter laugh. 'I had begun to hope he—' She bit her lip; she could see from Mary's compassionate face she had said too much already. 'You will not tell him,' she pleaded. 'I could not bear it if he knew—'

'But—' Mary began, and then sighed as she met Seraphina's panic-stricken gaze. 'Very well; I shall not say a word. Now, let us help you with your gown before you catch your death.'

# *Chapter Ten*

The Earl smiled as he stepped into the nursery and heard his son's peal of laughter from the inner room.

His smile faded as he reached the open door and saw Seraphina, kneeling among the rushes to retrieve a ball made of bright scraps of fabric from beneath a chest. The winter sun streamed through the window, making her cloth-of-silver gown sparkle like diamonds and turning her hair, which flowed loose down her back, to richest, fiery red.

Laughing, she rolled the ball back to Robert and then, seeing him look at something over her shoulder, she twisted to look behind her, her face haloed by a narrow braid of her glowing hair, threaded with pearls.

The Earl's breath stopped. Sweet heaven, she was beautiful, and in half an hour she would be his wife…

'Pretty,' Robert announced, holding up the ball.

'I couldn't agree more,' the Earl answered softly, his eyes on Seraphina's face.

'Thank you,' she said grittily, hating him, hating herself for the way her heart turned over at the sight of him, so handsome and lithe in his suit of bronze silk embroidered with gold. Did he think a compliment or two was recompense for what he had done the day before? Returning her gaze to Robert, she smiled. 'I must go; my mother and Bess will have the guard out looking for me by now, but we will play again soon; I promise—' She broke off and glanced up at the Earl defiantly, expecting him to argue. But he merely smiled and offered her a hand to help her to her feet.

'Apart from defying me, dare I ask what brings you here on your wedding morn?'

'I just came to bring Robert his new ball. Bess and I made it from scraps last night. I did not think to see you here.'

'I see.' He was silent for a moment. 'That was kind of you. But I wonder if you should be crawling among the rushes in such a costly gown.' He released her hand to pluck a stalk of grass from her wing sleeves.

'Probably not,' she agreed stiffly. 'But I shall not disgrace you. Bess will repair the damage. So, if you will excuse me? Goodbye, Robert.'

Robert lifted a pudgy hand, and then shrieked with laughter as a ginger kitten suddenly shot from beneath the bed and pounced on the ball.

'Wait!' The Earl followed her into the outer room and put an arm across the open door, preventing her from leaving. 'Yesterday...'

'What of it?' She met his gaze coolly, determined he should not know how he had hurt her the day before.

'You should not take too seriously what I said…did, in the heat of the moment. It meant nothing.'

'I never thought it did,' she answered stiltedly. If she had learnt nothing else, she had learnt that love-making was naught to him but another sport.

'I am glad.' The relief in his voice cut into her like a knife. 'There are too many misunderstandings between us.'

'Are there? I understand better than you think.'

'Do you?' He was startled and then, as he saw her expression, he groaned. 'I did not mean—'

'You seem to say very little of what you mean,' she interrupted sharply, then dropped her eyes. 'Now, if you will let me pass?'

She waited for him to move away from the door, but he had frozen, and was staring at her intently.

'Your hair? You are wearing it so?'

'Yes,' she grated, dropping her eyes.

'Like a maid? Do you mean Sherard never—' His arm dropped back to his side.

'Never,' she cut in brusquely. 'And I do not care if the world knows it!'

Before he could say another word, she picked up her heavy silver skirts and pushed past him.

Seraphina stared at the rowdy, glittering courtiers who filled the room. This was her wedding celebration and, apart from her family and one or two others, she scarcely recognised a face. She wished the Earl was still sitting beside her on the dais, but he was talking to people she did not even recognise. Soon it

would be time for the bedding. She took another swallow of her wine. She had never felt so alone, so afraid
of making a fool of herself. Still, at least the Queen
was absent. She had attended the ceremony in the
chapel, but business of state had taken her from the
celebration early. That was something to be thankful
for, and that the Queen had not spoken of her behaviour to her parents. She was jarred out of her thoughts
by the realisation that Grace, beautiful in ice-blue brocade, was standing before her, her face very pale and
set. What did she want? Seraphina wondered dully.
She had hoped to avoid having to speak to her again,
ever—

'How could you, Seraphina?' Grace said reproachfully.

'How could I what?' she asked recklessly, more
than a little light-headed from the wine she had consumed.

'Insult Edmund's memory,' Grace answered de-
spairingly. 'Wearing your hair loose like that as if you
were a maid that had never been wed! Do you know
what people are saying about him?'

'The truth?' Seraphina laughed nervously. 'An
hour from now half the court will know what he did
to me, when I am stripped of my clothes and put to
bed! Why shouldn't he share a little of the humiliation?'

'You were never worthy of him!' Grace said
thickly.

'Were you?' Her dark brows arched upwards. 'Bess
said she thought you had a desire to share his bed.'
The colour left Grace's rosebud mouth, until her lips

were almost white. Seraphina met Grace's furious blue gaze defiantly, half expecting, half hoping she would lash out with one of her small white hands and give her the chance to respond in kind.

But Grace looked away, avoiding the challenge. 'I do not know how you can say such a thing,' she said in a hurt tone. 'After all I did for you—'

'And was kissing my betrothed at the joust yesterday something you did for me?'

'You think I want *his* attentions?' Grace gave a hollow laugh.

'You do little to refuse them.'

'You think I have a choice?' Grace laughed again. 'My faith earns me no friends here. A word from him could consign me to the Tower, or worse—'

'You are afraid of him?' She was startled. 'You really do not welcome his attention?'

'No. Believe me.' Grace made a helpless gesture. 'I would have naught to do with him; I tried to tell him that yesterday, after the joust—'

'After the joust—' Seraphina repeated sickly. Had he gone straight from her arms to Grace?

'Yes.' Grace sighed as she saw her expression. 'On the eve of his wedding—'

'You're lying—' Her response was instinctive, desperate.

'No.' Grace pressed her hand briefly. 'Believe me, I wish I could say I was. I'm sorry, truly sorry.' Her voice became muffled and she turned away, a hand raised to her face.

With a sick sense of inevitability, she saw the Earl stop Grace as she hurried across the room, put his arm about her shoulders. She could not watch this. She stood up, overturning her chair in her haste as she stumbled from the dais and pushed through the crowd, ignoring the startled stares of strangers and her mother's frantic signals from the high table alike. She was halted by a tapestry-hung wall. In her panic to get away she had gone the wrong way. She sank down on a bench, her eyes filling with tears.

'Mead, m'lady?'

She took the proffered cup from a servant and drained it. She had drunk too much already in a vain effort to steady her nerves, but she no longer cared. She wanted to be numb, not to see, not to think. 'More,' she ordered curtly as the servant began to move away.

She raised the cup to her lips, only to find a gentle hand on her wrist and the cup removed from her fingers. She looked up in fleeting hope, but her eyes confirmed what her senses had told her already. It wasn't the Earl.

'Come and dance a measure; you'll find it does more for the spirits than this.' Robin Dudley smiled at her as he set the cup down.

'Does it?' Dizzy with wine, she almost tripped as he pulled her to her feet. Her eyes went to the Earl and Grace. 'He kissed me,' she blurted as they swirled into the galliard, 'and then went to her—'

'Shush!' Dudley warned her. 'At court it is wisest to pretend you do not care, so smile at me with your mouth if not with your eyes. Good,' he said approvingly, as she swallowed her tears. 'Nor should you believe all you hear. But if he did as you seem to think, I suspect it is merely because he wishes to prove to himself that he is not in love.'

'But if he doesn't love her, then why—'

'You don't know?' He gave her a startled look and then shook his head. 'It is Richard you had best ask, but in the meantime, lady, smile and dance, then at least your pride will be intact if your heart is not.'

'Thank you, my lord.' She swallowed her tears, knowing he was right, and gave herself up to the galliard. And, when that finished, let herself be swept off by another partner, then another, until she had lost count and all sense of time. She only knew that so long as she danced, she need not think, need not confront the truth: that it was him, not Grace, who was at fault.

The Earl bit his lip as he watched Seraphina laugh as a fair-haired young man pulled her into a galliard. Langham! That blasted popinjay!

'Easy, Richard,' Robin Dudley said beside him. 'She's not to know about Langham and Lettice.'

'No.' The Earl exhaled slowly and unclenched his fists.

'You're a lucky man,' Dudley added enviously, as he too watched Langham spin Seraphina through the air, sending her cloth-of-silver gown belling out and her hair flying like a silken banner. 'That hair, it's like flame, impossible to ignore. How long was she married to Sherard? A year?'

'Yes,' the Earl replied tersely. He knew what Dudley was hinting at. Her hair! There had been an audible gasp as she had gilded into the chapel, her head

bare except for a rope of pearls threaded into a braid
that was wrapped around her head as a band. The rest
of her hair had streamed down her back, rich and red
as burgundy wine in the sunshine that filtered through
the stained-glass windows of the chapel.

'I don't wish to interfere, Richard,' Dudley went
on. 'But I think it might be wise if you gave her a
little of the attention you've been lavishing on Mistress Morrison this last hour! Damn it, man! It is your
wedding night, and, by the looks of it, her first bedding! She was near enough in tears when I found her,
and drinking mead as if it were water.'

'Do you think I don't know it!' the Earl answered
savagely. 'She was shaking with nerves from the moment she stepped into the chapel!'

'So, it's naught to do with your fawning over the
Morrison chit, then?' Dudley said sarcastically. 'Perhaps it's just the bedding she's nervous about.'

'The bedding! Gates of Hell!' The Earl swore violently at his own stupidity. The bedding ceremony!
She must be dreading it, knowing the world would
see and speculate on what Sherard had done to her.
And he had given her precious little comfort with his
behaviour. The only wonder was that she had not
drunk herself into oblivion. 'I am a fool, Robin!'

'I'm glad you realise it,' Dudley laughed. 'If my
wife looked like her, I should not be spending time
with Grace Morrison.'

'Shut up, Robin!' the Earl retorted. 'Get Mary; I'll
need her help before—' He broke off as Seraphina
and Langham disappeared among a crowd of courtiers. 'Damnation! Come on!' He vaulted down from

the dais where they had been sitting and ran across the hall, elbowing aside men and women alike.

Bewildered and half amused, Dudley followed in his wake.

'No!' Seraphina's protest was instinctive as Langham and another man she did not know hoisted her on to their shoulders. She had tried to push this to the back of her mind, tried to drown out her dread with wine, but now she felt sick. To be mauled and then stripped, to endure the snide comments…

'Let me go!' She struck out at them, tried to throw herself down. They laughed, and pinioned her hands.

'The garter! The garter!' A dozen young men took up the chant. The scuffle to gain the bride's garter began. There were hands, rough and male, on her ankles, beneath her skirt. Her captors' hands dug into her cruelly. Hurting her. Like Edmund. Everything blurred. Langham became Edmund. Laughing, taunting, hurting her! She sobbed as hands clamped her legs, fingers fumbled and pinched at her thighs, pulling at the knot of ribbon that secured her stocking.

'Help me! Help me!' she could hear herself screaming, but no one seemed to hear. Just as they hadn't before… Frantic, she twisted, flailed in their grasp.

'Bitch!' A man swore as she bit his hand. The laughter was louder, the hands rougher.

'What the hell are you doing, Richard?' Dudley asked after he made a hasty apology to a knight whom the Earl had almost knocked to the ground. 'They're only after the garter, and the favours. It's only fun.'

'Does she look as if she's enjoying it!' the Earl

snarled. 'For God's sake, help me get her out of this mêlée!'

Dudley looked startled for a moment, but then followed.

She was chalk-white, half fainting, lolling like a rag doll, her gown half off her shoulder where someone had ripped off a favour.

'Let go of her!' the Earl roared as he reached the two young men that held her. 'Now!'

They were too drunk to see their danger. 'Give us a chance, Heywood; you were more generous with your last wife.' Langham grinned, delighted with his own wit. The others laughed appreciatively.

The Earl and Dudley moved at the same moment. There was the unmistakable crack of fist against jaw; the two gallants crumpled, groaning, on to the rush strewn floor.

'Richard...'

He caught her as she swayed forward, sweeping her up in his arms.

'It's all right,' he murmured as he strode through the ranks of stunned courtiers. 'I've got you.'

She shut her eyes, letting her head lie on his shoulder. The heavily embroidered bronze brocade was rough against her cheek, but she didn't care. His arms were around her. She was safe.

'You'll have to have some attendants, Richard,' Dudley said in a low voice, hurrying after him. 'This will cause talk enough as it is. Langham is a Duke's son.'

'I don't care if he is a prince of the blood!' the Earl growled. 'But I suppose you're right about attendants;

can you bring your sister? She can help Seraphina; you can act for me.'

'You need not fear Mary will gossip; she is no tattle-tongue,' the Earl said quietly, as he shut the door of the apartment the Queen had given them as a wedding gift, and barred it.

'No,' Seraphina said dully, pleating the edge of the silk sheet between her fingers and staring up at the ruched blue satin canopy of the tester bed. Mary's shock had been evident as she had helped her out of her clothes and into the bridal bed, but she had not asked a single question. 'I am sorry…to make such a scene. I don't know what happened. It was just as if—'

'Don't fret about it; it will be forgotten as soon as the next scandal breaks,' he interrupted softly, going to a side-table near the roaring log fire and pouring a beaker of wine. 'If I had been taking greater care of you, things would not have gotten so out of hand—' he added, sitting down on the edge of the bed.

'Would you like some?' He proffered the goblet.

'No.' Her mouth dried as she glimpsed his chest beneath the loose wrapping-gown of gold brocade. Despite what Grace had said, the desire to reach out and feel the warmth of his skin was almost overwhelming. 'I have drunk more than enough.'

'Yes,' he agreed with a half-smile, leaning back against the bolster and sipping the wine. 'Why don't you get some sleep? Your head will be the better for it in the morning.'

'Sleep…' she echoed dully. 'Aren't you coming to bed?'

'I think it would be better if I didn't,' he answered without meeting her eyes. 'Perhaps when we are better acquainted…' His voice tailed off as his eyes touched on her hair, spread against the white linen pillows. 'What happened between you and Sherard?'

'I am surprised Mistress Morrison did not enlighten you,' she replied bitterly. 'Did she not tell you what a disappointment I was to my former husband?'

'You refused him? Is that why he beat you so?' His tone was soft as he put down his wine.

'Refused him?' Wild laughter bubbled up in her throat. 'I begged him to lie with me as a husband should with his wife!' Somehow her laughter had turned into tears; she could feel them sliding down her cheeks, hot and salty as they rolled over her lips. She couldn't stop them, any more than she could stop the humiliating truth that came tumbling out. 'I thought if we had a child things would be better, he would be pleased. We had been wed a year and he had not come near me. He was angry with me all the time. Grace suggested that I should put on perfume and paint and go to his room. She lent me a silk gown that he had admired on her, but when he saw me he was furious. I tried to leave but he wouldn't let me. He just kept hitting me, calling me a whore. He wouldn't stop, and no one came…'

'Sera, hush sweeting; it's all right.'

Sera. No one had called her that for years. It made her cry harder as his arms wrapped around her.

'It's not!' She sobbed, trying to pull away. 'Yesterday, you were with her…after…and you wish you'd never met me…'

'That's not true!' His hands tightened on either side of her head as he tilted her face to meet his gaze. 'What the devil did you think I was talking about this morning!'

'Then why did you go to her last night? Why did you dance with her instead of me this night of all nights!'

'I—can't explain…' he said helplessly. 'Not yet. Trust me, Sera, please. There are good reasons for everything I have done, and my only wish is not to hurt you further than I have done already.'

'Then make me your wife,' she said, burying her head on his shoulder. 'Please…'

'No…' His voice was anguished as his arms tightened about her. 'Not tonight, not like this…not when you are angry and afraid, and I cannot promise you that I will have naught more to do with Grace Morrison. If I take you now, you will end up hating me.'

'What difference will it make?' She sobbed against his shoulder. 'Yesterday you had no such scruple.'

'Yesterday was a mistake…a sort of madness.'

'A mistake!' She lifted her tear-stained face and stared at him in disbelief. 'How can you say that? I hate you!' She flailed at him with her hands, hitting any part of him she could find. 'I hate you…'

'No, you don't,' he said wearily, rocking her in his arms as she subsided suddenly into racking sobs. 'You think so because I have hurt you and you have had too much wine. Now, lie beside me and sleep, it will seem better in the morning.'

'It won't. And I can't sleep…' she choked.

'Hush, hush…' he soothed as he got into the bed beside her. 'Come here,' he sighed as she rolled abruptly away from him. 'I said I would not make love to you tonight, not that I didn't wish to hold you.'

For a moment she lay rigid as his arm came about her waist, heavy and warm, and then, still crying, she turned into his arms, knowing only that here was comfort, safety.

He held her in silence, not moving, not speaking until she had cried herself into exhaustion and sleep. Then, and only then, did he move and settle her more comfortably in his arms. Then he sighed, and stared up at the ruched canopy of the bed. A week, Cecil had said. No more. He had a week to prove his suspicions were right or the girl in his arms would be arrested. It didn't matter if she were innocent, Cecil had said. An arrest, perhaps an execution might frighten other conspirators into acting hastily and making a mistake. Seven days. And, as yet, he had no real evidence to save her…

# Chapter Eleven

Seraphina picked up the paddle-shaped silk fan that hung from the gilt chain at her waist and fanned herself. It was hot and stuffy in the panelled room; the air was thick with perfume, candle smoke and sweat. Not all the courtiers, it seemed, shared the Queen's passion for bathing.

In the midst of a circle of chattering, jostling courtiers, a group of dancers performed a pavanne, led by the Queen, in a crimson velvet gown, and Robin Dudley. Men and women were dressed in enough silk, satin, velvet and lace to carpet half of England, and some were so laden with glittering jewellery Seraphina was amazed they could stand upright. The whole room reminded her of an overfilled jewel casket. Even the red- and green-painted panelling on the walls was ornamented with gilded bosses that shone in the light of the candles and the two huge fires which blazed in the stone fireplaces at either end of the room. She looked upwards at the great frieze painted on the wall above the panelling. Knights, maidens and unicorns frolicked in summer woodland.

It looked cool, green and peaceful. She wished that she were in such a place, out of sight of a hundred pairs of amused and cynical eyes, rather than in this overcrowded jewel box of a room. Sighing, she made herself count the number of birds in one panel, the number of roses in the next, anything to take her mind off the fact that the Earl had left her bed before dawn, that she had scarcely seen him all day and now he was dancing with Grace instead of her. One measure, he had said, as he had led Grace away. One. This was the third!

''Tis a sight worth seeing, is it not?'

She started as Sir John Malgreave spoke from beside her. On several occasions during the day she had been aware of him watching her with disturbing intentness.

'Yes,' she agreed with the barest politeness. She was not in the mood for conversation with a stranger.

'I like to come here and look at it when the chamber is empty. It puts me in mind of the woods around my home,' Sir John Malgreave continued in his soft Devon drawl.

'Are they full of unicorns and beautiful maidens?' She forced herself to smile.

'No.' He returned her smile shyly. ''Tis my wife's domain; she likes to walk there. Unicorns she might tolerate, but the maidens I doubt she would allow.'

'I suppose not,' she said, warming to him because of his obvious affection for his wife. 'She did not come with you to court?'

'No. Our first child is due in a month; besides, Nell would not like it here.'

'You don't either, do you?' she couldn't help saying as she noticed how strained he looked.

'No.' He rubbed his downy beard and looked at her thoughtfully. 'I wish I'd never left Devon. I want nothing more than the Queen's leave to go home, and that is where I must beg your help—'

'Mine!' She was taken aback. Surely it was obvious to all that her influence with her new husband and hence the Queen was negligible.

'Yes.' His voice dropped to a whisper. 'I must see the Earl privately. I need his advice before I approach the Queen. Tell him I shall be at the Bowling Green when the revels are over—please?' he added as he saw the doubt on her face.

'But why can you not ask him?'

'I dare not be seen speaking with him. It would be dangerous.'

'Dangerous? Whatever are you talking about?'

'You really don't know?' He looked as startled as she felt. 'I thought he would have told you—he must have realised it is not you. I knew the moment I saw you together.'

'Told me what?' she said, utterly bewildered.

'That—' he began, and then shook his head. 'No, perhaps it's best, safest that you do not know. But please, ask your husband to meet me.'

'Very well,' she sighed, touched by the pleading note in his voice.

'Thank you.' He looked as if someone had taken a millstone from his back. 'And, m'lady, as a favour to yourself, be careful of those close to you; people are not always as they seem.' His hazel eyes flicked to where hers had been focused a moment before upon the Earl. 'Your husband—'

'What about—?' She broke off; the relief had left his eyes and he was as white as the chalk beneath her native Wiltshire downs. 'Are you unwell?'

'No.' He swallowed and shook his head. 'But I must go; you will not forget what I have said?'

Not waiting for her answer, he backed into the crowd and disappeared. She bit her lip in puzzlement. He had seemed almost terrified, but why? He had simply been looking at the dancers. She let her eyes go back to the Earl. The pavanne had ended. It would be a galliard next, her favourite. Surely he would come and ask her to dance now? Grace met her stare and made a helpless gesture of apology as the Earl put his hand on her waist and pulled her into the next set. Seraphina jerked her head away, hating him, and hating herself for caring what he did. How could he do this to her again? she wondered sickly. Yesterday's humiliation had been hard enough to bear, but this evening he could not have made it more obvious that he preferred Grace's company to hers. *What man would not?* She could hear Edmund's bitter voice as if he were standing next to her.

The memory twisted in her stomach like a knife. Her vision blurred suddenly as she saw the Earl take Grace's small hand and raise it to his lips. She looked away, curling her hands into fists until her nails dug into her palm. Why did it have to be Grace?

'It is kind of your husband to take such an interest in Mistress Morrison, is it not?'

'The Earl is always kind.' She swallowed the hard

lump in her throat and turned her head to smile brightly at the man who had spoken from behind her shoulder. Green she might be in the ways of the court, but she would not be caught so easily by Lord William Denleigh. Grace had introduced her to him before her marriage and she had not liked him then, nor did she now.

Denleigh's rather full pink mouth curved in an insincere smile. 'Always? I scarcely call it kind to leave you standing all alone for so long. I should not if you were my wife.'

'But I am not.' Thankfully, she added beneath her breath, as she took in his suit of ice-blue satin, encrusted with gold embroidery, and lined with yellow silk.

'Alas, no.' His narrow blue eyes travelled downwards from her face. 'But I should be happy to stand in for the Earl on any occasion...' He gave a blatantly inviting look from beneath his stubby gold lashes.

She looked away hastily. He was comely enough in a way, with his tight gold curls and cupid's bow mouth, but there was something about him that aroused a faint sense of distaste in her. His pink and white skin was a little too pampered and smooth, his mouth a little too moist. And there was something disturbing in the way his eyes lingered on the neckline of her cinnamon and russet gown, something that made her lift her fan instinctively.

'I shall tell the Earl of your kind offer,' she replied with deliberate innocence. 'I am sure he will be pleased.'

Denleigh laughed a little uncertainly, showing small

white teeth. 'I see you like to tease, Lady Heywood, but if I have offended you, then you have my apology.'

'Thank you. But now, if you will excuse me?'

He put a hand on her sleeve, staying her. 'You cannot leave before the Queen.'

'No, of course not.' She felt flustered and foolish for forgetting such basic etiquette in her haste to escape from him.

'If you are bored, why not dance with me? They are just about to begin another set.' He gestured to the dancers, and smiled a little maliciously. 'It does not seem that your husband will object.'

She followed his gaze. The Earl's dark head was close to Grace's, so close she would swear his lips touched her throat. 'No,' she said thickly, as her anguish crystallised into rage. How could he humiliate her like this! Why not dance with Denleigh? What did it matter? Nothing mattered!

'Come then, my lord; they are about to begin!' She took his arm and pulled him forward with a suddenness that startled him.

The Earl looked up at that moment and stared, his tawny eyes unmistakably hostile as they touched on her hand resting on Denleigh's sleeve.

She ignored him. Head high, she clung to Denleigh's arm and smiled up at him.

As they took their place in a row of fluttering, chattering courtiers, she risked a glance at the Earl, who was in the opposite row. He seemed momentarily to have forgotten Grace. He seemed frozen, as if he had been carved from jet. Only his eyes moved, seeking hers. She met his gaze defiantly and then wished she had not. She had hoped to see annoyance, but found only contempt, black and infinite.

She jerked her head away as the dance began. How dared he judge her after the way he had behaved with Grace? How dared he! She danced with deliberate gaiety, laughing and smiling at her partners, responding to Denleigh's blatant flirtation every time the dance brought them together. And then, inevitably, the pattern of the dance brought her opposite the Earl.

His face was pale, almost expressionless, but his eyes were cold and dark. So he did not like the taste of his own physic, she thought triumphantly.

'What the devil are you playing at?' he hissed at her.

'Why, m'lord,' she smiled sunnily. 'The same game as you. Did you expect me to stand like a quintain in a deserted tiltyard all night?'

'I expect you to behave like my wife!' His hand tightened on hers, crushing her slender fingers. 'You're to have naught more to do with Denleigh, understand?'

'I'll consort with whom I choose!' she snapped at him. 'And let go of my fingers; you're hurting!'

'I'll do more than that if you don't stay away from Denleigh!' His grip tightened further.

'And are you going to stay away from Grace?' she retorted.

'My interest in Mistress Morrison is not what you think!'

'Isn't it? Then tell me; I don't understand!'

'No, you don't!' he rasped, spinning her through

the air again and catching her. 'And that is why you should do as I say and do it quietly. You are not in Wiltshire now.'

'And doubtless you wish I were!'

'Yes, I do!' he agreed with a savagery that shocked her. 'I wish you were a thousand miles away!'

'A sentiment I share!' she spat back, as they stepped and turned first one way then the other.

They danced in grim silence for several minutes, he with a face like thunder, she smiling a bright, bright smile that made her jaws ache to sustain it. She dared not relax for fear she would cry.

'What did Malgreave want of you?' The abrupt question caught her off guard and she stumbled. 'Well?' he asked roughly as he dragged her back into step.

'To meet with you privately tonight at the Bowling Green. He thinks you can help him gain audience with the Queen, but he did not want to be seen approaching you directly.'

'I see.' His eyes seared over her face. 'And what are your plans while I am so engaged?'

'To go to bed!' she snapped, angered by the unmistakable suspicion in his eyes.

'With Denleigh?' he drawled insultingly.

'You bastard!' Her voice rang out in a sudden silence. To her horror she realised that the Queen had signalled her intention to retire and the musicians had ceased playing. Half the court was staring at them, some with carefully composed faces, others smiling openly.

'Must you make fools of us both?' he hissed.

'Hypocrite!' she returned in a searing whisper. 'You have made a fool of me from the moment we were wed and before!' Furious, she wrenched out of his grasp and fell back with the other women to form a row opposite the men so the Queen might pass. She glowered across at the Earl. It was his fault! All his fault!

'Curtsy.' She jolted as Grace whispered urgently in her ear and realised the Queen had paused in front of her and was waiting for her obeisance. Scarlet-cheeked, she sank into a hasty curtsy and braced herself for a reprimand. Shaking inside, she straightened, acutely aware of the cool, dark gaze on her face. But the Queen said nothing. There was simply the faintest lift of one finely plucked brow before she moved on in a rustle of silk.

As the doors of the chamber swung shut behind the Queen, she thanked Grace stiffly for her reminder and then turned away abruptly. But Grace caught her arm, halting her.

'Don't go; we must talk,' Grace began softly.

'About what, my husband?' She could not keep the acid out of her voice.

'Seraphina, please; it is his doing not mine—'

'Is it?' She did not bother to disguise her doubt as she met Grace's anxious gaze. 'Is there really naught you can do to escape his attentions? You have no such difficulty with other men.'

'Please—' Grace's fingers tightened on her arm, 'I told you; I dare not offend him. He says he will tell the Queen I do not approve of her succession; he might as well accuse me of treason. It's the truth.'

She put her hand to the silver crucifix she wore. 'I swear it on this.'

Seraphina felt her heart turn to ice. Grace was far too devout to use such an oath lightly.

'I see,' she said flatly. 'I will tell him to desist or *I* shall go to the Queen—'

'No!' There was genuine terror in Grace's voice. 'He is her favourite; she'll be angry and blame me. Swear you will not.'

'Very well,' she agreed reluctantly. 'But, by God, I will tell him to leave you alone or he will find himself without a wife.'

'Tonight—you will tell him tonight; I want no more of his attentions.' The pathetic eagerness in Grace's voice fuelled her anger. How could he stoop so low as to threaten a woman?

'Yes, and I shall not wait a moment longer,' she replied grimly glancing at the Earl, who was deep in conversation with William Cecil.

'Thank you,' Grace said with relief. 'If you do not mind, I shall say goodnight. I shall see you tomorrow, perhaps?'

'Yes. Goodnight.' She responded mechanically, her eyes still fixed on the Earl. How could she have been so blind? How could she have believed him when he had said there would be no one else for him as long as she lived. He was a despicable liar and she would tell him so, and she did not care who heard!

'Seraphina—' Mary Sidney stepped in front of her as she began to move towards him. 'I could not help hearing what Mistress Morrison said just now.'

'What of it?' Seraphina said defensively.

'It is not true. I know Richard as well as any brother, and I *know* it is not true. As I think you do in your heart.'

'No,' she answered thickly. 'I know that I do not want to believe it, but how can I not when he pursues her for all the world to see?'

Mary frowned. 'I don't pretend to understand and I don't excuse his conduct, but he would not resort to threats to win Mistress Morrison.' Her frown deepened, 'And I do not believe he really wishes to—it is you he cares for. I am certain of that.'

'He has a strange way of showing it,' she answered with a choked laugh.

'He gave you Madrigal,' Mary said softly.

'Madrigal? What has she to do with anything?' Seraphina looked at her in bewilderment.

'She was to have been a New Year's gift for the Queen, one which she was most eager to have, but he gave her to you instead.'

'You mean…' She stopped, feeling a shock of pleasure, of hope. 'He put me before his ambition?'

'Aye,' Mary smiled. 'And if he means as much to you as I think, can you not sacrifice a little pride and try and settle your quarrel with him? It is never good to sleep on ill words. Now, I must go; I wait on the Queen tonight and she'll box my ears if I am not there to brush out her hair. As you will find when it is your turn to wait upon her. Goodnight, and good luck.'

'Thank you…' she said, still trying to make sense of what Mary had told her. There was only one thing to do: she had to confront him, demand the truth about Grace, about Madrigal…

Tentatively she glanced across to where the Earl had been standing a moment before, talking to William Cecil. There was no sign of him, but perhaps he had gone to the gardens, after all. If she hurried, she might catch him. Picking up her skirts, she sped towards the door. Lord Denleigh watched her, a half-smile on his lips and then strolled after her. William Cecil stood staring after them, a frown on his scholarly face.

Seraphina shivered as she stepped out of the palace and felt the bite of the night air against her overheated skin. She paused for a moment to let her eyes adjust to the darkness, and then began to walk briskly along one of the gravel paths which criss-crossed the Privy Garden. The garden was deserted, and a little eerie in the weak moonlight. The decorative columns surmounted by heraldic beasts loomed suddenly out of the dark as she passed them. She glanced upwards at a griffin, crouched with one savage clawed foot extended against the night sky. If you looked quickly you could almost believe it alive—she started as a peacock gave a blood-curdling screech from somewhere to her right. Fool, she told herself, as she felt her heart quicken. She had never been afraid of the dark at Mayfield and that had been country darkness, black as pitch, whereas here there were a hundred lighted windows in sight. Nevertheless, she increased her pace, until she was almost running and then halted abruptly as ahead of her, where another path crossed her own, a man stepped out from the denser shadow cast by one of the columns.

'Who is it?' Her voice was not so steady as she would have liked.

'There is no need for alarm, Lady Heywood.' Her heart sank as she recognised Denleigh's voice rather than that of the Earl as she had hoped. 'I saw you enter the garden and thought you might need an escort,' he continued as he came towards her. 'It is not wise to walk about Whitehall at night. With the public road running through the palace, one can never be sure who is about.'

'Yes,' she agreed nervously, realising that she was afraid of him, although she could not say why. 'You are right, of course. I was hoping to catch up with my husband—' she emphasised the last word '—but I think I shall wait for him at our apartment instead.'

'Then I'll accompany you,' he answered her smoothly. 'You're lodged near the Chapel, are you not? Come, I know a short cut.'

'I would not inconvenience you, m'lord,' she protested uncertainly, 'and I should rather go the usual way; it is better lit with torches, I understand—'

'You are a country girl, indeed.' Denleigh's teeth showed white in the moonlight as he laughed. 'Little wonder Heywood has begun to look elsewhere for excitement; next you will say you must have your mother's permission before you can take a walk with a friend.'

'I shall not,' she replied unevenly, stung by his words. 'But—'

'Then come along.' He took her arm.

For a moment she considered pulling away and

fleeing back the way she had come, but that would make her look hysterical and gauche, and she had the uncomfortable feeling that Denleigh would put the tale about court and make her more of a laughing stock than she was already.

'If you insist, m'lord.' Stiffly and against her instincts she let him lead her through the garden and into the maze of alleys and passageways which linked the sprawling buildings of Whitehall.

'Surely we have gone wrong,' she said uneasily as they entered a tiny courtyard and the moon came out from behind a cloud, illuminating a circular fountain in the courtyard's centre. 'This is where the fire was just after Yule. These apartments were gutted; the doors are boarded up; there is no way through—'

'Alas, no,' Denleigh gave a low laugh which made her skin crawl. 'And we are quite alone, quite hidden from prying eyes.'

His tone sent an alarm ringing in her brain. She recoiled too late. He caught her in his arms and clamped his mouth on hers in a kiss that crushed her lips painfully against her teeth. His lips were wet and cold, arousing nothing in her but a sense of nausea.

'Let me go! At once!' She struggled furiously, feeling the first stab of panic as his fingers dug cruelly into her arms.

'Don't be so coy, m'lady.' He sniggered, pulling her closer. 'You seemed willing enough earlier.'

'I am not—'

Her protest was cut short as his mouth smothered hers again. She twisted and flailed at him with her hands, but it was useless. For all the plump softness of his fingers, his hands were strong, pinioning her arms, while his mouth roved from her lips to her throat, nipping, so that she cried out at the pain. Her panic grew along with her sense of revulsion as he laughed and tried to force his tongue into her mouth. Then from nowhere a memory flashed into her mind. She, Dickon and Bess had gone to a fair years ago to watch the wrestlers. After the bout, Dickon had persuaded one of the wrestlers to show them some of the throws. Pretending to yield to his embrace, she slumped so that he was drawn forward by her weight. He laughed triumphantly and let go of her arms to shift his hands to her waist. Slipping one foot behind his foremost heel, she hooked his leg forward with all her strength while shoving at his chest at the same moment. Somewhat to her surprise, it worked perfectly; he went flying backwards. She found herself mesmerised as he teetered on the edge of the pool, arms milling in a frantic, futile attempt to regain his balance. The water plumed upwards as he hit the surface with a spectacular splash, soaking her gown. She began to retreat and then hesitated, fearing that he might have struck his head and drown. A moment later she wished she had not listened to her conscience.

Denleigh erupted from the water, and began to clamber out of the pool, foul oaths streaming from his tongue faster than the water from his clothes. The moon came out from behind a cloud at that moment and the whole scene was bathed in light that was almost as bright as day. His appearance was so changed that she almost dissolved into laughter. His hair was plastered to his head without a trace of a curl, his beautiful lace ruff was limp and shapeless as a wet rag, trails of dark weed clung to his soaked costume and his hose had sunk to a wrinkled mass about his ankles, revealing legs that put her in mind of peeled willow wands.

But then, as she glimpsed the fury in his face, she realised belatedly that she had been a fool to linger. He was between her and the entrance to the enclosed courtyard. Snatching up her skirts, she dodged past him, gasping as he caught a ribbon on her sleeve. It ripped, and she was past, running blindly, not knowing or caring where she was going so long as it was out of his reach. She turned into the first passage she came to, and then the next and the next until she was completely disorientated. She glanced at the dark walls of the buildings which had hardly any windows; the servants' quarters, and most of them would be still at work in the main palace. There was little point, perhaps even worse danger in screaming for help. She ducked beneath a low archway and found herself in another tiny cobbled courtyard. She halted, holding her side as she fought for breath. Denleigh was still coming after her, she could hear the wet slap of his shoes upon the cobbles, slow because of his wet clothes, but still faster than she could ever be in petticoats and skirts. And there was no way out—or was there? The gap between the corners of the buildings was tiny and overgrown with briars, but somehow, with a strength born of sheer panic, she scrambled and squeezed through. The thorns caught her hair, her hands, her gown, but then she was through, tumbling

on to smooth, flat grass. She stumbled to her feet, and
ran on towards the low, dark shape of a building, not
caring where she was, but simply blessing the fact
that there was grass to run on instead of cobbles. As
she came closer, she realised with a sinking heart that
the building was absolutely deserted and silent, but
perhaps it would at least offer a hiding place. She had
nearly reached it when the moon came out from behind a cloud, bathing everything in pale silvery light.
The bowling green and the pavilion! Then Richard
might be close. She opened her mouth to shout and
then felt a wild surge of relief as she saw the man
sitting quietly on one of the wooden benches the players used between turns. He stared at her, his eyes wide
and startled.

'Sir John, thank God!' Sobbing for breath, she ran
to him and clutched his arm. 'Please—'

Her voice dwindled, trapped by her constricted
throat as John Malgreave toppled forward and went
sprawling at her feet.

'No...' A low moan, scarcely audible, came from
her lips as she saw the gleaming hilt of a stiletto pro-
truding from his neck. She opened her mouth to
scream, too full of horror to register the almost silent
emergence of a man from the pavilion.

The hands that clamped over her mouth and the
arms that wrapped about her like iron bands, took her
utterly unawares. Excruciating fear numbed her for
the seconds that it took her assailant to drag her back
into the shadow of the pavilion. Then she began to
twist and struggle frantically, drumming her heels into

his shins, biting at the hand across her mouth; she would not go to John Malgreave's fate easily.

'Be still for God's sake! It's me.'

'Richard—' The low voice shocked her into stillness and then she went limp in his arms as terror gave way to relief. She could think of nothing except that he was here when she most needed him and she was safe.

'Denleigh...' she gasped against his palm. 'You were right. I'm sorry.'

'Hush. Not a sound...understand?' he murmured, his lips against her ear. 'You...we...must not be found here.'

She nodded, too numb to reason why or argue. He took his hand from her mouth just as the moon dipped behind another cloud, and the clearing became inky black again.

She dragged in a breath, and then held it as Denleigh floundered across the green, swearing viciously.

'Come out, you teasing bitch! I know you're there!' He began to work his way along the pavilion, kicking over the benches, striking out wildly at the posts of the front gallery with his fists.

She flinched involuntarily as he came closer to where they stood pressed into the doorway of the pavilion. The Earl's free hand went to his sword and she heard the tiny silken whisper of steel as he loosened it in its scabbard.

'Come on, woman; come out, damn you...'

Denleigh squelched nearer and nearer. She wanted to run. It was torture to stand and wait. Her heart thudded painfully against her ribs, so violently she was sure Denleigh would hear it. The Earl's arm tightened about her waist, a tiny gesture of reassurance which gave her the courage to stand still as Denleigh blundered past, almost brushing her skirts.

'Jesu!' The tone of Denleigh's swearing changed abruptly as the moon peeped out from behind its cloud and a shaft of silver light illuminated Malgreave's sprawled form. He halted and bent over the body and then, with a curse, turned and ran back the way he had come. His incoherent shouts about murder were followed almost immediately by the clamour of a bell, the sound of men shouting and the clatter of pikes.

'Come on.' The Earl shook her almost roughly as she slumped against him, shaking, her mind empty momentarily of everything except the fact that Denleigh had gone and she was safe. 'You mustn't be found here; come on—' he repeated, dragging her after him, his arm still about her waist.

'Malgreave—' she began uncertainly, as she almost tripped over the body.

'It's too late to do aught for him.' He was cold, impassive.

Poor John, poor Nell. She felt an overwhelming sadness as she looked down and then utter, choking fear as the Earl propelled her towards the other side of the green.

'He…he came here to m-meet you…' she blurted breathlessly as he pushed her through a gate and into an alley. 'D…Did you…' She couldn't form the rest of the question. It was too horrible, too sickening to voice.

'No,' he rasped impatiently. '*I* didn't kill him! Why should I? Did you?'

## Chapter Twelve

'Me?' She laughed hysterically. 'Why should I want to kill John Malgreave? I have never spoken to him before tonight.'

'Forget it,' he said curtly. 'Now, come on, before we are both arrested.' He pushed her through a gate 'We will have to run. The guards will be all over the place in a moment.'

Only when they reached the torchlit wooden gallery which ran along one edge of the Privy Garden did he slow his pace and allow her to catch her breath.

'Jesu! Whatever have you been doing?' he groaned as the flickering torch-light revealed the tattered state of her dress. 'Perhaps you'll think twice before arranging another assignation.'

'I didn't have…an assignation with Denleigh! I was looking…for you!' she retorted breathlessly. 'He followed me, and I pushed him in a fountain—'

'A fountain? How the devil did you manage that?'

'With a throw I learnt from Dickon years ago,' she muttered, thinking he would be as disapproving as her mother had been at the time.

'*You* threw Denleigh?' He coughed suddenly.

'Yes,' she snapped, too upset to catch the fleeting note of laughter in his voice. 'And then he chased me and then—and then—' Her throat closed as she remembered John Malgreave's startled, pale face.

'All right, we'll leave the questions until later.' He spoke briskly. 'There will be people on us in a moment. If anyone asks you, we were strolling on the farside of the gardens when we heard the alarm and came to see what the matter was. With luck, your dishevelment will be blamed upon my ardour.'

'But Denleigh—'

The Earl's mouth contorted into a harsh smile as a group of courtiers holding torches came into sight, led by the sodden Lord Denleigh.

'I do not think Lord Denleigh will be boasting how he came to be in such a state; he values naught more than his pride. Now, be quiet and leave the talking to me.'

She nodded, and was grateful for the support of his arm about her waist, since she was shaking from head to foot.

No one questioned the Earl's explanation of their presence in the garden, but her sense of unease grew as her mind became less numb with fear and shock. Why was he lying? And why had he asked her if she had killed John Malgreave?

Bess greeted them as they entered their apartment, her bright blue eyes widening as she took in the state of Seraphina's gown. 'Whatever have you been doing, m'lady?' she exclaimed. 'We'll never get those water-marks out.'

'Leave us, would you, Bess?' the Earl said tersely. 'You may see to the gown later.'

'Yes, m'lord.' Bess made a curtsy. 'Your night-gown's ready, by the fire, m'lady; if you need it,' she added with a grin.

'Thank you,' Seraphina managed to smile. Was that how they looked to the world? A pair of besotted newlyweds, eager to be alone? She gave a ragged laugh as the door shut behind Bess.

The Earl released her and went to the side-table and poured two goblets of red wine from a flagon.

'Here.' He held one out to her.

She shook her head and walked over to the blazing fire, making a pretence of warming her hands before she found the courage to turn and look him in the eyes.

'Why? Why did you lie? Why couldn't we tell the Captain of the Guard the truth about finding Mal-greave?' she demanded, watching his face as he walked towards her and dreading what she might see. 'And why was Malgreave so afraid of you? I saw it in his face when he looked at you during the dancing.'

'If he was afraid, then it was not my fault, and I told you I didn't kill him, if that is what you are thinking.' He sighed and lifted his glass goblet and took a swallow of the ruby wine before putting it down upon the mantel. He reached into a pouch which hung from his belt. 'I lied because of this.' He held up a length of fine gold chain from which dan-gled an emerald ring, glittering and sparkling in the firelight. 'Perhaps you recognise it?' He dropped it into her hand as she reached out to stop it from spinning.

'It is the dragon ring,' she said in bewilderment. 'All Sherard brides are given it as a betrothal ring; the tradition is well known.'

'Exactly,' he said drily. 'I found it clasped in John Malgreave's fingers. It seemed clear he had pulled it from the neck of his assailant.'

'But—' She struggled to make sense of what he was saying '—but I left it at Sherard House for Edmund's heir.'

'Can you prove that?'

'No,' she said, after a moment's thought. 'Bess or Grace might remember, but I doubt they could swear to it.' Then, as the truth surfaced in her mind, she laughed nervously. 'You lied because you thought people would think that I murdered John Malgreave! What reason would I have to do such a thing? There was no need for you to lie to protect me; I could have defended myself from such a ridiculous charge.'

'You think so?' His mouth twisted into an odd smile. 'It might have been more difficult than you imagine, as difficult as it is going to be for me to persuade Cecil.'

'Sir William?' She looked at him blankly. 'What has he to do with this? I don't understand.'

'You really don't, do you?' There was unmistakable relief in his eyes and voice as he stared down into her face 'God! For a moment tonight, I thought I was wrong.'

'About what?'

'Nothing you need know about; knowledge is dangerous.'

'You agreed with me once that there should not be secrets between husband and wife and now you are treating me like a child!' She lifted her chin to meet his gaze.

'I am protecting you.'

'I suppose it makes a change from humiliating me!' she said bitterly.

'Sera—' He exhaled slowly as he said her name. 'Listen to me; there is no time for quarrelling. If anyone asks how you think John Malgreave died, you will say you think he fell victim to one of the vagabonds who hang about the palace at night. Promise me?'

'But the stiletto was jewelled, a nobleman's weapon, and there was no sign of a struggle; he must have known—'

'Promise!' His fierceness frightened her into silence. 'If you care for me at all, promise...' he added more gently, the hawkish lines of his face softening as he saw how she dropped her eyes so that he should not read them.

'That's unfair,' she protested.

'I know,' he admitted slowly, 'but have I your word?'

'Yes.' She conceded defeat with a sigh.

'Thank you.' He surprised her by cupping her face between his hands and kissing her swiftly, before releasing her with a half-smile. 'And in return I promise you that soon you will not have so much cause to regret wedding me. Now get Bess to help you out of that gown and tell her to sleep on the truckle bed tonight.'

'You are going out again?' She could not hide her disappointment as he discarded his richly embroidered compass cloak of tawny silk and took a plain wool one from the clothes press. She was cold, tired and frightened, and part of her wanted to beg him to stay.

'Yes, and I would rather you were not alone.'

'I would not be,' she said as she crossed the room and went to sit at her dressing-table, where Bess had lit two stands of candles, 'if you stayed.'

Watching him in the candlelit glass, she saw him pause in the act of fastening his cloak.

'I can't,' he said after a moment. 'There is someone I must see.'

'At midnight? Who?' Her voice shook a little as she took her heavy topaz and gold jewellery from her ears and throat and let it fall upon the inlaid table. The clatter it made seemed to echo in the silence which stretched after her question.

His reflection was blurred and indistinct in the shadowy glass, but not so much that she could not see the bleakness in his face, confirming what his silence had already told her.

She turned slowly, her eyes wide and very green in her white face. 'Why?' she asked. 'You lie for me, give me Madrigal, and at times seem to find me pleasing enough, so why do you go to her?'

'Not for the reasons you think,' he said wearily. 'But, before you ask, I cannot explain—not yet.'

'Did I ask you to?' She swivelled back to her mirror, took up a flagon of honey-water, poured some on to a piece of linen and began to dab at her face. 'Well?' she asked as she saw he was still standing behind her. 'What are you waiting for?'

'Sera—' He took a step forward.

'Just go!' she said savagely as she put the honey-water down clumsily and it spilled across the table. 'Just go!'

It was only when the door had shut behind him she gave up her desultory efforts to mop up the spilled liquid and slumped forward, her head in her hands.

'M'lady?' Bess's tap on the door a little while later brought her to her feet.

'What is it?' she asked wearily as she opened the door.

'Robert, m'lady; I found him wandering along the corridor.'

'Oh, Rob, whatever are you doing up at this time of night?' Forgetting her own problems, she went down on her knees to pick up the woebegone little figure clad in a voluminous nightshirt and askew nightcap.

'Can't find Tawny.' Robert's round face crumpled. 'He ran in th'dapple and the dead people have got him 'cos he won't come out.'

'I'm not sure what he's talking about,' Bess said as she followed Seraphina into the room.

'He means his kitten is in the chapel, don't you, Rob?'

Robert nodded solemnly.

'He'll only be chasing the mice; he'll be back for his milk in the morning.'

'He'll be scared 'cos it's dark. He's always scared when nurse puts the candles out,' Robert said, looking at her with eyes which were very brown and dark like his father's. 'You get him. Pliss?' His plump little arms tightened about her neck and he put his head on her shoulder.'

'I see.' She exchanged a glance with Bess. 'It seems Tawny is afraid of being on his own in the dark. I'll go and find him, and you stay here with Rob. Put him in my bed until I get back, then we'll take him to his nurse.'

'Come on, Rob.' Bess held out her arms and took the little boy. 'Lady Seraphina will soon find your kitten, don't you worry.'

The chapel was deserted, midnight mass being over, and only the candles on the altar were still alight. Shivering a little in the cool air, she made her obeisance to the cross and called out tentatively for the kitten.

To her surprise and relief, there was an answering mew, a scuffle, and Tawny appeared, teetering on the edge of one of the high-sided box-pews where those of high rank could listen to services in complete privacy.

She laughed, and then stifled it. Somehow it never seemed quite right to laugh in chapel. Moving on tiptoe to lessen the noise of her shoes on the stone flags, she advanced slowly towards the kitten.

She was almost within reach when the kitten leapt off into space, landed, skidded and sped towards the altar. Horrified, she watched as it poised itself for a leap on to the altar.

'Tawny!' she hissed. 'Don't! Cats have been burnt alive for less reason that that!'

As if understanding her, the kitten sped off again and darted through the open door of another box-pew. She followed, shutting the pew door behind her. Catching him should be easy now, if only she could see. For a minute or so, she felt for the kitten in the shadows, trying hard not to think of spiders, the one creature which she could not abide to see or touch. Her breath caught as Tawny's velvet paw dabbed at her fingers and then was snatched back as she tried to grab him. Sighing she sat down upon the bench, deciding that a different approach was needed. For several minutes she sat silent and unmoving, and then she heard the soft thud as the kitten jumped on the bench beside her, and, a moment later, the pressure of its paws as it climbed on to her lap. She stroked it gently and was rewarded with a purr. Smiling, she picked it up, and settled it against her shoulder. She was about to stand up when footsteps and a voice made her freeze.

'I tell you it wasn't there. Jesu, if it gets into the wrong hands—'

Denleigh. Seraphina shuddered as she recognised the voice and thanked God for the instinct which had kept her still. He was the last person she wished to meet.

His companion gave a silvery laugh 'They will think it hers, fool.'

'I had not thought of that...' There was relief in

Denleigh's voice. 'But then I cannot think of much these days, seeing him with you…when I think of him in your bed.'

The woman laughed again. 'Contrary to appearances, my lord, Heywood has shown no desire to share my bed as yet, for which I thank God.'

'And if he had?' Denleigh asked roughly.

'Then I should.' The woman laughed coldly. 'I can think of worse sacrifices to make for the faith. But don't fret, my lord; in two days, all will be settled.'

'And then you will be mine, as you promised?'

'Perhaps…' The rest of her answer was lost as their footsteps receded and the chapel door opened and shut.

Seraphina sat frozen. Grace. Grace and Denleigh. The Earl was not with her, nor had been any other night. He was not Grace's lover, nor wished to be! For a moment she was full of joy and relief, and then her euphoria gave way to bewilderment. Then why had he made such a play of pursuing Grace, and why had Grace lied to her? None of it made any sense. Inexperienced as she was, she could not doubt the attraction between the Earl and herself was real. And if he did not want Grace…she sighed and stood up. In the morning she would demand an explanation from them both.

At the same moment, Sir William Cecil frowned at the Earl. 'You are telling me that you found your wife's ring in Malgreave's hand and you still do not think she is the woman you saw at the cottage?'

'No.' The Earl rubbed a hand over his close-cropped beard. 'I think Sherard's cousin put it there to make us think it was Seraphina. If you'd question Tregarrick or Wharton—'

'There is no time; they have both gone back to the west. And I see no need; one example should be sufficient.'

'Example! You would see an innocent woman used as an example?' The Earl's eyes blazed with contempt. 'God's breath, if we were alone, Cecil—'

'But you are not,' the Queen put in icily. 'And you have not yet proved her innocence.'

'Precisely,' Cecil said smugly. 'This theory of yours about Mistress Morrison is far-fetched. I saw your wife with Malgreave tonight; I saw her follow him into the garden. And do you think the likes of Tregarrick and Wharton would take orders from the daughter of an impecunious merchant?'

'You said yourself Tregarrick and Wharton are small-fry. I think they have been duped into thinking they were dealing with my wife and that this scheme has Carey support. She was veiled at the cottage; the only means of identifying her was the ring. And where did the information about the meeting at the cottage come from? I think it was fed to us deliberately so we should end up chasing our own tails. We were meant to believe it was my wife while the real traitor goes on unhindered.'

'But you followed the woman to the inn and had her followed to Mayfield.'

'I know,' the Earl grated. 'But the woman at the cottage was not as tall as my wife; she was wearing high-heeled slippers. I should have realised it at once.'

'High-heeled slippers! God's breath, my lord! The Queen's life is in danger and you expect me to hesitate because of a pair of silk slippers! Every other report I have had points to your wife as the contact with France.' Cecil lifted his pen and began to scrawl out a warrant.

'Madam.' The Earl turned to the Queen, who had been listening impassively as she toyed with the diamond rings upon her fingers. 'Please, I beg you wait. If I thought there was any chance at all she was guilty, I should not—'

'You would not have told us about the ring tonight, would you?' the Queen finished lazily as the Earl stopped in mid-sentence. 'What would you have done, Richard, if you had thought her guilty? Warned her? Let her go? Or assisted her?'

'Madam!' The Earl's drawn face became very white. 'My loyalty to you is paramount and always has been—'

'Yes…all right.' The Queen made a staying gesture with her slender white hand. 'That was unfair of me, Richard, and I am sorry for it; you have served me well when few dared support my cause.'

'Then give me a little more time, madam, I beg you.'

'It would give me no pleasure to cause you pain, Richard,' Elizabeth said slowly, her eyes veiled as they travelled over his face. 'But a man has died. I shall have to act. Bring me what evidence you have in her favour by sunset tomorrow, or I shall have no choice but to arrest her.'

'Thank you, madam,' the Earl answered grimly. He had less than a day to prove he was right. And if he failed—she would die. He had little doubt of that. Cecil would not wait long to make his example.

'I've left the candle standing in a basin of water, 'twill be safe enough like that,' Bess said as she tucked the coverlet more firmly over Robert's sleeping form. 'But I'll stay with him tonight. By the way, his nurse is snoring; I'd wager she's drunk a vat of ale.'

'Aye.' Seraphina frowned as she put the drowsy kitten down upon the foot of Robert's bed. 'I'll speak to the Earl about her tomorrow. Goodnight, Bess, and thank you for staying with Robert.'

'M'lady?' Bess touched her arm as she turned to leave 'What is it? You have looked so different— since you came back with the kitten.'

'Do I?' She gave Bess a swift smile. 'Perhaps it is because I have just found out that my husband and Mistress Morrison are not lovers and never have been. I overheard her with Lord Denleigh in the chapel.'

Bess's freckled face lit up. 'I told you he'd never prefer her to you.'

'Yes,' Seraphina said ruefully. 'I think I have been a fool, Bess. You were right; Mistress Morrison is no friend of mine, nor I think has ever been, and I shall tell her so in the morning.'

'If you don't, I shall,' Bess said happily. 'Now go

and change that gown before you catch your death of cold.'

Seraphina walked briskly back to her apartment. The door was ajar; she and Bess must have left it open when they had carried Robert out.

She pushed it shut behind her and walked across to the fire which had burnt down to a dull glow. She shivered, aware suddenly of the uncomfortable dampness of her gown. Taking off her cloak, she dropped it on to a chair and turned—into a hard, male body, clad in a wrapping robe and little else.

Her cry of alarm died on her lips as her body recognised him even before her eyes had registered the hawkish features of the Earl's face. For a moment, as her fear gave way to relief, she almost put her arms about his neck and hugged him.

'Where the devil have you been? I've searched half the palace for you!' He caught her shoulders as she tried to retreat a step from his disturbing near nakedness.

'I was with Robert. He was upset because his kitten was lost. I went to find it.'

'I see.' She felt the anger drain from him, but he continued to hold her tightly.

'He is sleeping now, but Bess will stay with him until morning.'

'Good. Thank you,' he answered mechanically, still staring at her face as if he had never seen her before.

'You were looking for me? Why?' she asked.

'To tell you—' he stopped. 'I was not with Grace Morrison tonight.'

'I know.'

'You do?' He was visibly startled.

'Yes, I heard her in the chapel with Lord Denleigh when I was searching for the kitten.'

'Denleigh...of course...' He exhaled audibly. 'What were you saying?'

'Does it matter?' she asked uneasily, wondering if he would believe her, or think she had invented it out of jealousy.

'More than you know,' he muttered, almost pushing her into a chair beside the fire. 'Tell me what they said, exactly.'

Unable to look at him, she dropped her eyes to the Turkey rug as she repeated what she had heard.

'God's breath, I *was* right!' She lifted her head; relief was the one reaction she had not expected.

'You do not mind about her and Denleigh?'

'Mind?' He looked at her blankly as if he had forgotten she was there, and then, as his eyes skated over her face, he shook his head. 'It is the best news I have had in days.'

'I don't understand...'

'No.' His eyes were dark, soft as they sought hers. 'I know you don't, and it is safest that you do not.'

'But where did you go tonight?'

'I cannot tell you; no more than I can tell you why I have been spending so much time in Mistress Morrison's company. All I can say is that it concerns the Queen. I can only ask you to trust me for a day or so longer. I will explain, I promise you.'

'Very well...' she agreed reluctantly.

'Thank you.' He gave her a half-smile that did not reach his eyes. 'I know I have done naught to deserve your trust...' He turned away abruptly, threw a log upon the fire and then leant against the mantel, staring down into the flames, his chiselled features bleak and drawn in the flickering light.

He did not notice as she got quietly to her feet and came to stand beside him. 'My lord,' she said tentatively. 'You look tired; is there aught you need? Some wine—'

He shook his head. 'I do not need wine, Sera; I need—' He broke off as he raised his head and looked down into her face. 'I need to know you will forgive me for—' he paused and rubbed a hand across his face '—for everything. I have never wished to hurt you...you do believe that?'

'Yes.' The desperation in his eyes and voice would have brought the same answer from her lips even if she had not believed it were true.

'Good...' The harsh lines of his face relaxed a little. 'Now get out of that gown before you catch cold; 'tis time you were in your bed.'

'Yes,' she said flatly, a lump rising in her throat at the dismissive note in his voice. She was tired, afraid and utterly confused. Confused about everything except an aching need to have him hold her close and feel safe and desired as she had when he had held her at the joust. She began to fumble behind her back for her laces, they knotted—and he was simply standing and watching her struggle—it was the last straw. 'At least help me with my laces—' Her eyes flashed up to his, part angry, part pleading. 'You did not seem to mind doing so before.'

Her voice died as he reached out and caught her to

him in one swift movement, holding her so tightly, so fiercely, she could scarce breathe. She lifted her head from his chest, a thousand questions on her lips and in her eyes. Questions that faded into irrelevance as his head dipped and he kissed her mouth, her face, her eyelids, with hard urgent kisses, urgent as his hands as he snapped the knotted laces and freed her of her gown and then her petticoats, sweeping them down over her hips, careless of buttons and stitching. She melted against him; whatever else was wrong between them, this was right…

She murmured a protest as his hands left her to remove the starched frill of lace from her neck, where it had impeded the downward path of his mouth. And then she felt him go very still beneath her hands. She opened her eyes. He was ashen, staring at the circle of gathered lace in his fingers.

'My lord?' she asked shyly. 'What is it?'

'Naught—just I had not realised what a little neck you have—' He gave a choked laugh, and then dropped the ruff and wrapped his arms about her, holding her so close that she felt the heat of his body searing through the silk of his robe and her shift. 'But I will not let him take you. I swear. I will not let you go…' His murmur was only just audible as he pressed his lips to her hair.

'I want no other, my lord.' A little bewildered and frightened by his intensity, she lifted her head from his chest wondering if he was thinking of his first wife's infidelities. 'None but death would part me from you, and then I should not go willingly—'

'Don't speak of it!' His voice was jagged, harsh. 'Don't even think of it—'

'Richard?' She said his name, her eyes widening into pools of bemused emerald as she held his gaze. She had never seen him so vulnerable before, so afraid. So afraid of losing her. The realisation made her want to weep and dance for joy at the same moment. Going on tiptoe, she kissed his taut mouth in a shy, soft kiss.

He groaned, burying his hands in her hair and dislodging what pins remained after her flight from Denleigh in the garden. The heavy mass tumbled down past her hips, glinting red where it caught the firelight. He lifted a handful of it to his face, inhaling the spicy perfume she always wore, the perfume that had so misled him at the cottage and the inn. He had been blind, and because of it she might die. He swore inaudibly and brought his hands up to either side of her face, making her look at him. 'Tomorrow, I want you to make ready a few things, no more than you can take upon a horse, in case we have to go away from here at short notice.'

'To the country?' She smiled at him dreamily as happiness welled up inside her. He must care for her. He must, or he could not look at her so, touch her so. 'I wish we could. I have already had sufficient of court to last me a lifetime.'

'Not the country—' His long black lashes dropped, veiling his eyes from her shining gaze. 'I meant abroad. France, perhaps.'

'France!' She struggled to hide her astonishment.

And then she asked warily, 'We would take Robert? I promised him tonight that he should live with us.'

'Obedient as ever, I see.' He gave a strained laugh. 'We shall take Robert.'

'The Queen wishes you to be her envoy?' she asked. 'Is that what has upset you? That she does not want you at her side?'

'Not exactly,' he said thickly. 'But there'll be time to talk of it tomorrow; until then, say naught to anyone, not even Bess. Swear…'

'Yes…' she said uncertainly.

'My poor love. I ask so much of you and give you naught in return.' He sighed softly as he saw the bafflement on her face.

His love. She stared at him for a moment, frozen with shock and joy, and then, with a new confidence, she reached up and stroked a lock of his black hair back from his face and let her palm rest against his cheek. 'I ask naught but to be your wife in truth as well as in name.'

'You shall be.' He caught her hand, cupping her palm against his lips and then as he swept her up into his arms gave a wry, soft laugh. 'A saint could not resist you, and I am far from that.'

She looked up at him with anxious eyes as he lay her gently upon the satin counterpane of the canopied bed and stared down at her. Even now, a tiny part of her was afraid Edmund had been right—a fear that vanished as he knelt and drew off her slippers, and then bent over her and undid the bow of silk ribbon which secured the gathered neck of her russet gauze shift. Her mouth and throat went dry as he drew the loose column of silk down over her coral-tipped breasts, which grew taut and heavy as his gaze lingered on them before following the path of his hands downwards. She shivered as he put a hand beneath her back, lifting her as he glided the shift down over her hips and legs until she was naked, but for her white silk stockings and ribbon garters. He made a low sound in his throat as he untied the garters; his fingers trembled against her thighs as he stripped off the stockings, sending an answering flutter of anticipation through her body. He paused for a moment, his eyes dark, blurred with desire as he looked at her, and then in one swift movement he threw off his gown and was beside her, his mouth seeking hers as his arms brought her into shocking contact with his warm body, so lean and hard and powerful...so different from her own softness. His kiss gentled as he felt her tense. He lifted his mouth and then, with infinite gentleness, as if she were made of glass and might break, he touched her, smoothing back the burnished waves of her hair from her face and shoulders with his fingertips, and then feathering downwards over her breasts and ribs to her tiny waist, over her hips and thighs and then back, all the while watching her face intently.

She lay quiescent, her momentary fear washed away by the waves of desire which flowed between them. Desire that was so evident in the taut lines of his face, in his hands. She watched him touch her, spellbound by the faintly abrasive caress of his weathered hands on her pale skin. And then, as he circled her breasts, almost but not quite touching their hardened tips, she could bear his tantalising restraint no longer, and reached up to link her hands about his neck and bring him down to her.

'Please...' Her plea was incoherent but it was enough. His head dipped to her breast. Her fingers moved blindly, instinctively on his muscled shoulders as his mouth closed on the peak of her breast, sucking, teasing, until she wound her fingers in his hair and pushed his head away from her aching breast, unable to bear the exquisite but painfully incomplete pleasure a moment longer.

Her eyes sought his, dazzled, pleading as she moved her hips against his in an invitation that was purely instinctive. He rolled, pinning her beneath him. There was no restraint now, in his hands or mouth, just the raw male need to possess; a need which matched the desire in her own body to give, to yield to his weight and hardness. She arched eagerly to his mouth, his hands as he claimed her body. Only when his hand parted her thighs and slipped between did she recoil. The sensation was so intense, so unexpected. But his weight held her captive as he continued the merciless, devastating caress, until she was shuddering helplessly beneath him as her body seemed first to pool and then dissolve. And then she gave a choked gasp as he moved, lifted her to him and pushed into her. There was a moment of resistance, a splinter of pain and then an explosion of fiery pleasure as he filled the aching, melting void inside her.

'Did I hurt you?' He was tender, anxious, as she

went still beneath him, lost for a moment in this new, unfamiliar world.

'No...' Her voice was slurred as she opened her eyes to his blurred, dark gaze. The pain she had heard so much talk of had been nothing compared to the pleasure. 'It is just I did not expect it to be—' She broke off, struggling to find the words to describe the wonderful sense of completeness, the joy of being so at one with him. 'Like this—' she finished inadequately, her breath catching as he began to move in her.

'It gets better,' he laughed softly, dipping his head and kissing her. 'I promise you...'

# Chapter Thirteen

And he had been right, she thought, smiling into her mirror the following morning as she fastened a peridot and silver necklace Richard had given her the previous week about her throat. Not that she had believed him at the time. The night had become a journey into pleasures she had not dreamed existed, would think she had dreamed if it were not for the tender places on her body. She picked up the note he had left her to apologise for leaving before she woke, and her smile deepened. He would be back in an hour or so. So, that left time enough for her to make things right with Grace. This morning she was ready to forgive anyone anything. Blithely, her heart soaring, she twirled away from her mirror, sending the leaf-green velvet skirts of her gown flaring out over the primrose silk kirtle. Spring colours for the beginning of a new life…

'I'm going to see Mistress Morrison,' she called out to Bess, who was in the adjoining room repairing the damage to her cinnamon and russet gown. 'I shall not be long.'

Outside her apartment, she almost cannoned into Mary Sidney, who took one look at her glowing face and laughed. 'I need not ask if you have made up your quarrel!'

'Yes.' Colour rose in Seraphina's face as she smiled; she had not realised her happiness was so obvious. 'Have you seen Mistress Morrison?' she asked, smiling. 'You were right, and I intend to find out why. Not that it matters now.'

'Then perhaps there is something else you should know,' Mary Sidney said reluctantly. 'Before you came to court there were rumours about your first marriage, and they were begun by Mistress Morrison.'

'It was her? But why should she?'

Mary shrugged. 'Jealousy, perhaps.'

'But she had no call to be jealous of me. God knows, if anything it should have been the other way about. Edmund worshipped the ground she trod upon...' She frowned and then laughed. Nothing could destroy her happiness this morning, not even Grace's odd behaviour. 'Then that is something else I shall have to ask her. Perhaps it was just that she was so upset at Edmund's death.'

'Perhaps,' Mary said doubtfully. 'I saw her but a few minutes ago. She was dressed for riding; if you hurry you should catch her. Oh, I near forgot; you are to take your place among the Queen's ladies next Sunday. If you have time tomorrow, come and take some refreshment in my room and I'll explain how she likes things to be done.'

'Thank you,' Seraphina said gratefully. After her recent encounters with the Queen, she had not been looking forward with great enthusiasm to the next. 'Until tomorrow, then.'

'Yes,' Mary smiled, and then, after taking a few steps, frowned and turned back. 'Seraphina, there is something about Mistress Morrison which worries—' She broke off, shaking her head in amused disapproval as she saw Seraphina was already out of earshot and fast disappearing down a flight of stairs at a pace no lady could manage with proper modesty. But, as she turned back towards the Queen's apartments, her frown returned.

The stableyard was deserted, but that was not surprising since the Queen was hunting that morning. Courtiers would have had the grooms bring their spare horses in case the first tired during the chase and the stableboys were no doubt making use of the chance to enjoy a little leisure. A whicker from one of the stables brought a smile to her mouth. Madrigal. She went across to the mare's stable and, seeing she had tangled her tether and could not reach the hay in the slatted wooden rack, went in to put it right.

She lingered for a minute or so, stroking the mare's ears and letting her blow softly at her face. It seemed she had missed Grace, but as she remembered the previous night it no longer seemed important. Richard Durrant loved her. He had said so, more times than she could count. The smile on her wide mouth faded as, through the open half-door, she glimpsed Lord Denleigh crossing the yard. She shrank back behind Madrigal as he came closer, wishing suddenly that there were more people about. He slowed his pace as he reached the door and her heart stopped, and then started again as he went past, and she heard him enter the next stable. She waited for a few minutes, expecting him to come out again with his mount. Denleigh had not struck her as the sort to take an interest in his horses. Several minutes later she sighed with exasperation. She could not stay here all morning hiding from Denleigh. Richard would be back soon. But, if she left by the door, Denleigh might see her. She glanced upwards. Above the hayrack in the low-boarded ceiling was the open trap leading into the hay-loft which would have a door and steps down at the far end of the building. She had climbed through its like often enough at Mayfield to join Bess and Dickon in enjoying the spoils of illicit trips to the kitchen garden, but never in a court gown. There was nothing for it but to stay put until Denleigh left or the yard was less deserted. She breathed a sigh of relief as she heard the adjacent door open. He was leaving—no, someone else was going in—and if he had an assignation with a serving wench he would be too busy to notice her leaving.

'About time.' Denleigh's annoyed voice carried clearly through the wooden walls. 'Have you got it?'

'Yes,' Grace's soft, cool voice replied, stopping Seraphina in her tracks as she began to move 'And for the love of God do not drop the vial; such poisons are not easy to come by without questions being asked. Are you clear as to what you must do?'

'I send the jewelled casket of sweetmeats and the note to Katherine Grey tomorrow morning when she is waiting upon the Queen,' Denleigh said wearily.

'Yes, with the poem about her beauty, exactly as I have written it here.' Grace laughed softly. 'The vain little chit will not be able to resist boasting of it to the Queen and showing her the casket, no more than Elizabeth Tudor will let her keep it.'

'Can you be sure of that?' Denleigh said doubtfully.

'Certain. There is no love lost between Elizabeth Tudor and Katherine Grey, especially when she behaves as if the throne should be hers.'

'But if the Grey girl eats one first...' Denleigh began, still sounding very uncertain.

'Then we have spared Mary Stuart the bother of getting rid of her and Elizabeth will be blamed and her *reputation,* of which she is so proud, will be ruined and we will be free to try again, and have more support for our cause.'

'But if it is traced to us—'

'It can't be. Just be sure there is no outward sign of tampering with the sweetmeats and that they are the sort the Queen favours most, then we cannot fail. Now go, my lord; I will follow in a minute or two. It is best we are not seen too often in each other's company.'

Seraphina stood clinging to Madrigal's mane, sick with a mixture of fear and anger. Everything she had been about to say to Grace faded into insignificance. What were lies compared to treason? She had known that Grace shared Edmund's passion for the old faith, but she would never have believed it would lead her to this. Murder! Grace—who would say a dozen penances if she missed a mass! She held her breath as

Denleigh passed, knowing with sudden, unerring instinct that this was why John Malgreave had died; he must have known something of this. Dear God, what should she do? The Queen was hunting. Who should she tell? Allegiances had changed so often these last few years, it was impossible to know where the sympathies of many of the council truly lay. She shut her eyes, trying to think. Cecil, or Mary Sidney. They were trustworthy. She would go to one of them as soon as Grace had gone. Dear God, what would she not give to have Richard beside her now.

Something soft brushed her hand. She opened her eyes and gave an audible moan as her mind emptied of everything except primitive, skin-crawling terror. A spider! Black, seemingly enormous as it crouched, malevolently upon her hand. She shook her hand frantically, her heart racing beneath her ribs as if she had run a furlong. It fell on to her skirt. With a stifled scream she flapped the velvet wildly, causing Madrigal to shy away. And then, after what seemed like eternity, but was no more than a second it flew off into the straw at her feet. Shaking, she backed to the door, almost tripping as she collided with an empty water bucket and sent it clattering on the bare cobbles near the door.

'Seraphina? Whatever are you doing?' She wheeled, new fear choking her as she saw Grace standing outside the stable door, watching her.

'A spider,' she blurted tersely. 'A spider fell from the ceiling!'

'Have you not got over such a foolish fear yet?'

Grace was dismissive 'It is not as if they are venomous.'

'Unlike you?' Still shaken, Seraphina replied without thinking as she opened the stabledoor and closed it behind her, wishing that there was someone else in the yard. There was something in Grace's stillness which gave her the same gut feeling of fear as the spider.

Grace exhaled slowly, her pale eyes suddenly very brilliant in her delicate face. 'You have been there all the time; you heard?'

'Yes,' Seraphina answered, realising there was little point in trying to pretend otherwise.

'And what do you intend to do?' Grace asked coolly as if they were discussing the weather.

'What do you think?' Seraphina snapped, as the implications of telling the Queen surfaced in her mind. Grace would be arrested and then—most like it would be the axe or the stake. She took in a deep breath as her eyes met Grace's half accusing, half apologetic. 'I have to go to the Queen; you must know that. I have no choice.'

'I saved your life at Sherard House, does that mean naught to you?' Grace said, smoothing her already immaculate silvery hair.

'Yes,' Seraphina swallowed. 'And because of that I will beg the Queen to be…merciful.' She made a helpless gesture with her hands as Grace gave a little laugh. 'Come with me now, of your own free will. If you confess all, then perhaps there is a chance—'

'I will not die.' Grace gave a strained laugh and glanced across the empty yard as she fiddled with her hair again. 'It is not a chance I care to take. So what will you do? Drag me there?'

'M'lady!'

Seraphina turned, jogging Grace's half-raised arm as she saw Dickon's dear and familiar figure striding across the yard. 'No,' she replied shakily, 'but Dickon will, if need be.'

Grace went very pale, then shrugged. 'I suppose it does not matter much, since you do not care for your husband.'

'My husband? What of him?'

'They are his instructions I am carrying out, surely you realise that.'

'What?' She stared at Grace and then laughed, 'Don't be ridiculous; everyone knows his loyalty is to the Queen. He went to the Tower rather than give evidence which might have incriminated her after Wyatt's rebellion—'

'And was released when so many of his friends died. Why do you think that was? Have you not learnt yet that he will do anything for a price and a pretty face? Mary Stuart was very taken with him when he was sent back to treaty after Calais fell, and he with her, by all accounts…'

'It is not true,' Seraphina said woodenly, as doubt rose in her mind like poison as she recalled his evasiveness and strange mood the previous evening and what he had said about France. Something she had entirely forgotten until now. Her heart twisted painfully beneath her ribs. If he was involved…how could she betray him? Send him to his death? Whatever else was false, after last night she could not doubt that he loved her. If she doubted that, she might as well be dead herself.

'As you like.' Grace sighed and dropped her blue gaze to the ground. 'You will discover the truth soon enough. I did not want any part of this at first; he made me join him with his threats.'

'If that is true, why did you not go to the Queen?' she asked desperately.

'Because who would have believed me against the great and powerful Earl of Heywood?' Grace's voice trembled. 'Even you, whom I have always counted a friend, do not. Your man is here, shall we go?'

'No.' Hating herself for her own weakness, she shook her head. 'I need to speak to my husband first, and, if you are lying, I should make use of the time to flee.'

'So, you have been fool enough to fall in love with him.' Grace's mouth curled into a derisive smile. 'And to think you might have had Edmund's heart if you had wanted it.'

'What?' Seraphina said in sheer disbelief.

'It doesn't matter.' Grace shrugged and turned away. 'Not now.'

'Sorry, m'lady,' Dickon began in breathless apology. 'I'd have saddled Madrigal if I'd known you meant to ride. Lord Heywood said—'

'It's all right, Dickon,' Seraphina said slowly, feeling as if she were trapped in a nightmare 'I do not wish to ride.'

'Oh, good,' Dickon said relieved, and then bent to pick up something which lay shining on the ground where Grace had been standing. He held up the long hairpin, shining and sharp as a—stiletto. 'You've dropped this, m'lady.'

'No.' She shook her head, the blood draining from her face as she recalled John Malgreave's death. Had that been Grace—or the Earl! 'It is not mine. Mistress Morrison must have dropped it just now when I jostled her.'

'Are you all right, m'lady?' Dickon said 'You look very pale.'

'Yes,' she said shakily 'Walk back with me to my chamber, Dickon; I feel a little unwell.'

'M'lady, what are you doing?' Bess exclaimed as she came into the apartment an hour later and found Seraphina kneeling on the floor amid a litter of parchments and books. 'These are Lord Heywood's papers, are they not?'

'Yes,' Seraphina said dully. She had discovered what she had dreaded finding some five minutes before. A piece of paper folded and slipped down the spine of a book. She looked at it again. A plan for a rebellion. A list of some of the greatest Catholic families in the land, and against each name a note. This man to provide men at arms, that one to escort Mary Stuart to London. Edmund's name was there, scored through, presumably when he had died, and at the top her own and Grace's with a query against each. Had he thought to win her to his cause? Was that why he had made love to her last night? No. The thought hurt so much she crumpled the paper in her hands.

'M'lady?' Bess came forward anxiously.

She waved her away. 'Leave me, Bess, please…'

Reluctantly Bess did as she asked. She waited until the door had closed then went to the writing table and took up a quill. She wrote rapidly, angrily, her hand shaking, telling him what Grace had said, and that now she had proof, she was taking it to the Queen and she never wished to see him again, ever. The point of the quill snapped and she flung it aside and then snatched up another to sign her name. Sanding the letter, she folded it inside a clean sheet to make a packet and began to melt wax for the seal. Then abruptly she put down the half-melted wax as her eyes touched on the great bed where last night he had held her in his arms…loved her. The pain in her stomach was physical. How could she let him go to a traitor's death, and what of Robert? Lifting the flap of the packet, she scrawled a postscript.

I shall wait until dawn tomorrow before I go to the Queen—you have a day's start. I shall take Robert to Mayfield. Sera.

She blew on the ink and sealed the packet, then, after writing his name on it, she propped it on the mantel. She would ask Bess to pack her things so as to be certain to avoid seeing him. After one glance about the room she turned to go. Her hand was on the latch when a loud knock upon the door made her start. She opened it to see a manservant, bedraggled-looking and breathless.

'Lady Heywood?'

'Yes,' she said warily. 'What is it?'

'Your lord, he got in the way of a crossbow bolt at the hunt—'

'The hunt!' She stared at him stupidly as her heart stopped. 'He was not hunting today—he is not—' Dead. She could not bring herself to say it.

'Not yet, but near it, and he's asking for you; you'd best hurry,' he said.

'Where is he?' she asked desperately, knowing now that what she had written in the letter was a lie. She had to see him once more. She had not ever told him she loved him and somehow that mattered more than his treason.

'I'll show you,' he said gruffly. 'Have you a horse?'

'Yes!' She was ahead of him, picking up her skirts and running along the corridor for the stairs, praying as she had never prayed in her life that he would not die before she reached him.


'Dear God, where are they?' she demanded of the manservant an hour later as they rode deep into the woods and were forced to a walk by the low branches and dense undergrowth.

'You have missed the way—'

'No. It's just through here; he's in the old warrener's cottage. You'll have to dismount—'

But she was already slithering off Madrigal's back, pushing her way through brambles and into the clearing where the dilapidated thatched cottage stood. She ran across the uneven ground, not stopping to wonder that there was not another horse or person in sight. Her mind was empty of everything but the need to see him, hold him, just once more. Only when she flung open the door of the cottage and found it deserted did the first thread of suspicion unwind in her mind. She turned, too late.

'You!' Her stomach contracted with fear as she watched Denleigh shut the door with deliberate care and then stand in front of it, his hands on his hips as he smiled at her. Some instinct told her that whatever else she did, she must not let him see she was afraid. She drew herself up and gave him her haughtiest stare. 'You have got me here on a fool's errand, so now you have had your revenge, m'lord, will you stand aside—' Her composure broke as he lunged forward suddenly, pinioning her hands behind her back and pushing her against one of the upright beams which supported the half-loft above their heads. 'Let me go!' She struggled furiously, twisting and kicking, until he shoved her so hard her head snapped back against the beam, leaving her sick and dizzy as he bound her hands about the pillar. 'Have you gone mad?' she groaned as the dizziness receded. 'Release me at once, or—'

'Or what?' Grace's cool, sweet voice froze her into immobility. 'I hope you are not expecting your husband to come to your rescue.'

'Where is he?' she demanded thickly. 'What have you done to him? I was told he was hurt—'

'He said that would bring you running.' Grace got up from the high-backed settle which had hidden her from sight and stroked some dust from her grey satin skirt before replying. 'He isn't here; there are some things, it seems, that even he has not the stomach for.'

'What do you mean?' Her fear turned to cold dread.

'You didn't tell me—' Denleigh began tersely.

'It is naught to do with you, m'lord. Leave us if you please.' Grace made a dismissive gesture.

'But you said I could have her—' he protested.

'There will be women enough for you later,' Grace said contemptuously. 'Now leave!'

Seraphina exhaled slowly, momentarily relieved as the door closed behind him. Then, her heart slowing, she forced herself to ask again. 'What did you mean? Why did you lure me here—'

'It was on your husband's orders He felt unable to rely upon your loyalty to him being greater than your misguided attachment to the house of Tudor. He is sorry, of course, and he does not relish being a widower again so soon, but—' she shrugged '—we all have sacrifices to make for the faith.'

'You're lying!' The denial tore from her throat. 'It isn't true! He would not harm me. He loves me—'

'But danced attendance on me at your wedding—' Grace's brows lifted.

'He isn't your lover. I heard you tell Denleigh in the chapel,' she said desperately.

'I lied. Denleigh's jealousy was becoming a nuisance.'

'No.' She moaned like an animal in pain.

'It hurts, doesn't it, knowing they have lied to you? Perhaps you understand now how I felt when Edmund fell in love with you.'

'With me?' She laughed hysterically, certain now that Grace was mad. 'He hated me!'

'No.' Grace's face contorted. 'He hated himself—

for wanting you. We were happy before you came; he had vowed to me no wife would ever take my place in his heart or in the bed we could not share because of the nearness of our blood and then you came and made him doubt everything with your heretic beliefs and your red hair!'

Seraphina stared at her with horrified contempt as understanding came with swift, sickening clarity. 'That is why you gave me your perfume, lent me your gowns, to remind him always of his vow to you, even when we were in our bedchamber. You wanted him to hate me.'

'Yes. It was easy at first,' Grace said complacently, as she went over to the fireplace. 'I knew him so well, and you were so eager for my advice. I told you to do whatever I knew would displease him most, and invented a little about our liking for the opposite sex. The thought of you with others kept him angry.' She toyed thoughtfully for a moment with the tinder box she had picked up. 'Too angry, perhaps. I never thought his infatuation with you would make him risk everything we had worked and prayed for.'

'Why did you save me that night, when you had goaded him into near killing me?' she asked numbly. What did it matter if Richard Durrant did not love her and never had?

'If you had died, your family would have been on us like hounds from hell to find the reason. The Careys can never let well alone. An investigation could have endangered this enterprise, so I had no choice but to save you,' she sighed 'A pity, really; it would have saved us much trouble if he had killed you.'

'I see,' she said, wondering how she could have been so blind to Grace's hatred for so long.

'You don't!' Grace's pale face blazed with sudden fury. 'I had to kill the only man I ever loved because of you!'

'*You* killed Edmund...'

'I had to.' Grace struck the flints from the tinder box savagely and lit a candle upon the fire mantel. 'He thought you were dead and that it was God's punishment for his treason. He tried to ride to the Lord Lieutenant and confess, to give his life as payment for yours so that he might escape eternal damnation. I rode after him to tell him you were still alive, but he was hysterical, insisting he must atone, so—' Her voice thinned a little as she picked up the battered pewter candlestick '—I killed him and saw to it that his horse dragged him to hide the wound. What else could I do?' She sounded almost plaintive. 'I could not let him betray his faith for you.' She sighed, and then almost casually touched the candle's flame to a pile of old straw heaped upon a rotting pallet. The flames leapt instantly, hungrily.

'Grace...are you mad? You have set the place afire!' Seraphina jerked at her bonds as Grace stood staring into the flames with an almost rapt expression upon her face as she took the crucifix from her neck. 'For God's sake, untie me—please—' Her voice dwindled as Grace came to her and she met her pale, blank gaze.

'You will think this cruel.' Grace smiled as she fastened the crucifix about Seraphina's neck and went to the door. 'But the flames are a heretic's only chance of salvation; you will have time to repent.'

'You will let me burn?' Seraphina's voice rose in terror. She had thought she would welcome death, welcome anything that stopped the pain of knowing Richard Durrant wanted her dead. But to burn! 'Grace!' she screamed as she heard the door shut and the key turn. 'Kill me first if you must, but don't let me burn!' But there was silence except for the crackling and roar of the flames. She looked about her hopelessly; there was no escape. The cottage was all wood and straw; it would burn like tinder. Already the flames were licking greedily up the wall to the hay-loft. She coughed as smoke began to fill the cottage. Frantically she wrenched against her bonds, twisting, pulling until her wrists were raw. It was useless; the leather thongs simply became tighter, so tight she was losing all feeling in her hands. She was going to die—die like the girl Edmund had burned for a heretic. She screamed, and screamed again, knowing there would be no one to hear, and then she was hoarse from the smoke, coughing, spluttering, as she struggled for breath. The smoke was everywhere, stinging, making her eyes gritty. They began to stream with tears, until everything about her was a blur of scarlet and gold as the flames leapt and spread, leaping from loft to thatched roof. Then clumps of burning straw fell, starting other fires about the room. One fell near her skirts, and she stamped it out, sobbing and coughing hysterically, and then slid down the pillar to the floor, drawing up her knees and burying her face in her skirts in a futile, instinctive attempt to shield herself from the suffocating, searing heat. Her skirt had begun to smoulder, slowly, because the hem was damp from where she had pushed through the undergrowth. She lifted her head, kicked at blackening silk velvet with her feet, sobbing hysterically. But it was useless. 'Dear God! Help me!' Her throat was so hoarse, her scream was no more than a whisper. She was going to burn...

'M'lord! M'lord!' The Earl frowned as he swung down from Pavanne's back and saw Dickon running towards him at full stretch.

'What is it, man?' he asked brusquely. So far the morning had brought nothing of value. Time was slipping away.

'The mare, my lord. She's just come back without Lady Heywood,' Dickon said breathlessly.

'What? She was not riding today—' The Earl strode to the stable, and glanced in at Madrigal, his face paling as he saw the brambles in her tail, and her snapped and trailing reins.

'She went to find you, my lord; a man said you were lying hurt in the woods.'

'Who was he?' the Earl rasped.

'I don't know—' Dickon began helplessly. 'I would have gone with her, but some fool had set my gelding loose and she was in a tear to get to you.'

'Get me a fresh horse, now! Then tell my man John to get my hound and start searching the western edge of the wood; I'll take the east—and ask Dudley and anyone else you can find to help.'

'Yes, m'lord.' Dickon left at a run.

\* \* \*

'Richard, this is useless,' Robin Dudley sighed several hours later. 'It's almost too dark to see. If she'd taken a bad fall, we'd have found her by now. I'll wager she's already back at the palace, safe and sound.'

'I should sell my soul to have you right,' the Earl said grimly. 'But I doubt it; someone lied to get her alone.'

'There's more to this than you have told me,' Dudley said, giving him a sharp look. 'You're really afraid for her. That business with Malgreave—you both knew more of that than you said, didn't you?'

'Yes,' the Earl cut in tersely. 'But don't ask me now, Robin; let's just keep looking.'

Dudley nodded. 'I can smell smoke; there must be charcoal burners nearby. I'll go and ask them if they have seen aught.'

'Charcoal burners…' The Earl looked upwards through the canopy of bare branches above their heads. The plume of smoke further to the west was only just discernible against the darkening winter sky. Then, with an oath, he put his heels to his horse's side. 'There aren't any charcoal burners in these woods,' he shouted to Dudley. 'Come on!'

The Earl stood in the charred, smouldering wreckage of the cottage, bile rising in his throat as he spread his cloak over the unrecognisable, twisted, blackened body. This wasn't her! This wasn't anyone—he shut his eyes, his fingers tightening on the besmirched and broken chain of peridots he had taken from the ghastly clenched hand. The peridots that told his mind what his eyes and heart refused to accept. God! Why hadn't he told her, warned her—?

'Richard!' He turned slowly, like a man who was drunk, as Dudley's horse crashed into the clearing.

'Have you found—' Dudley broke off as he saw the Earl's face.

'Yes, I found these on the body over there—' he said flatly as he walked to his horse and swung heavily into the saddle. 'They're hers.'

'Jesu! You mean—' Dudley paled as he glanced from the chains of peridots in the Earl's hand to the smoking ruins.

'Yes, she's dead.' He met Dudley's horrified gaze with blank, dark eyes. 'We'd best get back; there are things to be done. They'll need a litter for the body.'

'God's breath! Richard, I am sorry—' Dudley began helplessly, but the Earl had already wheeled his horse away and was urging it through the briars. Dudley watched him for a moment in shocked, helpless silence and then with a rough oath pulled his own mount round. 'Richard!' he shouted as he followed him out of the clearing and back into the wood. 'Haste will change naught. Slow down; you'll break your own neck in this light—'

The Earl reined in and swung to look at him, his face a savage mask. 'Do you think I should care if I did?' he asked bitterly. And then, putting his spurs to his horse, he rode on, ducking and weaving through the low branches at suicidal speed.

## Chapter Fourteen

Seraphina opened her eyes slowly; she ached, her mouth and throat were parched, unbearably sore as cold, moist air sliced into her lungs. She stared uncomprehendingly at the tangle of twigs and brambles a few inches above her face. What was she doing here? She pulled herself up on to one elbow and recollection came with sickening suddenness as the reek of smoke rose from her hair and clothes. The cottage. She shut her eyes; she remembered now. Remembered the heat and terror and being cut free, and being pushed through the door as her skirts had started to flame. Then the wonderful cool wetness of the grass as she rolled to smother the flames and beat at them with her hands—that was why they stung so—or had she burned them when she had tried to free Denleigh from the fallen beam which had missed her by a fraction? She shuddered, remembering how he had clutched at her, his fingers curling on her necklace as he had begged her to get him out. The chain of peridots had snapped; she had fallen back as the roof had collapsed inward in an explosion of flame. Denleigh had vanished into the crackling, roaring thunder of the fire and she had half run, half crawled into this old animal lair to hide, afraid that Grace would come back, or him.

She let her head drop back upon the earth. She did not want to think of that; it hurt, hurt a thousand times more than her hands and lungs. She did not want to move or think ever again; she wanted to stay here, curled against the sweet, musty smelling earth…but she couldn't. She had to warn the Queen.

The Queen! What time was it? It was still light, no, it was getting light—she had been unconscious all night. And that meant it was Friday…

She crawled out from her shelter of branches and dragged herself to her feet. If she headed east in the direction of the rising sun—she clutched at a sapling as her legs buckled and forced herself to drag in long painful breaths of the cold morning air, until sky and woods had ceased to spin about her. She had to get to the palace…she had to…

It was over three hours later when she at last reached the gates of Whitehall. She half scrambled, half fell from the dilapidated cart in which she had managed to secure a ride. Its ancient driver, who looked even older than the two snail-slow oxen which pulled his cart, looked at her curiously as she went sprawling in the dust and mud of the road. 'You'm can't go in there, m'maid.'

'I must—' she choked, dragging herself to her feet. 'And thank you. Here.' She took the earrings from her ears, having naught else to pay him with and pressed them into his gnarled hand. They were worth more than he would have earned in his lifetime, but he deserved them. A dozen others had passed her as she had lain upon the side of the road, incapable of moving another step, and whipped up their horses, afraid, no doubt, that she had the plague or some other ill they might catch.

She did not hear his delighted thanks, her mind was totally taken up with the effort of crossing the few yards to the servant's entrance, climbing the endless, endless steps. And then there was the gloomy labyrinth of passages and stairwells, where yards seemed to stretch into miles. People passed her, looked at her curiously, but she was only half aware of them, too exhausted even to think of asking their help. The Queen. That was all that mattered. She must reach the Queen and then she could rest, slide into the blackness at the edge of her mind. She stumbled on, her legs stiff and leaden, so each step jarred her aching head into shearing white pain.

She flinched at the clash of pikes which reverberated in her aching head. Pikes and guards...the Queen's apartments. Thank God. She leant against the wall, trying to force words from her dry throat.

'Get out of here!' One of them growled 'This is no place for drabs.'

It was only then that she realised what she must look like, her face, hands and hair dark with smoke, her clothes scorched and torn and muddied. 'Please...' she begged them hoarsely. 'Please, I have to see the Queen, it is a matter of life or death...'

'It'll be our death if we let you in—now get out.'

Defeated she sank to the floor, her head in her hands.

'What is happening here?'

'Mary!' She croaked out the name with joy as she lifted her head. 'Thank God—you have to help me to see the Queen.'

For a moment Mary stared at her without recognition and then her face lit with delight. 'Seraphina! How? We thought—Richard thinks you're dead!'

'Please,' she begged as Mary helped her to her feet, 'there is no time to explain now; I must see the Queen.'

'But you are hurt,' Mary said anxiously, steadying her as she swayed. 'Can it not wait?'

'No! She is in danger!'

Without further argument, Mary bid the guards let them pass and led her through the royal apartments, which seemed to become a blur of tapestry, silvergilt and silks as her faintness increased. And then they were in a dazzlingly sunny chamber, where three people stood talking, silhouetted against a great window. Her heart turned to stone as she watched one of them, learn, dark, unbearably familiar, hold out a casket to the Queen and saw the long, slender hand reach out and pick up a sweetmeat…

'No! Your Majesty!' Her scream brought them wheeling round as she wrenched free of Mary's supporting arm and flung herself forward and dashed the sweetmeat from the Queen's hand.

'Sera!' She had just time to be startled by the joy that sheared across the Earl's face before a crashing blow from a guard's pike sent her to the ground and into complete and instant darkness.

'Sera?' His voice was soft, tender, as she opened her eyes and found herself looking up at the canopy of their own bed. For a moment, before she remembered, she smiled. Then she jerked upright, retreating from him across the bed on her hands and knees as fast as the hampering folds of her voluminous linen nightrail would allow.

'Don't touch me—' she croaked in terror as he tried to reach out to her. 'Oh, thank God!' she gasped with relief, as Mary came into the room, a basin and cloths in her hands 'Get help—the sweetmeats are poisoned. Grace and—'

'Sera—' He sounded almost as hoarse as herself. 'Don't be afraid; I'm not going to hurt you…'

'Stay away from me!' She snatched up a candlestick from beside the bed and brandished it at him.

'Be calm.' Mary hurried to her side 'We know all about it, thanks to the letter you left for Richard; the Queen was but looking at the sweetmeats. She wishes to send their exact likeness to her cousin in France, without the poison, as a warning to keep her hands off the English throne.'

'And Grace?'

'She took her own poison rather than deliver herself into my custody,' the Earl said grimly. 'And 'tis well for her she did so, when she told me that she had left you to burn alive.'

'On your orders! You told her to kill me!' she said hysterically.

'No, no; you have it wrong,' Mary answered hastily as the Earl seemed at a loss for words. 'She lied to hurt you—she boasted of it when she was taken. Richard is no traitor, and he would not harm a hair of your head; you must know that.'

'It was not true—none of it?' The candlestick fell from her hand as her eyes searched his anguished face, and she knew with soaring happiness that it was not.

'None of it, fool,' he rasped as she flung herself into his arms with a half-sob 'None of it. I was acting *for* the Queen, not plotting against her.'

'Do you think this is the time?' Mary began doubtfully, then seeing neither of them had eyes or ears for any but the other, retreated quietly and shut the door.

'Did you really believe I would hurt you?' His voice cracked as he smoothed back a strand of hair from her face and touched his lips to her cheek.

'I did not want to, but I was so confused,' she said helplessly. 'When I found that paper—'

'Those were the notes I had made for Cecil.'

'Cecil?' she said blankly. Her head ached and she could not think straight.

'But…' she began again, utterly bewildered. 'Why did you talk of us running away to France if you were acting for him and the Queen?'

He sighed. 'Because after she killed Malgreave and left the dragon ring on his body, Cecil was threatening to arrest you.'

'Me! But why—' she asked, too startled to take in the fact that he had been prepared to leave court, give up everything, so she might be safe.

'Because Mistress Morrison had taken great pains to make us think *you* were leading the conspiracy. It served her purpose in several ways. She knew we would hesitate longer for acting against a Carey, and that waverers would be reassured if they thought the scheme had Carey support. It gave her more time and had us going in circles.'

She pulled out of his embrace as a thousand things which had puzzled her suddenly became very clear. 'You were ordered to seek my hand and persist in your wooing, despite all I did to put you off—'

'Yes.' He got up abruptly, suddenly finding he could not bear to watch the happiness fade from her eyes.

'I see.' She pleated the sheet between her fingers and then went on in a rush, 'You had no more wish to wed than I?'

'No.' He touched a single note on the virginal. 'Lettice had left me with no taste for marriage.'

'But it did not matter, since it was not to last,' she said bitterly. 'Little wonder you would have kept me from Robert. How you must have prayed that I was guilty and the block would free you!'

'That was never true!' He swung round. 'The Queen promised me an annulment, but since we have shared a bed…'

'None need know it so long as I am not with child.' She misunderstood his hesitation. 'I will know in a week and all being well you can have your annulment. You will recall I had no more wish to be wed again than you! And you have given me no cause to change that opinion. Now leave me; I would rest. God willing we need not meet again.'

'Sera!' He took a step towards the bed and then stopped and sighed as she rolled away and pulled the covers over her face. 'I do not blame you for being angry. I have explained this badly, but I had hoped you might forgive—'

'Just go!' she repeated furiously from beneath the covers. 'I never want to see you again, ever! Need I say it again?'

'No,' he answered hollowly. 'I'll send Mary in.'

It was only as she heard the door shut behind him that she began to weep. Silent tears which continued to slide down her face as Bess and Mary fussed over her, helping her wash the smoke from her skin and hair. Tears which did not stop until, utterly exhausted, she fell asleep.

'Seraphina?' She opened bleary eyes to see Mary standing over her, a candle in her hand. 'I'm sorry to wake you, but you must get up.'

'Why?' she demanded miserably. Sleep was her refuge from the knowledge that he had never, ever, loved her, that it had all been lies from beginning to end.

'The Queen would see you. Come, I'll help you dress.'

There was an urgent, anxious note in Mary's voice that brought Seraphina out of bed in one swift movement.

'Now? Why? It must be near midnight.'

'Past it,' Mary said as she hustled her out of her

nightgown. 'There's something amiss. She's been in a strange mood since Richard came to see her and then stormed off, heaven knows where.'

'Come in, Lady Heywood; I do not bite,' the Queen bid Seraphina impatiently as she stood uncertainly at the entrance to one of her private chambers. 'You may leave us, Mary, and close the door.'

Seraphina made a low curtsy and then walked forward, to where the Queen sat in a cushioned chair near the blazing fire. Her stomach knotted. Even clad in her simple purple velvet wrapping-gown, Elizabeth Tudor looked as regal and terrifying as she could in her presence chamber. The Queen eyed her coolly, seemingly taking in every detail of her appearance from her crackling newly washed hair which had defied all Bess's efforts to tame it, to the bandages upon her hands.

'Your husband tells me you want your marriage annulled? Why?' Elizabeth snapped suddenly, making her flinch.

'With respect, Your Majesty, you must know the answer to that as well as I. He has no wish to be wed to me and never had.'

'And you?' Elizabeth silenced her with a gesture, 'Have you no wish to be wed to him?'

'I—I think it scarcely matters in the circumstances,' she said, avoiding the Queen's steely eyes.

'No, perhaps not. Now sit, before you fall.' The Queen gestured impatiently to a cushioned stool. 'You look ill. Are your hands painful?'

'A little, Your Majesty,' Seraphina admitted as she

sat down, folding her hands in her lap to disguise their shaking.

'I understand you are lucky to have escaped me lightly.'

'Yes, madam.'

'Just as well,' the Queen said drily. 'To send a sick woman to the Tower and throw away the key would not enhance my reputation.'

'The Tower…why?' Seraphina's eyes came up from her lap, wide and astonished 'What have I done?'

Elizabeth held up the outer sheet of the letter she had written the Earl about the conspiracy. 'You recall writing this, I take it?' she drawled, waving it idly to and fro. 'Your spouse was too distraught to notice it, but I, however, did…'

'Yes.' The blood left Seraphina's face as she saw what was coming.

'You warned one of my enemies so that he might escape? Supposing he had brought his plot forward?'

'But he wasn't your enemy—'

'You did not know that at the time.' The Queen was suddenly silky-sweet. 'So why did you do it?'

'Because I—' She stopped, unable to go on. It was one thing to be a fool, another to admit it to a woman with a mind like a rapier, and a heart of ice.

'You love him?' Elizabeth's mouth curled as her eyes fastened on Seraphina's face, daring her to lie.

'Yes,' she confessed hopelessly.

'More than your Queen?' The question was as sharply edged and swiftly aimed as an axe. 'A sweet treason indeed, but still treason, as you must well know.'

'But—'

Elizabeth silenced her with a gesture as she stood up and clapped her hands sharply. 'I cannot let treason go unpunished for the good of the realm.'

From another door, four pikemen entered with their captain.

'Your Majesty?' The captain of the guard bowed.

The Queen pointed to Seraphina. 'This lady has admitted her guilt, so you know where to take her, and be sure to give this warrant to her warder.'

'Yes, madam.' The captain smiled as he took the sealed parchment the Queen handed him and tucked it in the front of his jerkin.

'Do you not wish to know what is in the warrant?' Elizabeth's cat mouth curved into an odd smile as she watched Seraphina go ashen and rise to her feet. 'Most, in such circumstances, would at least plead their case and beg for mercy.'

Seraphina shook her head. 'I do not care overmuch what befalls me now and I have made fool enough of myself already.'

'I could not agree more.' Elizabeth gave her a swift, utterly surprising smile, before nodding to the commander of the guard and turning away.

Seraphina paced about the small stone-walled chamber, sat down for a moment upon a comfortably cushioned settle and then stood up again. She didn't understand why she had been brought here to this small, cosy manor house instead of the Tower. Perhaps they had only come to deliver the warrant into the hands of her warder. Despite her statement to the Queen, she could not prevent a surge of panic as she heard footsteps approaching and then the latch on the door lift. Struggling to appear calm, she turned slowly to face the open door, her eyes widening as she took in the tall, black-velvet-clad figure.

'Richard?' Her heart lifted instantly, irrationally, as it always had at the sight of him. 'What are you doing here?'

'It is one of my manors. It seems I am to be your keeper.'

'You…' Her voice dwindled as he shut the door. 'She would not be so cruel.'

'You had best read this,' he said gravely, handing her the warrant. 'It concerns your life.'

'My life…' Her voice wavered as he took her arm and drew her to sit beside him upon the settle. 'Just tell me—' she blurted, wanting it over with. He shook his head, and for a moment, she thought she saw laughter in his eyes. Laughter? When he spoke of a warrant and her life? Her fingers were clumsy from nerves and the bandages as she tried to unfold the parchment. He smoothed it out for her upon her knees, watching her face intently as she began to read the first few lines with growing incredulity.

This was no warrant. It was a letter, tart in tone, saying in no uncertain terms that the Queen considered them both the greatest fools she had ever had misfortune to meet. Seraphina lifted her head, shocked, at what the Queen had written in her elegant, flowing hand. 'Is this true? Were she and Cecil really afraid that you might betray them because you had—' she paused, her pulse racing as she let her eyes meet his warm, golden gaze '—fallen in love with me from the first…'

'Apparently,' he said softly, 'and they were right to be. I did love you, almost I think from the first, so much it seemed that everyone could see it but me.'

'And me,' she said as sheer, dazzling joy filled her heart and mind. Then with a pretended frown, she asked, 'Almost?'

'At the inn I was angry with you,' he explained softly.

'The inn?' she said blankly, and then memory came flooding back and with it realisation. 'It was *you* on the mounting block. You caught me—I remember feeling as if I belonged in your arms…'

'Then your instincts were better than mine.' His eyes darkened as he stared down into her face. 'It was not till we met at Mayfield that I knew you belonged to me; that was why I offered your betrothed a place on my estates when I did not know who you were. I knew I could not simply let you go and never see you again. You can imagine how I felt when I discovered you were the traitress I had been sent to trap…'

He was silent for a moment as he put an arm about her waist and drew her close. 'Those days at Mayfield were torture. Wanting you, finding you more beautiful, more desirable every time I saw you, and knowing that I was going to be responsible for sending you to the block or the stake. I had meant to seduce your secrets from you—'

'I wish you had—' She smiled at him. 'I thought you did not want me…'

'My conscience would not let me make love to you when I thought I might send you to your death.' He hugged her closer. 'I was afraid of losing you even then, even before I knew you were not the traitress. I insisted you marry me, not because Cecil ordered it, but because it was the only way to protect you. I knew if I did as he asked and kept you under close watch, then he would hesitate before resorting to rougher, less discreet methods of getting at the truth.'

'When did you know I was not the traitress?' she asked, letting her head rest against his shoulder as quiet, deep happiness rolled over her, washing away all the pain and doubt of the last weeks.

'The first day you arrived at court when you spoke of Mistress Morrison and your husband being alike as twins. I realised that, although it was you I had seen at the inn, it was *not* you I had seen meeting the conspirators the night before. Only the clothes were the same.'

'She borrowed my clothes?'

'Exactly—after that it became a matter of proving that my suspicion was correct.'

'And that was why you flirted with her and paid her so much attention.'

'Yes, when all the time I could only think of you. Which was probably why I failed to convince her that I was smitten and she guessed what I was about. She did her utmost to distract my attention, getting Denleigh to flirt with you and even trying to kill Robert.'

'She did that deliberately, let him wander into the

path of the horses?' She felt sick with sudden horror that any woman could do such a thing.

'Yes, that was something else she told us before she swallowed the poison. She seemed to feel she had to confess for the sake of her soul.' His mouth twisted. 'But I doubt she had one.'

'I don't want to think of her, not now,' she said suddenly, putting her arms about his neck.

'Nor I.' His arms tightened about her and he touched his lips to her forehead. 'Now tell me, fool, if you love me as much as this suggests—' he caught the parchment as it began to slide from her lap, and pointed to where the Queen had quoted the postscript of her letter to him '—why did you say you wanted our marriage to end?'

'Because I thought it was what you wanted. I thought you were trying to say you wanted to be free of me.'

'Did I make such a mare's nest of it?' he groaned, and kissed her. 'I have no wish to live without you, don't you realise that yet? God! When I found your necklace in the ashes of that blasted cottage—' he broke off. 'How did Denleigh come to be there in your place?'

'Grace had sent him away, but he came back to get me out.' She shuddered at the memory. 'There were flames all about the door, he pushed me through them, was almost through himself when the beam fell and trapped him. I tried to pull him out, but the roof fell in—' She frowned. 'I don't know why he came.'

'I doubt he had much good in mind,' the Earl

growled, stroking her hair, 'but I'll buy a few masses for his soul. If it was not for him—'

'Don't let us talk of such things now.' She nestled against him. 'I just want to be with you...'

'And you shall be, forever. Have you not read the close yet?'

She did, and then laughed. 'So, the Queen has sentence me to a lifetime in your custody.' Then, as he stood up, lifting her with him into his arms, she laughed again. 'And you to a lifetime of my housekeeping when we are not at court. I wonder which of us is being punished the most, my lord?'

'Are you telling me that you do not know how to make your mother's pastries?' he asked with a severity that was totally betrayed by his eyes, as they swept over her upturned face. 'You do realise that was my real motive for wedding you?'

'Oh, I know how to make them,' she said blithely as he carried her through the door and up a short flight of shallow stone steps into a bedchamber. ''Tis just they always turn out so hard and black...'

'Then you had best get to bed and sleep, wife, so that you can begin practising your culinary skills in the morning,' he said against her ear, making her skin shiver deliciously, as he kicked the door shut behind them.

She looked up into his eyes as he lowered her on to the soft feather bed, all innocence. 'I cannot sleep in my gown, my lord. Will you help me with the laces...?' She lifted her hands to free her hair from where it was trapped beneath her shoulders, her mouth curving as she saw his eyes follow the upward movement of her breasts, and flare with sudden fire.

'Mmmm...' He smiled slowly, as he lay down beside her and picked up a handful of her hair, winding it in his fingers. 'You seem to master other skills quickly enough...'

'Oh, no.' She shook her head vehemently. 'I am a slow learner.' She moved closer to him and touched her lips to his throat. 'I fear this might take all my time...'

His smile deepened as he folded her into his embrace. 'Forever, perhaps?'

'Yes,' she said happily against his mouth. 'Forever...'

\*    \*    \*    \*    \*

# THE DESERTED BRIDE
## by Paula Marshall

Reader letter to come at later date

# *Chapter One*

He was her husband. He had been her husband for ten years, and all she had ever had of him was the miniature which had arrived that morning.

And the letter with it, of course.

The letter which simply, and coldly, said, "My Lady Exford, I am sending you this portrait of myself in small as a token of my respect for you. I am in hopes of paying you a visit before the summer is out. At the moment, alas, I am exceeding busy in the Queen's interest. Accept my felicitations for your twentieth birthday now, lest I am unable to make them in person. This from your husband, Drew Exford."

Elizabeth, Lady Exford, known to all those around her as Lady Bess, crumpled the perfunctory letter in her hand. All that it was fit for was to be thrown into the fire which burned in the hearth of the Great Hall of Atherington House. At the very last moment, though, something stayed her hand. She smoothed the crumpled paper and read it again, the colour in her cheeks rising as her anger at the writer mounted in her.

About the Queen's business, forsooth! Had he been

about the Queen's business for the last ten years? Was that why he had never visited her, never come to claim her as his wife, had left her here with her father, a wife and no wife? She very much doubted it. No, indeed. Andrew, Earl of Exford since his father's death, had stayed away from Leicestershire in order to enjoy his bachelor life in London, unhampered by the presence of a wife and the children she might give him.

The whole world knew that the Queen liked the handsome young men about her to be unmarried, or, if she grudgingly gave them permission to marry, preferred them not to bring their wives to court. And from what news of him came her way, the Queen had no more faithful subject than her absent husband.

How should she answer this? Should she write the truth, plain and simple, as, "Sir, I care not if I never see you again?" Or should she, instead, simply reply as an obedient wife ought to, "My lord, I have received your letter. I am yours to command whenever you should visit me."

The latter, of course. The former would never do.

Bess walked to the table where ink, paper and the sand to dry the letter awaited her, and wrote as an obedient wife should, although she had never felt less obedient in her life.

And as she wrote she thought of the day ten years ago when she had first seen her husband...

"Come, my darling," her nurse had said, on that long-gone morning, "your father wishes you to be wearing your finest, your very finest, attire today. The damask robe in grey and pink and silver, your pearls, and the little heart which your sainted mother left you."

"No." Ten-year-old Bess struggled out of her nurse's embrace. "No, Kirsty. Father promised that I should go riding with him on the first fine morning, and it is fine today. Besides, I look a fright in grey and pink, you know I do."

Her nurse, whom Bess was normally able to wheedle into submission to her demands, shook her head. "Not today, my love. I cannot allow you to have your way today. Your father has guests. Important guests. They arrived late last night after you had gone to bed, and he wishes you to look your very best when you meet them."

Kirsty had an air of excitement about her. It was plain that she knew something which she was not telling Bess. Bess always knew when people were hiding things from her but, even though she might be only ten years old, she was wise enough to know when not to continue to ask questions.

So she allowed Kirsty to turn her about and about until Bess felt dismally sure that she looked more like a painted puppet dressed up to entertain the commonalty than the beautiful daughter of Robert Turville, Earl of Atherington, the most powerful magnate in this quarter of Leicestershire. She disregarded as best as she could Kirsty's oohings and aahings, her standing back and exclaiming, "Oh, my dear little lady, how fine you look. The prettiest little lady outside London, no less."

"My clothes are pretty," said Bess crossly, "but I am not. I am but a little brown-haired thing, and all the world believes that fair is beautiful, and I am not fair at all—as well you know. And my eyes are black, not blue, so no one will ever write sonnets to *them*."

Useless, quite useless, for Kirsty continued to sing

her praises of Bess's non-existent beauty until aunt
Hamilton, her father's sister, came into the room.

"Let me look at you, child. Dear Lord, what a poor
little brown thing you are, the image of your sainted
grandam no less."

Far from depressing Bess, this sad truth had her
casting triumphant smiles at the mortified Kirsty, who
was cursing Lady Hamilton under her breath. Fancy
telling the poor child the truth about herself so harshly.
It couldn't have hurt to have praised the beautiful dress
m'lord had brought from London for her, instead of
reminding her of the grandam whom she so resembled.

For Bess's grandam had been the late Lady Atherington, who had always been known as the "The
Spanish Lady". She had accompanied Catherine of
Aragon when she had arrived in England to marry the
brother of the late and blessed King Henry VIII, the
present Queen's father. The then Lord Atherington had
fallen in love with, and married her, despite her dark
Spanish looks, and ever since all the Turville daughters had resembled her, including the brisk Lady Hamilton. Brown-haired herself, and black-eyed, she had
still made a grand marriage, and the sonnets which
Bess was sure would never come her way, had been
showered upon her.

"Golds," she was exclaiming, "and vermilions, or
rich green and bold siennas, are the colours which
your father should have bought you. Trust a man to
have no sense where women's tire is concerned! Never
mind, child, later, later, when I have the dressing of
you, we may see you in looks. This will have to do
for now. Come!"

She held out a commanding hand, which Bess took,
wondering what the fuss and commotion was all

about. She had been living quietly at Atherington House as she had done for as long as she could remember—which admittedly at ten was not very long—until yesterday, when her father had arrived suddenly, with a trunkful of new clothes for her, and a train of visitors who had stared at her when she was brought into the Great Hall after they had dined.

Bess had never seen so many people all at once, but she had smiled at them bravely, relieved when, after being seated on her father's knee for a little space and been fed comfits by him, she had been allowed to retire to her room.

And now, if Kirsty was to be believed, another bevy of guests had arrived. Oh, she had heard the noise just as she was going to sleep, and could not help wondering what all the excitement was about. It seemed that she was soon to find out.

For, as she descended the staircase into the Great Hall, she saw that all the servants were assembled at one end of it, and a large body of finely dressed men and women were at the other. Her father was standing a little in front of them, her uncle, Sir Braithwaite Hamilton, by his side, with a pair of attendant pages hovering in their rear.

"Come, my lady," her father said, smiling at her as her aunt Hamilton let go of her hand and pushed her towards him, "we are to go to a wedding. In the chapel."

At this, for some reason unknown to Bess, the company all laughed uproariously, led by uncle Hamilton. All, that was, except aunt Hamilton, who primmed her lips and shook her elegant head. Like all the guests she was richly dressed and Bess could only imagine that it was her father's wedding to which they were going with such ceremony.

Gilbert, the Steward, importantly carrying his white wand of office, marched solemnly before them. Tib, the smallest page, with whom Bess daily played at shuttlecock, was his attendant, looking as solemn as Giles, not at all like the rowdy boy who was her shadow.

The processional walk to the chapel did not take long. Not all the guests would enter it with them, for it was small. Above the altar was a painting brought from Italy, beneath a stained glass window showing Christ in his glory. Master Judson, the priest, stood before it.

But where was the bride?

Bess looked about her. Where the bride should stand were several richly dressed men—and a tall boy who appeared to be about sixteen years old.

The boy was as beautiful as Bess was plain, and he was as fair as the god Apollo on the tapestry in the Great Hall. His hair was silver gilt, and curled gently about his comely face. His eyes were as blue as the sky on a summer morning, and the pink and silver colours of his doublet, breeches and hose not only suited him better than they suited Bess, but also showed off a long and shapely body. He resembled nothing so much as one of St Michael's angels come down to earth to adorn it.

As she entered on her father's arm the boy was looking away from her. The man at his side, no taller than he was, whispered something in his ear, and he turned to look at her.

His eyes widened. The handsome face twisted a little. He swung round to the man who had whispered to him and muttered, "Dear God, uncle Henry, you are marrying me to a monkey!"

No one else but Bess, and the man, heard what he said. Bess's father was a little hard of hearing and aunt Hamilton and the train behind her were too far away to catch his words.

But Bess heard. She heard every bitter syllable. And from them she learned two things. That it was not her father who was to be married, but herself…

And the beautiful boy to whom she was to be tied for life thought that she was ugly and had not hesitated to say so to his attendant.

No! She would not be married to him. She hated him. She hated his beauty, and his unkindness. He had not meant her to hear what he had said, and he was not to know that her hearing was abnormally acute. Even so, he should not have spoken so of her, and she would not marry him, no, never! Never!

Bess wrenched her hand from her father's grasp, swung round on him, and said, as loudly as she could, her voice breaking between shame and despair, "If you have brought me here to be married, sir, then know this. I have no mind to be married. Indeed, I will not be married. Least of all to *him!*"

And she sat down on the stone floor of the chapel.

Such a hubbub followed, such an uproar as had never before been heard in Atherington's chapel. Master Judson looked down at her, astounded, nearly dropping his prayerbook at the sight of such unmannerly behaviour. The boy—and who could he be?—looked haughtily down at her as she sat there, now weeping bitter tears. He said, his voice like ice, "And I have no mind to marry you, either, but I obey my elders and betters at all times—which plainly you have never been taught to do.''

Oh, the monster! She hated him. Yes, she did. A monkey! He had called her a monkey. Well, she would dub *him* monster.

''Handsome is as handsome does—and says,'' she flung at her as her father put his strong hands under her arms and lifted her up.

''Shame on you, daughter, for behaving so intemperately. You shall be beaten for this, I promise you. But only after you have married Andrew, Lord Exford, whom you have so vilely insulted. And since you are so free with maxims, let me remind you of one which you have forgotten, 'Little children should be seen and not heard.'''

Sobbing now, and trying to hide her face, for she felt so humiliated that she could look no one in the eye, Bess found herself being gently lifted away from her father. It was her aunt Hamilton who set her upon her feet again, and bent down to speak softly to her so that none other should hear what she had to say.

''Come, niece. I told your father that he should have prepared you for this day, but he believed that it would be better for you not to be forewarned. See, it is a handsome boy you are marrying, and a great family. Your father has done well for you. Now do you do well for him. Dry your tears and behave as a great lady should.''

A great lady. She wasn't a great lady. She was simply poor Bess Turville who was to be married against her will to someone who despised her.

What of that? Could *she* not despise *him?* After all, it was likely that, after today, she would not see him again until she was old enough to be truly his wife and able to bear his children.

Slowly Bess nodded her head—to her aunt's great relief—to say nothing of her father's. The only person not relieved was Andrew Exford himself, who had been hoping that this unseemly child's equally unseemly behaviour might rescue him from this marriage which had been forced upon him by his uncle and guardian, the man who stood at his elbow.

It was all very well to talk of money and lands and the right to give the title of Earl of Atherington to his eldest son when the father of the heiress whom he was marrying died, but his uncle wasn't having to marry a midget who resembled a monkey. Useless for his uncle to murmur in his ear that the child would grow and might, when older, come to resemble her handsome aunt.

As Bess already knew, blonde was beautiful in Andrew Exford's world, and Bess was far from blonde.

But Andrew—as he had told Bess—knew his duty, and since his duty was to increase the lands and wealth of the Exfords, he would do it. But the good God knew that he would not enjoy the doing.

Her eyes dried, a cup of water brought to her to drink, her aunt's comforting hand in hers, and Bess was ready to be married. Her father snorted at Master Judson, ''Begin, man. Forget Lady Elizabeth's childish megrims—she will soon grow out of them—and do your duty.''

Thus was the Lady Elizabeth Turville married to the most noble the Earl of Exford. Later that day, after a banquet of which she tasted nothing, for all the beautiful food put before her might as well have been straw, she was ritually and publicly placed in her husband's bed, a bolster between them. For this short public occasion they had been granted the Great Bed of Honour in which Robert, Lord Atherington, usually slept.

Neither Drew Exford nor his bride had spoken a word to the other since the wedding ceremony. It was quite plain to Bess that he had tried to avoid looking at her at all. Bess, on the other hand, when she did allow her eyes to stray to his face, glared her hatred at him.

That he should be so beautiful—and she so plain! His beauty, which she should have joyed in, hurt her. She lay stiff in the bed, her back to him, and when, a little time later, the ritual having been performed, her aunt returned to take her away, she gave him no farewell.

Nor did he say farewell to her.

Two days later Bess had watched his train leave the House, making for the distant south which she had never visited. Before he left he had taken her small hand and placed a kiss on it. His perfect mouth had felt as cold as ice, so cold that she wanted to snatch it away, but dare not.

"I shall see you again when you are grown, wife," were his last words to her.

Bess had nodded at him, and curtsied her farewell. She could not speak, and sensed her father's exasperation at her silence, but for once she would not obey him. All that she could think of was that she would soon be rid of her unwanted husband, whom she would only see again when, as he had said, she would be grown, ready to be his true wife and bear his child.

Once he had disappeared down the drive, Bess knew that she must face her father's anger at her misbehaviour. Before Andrew Exford's arrival it would have saddened her to be at odds with him, but, all unknowingly, he had lost the power to distress her. It was, Bess thought, back in the present again, as though in one short moment in the chapel she had grown up, had learned the arbitrary nature of her life, and that her father's love for her had its limits.

What her aunt had said was true. He should have warned her, prepared her for such a major change in her life, but he had, as he told his sister when the Exfords had left, "No time to trouble with a child's whimwhams. She should be grateful for the splendid match I have made for her—and for Atherington."

"And so I told her," Mary Hamilton said, her voice sad, "but she is only a child after all, and for some reason which I cannot fathom, and which she will not confess to me, she has taken against him. Which surprises me not a little, for he is a beautiful youth, well-mannered and courteous. I would have thought she would have received him as happily as though he were a prince who had wandered out of a fairy tale, not met him with hate."

"Hate!" exclaimed Robert Atherington. He was a choleric man, who loved his daughter but would never understand her. Since neither he nor his sister had heard Andrew Exford's harsh words about her, Bess's dislike of him seemed wilful and beggared belief. They were both united in that.

"Hate," he repeated. "Well, Lady Elizabeth must learn to tolerate her groom. It will not be many years before he returns for her, and she must be ready for him."

But Andrew Exford did not return. The years went by. Bess's father died of an ague, leaving Bess mis-

tress of the House and all the Atherington lands, with
her uncle Hamilton as her guardian. Soon afterwards
he had a fall in the hunting field, and became a cripple,
helpless and confined to his room. Aunt Hamilton became her niece's constant companion, and if Bess was
a queen in Leicestershire, much as her namesake,
Queen Elizabeth, was Queen of England, aunt Hamilton was in some sort her Queen Mother.

With the help of the vast staff, numbering over three
hundred souls, which Robert Atherington had trained,
Bess reigned over her small kingdom. Accounts and
details of the estate which he owned, but never saw,
were sent to her husband, and occasional monies
which he needed to keep up his position at court. They
were all acknowledged by his secretary, never by him.
So far as Bess was concerned, he did not exist, and
she had no wish to see him.

Looking back over the years to her wedding day,
Bess stifled a sigh. How different her life would have
been if she had not overheard Drew Exford's sneering
comment. Not that she had any quarrel with her life.
There was always so much to do, so little time to do
it. She had become expert in the running of her estate,
and enjoyed herself mightily in performing all those
duties which her husband would normally have carried
out. Never having known him, she did not miss him,
and hoped that he would stay away forever, as her
distant cousin Lucy Sheldon's absent husband had
done.

One thing which she never did was look in a mirror.
And if, occasionally, aunt Hamilton said, "Bess, my
dear, you grow more handsome every day," Bess put
such an unlikely statement down to her aunt's kindness. Her aunt had mellowed with age, and she and

Kirsty were a good pair of flatterers, as Bess frequently told them.

And now Drew Exford was proposing to visit her—if she could believe him. Useless to worry about how she was to greet him. "Sufficient unto the day is the evil thereof," she said aloud. "I'll think about that when he arrives."

"Damn it, Philip. Why can't I be like you, unencumbered?"

Drew Exford was towelling himself off after a hard game of tennis against Philip Sidney, who had been his friend since they had spent part of the Grand Tour of Europe together shortly after Drew had been married.

Philip smiled wryly. "Unencumbered is it, dear friend? I think not. I am most encumbered since the Queen took Oxford's part against me after our recent fracas on the tennis court. I am encumbered by her disfavour and her dislike, particularly since she knows that I am much against her flirtation with the notion of a marriage to the French Duc d'Alençon. I am thinking of retiring to Wilton. Why not come with me? The air is sweet there, and most poetical. But what is it that troubles you? After all, you retain the Queen's favour, you are your own master and may do as you please."

Drew buried his face in his towel. Philip was a good fellow, and although his pride was that of the devil he had a sweet nature, and a kind heart.

"If you must know, I am envying you your single state."

"Eh, what's that?" Drew's voice had been muffled by the towel and Philip was not sure that he had heard aright. ''I thought that you were single, too. And I am beginning to lament my single state.''

Drew emerged from the towel. ''Oh, I was married in a hugger-mugger fashion ten years agone, before we posted to Europe together and spent our wild oats in Paris.'' He paused, and made his confession. ''I have not seen the lady since.''

His friend stared at him. ''Ten years—and not seen her since? That beggars belief. Why so?''

He might have known that Philip's reaction would be a critical one. Philip Sidney liked—and respected—women. If he had affairs, he was so discreet that no one knew of them. His kindness and gentleness in his relations with the fair sex were a byword.

''She was but ten,'' Drew said, almost as though confessing something, he was not sure what. He could not tell Philip that for some little time his adventurous life had begun to pall on him, and the game of illicit love, too. He had begun to dream of the child he had married. Strange dreams, for she was still a child in them, who must now be a woman. A woman who could be the mother of his children. His uncle had railed at him recently for not providing the line with an heir.

''She didn't like me,'' he said, somewhat defiant in the face of Philip's raised brows, ''and she…'' He stopped. He could not be ungallant and repeat exactly what he had said ten years ago to his uncle—''You are marrying me to a monkey''—but he thought it.

''And all these years, whilst you jaunted round Europe and sailed the Atlantic, and ran dangerous diplomatic errands in France for that old fox Walsingham, I thought you single! Was she dark or fair, your child bride who didn't like you? I thought all the world, and the Queen, liked Drew Exford!''

''Well, *she* did not. And she was dark. I remember at the banquet after the wedding ceremony, she ate little—and rewarded me with the most basilisk stare. I thought that the Gorgon herself had brought forth a child, and that child was trying to stare me stone dead!''

''And did you bed the Gorgon?''

''After the usual fashion. They put a bolster between us for some little time. She turned her back on me, and never looked at me again. For which I was thankful. She was not pretty.''

''Poor child!'' Philip's sympathy for Drew's neglected child bride was sincere. ''And where is she now? I suppose you know.'' This last came out in Philip Sidney's most arrogant manner, revealing that he thought his friend's role in this sad story was not a kind one.

''At Atherington House, in Leicestershire. Her father died; her uncle acts as a kind of guardian to her in my absence.''

He strolled restlessly away from Philip to stare across the tennis court and towards the lawns and flowerbeds beyond. He remembered his anger at the whole wretched business. His uncle had sprung the marriage upon him without warning, and had expected him to be overjoyed. He had not felt really angry until that fatal morning in Atherington House's chapel when he had first seen his bride.

An anger which had finally found its full vent when he had been left in the Great Bed with his wife. I have been given a child, he had thought savagely, not yet to be touched, and what's more, a child who will never attract me. I do not like her and I fear that she does not like me because, somehow, she overheard what I said of her.

Lying there, he had made a vow. In two days' time he would journey to London to take up his life again, leaving his monkey wife in the care of her father until she was of an age to be truly bedded. Once he had reached London and the court he would make sure that he never visited the Midland Shires again, except on the one occasion in the distant future when he needed to make himself an heir.

Now, in his middle twenties, that time had come, compelling him to remember what he had for so long preferred to forget. For to recall that unhappy day always filled him with a mixture of regret, anger, and self-dislike. His friendship with Philip Sidney had made the boy he had once been seem a selfish barbarian, not only in the manner that he had treated his neglected wife, but in other ways as well.

*"Preux chevalier"*, or, the stainless knight, he had once mockingly dubbed Philip—who was not yet a knight—but at the same time he had been envious of him and his courtly manners.

Drew flung the towel down, aware that Philip had been silently gazing at him as he mused.

"What to do?" he asked, his voice mournful. "The past is gone. I cannot alter it."

"No," returned Philip, smiling at last. "But there is always the future—which may change things again. A thought with which I try to reassure myself these days. We grow old, Drew. We are no longer careless boys. I must marry, and I must advise you to seek out your wife and come to terms with her—and with yourself. The man who writes sonnets to imaginary beauties, must at the last write one to his wife.''

''Come,'' riposted Drew, laughing. ''Sonnets are written to mistresses, never to wives, you know that, *chevalier* Philip. But I take your point.''

''Well said, friend.'' Philip flung an arm around Drew's shoulders as they walked from the tennis court together. ''Remember what I said about visiting me at Wilton some time. It is on the way to your place in Somerset. Tarry awhile there, I pray you.''

''Perhaps,'' Drew answered him with a frown. For here came a page with a letter in his hand which, by his mien, was either for himself or for Philip. He stopped before them to hand the missive to Drew.

''From my master, Sir Francis Walsingham,'' he piped, being yet a child. ''You are to read it and give me an answer straightway.''

Drew opened the sealed paper and read the few lines on it.

''Simple enough to answer at once,'' he said cheerfully. ''You will tell Sir Francis that Andrew Exford thanks him for his invitation and will sup with him this evening.''

Philip Sidney watched the boy trot off in order to deliver his message. ''Well,'' he said, smiling, ''at least, if Walsingham knows that you are already married, he will not be inviting you to supper in order to offer you his daughter, who is still only a child!''

Drew made his friend no answer, for he suspected that Sir Francis Walsingham was about to offer him something quite different. Something which might require him to journey to the Midland Shires which he had foresworn, and to the wife whom he had deserted ten years ago.

# *Chapter Two*

"I cannot abide another moment indoors, Aunt. I have ordered Tib to saddle Titus for me. I intend to ride to the hunting lodge and break my fast in the open. The day is too fair for me to waste it indoors."

Aunt Hamilton raised her brows. Bess's teeming energy always made her feel faint. That her niece was wearing a roughspun brown riding habit which barely reached mid-calf, showing below it a heavy pair of boots more suited to a twenty-year-old groom than a young woman of gentle birth, only served to increase her faintness.

"Must you sally out garbed more like a yeoman's daughter than the Lady of Atherington, dear child? It is not seemly. If you should chance to meet…"

She got no further. Bess, who was tapping her whip against the offending boots, retorted briskly, "Who in the world do you imagine I shall meet on a ride on my own land who will care whether I am accoutred like the Queen, or one of her servants? I am comfortable in this, and have no intention of pretending that I am one of the Queen's ladies. Everyone for miles around Atherington knows who I am—and will treat me accordingly.''

Useless to say anything. Bess would always go her own way—as she had done since the day she was married. Mary Hamilton sighed and walked to the tall window which looked out on to the drive and beyond that towards Charnwood Forest. She watched Bess ride out; Tib and Roger Jacks, her chief groom in attendance.

If only her errant husband would come for her! He would soon put a stop to Bess's wilfulness, see that she dressed properly and conducted herself as a young noblewoman ought. Her niece behaved in all ways like the son her late brother had never managed to father, and the dear God alone knew where *that* would all end.

Bess, riding at a steady trot towards the distant hill on which the lodge stood, was also thinking about her absent husband. It was now a month since his letter had arrived and there was still no sign of him. She had hung his miniature on a black ribbon and wore it around her neck when she changed into a more lady-like dress on the Sabbath in order to please her aunt.

Occasionally she looked at the miniature in order to inspect him ''in small'' as he had called it in his letter. She saw a slim, shapely man with a stronger face than the one which she remembered. If the painter had been accurate, his hair had darkened from silver gilt into a deep gold, and his mouth was no longer a Cupid's bow but a stern-seeming, straight line. It would be as well to remember that he was twenty-six years old, was very much a man, no longer a child. Bess felt a sudden keen curiosity to know what that man was like:

whether the spoiled boy—she was sure now that he had been spoiled—had turned into a spoiled man.

They were almost at the small tower, which was all that the lodge consisted of. It stood high on its hill above the scrub and the stands of trees, for Charnwood Forest was thin on Atherington land, merging into pasture where cattle grazed. The open fields of nearby villages had been enclosed these fifty years and charcoal burning had stripped the forest of many of its trees. Over the centuries, successive Atherington lords had run deer for the chase, and the deer had attacked and stripped most of the trees which the charcoal burners had left.

"Shall you eat inside the tower—or out, mistress?" Tib asked her.

He had called her "mistress" since they had been children together, and Bess had indulged him by allowing him to continue the custom when the rest of her servants had learned to call her Lady Bess. Another of her many offences, according to her aunt.

"After all," Bess had said sensibly and practically, "my true title is m'lady Exford, but since I do not care to use it, then any name will do, for all but *his* are equally incorrect."

Aunt Hamilton knew who *his* referred to and was silenced. A common occurrence when she argued with her niece.

"Outside," Bess told Tib, "at the bottom of the hill. My uncle Hamilton once told me that the Queen picnicked in the open, and I am content to follow her example. All that will be missing will be her courtiers."

Tib grinned at her. "Roger and I will be your courtiers, mistress."

Roger grunted at that. "You grow pert, lad, and forget yourself."

Really, to bring Roger along was like bringing her aunt with her! He was nearly as insistent on reminding her of her great station as she was. Nevertheless, Bess smiled at him as she shared her meal with them. Inside a wicker basket lined with a white cloth were a large meat pasty, several cold chicken legs, bread and cheese and the sweet biscuits always known as Bosworth Jumbles, and wine in a leather bottle. A feast, indeed, all provided by the kitchen for her and her two grooms. All her staff were agreed that the Lady Bess was a kind and generous mistress.

"Food in the open always tastes much better than food in the house," she declared, her mouth full of bread and cheese, "and wine, too." She threw the bread crusts and the remains of the pasty to the two hounds which had followed in their rear, before lying back and sighing, "Oh, the blessed peace."

She could not have said anything more inapposite! The words were scarce out of her mouth when the noise of an approaching horse and rider broke the silence Bess had been praising. They were approaching at speed through the trees, and as they drew near it was apparent that the horse, a noble black, which was tossing its head and snorting, was almost out of his rider's control.

Foam dripped from its mouth: something—or someone—had frightened it, that much was plain. But its rider, a tall young man, was gradually mastering it, until, just as he reached Bess's small party, his steed suddenly caught its forefoot in a rabbit hole, causing it to stumble forward. His master, taken by surprise, was thrown over his horse's head—to land semi-conscious at Bess's feet.

She and her two grooms had sprung to their feet to try to avoid a collision. Their horses, tethered to nearby trees, neighed and pranced, whilst Bess's two hounds added to the confusion caused by this unexpected turn by running around, barking madly.

One of them, Pompey, bent over the stunned young man to lick his face. The other, Crassus, ran after the black horse which, hurt less than his rider, had recovered itself, and was galloping madly away. Roger untethered his mount and chased after it. Bess and Tib joined Pompey in inspecting the young man, who was starting to sit up.

Bess fell to her knees beside him, so that when, still a trifle dazed, he turned his head in her direction, she looked him full in the face.

Could it be? Oh, yes! Indeed, it could! There was no doubt at all that sitting beside her was the husband whom she had not seen for ten long years. He had stepped out of the miniature, to be present in large, not in small. If he had been beautiful as a boy, as a man he was stunningly handsome, with a body to match. So handsome, indeed, that Bess's heart skipped a beat at the mere sight of him, just as it had done on the long-ago day when she had first seen him.

What would he say this time to disillusion her? To hurt her so much that the memory of his unkind words was still strong enough to distress her?

He gave a pained half-smile, and muttered hoarsely, "Fair nymph, from what grove have you strayed to rescue me?" before dropping his head into his hands for a moment, and thus missing Bess's stunned reaction to the fulsome compliment which he had just paid her.

It was quite plain that though she had known at once who he was, he had not the slightest notion that she was his deserted monkey bride!

Drew Exford had left London for Atherington a few days earlier. His supper with Sir Francis Walsingham had, as he had suspected, brought him a new task.

After they had eaten, and the women had left them alone with their wine, Sir Francis had said in his usual bland and fatherly fashion, ''You can doubtless guess why I have summoned you hither this night, friend Drew.''

Drew had laughed. ''I believe that you wish to ask me to do you yet another favour. Even though I told you two years ago that I had done my duty by my Queen, and would not again become involved in the devious doings of the State's underworld, as I did when I was with the Embassy in France.''

Sir Francis nodded. ''Aye, I well remember you telling me that. Nor would I call on you for assistance again were it not that you are singularly well placed to assist me to preserve our lady the Queen and her blessed peace against those who would destroy it—and her.''

Drew raised his finely arched brows. ''How so?''

Sir Francis did not speak for a moment; instead, he drank down the remains of his wine. ''Your wife, I believe, lives at Atherington on the edge of Charnwood Forest. There are many Papists in the Midland counties who are sympathetic towards the cause of Mary, Queen of Scots, and would wish to kill her cousin, the Queen, and place Mary on the throne instead. Each summer the Queen of Scots is allowed by her gaoler, the Earl of Shrewsbury, to visit Buxton, to take the waters there. Her sympathisers from the surrounding counties visit the spa, and plot together on her behalf.

"I have reason to believe that this plotting has become more than talk. It is not so long since another party of silly Catholic squires from roundabout were caught trying to rebel against the Crown—and were duly punished for their treason. Alas, this has not, we now know, deterred others from trying to do the same."

Drew leaned forward. "A moment, sir. Are you telling me that my wife is one of these plotters?"

Sir Francis shook his head vigorously. "No, no. The Crown has no more loyal servant than the Turvilles of Atherington. Your wife's father was a friend of the Queen and helped to seat her on the throne. What I wish you to do is to go first to Atherington and thence to Buxton to find out what you can of this latest piece of treason—and then inform me through one of my men who will arrive some time after you do. You will know that he is my man and that you may trust him because he will show you a button identical with those I am wearing on my doublet tonight.

"You may give it about that your real objective in the Midland counties is to take up your true position as the lady's husband. Consequently, no one will suspect that you have an ulterior motive for journeying there. Thus you will kill two birds with one stone. You will do the state some service—and get yourself an heir at the same time."

"Most kind of you," riposted Drew somewhat sardonically, ''to consider my welfare as well as that of the Crown.''

''Exactly so,'' returned Sir Francis, taking Drew's comment at face value. ''It is always my aim to assist my friends, and despite the difference in our ages, you are my friend, are you not?''

Drew thought it politic to signify his agreement.

His host showed his pleasure by pouring his guest another drink, and saying, ''You are a promising fellow, Drew. You have outgrown your youthful vanity—if you will allow me to say so—and you have a commendable shrewdness which has been honed by your journeyings to both the New and the Old World. I would wish to think of you as one of my inheritors. England needs such as yourself when Burghley and I are gone to our last rest.''

Drew laughed, his charm never more evident. ''There is little need to flatter me, sir. I will do your errand without it. But this will be the last. I would prefer to perform upon a larger stage—and not be suspected of being a common spy!''

''And so you shall. I repeat, I would not ask you were it not that your presence near to the Queen of Scots will be thought to be the result of your family circumstances—and for no other reason. Drink your wine, man, and pledge with me confusion to that Queen. I fear that, as long as she lives, our own Queen's life is not safe.''

That was Walsingham's coda. Afterwards they joined Lady Walsingham and her daughter and talked of idle and pleasant things.

And so Drew had no other choice than to see again the wife whom he had avoided for ten long years. He was not sure whether he was glad or sorry that meeting her was part of the duty which Walsingham had laid upon him. Each mile that he covered once London was left behind found him still reluctant to commit himself to Atherington House and its lady.

So much so that, when he had come almost to its gates, he and his magnificent train had stopped at an inn instead of journeying on, and he had taken Cicero out into the forest to try to catch a glimpse of the House, as though by doing so he could gauge the nature of either his welcome, or that of the greeting he would give her.

Except that Cicero, usually the most well-behaved of horses, saw fit to take against the whole notion of riding through the forest, and whilst trying to control him, he had lost control himself. As a result he was now sitting, shaken, not far from the House, and looking into the great dark eyes of a beautiful nymph who seemed to have strayed from the Tuscan countryside which he had visited with Philip Sidney and whose glories he had never forgotten.

By her clothing she was the daughter of one of the yeoman farmers who frequented these parts, and he wondered if they knew what a treasure they had in their midst. Well, if boredom overtook him at the House, he would know where to look for entertainment!

Something of this showed on his face. Bess, agitated, turned away from him in order to rise to her feet, so that she might not be too near him. He was altogether so overwhelming that she was fearful that she might lose the perfect control which had characterised her life since the day she had married him. He was not so shaken that he was incapable of putting forward his perfect hand and attempting to stay her.

"Nay, do not leave me, fair nymph, your presence acts as a restorative. You live in these parts?"

Bess, allowing herself to be detained, said, "Indeed. All my life." She had suddenly determined that she would not tell him her name, and prayed that neither Tib nor Roger, when he returned, would betray her.

"Send your brother away, my fair one, and I will give you a reward which will be sure to please you." The smile Drew offered her was a dazzling one, full of promise, and he raised his hand to cup her sweet small breast, so delicately rounded.

Tib! He thought Tib her brother, not her servant! Aunt Hamilton had been right for once about the effect her clothing would have on a stranger. For was he not promising to seduce her? He was busy stroking her breast, and had blessed the hollow in her neck with a kiss which was causing her whole body to tremble in response. Oh, shameful! What would he do next? And would she like that, too?

She was about to be seduced by the husband who had once rejected her! Was not this strange encounter as good as a play? Or one of Messer Boccaccio's naughty stories?

She must end it at once. Now, before she forgot herself. Bess escaped his impudent hands and rose to her feet, putting her finger on her lips to silence Tib who, full of indignation at this slur upon his mistress, was about to tell their unexpected guest exactly who she was.

"Not now," she murmured, smiling coyly at Drew, her expression full of promise. "Another time—when we are alone."

"Ah, I see you are a practised nymph, but then all nymphs are practised in Arcadia, are they not?"

smiled Drew, enjoying the sight of her now that his senses had cleared. For not only was she a dark beauty of a kind which he had learned to appreciate in Italy, but she had a body to match, of which her rough riding habit hid little, since she was wearing no petticoats under it, nor any form of stiffening designed to conceal the body's contours. He had not thought Leicestershire harboured such treasures as this.

Bess's reply to him was a simper, and a toss of the head. She was astonished at herself: she had not believed that she could be capable of such deceptive frivolity.

But I am, after all, a daughter of Eve, she thought with no little amusement, and, faced with a flattering man, Eve's descendants always know how to behave. Perhaps it might be the thing to flounce her skirt a little as she had seen her cousin Helen do when she visited her and wished to attract one of the gallants whose attentions Bess always avoided, she being a married woman.

Also present was the gleeful thought, How shocked he will be when he learns who I really am, and that he was offering to seduce his own wife!

She watched him stand up with Tib's help, which he did not really need, although he courteously accepted the proffered arm. By his manner and expression he was about to continue his Arcadian wooing, but, alas for him, even as did so he heard in the distance a troop of horse arriving.

Drew stifled a sigh. It was almost certainly part of his household who had followed him at a discreet distance to ensure his safety, even though he had repeatedly told them not to.

"Yes, it must be another time, I fear, that we dally among the spring flowers," he said regretfully.

His cousin Charles Breton, his mother's sister's son, arrived in the small clearing, at the head of his followers, exclaiming as he did so, "So, there you are, Drew. But where is your horse?"

"He unshipped me most scurvily," Drew told him, no whit ashamed, Bess noted, at having to confess his failure to control his errant steed. "But I have been rescued by the shepherdess you see before you—and her brother," and he waved a negligent hand at Tib. "They have not yet had time to offer me a share of their picnic, else my pastoral adventure would be complete. Ah, I see that they have even rescued Cicero for me."

So they had, for Roger rode up, his face one scowl, with Cicero trotting meekly along beside him, apparently unharmed.

"Here is your horse, young sir," he growled, "and another time show the forest a little more respect. It is not like the green lanes of the south where a man may gallop at his will!"

"How now, sirrah?" exclaimed Charles. "Do you know to whom you speak? Show a proper humility towards your betters!"

Roger opened his mouth, ready to inform him that he knew who his betters were, and furthermore, that they included Lady Exford who stood before them, and around whom Drew had now placed a familiar arm. In vain, before he could speak, his lady forestalled him.

"Oh, my groom has a free spirit, sir, as all we dwellers in these parts have. And now I must bid you adieu, for my duties await me. The cows must be fed, and the day wears on.''

Adroitly, she wriggled out of Drew's half-embrace and, without either Tib or Roger's assistance, swung athletically on to her horse. Seeing Roger about to speak again, she said smartly, ''Silence, man. You must not offend these great ones. And you, too, brother.''

Tib's answer to that was a grin. He possessed to the full the countryman's desire to make fools of townies and, by God, these were townies indeed, with their fine clothing and their drawling speech. Particularly the one whose horse had thrown him, who had been so busy making sly suggestions to his mistress.

He and Roger mounted their horses, whilst Drew, seeing his nymph ready to abandon him—rather than simply turn herself into a tree, as Daphne had done when pursued by Apollo—seized the bridle of Bess's horse, and exclaimed, ''Not so fast. I am Drew Exford, and I would know who you are.''

Bess looked down into his perfect face, and, giving him a smile so sweet that it wrenched his heart, she said softly, ''But I have little mind to tell you, sir. You must discover it for yourself. Now, let me go, Master Drew Exford, for I have no desire to be be-hindhand with the day.''

He could not be so ungallant as to insist, especially with Charles's amused eyes on him, and the snickers of her two companions, who were enjoying his discomfiture plainly audible. There was nothing for it but to stand back and watch her tap her whip smartly on her horse's flank and ride off, the two men behind her, leaving Drew to gaze after her.

''Was she real, or are we dreaming?'' he said, turning to Charles, who had dismounted and was staring at him as he added energetically, ''Come, let us follow them.''

Only for Charles to place an urgent hand on his sleeve. ''Nay, Drew. You have had a fall, the day grows old and we must ready ourselves to be at Atherington on the morrow. You do intend to visit your wife, do you not? Hardly the perfect start to your visit, to seduce one of her tenant's daughters before you even bid her good day.''

Drew nodded his head reluctantly. ''I suppose that you have the right of it. But have you ever seen such a divine face and form? Dress her in fine clothing and she would have half London at her feet.''

''Now, Drew, you do surprise me,'' drawled Charles as the pair of them remounted. ''I had thought that your wish would be for her to have no clothes on at all!''

# Chapter Three

"So, he is here, at last," twittered aunt Hamilton, shaken out of her usual calm when a courier arrived with m'lord Exford's letter for her husband, Sir Braithwaite Hamilton, informing him that he was lying at an inn nearby and proposed to arrive at Atherington House shortly after noon. He would be grateful if Sir Braithwaite would apprise his niece, Lady Exford, of the news, and also make Atherington House ready to entertain his train.

She continued excitedly, half-expecting her niece to refuse to do any such thing, "And when you meet him you must be dressed in something more appropriate to your station than that old grey kirtle you have seen fit to wear today."

"Indeed, indeed," agreed Bess equably and surprisingly. She had every intention of being as splendidly dressed as possible to receive her husband, if only to disconcert him the more when he realised who the nymph of Charnwood Forest really was.

"Does he not know that my poor husband has been unfit to arrange anything these past five years?" aunt Hamilton continued, still agitated, and quite unaware

that Bess had kept this interesting fact from her husband lest he send a steward—or, worse still, arrive
himself—to manage Atherington's affairs. He was
quite unaware that Bess had been in charge since Sir
Braithwaite had lost his wits after his accident—another surprise for him, and perhaps not a welcome one,
was Bess's rueful thought.

He was sure to demand that some man should replace her, even though Bess had managed Atherington
lands more efficiently than her uncle. In that she was
similar to another Bess, she of Hardwick, who was
also Countess of Shrewsbury, and who ruled her husband as well as their joint estates.

"He has probably forgotten," prevaricated Bess,
who had long developed a neat line in such half-truths.
"He has such a busy life about the court—and elsewhere," she ended firmly, although she had not the
smallest notion what her husband had been doing during the long years of his absence.

"Nevertheless…" Her aunt frowned, prepared to
say more had not a well-known glint in Bess's eye
silenced her. She decided to concentrate instead on
arranging for her usually wild niece to look, for once,
like the great lady which she was by birth and marriage.

"And you will receive him in the Great Hall as soon
as he arrives, I suppose?"

"Nay." Bess shook her head. "I am sure that he
and his train will wish to change their clothing and
order themselves properly after their long journey.
Only after that shall I welcome him—and then in the
Great Parlour. I have given Gilbert orders to lay out a
meal in the Hall for a score of us. Lord Exford—" she
would not say "my husband" "—writes that he is

bringing six gentlemen of his household with him, as
well as his Steward, and Treasurer, and Clerk Comptroller—to inspect our finances, no doubt. His servants, of whom there are a dozen, may eat in the kitchens. It is fortunate that since he wrote that he might
visit us I have arranged for a greater supply of provisions than we usually carry. I suspected that he
might arrive without warning.''

Aunt Hamilton said, almost as though regretting it,
''You are always beforehand with your arrangements,
my dear.''

''Oh, I have a good staff who only cross me when
they are sure I am wrong,'' returned Bess, who had
spent the morning with her Council discussing how to
ensure that m'lord Exford's visit was a success. They
were all men, so Bess's lady-in-waiting, Kate Stowe,
always sat just behind her to maintain the proprieties.

At first, when Sir Braithwaite had become incom-
petent, they had been wary of Bess taking his place,
but she had soon shown how eager she was to learn
and, despite her lack of years, had shown more commonsense than Sir Braithwaite had ever displayed—
even before he had lost his wits. Three years ago she
had insisted on reducing her household from nearly
three hundred people to little more than a hundred and
fifty, arguing correctly that Atherington was beginning
to run into needless debt by providing for so many
unnecessary mouths.

''But you have a station to keep up, my child,'' aunt
Hamilton had wailed. ''We great ones are judged by
the number of those we gather around us.''

''Nothing to that,'' Bess had replied firmly, ''if by
doing so we run headlong into ruin. If we continue as
we are, we shall eventually arrive at a day when we

shall lose our lands, and scarcely be able to employ anyone. How should that profit Atherington?''

Nor did her household know that she had failed to inform her husband of Sir Braithwaite's misfortune, for she had quietly destroyed the letters of her Clerk comptroller telling of it, and substituted others with the documents and accounts which were sent south.

And now, at last, the day of reckoning was here, and to the half-fearful excitement of meeting her husband in her proper person was added that of facing both him and her staff when they discovered her deceptions. Unless, of course, she managed to conceal them. How, she could not imagine.

No one could have guessed at the contrary emotions which were tearing Bess apart. She seemed, indeed, to be even more in command than usual when she spent her early morning with her Council. And this unnatural calm stayed with her during a late-morning session with aunt Hamilton and Kate Stowe—as well as sundry tiring maids—being dressed to receive the Exford retinue in proper style.

Usually Bess greeted being turned out "like a maypole in spring", as she always put it, with great impatience. Today, however, aunt Hamilton was both surprised and gratified by her willingness to please, and her readiness to wear the magnificent Atherington necklace which her niece had always dismissed as too barbaric and heavy, even for formal use. Perhaps it was the prospect of meeting her husband which was causing her to behave with such uncharacteristic meekness.

If so, aunt Hamilton could only be pleased that Bess was at last going to behave like the kind of conventional young woman whom she had always wished her to be.

She was not to know that her niece was gleefully preparing, not to be counselled and corrected by her husband, but rather to wrongfoot him with the knowledge of exactly who it was that he had been so eager to seduce on the previous day!

Contrary emotions were also tearing at Drew Exford. The flippancy of his cousin Charles—which he usually encouraged to lighten the burden of his great station—grated badly on him the nearer he approached the time to meet his long-deserted wife.

Of what like was she now, m'lady Exford? Was she still as plain as the child he had abandoned? He prayed not, but he feared so. But this time he would be kind, however ugly she might prove to be.

He remembered Philip Sidney saying of a plain woman, "She does not deserve our mockery, but our pity. For we see her but occasionally, whilst she has to live with her looks forever. Always remember, Drew, that she has a heart and mind as tender as that of the most beautous she. Nay, more so, for she lives not to torment our sex by using her looks as a weapon, but practises instead those other female virtues which we prize not in youth, but value in age. Loving kindness, charity and mercy—and the ability to order a good household!"

Easy enough to say, perhaps, but hard to remember when a young man's blood is young and hot. Perhaps here, Drew hoped, in leafy Leicestershire, away from the temptations of London and the court, he might find in his wife those virtues of which Philip had spoken.

"You're quiet today, Drew," Charles observed as

he drew level with his cousin who had ridden ahead of his small procession. "Thinking of your bride, no doubt, who probably does not resemble the Arcadian shepherdess of yestermorn very much."

This was too near to the bone for Drew to stomach. He put spurs to his horse and left Charles and the rest behind, and stayed ahead of them until Atherington House was reached.

And a noble pile it was. Square and built of red brick, a small tower had been added on each corner to remind the commonalty that although a castle no longer stood on high to menace them, power and might in this part of Leicestershire still belonged to the Turvilles.

There was a formal garden on one side of the house, and stables at the back. It had been built around a central quadrangle filled with a lawn which was bordered by beds of herbs and simples. An arcaded walk had been added to one wall. A small chapel stood at a little distance from the main building.

But all this was yet to be discovered by the visitors. Drew waited for his people to catch him up, whereupon he sent the most senior of his pages before him as a herald to inform Atherington that its master had arrived. But even before the page reached the main entrance with its double doors of the stoutest oak, they were flung open and a crowd of servants appeared, opening up an avenue for Drew and his gentlemen to walk through when they had dismounted. A burly Steward, carrying a white staff of office, came forward to meet them.

He bowed low to Drew and his company. "My mistress, your good lady, bids me greet you, my noble lord. Knowing that your journey from London has been both long and hard, she has arranged to meet you, m'lord, and your gentlemen, in the Great Parlour, after you have had the ordering of yourselves. I most humbly beg you to follow me to your quarters.'' He bowed again.

Drew heard Charles give a stifled laugh. Himself, he wanted to fling the man on one side and demand to be taken immediately to his wife. His self-control and temper hung in the balance—and, what was more, Charles and the others knew it. Self-control won. After all, what matter it that he met his wife early or late, when as soon as they did meet he would make it his purpose to show her that he was the master at Atherington.

''I thought,'' murmured Charles in his ear, ''that you told me that your wife's uncle was Regent here for you. But yon popinjay made no mention of him. Would you wish me to remind him of who rules at Atherington?''

Charles was merely saying aloud what Drew was thinking. Nevertheless he shook his head. ''No, I do not wish my own rule to begin in dissension and unpleasantness. Later we will arrange things to my liking. For the present we go with the tide.''

Again, easy to say, but hard to do.

It was, therefore, some little time before Drew and his gentlemen were escorted by the same Steward from their quarters in one of the towers down the winding staircase towards the entrance hall and the double doors which led first to the Great Hall. From thence they processed to the Great Parlour—the room where the owners of Atherington took their private leisure. These days the Great Hall was reserved for more formal functions.

Drew had dressed himself magnificently in cloth of the deepest silver with a hint of cerulean blue in it. The colours emphasised—as they were intended to do—his blonde beauty. His doublet had the new peasecod belly. His breeches were padded with horse-hair, and his long stockings of the palest cream were visible until just above his knee where they were supported by garters made of fine blue and silver brocade.

His ruff was also of the newest fashion, being oval in shape, rather than round, and was narrow, not deep. It was held up behind his head by an invisible fine wire frame. His leather shoes had long tongues and small cork heels. A sapphire ring decorated one shapely hand; a small gold locket hung around his neck, its case adorned by a large diamond.

Charles and his other gentlemen were similarly dressed, but not so richly. They formed the most exquisitely presented bevy of young male beauty such as Atherington had not seen for many a long year.

They marched in solemn procession through the Great Hall, already laid out for a formal banquet, and then through an oak door richly carved with the Tree of Life, and into the Great Parlour, a large splendidly furnished room, whose leaded windows looked out on to the central quadrangle.

Facing them was a group of people as richly dressed as themselves, although not quite in the latest fashion. All but two of them were men. In front of them, with another, and older woman, standing a little behind her, stood a young woman of middle height as richly and fashionably dressed as he was, in a gown whose deep colours of burnt sienna, rich gold and emerald green were in marked contrast to the pastel hues of Drew and his train.

As though she were the Queen she made no effort to walk towards him, but stood there, waiting for him to approach her, her head held high, her face concealed by a large fan, so that all that Drew could see of her was her rich dark hair, dressed high on her head, and a single pearl resting on her forehead above the fan's fluted edge.

At last, reluctantly, he moved forward, bowing, as did his followers. Straightening up, he found that he had no wish to see the face which was hidden behind the fan. He had a form of words ready for her, which would contain no reference to what had passed between them ten years ago, or to her looks—for that might be tactless.

"Madam," he began—and then paused for a brief moment before he spoke the words which flowed from him almost against his will. "We meet at last, m'lady Exford."

On hearing this, his wife slowly lowered the fan to show him her face for the first time.

Drew stood there paralysed. For the face before him was that of the beautiful nymph whom he had lusted after—and had offered to seduce—in Charnwood Forest on the previous day.

But the nymph had worn rough clothing and had moved and spoken with the wild freedom of a creature of the woods. This woman was a lovely icon, standing stiff and proud in her formal clothing. But, oh, her face was the perfect oval he remembered, the lips as crimson, shapely and tender, the eyes as dark, and her complexion, yes, her complexion, was of the purest and smoothest ivory, with the faintest rose blush to enhance its loveliness. And beneath her stiff clothing her body was surely as luscious and inviting.

Drew, standing there, dumbstruck, all his usual rather cold command quite gone, heard his cousin Charles give a stifled groan—turning it into something between a cough and a laugh as he, too, recognised the woodland nymph. The sound brought him back to life again, even as he wondered what in the world had happened to the dark monkey-like child of ten years ago.

Had his wits been wandering then? Or were they wandering now?

Had it been a changeling he had seen? Or was this woman the changeling? Without conscious thought, courtier-like, as though greeting his Queen, Elizabeth herself, he went down on one knee before her and took into his own hand that of his wife's which was not holding the fan.

Turning it over, he kissed, not the back but the palm of the hand—a long and lingering kiss—and thought that he detected a faint quiver in it. But as he looked up there was no sign of emotion in the cold, aloof face of the woman before him.

Why did she not speak? As though she had picked his thought out of the air, she said at last in the wood nymph's honeyed tones, "As the old adage has it, better late than never, m'lord. Permit me to introduce you to my good counsellors—and yours—who have served you well these many years."

She had looked him in the eye for one fleeting moment before she began to name the men around her. Her manner reminded him again of that of his Queen. But that Elizabeth was a ruler, and this woman ruled nothing. He waited, as she introduced them one by one, for her to name the Master of her Household, Sir Braithwaite Hamilton, but although she introduced his wife to him, his name did not pass her lips, and he was not one of the men around her, either.

He murmured his acknowledgments, as did those gentlemen of his train whose duties matched those of the men around his wife, before he questioned her.

"And Sir Braithwaite Hamilton who rules here, where is he?"

Drew was not prepared for the manner in which his question was received. The heads of Atherington's male Council turned towards him in some surprise. His wife gave him a cool and non-committal smile.

She raised her fan and said to him over it, "You forget, m'lord. As I informed you at the time, Sir Braithwaite has been an invalid bereft of his wits these five long years, and my Council and I rule in his place."

Bess had expected his question, and was prepared to offer him a brazen lie in answer to it. Oh, this pinked and perfumed gallant who plainly thought that every pretty woman he met was his rightful prey, who had recognised her immediately, and on whose face she had read the shock he had received on learning what his ugly child bride had turned into during his absence, did not deserve that she should be truthful with him.

Drew's face changed again, as he received this second shock—the first having been the changed face of his wife. It was as though he were standing on one of the Atlantic beaches which he had visited during his merchant adventurer years, watching the surf come rolling in, each wave bigger than the last.

How he kept his composure he never knew. The hot temper which he had so carefully controlled these many years threatened to overwhelm him. He mastered himself with difficulty as he bade it depart, so that, like a dog retiring to its kennel, it slunk into a corner of his mind where it might rest until he was ready to indulge it.

He said, or rather muttered to her, "I see that we have a deal of matters to discuss in private, madam."

If he had thought that visiting—and disposing of—his wife was going to be a simple matter beside the duty which Walsingham had laid on him, he was rapidly being disabused of any such notion.

The smile his wife gave him in reply was, he noted, as false as Hell, as false as the letters he had received from her over the years. "Indeed, and indeed," she murmured sweetly, lowering her fan, and showing him the glory of her face, "there is much of which we have to speak."

"Beginning with honesty." He made his voice as grim as he dare without causing an open affront. He had no mind for a public altercation with the double-dealing bitch before him. But, oh, how he longed for them to be private together!

"Oh, honesty!" Bess carolled, displaying animation for the first time. "It is a virtue which I prize highly. Like chastity. Another virtue which I am sure, knowing you, that you prize also, my dear husband."

He heard Charles's stifled laughter behind him again.

Drew thought of yesterday's unconfined behaviour of the demure woman before him. "You would give me lessons in it, wife?" he riposted, his voice now dangerous as well as grim.

"Aye, sir. If you think that you need them. My acquaintance with you is not sufficiently lengthy for me to be able to make a judgement on the matter."

She paused, leaned forward and tapped his chest provocatively with her fan. "They say that first impressions are frequently faulty, m'lord! What do you say?"

Drew wanted to say nothing. What he wanted to do was to place the impudent baggage across his knee and give her such a paddling as she would never forget.

But he was hamstrung by the formality of the occasion, and by the fact that so far she was wrongfooting him at every turn, so that he was finding it difficult to gain any verbal advantage over her. Much more of this and Charles would be openly laughing at him—and he could well imagine the smirks of his gentlemen.

Oh, what a fine play this whole wretched business would make with a title along the lines of, *The Nymph and the Satyr,* or, *the Man Who Tried to Seduce His Own Wife.* How much he would enjoy this situation if only some other poor fool was in the middle of it, and not himself.

He spoke at last, conscious that he had been silent for some time. He was surprised at how bored and indifferent he sounded. "Why, madam, that is one matter which I would prefer to discuss in private with you. I cannot say how much I look forward to doing so."

He let his gaze rove around the room, taking in the men standing watching them, more than a little bemused by this byplay, and said, in a low voice which none other but she could hear, "And your youthful escort, madam, who follows you to play with you in the woods, where is he? I see him not here."

What, was he jealous? This was delightful, was it

not? Bess could see that every word she uttered was a dart striking home. He had come to lord it over her, to stress his superiority and by his own wilful and lustful behaviour, and her wicked conduct in not enlightening him as to who she was, she had him at a disadvantage—who should have been at a disadvantage herself.

"Oh, you shall see him soon—when you are introduced to the rest of my servants. In the meantime I have instructed my Council to have ready for you and your Comptrollers all the books and accounts relating to Atherington's affairs. First, perhaps, we should eat. A feast has been prepared in your honour."

"So I see, madam." He was glacial now. "But permit me to correct you. First I should like to be taken to see Sir Braithwaite—to reassure myself as to his condition."

Aunt Hamilton, who had been listening with increasing agitation to the hostilities being conducted in her presence, took it upon herself to say, "Oh, m'lord, I can assure you that his condition is as was described to you when he first fell ill after his accident. He has not improved."

Drew's blue gaze was stern. "I thank you for that reassurance, Lady Hamilton, but I would prefer to see him for myself. My cousin Charles, who is my Chief Comptroller, will accompany me. There is no need for either of you two ladies to do so. Only after I have paid him my respects shall I break bread. Pray order the Steward, Lady Exford, to conduct me to him."

"Willingly, husband," Bess said, dipping him a deep curtsey. "I am always yours to command."

"See that you are, madam, see that you are. I do

not care for wilful, forward women who think they know better than their husbands.''

Oh, yes, she had stung him, and seeing his grim face Bess knew that she was going to pay for it. But for the present she had enjoyed herself mightily—and in the end everything had to be paid for. Which was a maxim her father had taught her. What he had been unable to teach her was what form payment might take!

Charles began to speak to his cousin the moment that they were safely out of the Great Parlour and walking towards the main staircase. Drew stopped, took him by the arm and said roughly, ''Not now, later. When we are alone. For the present we are to see Sir Braithwaite Hamilton, who, until a few minutes ago, I thought was in charge of my lands here. After that we may talk.''

Sir Braithwaite was, as his wife and niece had said, a helpless invalid. He was incapable of coherent speech, and physically little more active than a baby. He stared affably at Drew and Charles from a great chair placed before a window overlooking the kitchen gardens after his attendant had nudged him and pointed to his visitors. He spoke, but his speech was a babble. Drew thought that by his appearance he was not long for this world, but later the doctor attending him said that he had been of this countenance since his accident.

So, his lady wife had been deceiving him—and by the looks of it—her own Council, ever since Sir Braithwaite had become witless, by not informing him of her uncle's condition! He was certain that she had never sent him any letter reporting the true facts of it, however much she said to the contrary.

He dismissed the Steward when he reached the bottom of the stairway which led into the entrance hall, and pushed Charles into a room which opened off it.

"Now, Charles, what the devil has been going on here? The man I thought was my Comptroller is a blinking idiot, and my lady wife is not only running the household and the estates, but is riding around the countryside dressed like a milkmaid inviting seduction."

Charles said, choking with laughter, "Your face, Drew, your face when you saw that the nymph you tried to seduce was your own wife! A beauty, though, a very Helen of Troy. Whyever did you tell me that she was plain?" and he began to laugh helplessly.

Drew grasped his cousin by the shoulders and turned him so that they were face to face, eye to eye. Charles was still trying to control his amusement, whilst Drew was as grim as Hercules about to embark on another of his labours—as Charles told him later.

He hissed at his cousin, "If you laugh, Charles, I shall kill you! That is a promise, not a threat!"

Charles rearranged his face, and said, as solemnly as he could, "What, laugh? I laugh? No, no, I merely choked a little—from surprise, you understand. This is a grave matter, a very grave matter, m'lord."

"And do not m'lord me, either. Damnation and Hell surround me and every devil with a pitchfork is sticking me with it. How in God's name was I to know that that wanton nymph in the woods yesterday was my wife? And he I thought her brother—in Hell's name, who was he? Was she wantoning with him in the greenwood? I can believe anything of her after the way in which she taunted me just now."

"Most strange," agreed Charles, his face solemn,

but his eyes had an evil glint in them as he savoured Drew's discomfiture. "As I said earlier, repute had it that she was plain, and you did not deny it, on the contrary."

"Hell's teeth," roared Drew who had lost all his usual calm control and the measured speech which went with it. "She resembled naught so much as a monkey ten years agone. What alchemist has she visited to turn herself into such a...such...?" He ran out of words.

"A pearl?" Charles finished for him, still as grave as a parson.

Drew raved on. "I was prepared to be patient with her, and kind, because she was so plain, you understand. But what shall I do with her now that she has caught me trying to seduce a woodland maiden who turned out to be my own wife? She never said a word to enlighten me, into the bargain, but inwardly enjoyed the jest at my expense. And after *that,* she had the impudence to twit me with her chastity—and my lack of it."

Charles could not help himself. He began to laugh until the tears ran down his face. "Confess, Drew, what a fine jest *you* would think this if it were happening to someone else!"

Drew stared at him, and then, as his cousin's words struck home, he began to laugh himself at the sheer absurdity of it all. Laughter dissipated his rage—it slunk back again into its kennel. When he spoke, his voice showed that he had regained his usual cold command.

"Merriment purges all, Philip Sidney once said. You were right to laugh, Charles, at the spectacle of my High Mightiness brought low by a woman. Now

I am myself again, and by my faith, the best way to treat my lady wife will be to behave as though yesterday was a dream—which I did not share. More, I shall sort out her deception over the ruling of Atherington in such a way as will offer her no satisfaction, no chance to enjoy any more secret jests at my expense.''

"Oh, bravo! That is more like yourself, Drew. Come, let us to the feast."

"Aye, Charles, where I shall behave like a grave and reverend *signor* who would never attempt to tumble a chance-met wench in the greenwood!''

# Chapter Four

"Bess, my dear, I cannot understand how it was that your husband did not know of Sir Braithwaitte's illness! I distinctly remember that he was informed. You said that he might have forgotten—but how could he forget a matter of such importance? It would be most careless of him, and he does not appear to be a careless person. I was always surprised that he appointed no one in my husband's place, but allowed you to take over the governance of Atherington!"

Aunt Hamilton had been twittering away to Bess on this undesirable subject ever since Drew and Charles had left them. Walter Hampden, her Chief Comptroller, had also approached her, frowning heavily, as they awaited her husband's return to the Great Parlour. Bess had silenced him by immediately turning on her heel and ordering Gilbert to arrange for goblets of sack to be brought through to the company, ostensibly to help them while away the time until dinner, but actually to keep them from questioning her.

Even so, Walter, a neglected goblet of wine in his hand, had not taken this none-too-subtle hint, but began immediately to question her, saying, "Madam, I would have a word with you. I remember that we wrote several times to Lord Exford informing him of Sir Braithwaite's sad mishap, so how was it that he knew nothing of it? Most strange, most strange.'' He shook his old head in wonderment as he finished.

He had been Sir Braithwaite's trusted right-hand man, and had continued as Bess's after it was plain that Lord Exford, by his silence, seemed happy for matters to continue as they were, without sending his man to oversee Atherington's affairs.

Atherington, under his and Bess's guidance, with the help of the Council, had subsequently become so prosperous that after a time Walter had ceased to question this somewhat odd arrangement. As Bess had feared, however, Drew's apparent ignorance of the truth about Sir Braithwaite's condition was beginning to trouble him.

''Oh, I am sure that this is but a misunderstanding,'' Bess proclaimed feverishly, wishing that Drew would return so that they could repair to the Great Hall and set about the banquet. Her husband could scarcely expect her to begin discussing matters of business whilst they were eating and drinking their way through Atherington's bounty.

His grim face, however, when he returned from Sir Braithwaite's tower room, gave her no reason to expect that she was going to receive much mercy from him, either at the banquet—or anywhere else. His cousin Charles, by contrast, had an expression on his face which showed that one person, at least, was deriving some amusement from the situation.

''I am at your service, madam,'' Drew announced. ''Bid your Steward to escort us to the Hall.''

He held his hand out to take hers as though nothing

was amiss, but his mouth, set in a hard straight line, was an indication that their private life, like their public one, was to be as coldly formal as his voice.

Gilbert the Steward, however, was delighted. If he had a complaint about Lady Bess's rule, it was that she was too easy in her conduct of it. All the heavily manned little ceremonies which Sir Braithwaite had insisted upon had been done away with. And, since they mostly centred around Gilbert's affairs, he had felt that his station in the Atherington household had been demeaned.

Plainly his new master thought differently, and so they all processed majestically into the Hall, where pages, at Gilbert's instructions, ran forward with napkins and bowls of water. The napkins were to protect the guests' fine clothing, and the water was for them to rinse their hands in after they had eaten of the roast beef, the chickens, the pigs' trotters and all the other delicacies carried in on great platters by another half-score of obedient pages. The napkins then found their further use in drying wet hands, although some still preferred the old custom of waving them in the air. Gilbert was beside himself with joy.

Not so Bess. She hated ceremony, considering it a waste of precious time. For her, informality was all. She wondered what Drew's preference was. The fact that he was being so correct in his conduct today was not necessarily a guide to his character if she remembered how lustily—and improperly—he had set about her yesterday!

She stole a look at his noble profile as he sat beside her. It was still grim, and his mouth was set in stern lines. She wondered if she dare try to soften it. She would have to go carefully, for seated as they were in the place of honour in the middle of the long table, all eyes were upon them, save for those few of their senior officers who shared their side of it.

She was about to speak when Drew forestalled her.

"I desire an explanation from you, madam my wife, as to why you did not see fit to inform me of your uncle's grave and disabling accident."

So, war had been declared, had it? There was to be no peace over the dinner plates. The best form of defence, Bess had long ago concluded, was attack. She went on to it, keeping her voice low, but firm.

"Not so, m'lord husband. You were kept fully informed. Do try the chicken legs, I beg of you. They are tenderer than most because of the delicate food-stuffs Dame Margery insists on. Meat cannot be tender, she avows, if what is put in the animal to make it grow is tough." The gaze she turned on Drew was a melting one.

Drew was not melted. "To the devil with Dame Margery—and her chicken legs, too," he said roughly. "Do not seek to deceive me, wife. I am of the belief that you lied to your Council and to me."

"Now why should you think that, husband? And it is unkind of you to curse Dame Margery. She is a very hard worker, and loyal to Atherington—as are all my servants."

"And is she a liar, too? Does she also go running around…?" Drew stopped himself and cursed inwardly. He had not meant to refer to yesterday's contretemps, and here he was reminding her of it! Not a very clever ploy. In life, as in chess, one did not give the enemy an advantage. He swallowed his words and started again.

"You may be sure that I, and my advisers, will

examine your books and documents with the utmost care, and if I find any maladministration, I shall know full well who is to blame.''

Attack! Attack! Trumpets were blowing in Bess's brain. ''And you will not blame yourself, husband—if you do find anything amiss, which I doubt—that for ten long years you have ignored Atherington and left us to our fate? I have been a woman for six full summers, ready to do a wife's duty, and bear your children. Address your reproaches to the one who deserves them, sir, which is not my good self, but one who is nearer home to you!''

Oh, sweet Lord! Now she had done it. She had lost her temper—as, by his expression, he was losing his. He leaned forward, food forgotten, and said between his teeth, ''Do you not fear a day of reckoning, my lady wife? For you should.''

''No more than you should,'' returned Bess hardily.

How dare he reproach her, how dare he? Her eyes flashed at him, as they locked with his, stare for stare. Not only their food, but the spectators were forgotten.

''Oh, indeed,'' he sneered. ''And that youth who was with you yesterday—is all seemly between you?'' He had meant to save this for the privacy of their room, but the woman would tempt a saint to misbehave, for even as they wrangled he wanted to fall upon her and have his way with her; the way which he had been denied yestermorn.

For she was temptation itself. How could he be moved by one who was so unlike all the women whom he had favoured so far? She was black, not blonde, her eyes were dark, not blue, her complexion was pale, not rosy, she was not small, but was of a good height—and instead of being meek in speech she had a tongue like the Devil. Nor did she fail to use it at every turn.

By God, it would be a pleasure to master her, to ride her to the Devil who had blessed, nay, cursed her with that tongue. Aye, and beyond him to the lowest pit of Hell where only the demons lurked, forgotten even by their unsavoury Lord! The very thought of using her so was doing cruel and untoward things to his body.

Drew tried to calm himself. He must not let her catch him on the raw every time she spoke.

"I think you mistake a woman's place, madam. It is to be quiet, to obey her lord, to be meek at all times…"

"I'd as lief be dead!" Bess could not help herself. The words flew out of her, interrupting him in his catalogue of what a good woman should be.

"I have no mind," she exclaimed in ringing tones which the whole table could hear, "to be like patient Griselda in Master Chaucer's poem, who pitifully thanks her husband for his mistreatment of her."

"Nor am I minded to be the husband of a nagging wife, always determined to have the last word." Drew roared this as though the demons he had conjured up were at his back, prodding him with their pitchforks.

Well, at least formality had flown out of the window and honesty had taken its place, thought Bess, stifling a smile at the sight of all the shocked faces around the table.

Worse, aunt Hamilton was quavering at her, "Oh, my niece, my dear niece, remember that your husband stands in the place of your God—to be obeyed at all times… This is no fashion in which to conduct yourself…and in a public place, too."

Little though she cared to admit it, Bess knew that aunt Hamilton was right—at least as regards the place in which her differences with her husband ought to be aired.

She gave an abrupt laugh, and put her hand out towards Drew's, saying, "How now, my lord, let us cry quits for this meal, at least—and shake hands on it. We are not players on a stage, paid to entertain an audience."

His wife had spoken as frankly and freely as any boy, and her manner was smilingly confident as she did so. The moment—and the relationship between the pair of them—swung in the balance. Drew was aware that he could base his answer on his own masculinity and his consequent right to rule his wife, and thus reject her offer outright. All between them would then lie in ruins. Or, he could forget his husbandly rights, take her offered hand, cry truce—and let the game start again.

Even as he wavered Bess said, still frank and as though she had read his mind, "Come, m'lord, let us set the board out for a new game and forget the old one."

As though of its own will, and not his, Drew's hand thrust itself forward, and grasped her smaller one, enclosing it in his where it fitted so warm and sweetly, that he felt his anger leaching out of him.

"Quits," he said. "But I cannot promise what will happen on another day."

"No," shot back Bess. "But then, no more can I!"

"A strange truce," smiled Drew, determined not to lose his self-control again, "when the two principals who have agreed it are still at war!"

"*I* am not at war," announced Bess, picking up one

of Dame Margery's chicken legs and throwing a sideways glance at Drew as she did so. "On the contrary, I am enjoying my dinner, and am consequently at peace."

Her sideways glance nearly undid Drew, it was so full of fun and mischief. He gave a little groan, and then leaned forward to take the half-eaten chicken leg from her hand and to begin to eat it himself, his eyes on hers. "What does Dame Margery baste her meat with that it has one effect on you, madam, and quite another on me?"

Bess smiled crookedly at him. "Why, you must to the kitchens, sir, and ask her. Though whether she will have an answer to satisfy you, is quite another thing." Her smile, unknowing to her, was provocation itself.

A witch! A very witch! Had there been a potion in the goblet which the eager page boy had handed to him as he sat down? Only that could explain why she was keeping his hot blood on the boil. Used to meek women, determined to please him, to meet one who met him with defiance—and smiled so sweetly at him in the doing—was having the strongest effect on Drew. He could not wait for the evening, to have her in the Great Bed which was sure to be in the master bedroom above him.

His wife was suffering from the same fever. The beautiful boy who had despised her had turned into a man who stared at her with eager eyes even as he reproved her. He waved his stolen chicken leg at her before eating it slowly, his blue eyes on her face exactly as though it were she whom he was devouring.

Well, Bess knew a game worth two of that! She leaned forward to take his wine glass, lifted it to her lips and drank it as slowly and sensuously as she could, her eyes on his, so slowly that Drew could have sworn he could see the crimson liquid staining her skin as it slid down her throat.

And then, glass in hand, she took his bread and its attendant cheese from the pewter platter which lay between them, and ate that, too. "Tit for tat, my lord," she murmured. "Your bread, cheese and wine for my leg. A fair exchange? Say Yea—or Nay."

Aware that his cousin Charles, eyes wide, was avidly watching this little scene, Drew hooded his own eyes, clasped the wrist of the hand which held the wine glass, now half empty, and putting his lips where hers had been, drank from it until all the wine was gone.

"Neither Yea nor Nay, madam, but half and half, and somehere in between. You shall not best me!"

"Nay, sir, but I must try. I am not Griselda."

Oh, Bess knew that it was unwise to tease him so. But yet she must, and knowing little of the game of love, as yet untouched by a man's hands or lips, for Tib and the others had worshipped her from afar, how was it that she knew how to drive a man to distraction?

For Bess had no doubt that that was what she was doing, and even as she led him on with one ploy her busy mind, obeying her body's urgings, was driving her on to another. Some time in the future he would force a reckoning on her, she knew that, and her body throbbed at the very thought. But he was answering her and she must attend.

"Now, that I already know," Drew murmured, "that you are not Griselda. But are you Mother Eve who has already tempted—and taken—a man to lie on your breast, so knowing are your arts?"

"I have no arts, husband, other than those which Mother Eve gave me when I was born. And no man has known me either. I am as untouched as Eve was when the Lord God took her from Adam's side.''

Could he believe her, so frank and free was she? He was not to know that all of the Atherington household was watching their lady with the deepest astonishment. They had never seen her behave like this before. But then, she had never sat beside her husband before. Drew, trying to maintain his self-control, shrugged. He would pursue the matter of Tib, and his wife's familiarity with him, in private.

''Leave that, wife,'' he told her curtly. ''We have other, more pressing matters, to discuss. After this meal is over we must have an accounting, you, your Council and myself. I shall be most interested to hear an explanation from you all as to why I was never informed of Sir Braithwaite's incapacity.''

One thing was plain to Bess. For all his easy surface charm—and there was no denying it—her husband was like a determined terrier with a rat in his jaws who would never let go, however much he was distracted, when he had set his mind on obtaining an answer to something which puzzled him.

''Oh, I think that you are mistook over that, sir. These mistakes will happen, will they not?'' And now it was Charles Breton, sitting on her left, who received her charming sidelong glance.

''Oh, aye, indeed,'' returned Charles, with a humorous duck of his head. ''Most like the letter was lost, either on its way to us, or perhaps, after it was received.''

''Very helpful of you, Charles,'' commented Drew, his voice dry. ''I scarcely think, though, that my wife needs your assistance in explaining away the odd circumstances which appear to surround Atherington's affairs.''

Thus rebuked, Charles smiled and changed the subject. It would not do to provoke Drew so hard that he lost his temper. Drew scarcely ever did so, but he had been a rare sight on the few occasions when he had lost control of himself. He wondered what it could be that was disturbing his cousin so strongly. Knowing of Atherington's stalwart Protestantism, he asked a question to which he thought Drew could make no objection.

''Are there are many gentry families around Charnwood, Lady Exford? I had heard in London that there were—and that a number of them held to the old Catholic faith.''

Even as Bess began to reply, Drew swung around sharply to watch her as she spoke. Charles, he was sure, had no knowledge of the real reason why he was visiting Leicestershire, and was therefore, unknowingly, doing him a favour by raising the matter. It would save him from needing to ask such a question himself. He listened with interest as Bess agreed that there were a large number of gentry families in the county, some of whom were Catholic.

''But not so many, I believe,'' she ended, ''as in Derbyshire, where the Babingtons, my distant relatives, who are settled at Dethick, still hold to the old Faith. Most living hereabouts, though, are Protestant.''

''And are those around Atherington mainly Protestant, and therefore loyal, madam?'' asked Drew, apparently idly.

''Assuredly.'' Bess answered him eagerly; she wanted him to know that there were no traitors in Leicestershire. "We are all, Catholic and Protestant alike, loyal subjects of our Queen."

Drew knew this to be true in the main. There had been many plots against the Queen designed to assassinate her, and replace her by her imprisoned cousin, Mary, the Catholic Queen of Scots, but few English Catholics had been involved in them. They had mostly been hatched abroad. This lay behind Walsingham's uneasiness over the reports he had received, for they seemed to hint at a purely English conspiracy—a most disturbing development.

Bess had, quite deliberately, spoken to be heard by all, not simply her husband, and as a result all heads had nodded in agreement when she had finished speaking. Her Comptroller, Walter Hampden, sitting not far from them, raised his goblet of wine and said, "With your permission, my Lord of Exford, I beg that on this auspicious day of your arrival we may all rise to toast, not only our good Queen Elizabeth, but the Protestant Faith."

Drew rose and held his goblet high. "With all my heart, my good sir. I give you Good Queen Bess and the Protestant Faith. Drink up, I beg you." He threw his handsome head back and drained his goblet to the lees.

The whole room echoed him, but Walter had not finished. He called on the servitor to refill his goblet, saying, "Again with your permission, my lord, I ask that the company may now be allowed to toast both you and your good lady, who has guarded Atherington's interests so bravely on your behalf."

Now, what could he say to that, but, "Most excellent and all good cheer to you, sir. I will allow your toast—but only if you will omit any salutation to me so that I may be allowed to drink to my lady wife also.''

A hum of delight ran round the table. Some of Atherington's people, watching their new lord, had feared that he and his lady might be at odds, but such a statement cleared their minds of worry. As for Drew's followers, including Charles, they were noting with some amusement that their master was using his notorious charm to win over his new subjects.

Bess, somewhat nonplussed by Drew's apparent change of heart, smiled up at him as he bent down to kiss her on the cheek before he led the company in the toast to her. ''Is this reconciliation, my lord? Or have you some other aim in mind?''

Oh, she was a clever minx, his wife! She did not trust him in the least—as he did not trust her. He whispered in her ear as he sat down again, ''It is not to Atherington's benefit for your people to think that we are out of humour with one another—even if we are. Smile, my lady wife, as I do—and thus we make our world happy. We may pursue our real ends when we are alone together.''

Alone together! The mere thought of it had Bess quailing inwardly. No doubt about it, he would be the terrier and she would be the rat. But if so, why, as well as fear, did she feel a strange exhilaration? It was as though she had never lived until she had met him. She was on fire—and knew not why. She only knew that her husband was looking at her strangely, his blue eyes growing larger and larger as they drew nearer and nearer to her.

Panic rose in Bess's breast. She was sailing into unknown waters, a mariner lost in the steep Atlantic stream of which the poets wrote. To break his spell, deliberately woven, she was sure, to snare her, she turned away from him to see her great hound, Pompey, sitting up before one of the arras, his liquid eyes begging her to feed him.

"Oh, Pompey," Bess exclaimed, "I have quite forgot you in this hubbub." She snatched a gnawed beef bone from the great platter before her, turned and tossed it to him, anything to escape her husband's compelling eyes. Pompey, snarling, leapt upon it, and laying it before her, began to worry at it.

"The hound which licked me yesterday, I suppose," offered Drew smoothly, showing no sign that he had been thwarted in his desire to bend his wilful wife to his will. A line fit for a poet to use, he thought—so many meanings were there in it.

"Aye, husband, and a faithful one. He honoured you, for until yesterday he chose to like none but myself."

The moment she had spoken she wished she had not made such an admission, for he pounced on it immediately. "An omen, think you, wife?"

Before Bess could answer him, Pompey picked up the bone, now meatless, and trotted over to lay it at Drew's feet.

"Oh, traitor hound," sighed Bess softly, "to transfer your affections with such speed." As though he had understood what she said, Pompey rose, laid his head in her lap—and then promptly returned to worship at Drew's feet again.

"They say," remarked Bess, as platters of sweetmeats and sweet wine to drink with them were laid on the table before them, "that dogs can see into the true hearts of men and women. What does he see in yours,

husband, I wonder? A pity he cannot tell me.'' The
eyes she turned on him were mirthful and artless.

Drew retaliated by plucking a small cake from the
platter and popping it into her mouth, not his, so that
she could not soon answer him.

''That for your silence, wife. He would say only
that he approves of me—or that he knows his true
master when he meets him. Nay, do not try to answer
me with another witticism, for your well of wisdom
will soon run dry if you draw on it too often!''

And now his eyes were mocking hers again, and the
excitement which boiled inside Bess rose higher and
higher. Did he know what he was doing to her? Of
course, he did, and it was done with an end in view;
to subdue her, to bend her to his mental as well as to
his bodily will—for was not that seduction's aim?

Unable to speak, Bess stared at him. He stared back.
She swallowed, and the action set her long white
throat working after a fashion, which, had she but
known it, was seducing *him.*

Bess shivered. Suddenly she was frightened of the
powerful attraction he had for her. Unused to the company of young men, let alone handsome and powerful
young men, she had never learned those arts which
women used, either to attract them, or dissuade them.
So far Mother Eve had helped her, but she was approaching dangerous territory where that alone would
not be sufficient to save her from him.

Save her! Almost hysterical laughter bubbled up inside Bess. Nothing could save her, for was he not her
husband who might do as he pleased with her?

And would.

Any hope that he might be repelled by her as he
had been ten years ago, and might not wish to touch

her, let alone make love to her, had disappeared. It was difficult to know what he really thought of her—except, of course, that yesterday, not knowing who she was, he had addressed her in most flattering terms—and then tried to seduce her! But what did he think of her now that he knew that she was his wife?

And what did she truly want from him?

Bess swallowed again, and Drew looked away. Against everything which he might have expected as he had thought of this day on the way to Atherington, the wife he had delayed meeting for so long was rousing him simply by sitting beside him—and defying him! What had Philip Sidney once said to him? ''There is more pleasure to be gained from a woman who can meet and match you, than in one who is meekly resigned to endure whatever you have to offer her.''

Drew grinned to himself. Philip should meet his wife. They would make a good pair. On second thoughts, perhaps not. He wanted this high-spirited termagant for himself to tame—and to test whether Philip was right in his assessment of the extra pleasure to be gained from mastering such a skittish filly. Except that Philip had not said mastering, he had said meeting.

''Silent, sir?'' queried Bess who had just finished eating her extremely sticky sweetmeat. She was beginning to learn that in an untried maiden desire and fear went hand in hand. She had asked herself what she wanted from him, and the answer was, she did not yet know. But the desire to tease him, to see the blue eyes burn at her, was strong in her. For if she could provoke him, why, then she had power over him.

''I was thinking,'' Drew announced, ''of my friend Philip Sidney, who is a courtier, a scholar and a poet.''

"A paragon, then," quipped Bess naughtily.

"Indeed," returned Drew, who was beginning to realise how much he was enjoying this lengthy sparring match with her, carried out, as it was, in public. "He has a high regard for the capacities of women, which I assure you, is rare at the Court, or anywhere else in England for that matter."

"No need to tell me *that,* sir. Although we here at Atherington are not so dismissive of women's understanding."

"So I see, wife, for it is plain that you have your Council eating out of your hand. I am curious to know how you have accomplished that."

Bess was airy. This interminable meal was nearly at an end, and she was flown with good food and wine, and the exhilarating sensation of danger which surrounded her husband.

"Why, sir, that is easily done. One treats them as one treats Pompey, you understand. A little petting, good food, flattery—and the will to show them who is master here whenever it is necessary."

Bess was immediately aware that this frivolous answer was an unwise one, but it had slipped out of her, and his answer, she was later to understand, was typical of him—for he took her meaning and embroidered upon it—as a good fencer may turn his opponent's skill against him to secure a hit.

"Mistress," he said softly, leaning forward to take her goblet of wine from her. "You mean mistress, not master—but I take your meaning, and I promise you I shall be very wary of you if you attempt to pet me, feed me, or flatter me—and then try to prove to me who is master here—or is it the other way round, lady, and you wish to be mistress?"

"Any way which you wish," said Bess, full of good food, good wine and magnanimity, "for you have the right of it—seeing that Atherington now has a master, as well as a mistress. Be brief in your answer, sir, I see that the feast is over, and Gilbert is unsure which of us should rise to say so."

Drew laughed, and the sound of it echoed in one of those strange silences which often fall in the company of men and women assembled together. He took her hand and urged her to her feet.

"My friends," he announced. "We have eaten well. My wife and I bid you adjourn to the Great Parlour where I am told that musicians are assembled to play to us as we recover from the pleasures of the feast. Lead on, Gilbert, and let the company follow us."

# Chapter Five

Be damned to it! Drew had spent the whole afternoon with his wife and her Council, he and his Comptrollers examining books, papers and accounts, and at the end of it none of them could discover anything untoward with which she and they might be reproached. On the contrary, it appeared that Atherington was being more efficiently run than any of Drew's other estates.

His lawyer and principal man of business, John Masters, had been particularly severe in his questioning, especially over the matter of Sir Braithwaite Hamilton, but he could not shake the men before him. They stoutly maintained that m'lord had been sent all proper and pertinent details of his illness and their response to it, and it was not their fault if matters had gone awry at the other end.

Bess had said little, Drew noted glumly, leaving her advisers to speak for her. She had intervened only on one occasion when Masters had complained that some vital accounts relating to the sinking of new coalpits near Bardon Hill had been lost.

Before Walter Hampden could answer she had said, "Oh, I ordered that a new book should be opened in another name, so that what was going into and out of the pit in terms of money should be clearly distinct from our other affairs. I believe it to be in the small pile before you. It is the new one in the blue cover.''

So it was, and John Masters was left to retreat as gracefully as he could, to his own and Drew's annoyance. Was there no way in which he could turn the tables on the wench? He had hoped that all the food and drink which she had consumed at the banquet would have made her sleepy, but no such thing.

Instead, as at the feast, she seemed to have an answer for everything. Well, it would be interesting to find out what answer she would have for him this evening, in the Great Bed when they were at last alone.

His temper was not improved by John Masters saying to him in a resigned fashion after the meeting, ''Our fears that matters might be awry once we learned of Sir Braithwaite's incapacity and your lady taking over the reins were groundless. On the contrary, Atherington is a model of how an estate should be run.

''I would have thought that it might be all her Comptroller's doing, but he assured me at the feast that it was she who insisted on prospecting for coal after she had learned that the Willoughbys of Wollaton in Nottinghamshire were increasing their income mightily by exploiting their pits by selling coal both locally and as far away as the East Coast. And it was she who insisted on cutting the staff and running the House more economically.''

''A wise lady, my wife,'' returned Drew, who did not know whether to be glad or sorry at the news. How would she take giving up the power which she had wielded for the past five years and having to become a mere wife and mother instead? Perhaps he ought to give over to her the running of all his estates, as Lord Shrewsbury was reputed to have done to his wife.

Well, he was not George Shrewsbury, to be a door-mat for a woman, even a clever one, and he was now resigned to the fact that his wife was clever as well as beautiful. A paragon, she had said mockingly of his friend Philip Sidney, and he could say the same of her—but he would not say it *to* her. A wife must learn her place.

"Husband?" There she was, before him, looking as bright and eager as ever. Tiredness seemed to be un-known to her. "Husband, you are silent. I trust that you are not dissatisfied with what you have learned this afternoon?"

"On the contrary, my man, John Masters, and I, are in agreement that Atherington, like yourself, appears to be in the best of health. Your Comptroller is an excellent man of business, and his mistress appears to have an old head on young shoulders."

Bess dipped him a great curtsy. "You flatter me overmuch, husband."

"No, indeed, no flattery is too great for the woman who so cunningly contrived to conceal the true gov-ernance of Atherington from me for so long. Tell me, madam wife, did you burn the letters which your Comptroller caused to be written to me relating to Sir Braithwaite, or did they find their way to the cesspit rather than to my office?"

"Oh, husband—" Bess eyed him reproachfully, de-ciding yet again that attack was the best form of de-fence. "—how can you accuse me of such shameless double-dealing?"

"Easily, my wench, easily. For that is what I would

have done in your case so that I was not subject to someone from outside lording it over me.''

She would not waste her time in useless denials. Instead, her eyes hard on him, she said merrily, ''And your advisers, husband, do they agree with you over this? I should like to know whether I am universally damned.''

''Wife, they do not yet know you as well as I. Your advisers—whom you have also tricked—were so patently honest that their explanations were believed. But I do not believe them, and I shall never believe in anything you tell me unless I have first checked and double-checked its truth.''

''And I, husband,'' Bess riposted, ''will do you the same honour—if so it may be called.''

The expression on her face was so mischievous as she came out with this that Drew began to laugh. Bess watched him a little before primming her face and saying soberly, ''I have told Gilbert to set out cooling drinks and a light collation for the two of us on the roof leads. From them you may see Charnwood and the hills beyond, almost, they say, to Northampton-shire on a fine day. I trust you approve of my orders. I thought that you might like to look over your lands and be alone with me for a little.''

''Excellent, wife, although I must remind you that we shall be alone together for a long time this night, and I shall not be admiring the view *from* Atherington, but that *inside* Atherington!''

Bess blushed! She could not help herself. For all her self-command she was but maiden yet. She felt the blush spread over her whole body so strongly that for a moment she felt, as she stood before him, that her clothes had all flown off, and she was as naked as Mother Eve before the Fall.

She turned away from him; away from his burning blue eyes which looked so passionately into her dark ones. Oh, he lusted after her—he had not been deceiving the poor wench that he had thought she was yester morning—but that did not mean that he *felt* anything for her.

Drew knew that he had stared her down, and for the first time had, if only for a little, mastered her. Exhilaration filled him. He took her hand, "You will lead me to the roof, wife, if you will, for I long to see your view."

Again Bess took his double meaning, but this time did not let it trouble her. "Through this door, then. Up a winding staircase, and so we gain the leads."

The stair was narrow, as well as winding, and dark. At one of the landings Drew took advantage of the dark and their nearness to turn her into his arms and do what he had been longing to do all day.

He kissed her, not simply on the lips but on the mauve hollow just above her tight bodice which betrayed where the cleft between her breasts began. To Bess's surprise this last kiss was more exciting than the one on her lips. Her whole body dissolved under it—as snow melts beneath the sun.

"You are my sun," she wanted to say, but that would mean that she had submitted to him, and she had long determined, even before she had met him again, that she would never do that.

Instead she mewed like a kitten, so that Drew, beginning to be fully roused, stepped away from her. "Not here," he said, his voice hoarse. "Later, later, we shall have all the time in the world."

Unsteadily, Bess resumed her climb, which was more difficult for her in her fine stiff clothing than in her usual informal dress which her aunt so deplored. Drew, in some discomfort as he followed her, willed his body to behave itself, only for it to turn mischievous again when they reached the top of the steps and walked into the full afternoon sun which streamed across the leads.

For the sun gilded his wife's face and body as, unknown to him, it gilded his, so that both held their breath a little in admiration as they turned to look at the other.

"Arcadia," exclaimed Drew, looking away from her to break her spell and admiring the view which lay before him. "Arcadia seen from the rooftop of a Midlands mansion."

"Indeed, a splendid sight," agreed Bess as they looked across fields, woods and hills into the pale blue distance. The only sign of the habitation of men was the sheep which dotted the distant fields as they turned around to look at the valleys of the north, the hilly land being all in the south.

"I must agree with you, wife," smiled Drew, but the view that he was now admiring was the one of Bess as she stood, arm outstretched, pointing into the distance. "But I think that I prefer the scenery nearer home."

And he took her into his arms.

"We are alone, wife. Let us dally a little."

Oh, but dallying with Drew was delightful, even if love was far away and lust very near. He was kissing and stroking her, and gently cursing the stiff bodice which denied him the glories of her breasts.

It was when he began to lift the heavy skirts of her

dress to caress her other treasures that Bess sprang away from him.

"No," she exclaimed breathlessly, her face flushed with arousal, her dark eyes seeming larger than ever. "The servants will be here shortly to serve us. They must not find us…" She stopped.

Bess saw that Drew was not in full command of himself. He put out a hand to pull her back to him, then he, too, stopped. He was breathing as fast as she was, so fast that he turned away from her to brace his hands on the parapet which ran round this part of the roof.

"I had thought that you meant us to be truly alone—so that we might be husband and wife," he ground out at last.

Seeing him thus, Bess thought to wreak a small revenge on him for his demeaning words about her on their wedding day. "What, husband? Can you possibly be so impatient to bed me as not to wait for the night when you have allowed ten long years to pass without seeing me, or writing to me a word unconnected with the business of Atherington?"

She saw him stiffen, saw his hands leave the parapet to curl themselves into fists before he unclenched them and turned to face her.

"I did not know…" he began.

"Know what?" asked Bess coolly. "That Arcadia, that golden rural paradise, and its nymphs awaited you here?" She would have been less than human, she thought later, if she did not try to hurt him a little as he had once hurt her. The memory of her wedding day still returned, if less frequently, to haunt her.

She saw him flinch, his pride wounded. Perhaps he had thought that he merely had to smile at her to win not only her acquiescence, but also her trust, if not her love. Was he accustomed to easy conquest? Bess thought that perhaps he was. However much he attracted her, and he did, she would not surrender her essential self to him until he gave some sign that he was offering her more than the opportunity to be pleasured—and then forgotten again.

Would he depart for another ten years if once he gave her a child? If so, she must guard herself so that when he left her again their parting would not break her heart.

"There is no Arcadia," he declared almost savagely. "It does not exist on earth save in the minds of men and women. They make their own heaven—as they make their own hell."

It was the very last thing which Bess expected him to say, and oddly enough, for all its savagery, it gave her hope. She began to answer him, to offer him perhaps, as the dove had offered Noah, an olive branch, but behold the servants were arriving, and they must be formal Lord and Lady Exford, taking their pleasure on the leads.

So the day wore on. They were never alone, which was the common fate, Bess was beginning to discover, of being a great one, a personage of power to whom servility was constantly offered. She had never lived her life so much in public before, for at Atherington there had been little need: her and her aunt's wants had been simple, and were simply served.

During their time on the roof she said as much to Drew. He smiled wryly before answering her. "Ceremony," he said, "laps the life of such as we. It is expected. It is what earns us the respect of those whom we govern since they are never offered it themselves. And the ceremony my companions offer to me is small compared with that offered to the Queen at court. Surely, though, wife, you have experienced this before our arrival.'' He waved a hand at those who surrounded them, adding, ''They exist but to please us.''

''It does not please me,'' Bess returned.

''No?'' His manner to her was courteous, but she saw that he was surprised. ''Very well then, wife. When we visit the stables I shall dismiss our train, and you alone will accompany me and introduce me to Tib—whom I thought your brother—and to the groom who also accompanied you yestermorn.''

Bess was suddenly fearful, made so by this seeming concession. ''You will not turn them away? After all, it was I who ordered them to accompany me so informally—as I am wont to do, seeing that we are peaceful here. No beggars or cutthroats populate our woods and fields.''

Drew made no answer to that, and later, when he had been as good as his word and sent his train away, he escorted her to the stables where, one by one, he was introduced to all who worked there, from the head groom down to the merest stable lad. He had a friendly word with each one, something which surprised Bess a little after his having said so firmly, ''They exist but to please us.''

To Roger he merely said, ''I trust you to guard my lady at all times, and in future you will ensure that she has a proper escort—unlike her habit in the past.'' Roger made no attempt to answer him, merely offering his new master in the present as surly an acquiescent nod as he had offered his former mistress in the past.

Tib was the last in the long line to bow to the new

lord. He and Roger had seen him arrive earlier in the day and to their dismay had recognised him as the young gallant whom they had assisted yestermorn! Of the two of them Tib was the more fearful of being turned away, since he had unwittingly aided his lady in the deception of her lord.

His lady he hardly recognised, so fine and fair was she. His silent worship of her turned into even greater adoration, but his knees knocked a little when the fine gentleman before him drawled, "I see that you are not so forward in your speech, lad, as you were yestermorn. Has the stable-yard cat got your tongue?" The cat of which he spoke was rubbing his black furry back and sides against Drew's fine silk stockinged legs, evidently liking the sensation.

"No, noble sir." And then, inspired by his native wit, for Tib, unlike many of Atherington's staff, was lettered, he stammered, "I am blinded by the sun of your presence, noble sir. Mine eyes are dazzled, and my tongue silenced."

Unknown to Bess and those among whom he now lived, he was the only son of a ruined country gentleman who had hanged himself, leaving Tib penniless, alone in the world, and needing to find any work, however humble, in order to survive.

Bess gave a stifled groan. Pray God that her husband did not regard Tib's pretty speech as insolence, and turn him away at once as he had earlier half-threatened. For a moment Drew was of a mind to do exactly that, but something odd about the lad stopped him.

"Look at me, fellow," he commanded curtly, for Tib, certain that he was about to be dismissed and waiting for the blow to fall, had dropped his head.

"Your speech is not that of a stable hand. What are you doing here? And what is your name? Besides Tib, that is."

"I am called Jack Theobald, but my fellows always call me Tib. Because my father, who was a gentleman, died leaving me without any money or a family to care for me, I needed to find work lest I starve. I have always liked horses, and so I came here to work with them." He dropped his head again.

"Hmm." Drew regarded him for a long moment. "You may remain as you are—for the present. I shall decide what to do with you later. Meantime, treat your mistress with the respect which she deserves, and all will be well with you."

Scarlet mantled Tib's face. He swallowed, and seemed about to say something, but Drew had already turned away, taken his wife by the arm, and was gently walking her back towards the house.

"You were kind to him, husband, for which I thank you." Bess was indeed grateful that Drew had not dismissed or punished Tib. In her limited experience, fine gentlemen were hard on those servants who might have seen them humbled, even though by chance. Drew made her no immediate answer. He frowned a little, and said, still curt, "The fellow intrigued me. He speaks well, not like a peasant—or had you not noticed?"

Bess said slowly, "I suppose I had. But so do some others whom I know to be of simple birth."

"Lettered, too, most like," continued Drew thoughtfully. "He's wasted in the stables—even though he says that he loves horses."

"Which I know to be true. He is very good with

them. And Roger and Simon, my chief groom, both
agree with me on that.''

"No matter. That is enough of him for now. Mind,
though, that you do not rove the countryside again,
alone with him.''

"I was not alone with him, husband, I had Roger
with me, remember?''

"You know what I mean, wife—and see to it.'' He
released her arm, and was distant with her again.
Goodness, thought Bess, what can be making him as
crabby as an apple tree in the autumn? Surely he
cannot be jealous of Tib?

But he was, for Drew did not care to think that a
personable lad, nearer to his wife's age than he was,
was wont to spend much time with her on familiar
terms. The sooner he bedded his lively wife, curbed
her roving ways, saw that she was decently dressed at
all times, and made a suitably obedient woman of her,
the better. She might then not wish to pretend to be
Atherington's lord rather than its lady.

He gave her a sidelong glance. She looked thoughtful, but not unhappy. It occurred to him that the best
way to break her in to her new life—he could find no
more gallant way of describing what he meant to do—
was to take her away from Atherington altogether, as
far away as possible from the officers and servants
who were only too willing to serve her.

And what better, then, than to begin to do Walsingham's business for him by arranging for them to
visit Buxton as soon as possible as part of a bridal
tour. By what had been said during the day, she had
never been more than a few miles from Atherington.
Thus he would kill two lively birds with one stone,
train his wife in the way she should go, and find Wal-

singham's spy for him! He would speak to her on the matter before others so that she might be less inclined to begin arguing with him.

"Go to Buxton to take the waters! But you have only just arrived here, husband! I shall have no time to show you your lands and tenants, or the new coalpits and the iron works nearby."

"I have not the lightest desire to visit coalpits," returned Drew testily to a wife who had, once again, disappointed him by her refusal to agree immediately to his wishes. "You may tell me about them, and that will be enough. One pit looks very like another—and the same goes for the ironworks. So long as they are well run, and bring in the money to keep the estate solvent, I would be quite content never to see them at all. No, I am determined on a visit to Buxton where you may mix a little with your peers. You have spent too much of your life alone with servants—and thinking about coalpits."

"Not alone surely, husband," retorted Bess, "You forget. I have always enjoyed aunt Hamilton's company—and she never thinks about coalpits, do you, Aunt?"

She waved a hand at her agitated aunt, who was scarcely able to conceal her distress at the sight of her unruly niece arguing once again with her husband. She said, her voice trembling, "Oh, I take your husband's meaning to be that you have not mixed with those whom you may have to meet when he takes you to London, my dear. Your husband is but considering your happiness, I am sure. As for coalpits, I assure you, Lord Exford, that I have never thought about them once—nor encouraged my niece to do so."

"That I can well believe." Drew was sardonic. "But I also believe that my wife does not need encouragement in her wilfulness. You may be certain, though, that I shall have my way in this.

"Charles," he ordered, turning towards his cousin, who could barely suppress a grin at the spectacle of Drew being, for once, unable to charm a woman into instant submission, "tell my household, as well as that of Atherington's, that all must be made ready for their lord and lady to leave for Buxton by a fortnight's end."

So, it was a *fait accompli,* was it? Her wishes were to count for nothing. Charles was already speeding on his way to carry out his master's orders. Her husband watched him go, a grim smile on his face, before he said to her, "It seems to me, wife, that to indulge yourself in Buxton's warm water might serve to soften your temper a little, and prevent me from losing mine."

It was something of an olive branch and, a little ungraciously, Bess accepted it. "Very well, husband. So long as my aunt may accompany me as my chief attendant."

"Assuredly, wife, for I am certain that her choice of conversation will exactly accord with mine, rather than with yours." A statement which proved that the olive branch had a few thorns attached to it.

Later alone, being prepared for bed, prepared for *him,* Bess was to ask herself with some bewilderment why she had been so resolutely opposed to visiting Buxton, for had she not frequently wished to do exactly that herself and had not done so because some problem at Atherington had always intervened? It was all *his* fault, of course, throwing orders at her and expecting her to jump eagerly to fulfil them every time he did so. Which had her contradicting him even when he was proposing something which she had always wanted to do!

And now, here she was, decked out like a boar's head being prepared for a feast, ready to be carried in on a platter for the lord to consume! Not an unlikely simile at all, for at aunt Hamilton's command her attendants had crowned her with a wreath of flowers, painted her face, plaited her hair, and dressed her in a nightgown so elaborate that she was sure that she could have gone to court in it. In short, they had done everything but stick an orange in her mouth and put *her* head on a platter.

It was only by brooding on this that Bess could prevent herself from worrying about what was going to happen in the Great Bedchamber when all this prinking and painting was over. First of all, of course, she would be led into the big anteroom at the end of the suite of rooms where Drew would be waiting for her. Were they dressing *him* as though he had no hands to help himself with? What would he be wearing? What would he think when he saw her dressed like this?

Well, she would know soon enough what it was to be Drew Exford's wife, for aunt Hamilton had handed her a posy of spring flowers and taken her by the hand to lead her through each room until they reached the anteroom.

And there he stood, so handsome that he made Bess feel quite faint. He was wearing a bedgown of such rich material that he glowed like the sun. Behind him stood his cousin Charles and his immediate entourage.

Behind them stood a crowd of folk who overflowed the anteroom, the landing, and the great staircase which led to it.

All come to see her and Drew bedded.

Did they expect to remain until Drew had, in Aunt Hamilton's words, "done his duty by her"? Years ago, they had done so, and ripped the sheet from the bed immediately afterwards to see whether or no the bride was virgin.

Surely Drew was too civilised for that? She would soon find out. With Charles on his right, and a handsome young page on his left, he advanced towards her, to take her hand so that she might stand beside him.

Charles and the page disappeared into the throng. And suddenly, from nowhere, Gilbert arrived, his white staff in his hand, to lead them to the bridal chamber. Hysteria threatened Bess. This was even more of a ceremony than when she had been married. But, of course, then she had been a child.

Hysteria had her muttering to her groom, "I wonder that you did not employ a minstrel with a lute to go before us."

Drew whispered back at her, "Had I known that you wished that, then I would have done so," thus neatly turning the tables on her mockery.

"Ahem, ahem," murmured Bess, her hand before her mouth, trying to stifle her laughter and, at the same time, look as grave as the ceremony demanded. Hand in hand they reached the bedchamber again, where the bedcovers had been thrown back, and steps had been put out for them to climb into the Great Bed's deep embrace. Which they did, and sat stiffly, side by side, as though they were already stone effigies on a tombstone while the company cheered them repeatedly and wished them a long life and many children.

At a signal from Gilbert, who was relishing all this unaccustomed ceremony, one by one, and in proper order, the humblest first and the greatest last, they all filed out...until she and Drew were finally alone...

For a moment neither of them moved or spoke. Bess was wondering what would come next and how soon Drew would turn to take her in his arms and do *that* to her. She knew perfectly well what *that* entailed, being a country girl who had lived among the animals and who had listened to the women servants laughing and tittering about the behaviour of the men with whom they worked.

What had always puzzled her was why any sensible young girl would wish to commit such an unlikely act so much that she risked being encumbered with an unwanted child and sent away from the protection which being on Atherington's staff gave them?

Whenever she had tried to broach the matter with her aunt Hamilton, her aunt had always told her firmly that such matters were not for young ladies of rank to discuss. "Wait until you are married, my dear," she had always replied, rolling her eyes to heaven to suggest to God that, once again, her niece was being a troublesome nuisance.

"But I am married, aunt, so that cock won't fight," Bess once retorted, meaning that her aunt's explanation was faulty.

"Really, Bess, from where do you get such dreadful language? I would forbid you the stables only I know that you would disobey me. What I mean is—when your husband arrives, he will instruct you in what it is to be a wife."

And that was always that. And tonight, presumably, Drew was going to instruct her. She had once asked Annis, who was a pretty girl and her personal maid, the question which her aunt had refused to answer. "Shall I like it?"

Annis's reply had been robust. "Oh, aye, though perhaps not the first time. That usually hurts." She had said no more, for her aunt had come in suddenly, and heard Annis's answer. Shortly afterwards Annis had been sent to help in the kitchens, and a rather plain maiden lady had been promoted to be her maid.

So Drew would not only instruct her, he was likely to hurt her. The only thing which puzzled her was that whenever, during the day, he had touched her, she had found herself strangely excited and wanted him to continue doing so. Coupled with that had been an overwhelming desire to tease and provoke him. Life was really very strange if it gave rise to such contrary desires.

It grew odder still, for when Drew did move it was to jump out of the bed, to cross the room, untie his bedgown's sash and tear off the gown, throwing it on to the great chest which stood at the bottom of the bed.

Bess wondered whether she ought to avert her eyes from him, never having seen a naked man before, but she had no need to worry, for beneath the bedgown he was wearing a long shirt of thin linen which nearly reached the ground. It had a deep collar, with lace edging, so that now he looked like an archangel in the painting above the altar in Atherington's small chapel. His fair hair curled in waves and ringlets about his perfect face.

"That's better," he exclaimed, and then he dived—

it was the only word—into the bed again, to land beside her, and throw off the bedcovers to reveal her over-elaborate night rail.

"Come," he said, laughing, "you are as encumbered as I was. We were both attired ready for a masque at court, and not for the nuptial bed. But do not despair, we shall shortly be Mother Eve and Father Adam together before the Fall. Look, I have bought a painted apple for you, seeing that there are none ready to eat at this time of year!"

He turned away from her, leaving Bess to wonder what he meant, whilst he lifted from the small cupboard standing beside the bed something thin and square, wrapped in a blue cloth.

"Charles put it here for me this afternoon," he told her, as he handed it to her. "Open it, wife, your second present from me, the first being my picture in small. Here is another, by the same limner, and it is a little masterpiece, I assure you."

Whatever Bess had expected from him, she had not expected this. She untied the ribbon which bound the packet, and opened the cloth covering it to reveal a tiny painting of Adam and Eve, quite naked. Eve was handing Adam a rosy apple, and a miniature serpent was leering at them from the tree around which it was entwined.

"Oh, it's beautiful," Bess exclaimed reverently. No one had ever given her a present before. Her pleasure was so naked and so genuine that it quite overwhelmed Drew. Her eyes had widened, her lips had parted, and her whole face glowed in the candlelight. Desire roared through him.

"The woman tempted Adam and so he fell," he whispered into Bess's ear, taking her chin into his hand as he did so. "Will you tempt me, wife, that I may fall?"

Bess, still holding the little picture, whispered back, "But the serpent hath not tempted me, husband, so how may I bring about your loss of Eden?"

"Let me be both serpent and Adam to you," he told her, tipping her face so that they were looking into one another's eyes, "since for men and women to love one another and to know carnal desire was worth the loss of Eden, for that was the price we had to pay for it."

At the touch of his hand Bess began to tremble so that Drew dropped it from her chin, took the little picture and returned it to the cupboard's top. Her trembling grew the more when he took her chin in his hand again, and kissed the parted lips beneath the wondering eyes. "Do not be frightened," he said. "I shall try not to hurt you."

Which, Drew thought, might be difficult, for he had rarely, if ever, bedded a true virgin, and he did not know whether he was going to be able to restrain himself, if restraint were needed.

"Wife," he began, at last, "the father and the mother of us all went naked to their nuptials—"

Only for Bess to interrupt him with a little laugh, as he began to loosen her gown from her shoulders. "Not so," she said. "They made themselves aprons— or so the Bible saith."

Drew threw back his golden head and laughed, as much to break the tension which was beginning to build up in him, as to express his mirth. "I see that you are learned as well as practical, wife. I also see that I shall have to be careful if I chop logic with you in future."

"Is that what we are doing now?" queried Bess slyly.

"Indeed, no. This is instruction in Cupid's arts which I am about to offer you. The arts of the little god of love himself. Allow me, madam, and help me a little, I pray you. I prefer to see my wife, not the arts of her sempstress."

So saying, Drew tugged at her nightgown, and shyly, Bess began to help him to undress her, her whole body aquiver with she knew not what. To have a man's hands stroke and caress her as he stripped her last piece of clothing from her was beginning to make her understand why so many of Atherington's maids had risked all in order to lie with their lovers. It was as though she had never lived before, never known that her body could begin to sing an age-old song under a lover's ministrations.

As once before she mewed like a kitten, expressing her pleasure so frankly and artlessly that Drew found himself trembling. He had meant to have her strip his nightshirt from him, but he found that he could not wait. He tugged it off himself, so that for the first time Bess saw the splendour of his naked torso, the blond whorls of hair on his strong chest, the muscles on his shoulders, back and arms which his elaborate clothing had hidden.

Her mewing turned into a strong cry as he took her in his arms, and began to stroke the length of her body. New to lovemaking, Bess lay passive whilst he pleasured her, his stroking and kissing growing ever more intimate, ever stronger, until she was writhing beneath him, her hands clutching at him until she clutched and stroked his rigid sex, so that he almost spilled himself into the bed, not into her.

The serpent himself, he thought afterwards, must have instructed her in what to do to bring a man low! "No," he whispered, his breath growing ever shorter, "not now. Not this time, another. Give yourself to me, wife, let me make you mine," and like the stallion, the stag and the other animals—both tame and wild— he made her his own.

And in the doing, as Annis had said might happen, he hurt her, even though he tried not to, tried to prepare her, to pace himself, but she was truly virgin and her body resisted him, so that she cried out.

But when he would have stopped, she clung to him the more, saying, "No, what Eve could endure, I can," until the age-old rhythm of love brought them both to climax.

# Chapter Six

So this was marriage, Bess thought drowsily as she awoke in the Great Bed, secure in her husband's arms. For the moment whether she loved him, or he loved her, scarcely seemed to matter. Simple comfort was everything.

They were naked still—like Father Adam and Mother Eve—and whether their remote ancestors had loved one another in the poets' sense of the word was immaterial. Half sitting up, watching Drew as he lay quiet and sleeping as peacefully as a baby, she remembered how kind he had been on the previous night when, after their ecstasy was over, he had discovered that—as Annis had hinted—she had been hurt.

"Nay, wife!" he had exclaimed at the sight of her blood on his hands and on her body. "I had not meant to be cruel to the virgin that you were—and to have hurt you so grievously was never my intent."

Bess had smiled up at him. "Oh, I am proud to show you that I *was* virgin, and the hurt was only for a short space, and was preceded and followed by such pleasure…" She stopped, and turned her head away, not liking to confess how great her pleasure had been, and how surprising.

Drew had found such charming modesty pleasing— it was so new to him. "Nevertheless," he had told her firmly, "we must stanch your wound at once, and I must wait until you are healed before I pleasure you again." He had sprung out of bed immediately, and Bess noticed once again how purposeful he was, how athletic in all his movement, how superb his naked body was.

"There are nightgowns and linen cloths in the big chest opposite to the bed," she told him. "We can make a bandage for me from one of them."

"Not we," he said, "I must also help to bind up the wounded soldier in Cupid's wars." He was astonished to discover how unhappy he was at having hurt her, particularly when she lay there looking at him with such soft eyes. She seemed very different from the argumentative puss with whom he had wrangled the day before.

He brought a large piece of linen over to the bed and began it to tear it into strips, one of which he gave to her, jumping back into bed to watch her at her work.

"And in the morning we shall ask for some healing salve from the physician whom I have brought with me," he added when Bess had finished, smiling a little at the slow blush which spread over her face and body as he spoke.

"Come, my lady wife," he said, kissing her, "do not be ashamed. The whole world should know that the lord's lady came to him pure and whole—no need for shame there, but pride instead. And if we are blessed with a babe after this night's work then I shall know that it is truly mine—which is more than many men can claim of their children!''

He had, Bess remembered, sinking back on to her pillow again, said no word of love. But what matter of that? He had given her of himself, and taken something from her, and if between them they had, indeed, made a child, then what more could she ask from him?

''A boy, husband? You wish me to give you a boy?''

Drew paused a moment. What answer would please her the most? This was a new thought for him, and a new action, too, for though he had always been kind to his bed-partners, that kindness had been impersonal, not deeply felt.

So when at last he spoke it was slowly and carefully, with no hint of the cavalier manner which he had used to her so far.

''For my first,'' he told her, ''either boy or girl will do, but after that, I would wish an heir.''

He had his reward. Bess gave him a brilliant smile. She had feared that he would demand a boy from her—something which she could not influence, since only God knew whether a boy or a girl was created by the act of love, and poor human beings had no choice in the matter.

Thinking thus, she went to sleep again, to wake to find that her husband had gone, and that the bed was strangely empty without him. What had woken her was the arrival of her aunt Hamilton and a bevy of her ladies and ladies' maids. The maids were carrying basins and cans of hot water, soap and silk towels. Two footmen followed them carrying a large wooden tub for the hot water.

''Good morrow to you, niece,'' exclaimed aunt

Hamilton. "Your husband said that he thought that you would be prepared to greet the new day."

Bess sat up while aunt Hamilton came over to her and threw the bedcovers back, to reveal the blood-stained sheet. She helped Bess officiously down the steps, and out of the bed as though she were an invalid, before ordering the leading maid to strip the bed of the sheet and hold it up to the assembled company.

"Behold your lady's virtue," she cried.

Bess had an insane desire to laugh, something not shared by all her staff who gazed at her reverently. Since everyone in the room must have been well aware how chaste her life had been since birth, their reaction seemed a little extreme to her. They surely could not have been surprised.

After that, the footmen having filled the bath and retired, she was washed and dressed and her hair was formally arranged. Finally she was led out of the room and down the stairs, the leading maid still carrying the stained sheet.

Bess would have liked to break her fast in the kitchens, something which she had frequently done in the past, but which she was dismally sure she would never be permitted to do again. And where was her husband? And why had he left her alone?

She was soon to find out.

He was waiting for her at the bottom of the Great Staircase, Gilbert in attendance, as usual; his white staff in his hand. The only surprising thing about the last ten hours or so was that Gilbert had not been present when her husband had finally pleasured her in order to announce his success to all the world!

This thought set Bess smiling: a sight which pleased her husband. Drew was finding that his visit to Leicestershire and the act of making his wife his own was vastly different from his forebodings before he had set out. Then he had been expecting to find a plain young woman who, when he came to bed her, he would have been unable to pleasure, because without desire for her he would have been unable to perform his husbandly duties.

That would have been the polite way of putting it! For Drew, like his friend, Philip Sidney, was fastidious and, unlike many men, they both needed a woman to attract them before they could pleasure her.

Instead, he had found a woman who was not only beautiful, but possessed an attraction for him so powerful that he wondered at himself and his strong reaction to her.

And from wanting at first to show her who was master he had discovered, once he was in bed with her, that it was her pleasure, not his, which was important.

"Welcome, wife," he said, taking her hand. "We are to eat in the small parlour. I told your Steward that I thought that you might wish to be private with me this morning, so he has arranged that we should eat only with our two Comptrollers—and your good aunt, of course, and leave the others to the Great Parlour. We may then discuss our setting out for Derbyshire, and a little of our future lives together."

Bess's smile grew. She had not wanted to be surrounded by the stares of the curious who would watch her to guess how she had survived the night when she had ceased to be a maiden.

Breaking her fast with him, listening to him talk to Charles and to Walter Hampden, she was beginning to forget a little the long years of hurt after his dismissal of her on their wedding day as his monkey bride. Whether he loved her or no, he was plainly reconciled to having her for his wife, and by the manner of his speech he was prepared to take her not only to Buxton, but to London.

"You must send orders to London, Charles," he was saying, "causing Exford House to be made ready for a mistress, as well as a master. My wife will wish to live in a home, not a barracks fit only for the use of men. You will understand, Lady Exford," he told her, "that both my father and myself have lived there for long years without a woman's soft touch. All that must change in future. Perhaps, like Bess Shrewsbury, you will wish to oversee the ordering of the house yourself."

He looked around the small and gracious room in which they were taking their ease. "Yes, I am sure you will, seeing that Atherington is all a home should be. Full of warmth and comfort."

"Such," said Walter Hampden, "is owing to your lady, my good lord. She has always insisted on the comfort of others, besides herself, being considered."

"Then from now on she must consider mine," said Drew, offering Bess his most dazzling smile, "as I must consider hers."

Oh, it was all so different from what Bess had feared, especially after her first unfortunate meeting with him. She had seldom in her short life felt so mindlessly happy as she did on this bright summer morning. Pompey, couched by the door, must have sensed her pleasure, for he came running to her to push his wet nose into her hand, and to receive a titbit from her plate. And when Drew bent to stroke him, traitor that he was, Pompey again transferred his affection to him immediately.

"So, you continue to charm my dog as well as me," whispered Bess to her husband. "Will you leave me aught of my own?"

Drew raised his pewter tankard of good Leicester-shire ale. "Husband and wife are one in the eyes of God and the law, but I trust that I shall not be an overbearing husband."

Well, that was for her to find out in the future, was Bess's wry inward response. Aunt Hamilton had once said that the true test of a husband was not in the early days of marriage, but later, when custom and usage had begun to take their toll. Then a husband must become a friend as well as a lover—as poor Sir Braith-waite had been to her aunt before his accident had made him less than a man, and no kind of a companion.

Perhaps it might be a good thing for them to repair to Buxton, there to learn one another's ways in surroundings which would be new to both of them. Meantime, there was the present—particularly the nights, when Drew shouted himself a kind and inventive lover, and Bess roved the wide seas of passion in his company. At dusk all cats are grey, the proverb said, and in the dusk of the bedroom what mattered was not her and Drew's looks but the meeting of their minds as well as their bodies.

Bess was beginning to discover that passion had many dimensions, and in one of them she found that she had recovered the shock of delight which she had felt on that long-ago day when she had first seen her husband, before he had seen her, and said the unsay-able.

And yet, always, even in her nightly joy and her daily happiness in his company, there still lurked at the back of Bess's mind a shadow, a dim memory of those unhappy words of his which could never be unsaid. She had once read that at Roman feasts and celebrations, the participants were always reminded by an acolyte whispering warning words into their ear, that life had its pains as well as its pleasures. Nothing was to be taken for granted: the present was to be enjoyed, and the future…would happen when it happened.

A strange thing was happening to Drew—something he had not foreseen. Beforehand, he had always thought his time at Atherington would be a boring rural interlude, something to struggle through before he went on to the real business of his life at Buxton, but, as time went on, everything changed. He fell easily into the natural rhythms of country life. Atherington, he discovered, was always busy—though not after the fashion of the Court or the Town.

He rode out into the countryside with Bess, even visiting the coalpits of which she had spoken so proudly and, despite what he had said earlier, he displayed an intelligent and informed interest in them.

And daily he jousted with Bess after a fashion that was quite different from his previous dealings with women. She was, by turns, exasperating, infuriating, and argumentative. She refused to pander to his every whim, and proved herself to be both brave and clever. And everything she did was informed with the greatest good humour and such smiling impudence that she attracted him so much that whenever he was with her, even in the day, he could scarce keeps his hands off her.

At night she had become his lusty and inventive lover so that with her he reached heights of passion such as he had never known before.

"They called your grandam 'The Spanish Lady', wife," he gasped at her once, as they lay entwined, their hair and their bodies moist with the force of their mutual passion. "By what name shall I call you?"

"Call me no lady at all," she replied sweetly. "I am simply Drew Exford's wife!"

At which he took her in his arms again…

The two weeks to be spent at Atherington became three, and it was Drew who put off their departure, excusing his delay by claiming that letters of business had come from London and needed to be attended to properly and not in haste: Buxton could wait.

"Must we go at all?" Bess asked him in the dark watches of the night. "We are so happy here."

Drew sighed. His duty called him, if only feebly. He knew that he ought to arrive at Buxton before the Queen of Scots did, and he was risking that by his delay in leaving.

He turned and kissed her. "I have promised you a holiday from care, wife, and a holiday you shall have."

Bess sat up. "Care? What care? For the last two weeks I have had no care at all."

"Nevertheless, wife, you deserve to be waited on, to be truly idle. We must be away at the end of this sennight."

Were it not for his mission he would have given way to her pleadings, for in these early days of marriage Drew had found his Arcadia and did not wish to lose it by engaging in the sordid intrigue to which he was committed. Nevertheless…as he himself had said…nevertheless…

He made a sudden decision. His roving and adventurous days were over, the days when nobody and nothing depended on him. This enterprise would be the last of its kind.

To Bess he simply said, "Grant me this wish, wife, that we have our bridal tour together in the fair Peak District of which I have heard so much." For the first time he felt himself a cur because he could not tell her the true reason for their visit to Buxton.

And then, at last, all was made ready. The long train of coaches, carts, wagons and horsemen set off for Buxton so that m'lord and his lady might take the waters in the company of their peers. Atherington, which Bess had never left, was left behind, and the future which she half-welcomed, half-feared, lay before her.

"Where do you think we are, Aunt? I thought that my lord said that we should not stop for another hour, and here we are, not ten minutes agone, and at rest again."

Aunt Hamilton, seated in the coach with Bess, and one of her ladies, shook her head. "I'm sure I don't know, child. I have not been so far this way before. I think that we have passed the Derbyshire borders, but have not yet reached the hills amongst which, I believe, Buxton lies."

Impatient, and eager to be on their way, Bess put her head out of the crude unglazed window in the coach's door. The coach itself was little more than a simple enclosed box mounted on a farm cart's frame, unsprung, and consequently very uncomfortable. Since the day was fine Drew, together with most of the men, was on horseback, and she put her head through the window to try to find him.

The road, now that they had left the main road north, was nothing more than a rough track between fields, and they had reached a sharp turn in it. A stand of trees sheltered it so that Bess could not see the track beyond it. Nor could she see Drew and Charles, or the outriders who preceded them to clear the way for the most noble the Lord and Lady Exford. She could, however, hear neighing horses, raised voices, and shouting, but could not distinguish anything which might reveal what all the commotion was about.

Bess opened the coach door and, ignoring aunt Hamilton's wailings, she began to walk along the track, picking her way through the horsemen who were patiently waiting for their orders to start off again. Tib, who had become Charles's page—the one whom he had brought with him from London having broken his leg before they left Atherington—was holding his master's horse. He saluted her with a raised hand, and a short, "Mistress," before turning his head away.

"What is it, Tib? Why have we stopped?"

Tib had been told by both Drew and Charles that Bess was out of bounds to him, and that his future with Atherington lay in remembering his own low station and Bess's high one. Accordingly, instead of answering her, he shook his head and shrugged indifferently.

So be it, thought Bess sadly, watching the easy days of her youth disappearing with her former happy relationship with him. She was truly Lady Exford now, and she would not make trouble for him, so she walked on until she reached the trees. And there, beyond the bend, was the reason for the sudden end to their rapid progress towards Buxton.

Half across the muddy track—for it had rained on the preceding day—a coach and a large covered wagon had, by some accident, come together. The coach, being smaller and of unsteady balance, had fared the worst, and was lying on its side on the track, blocking the way. The wagon was tilted askew against a tree.

Richly dressed men and women were sitting and standing in the shade of the trees. Charles and Drew, a little way away, were talking to a large middle-aged man in clothing as splendid as theirs. One motley crew of attendants from both parties was engaged in trying to right the coach, another was pulling the wagon free, and a third was trying to control the frightened horses which had been pulling them.

Except that one horse lay still on the ground—its right foreleg was twisted beneath its body, obviously broken; the other foreleg was twitching. It was, Bess suspected, the one which she had heard neighing its anguish, although it had fallen silent now. A page was standing miserably by it, and failed to see her until she dropped on her knees by its head. She put out her hand to stroke it, even as the page exclaimed, "No, mistress. Do not put yourself in danger."

To Bess it was suddenly as though an illuminated picture in a book which she had been reading had come to life. She had been outside the scene, but was now part of it. Drew, his attention drawn by the page's shrill shout, swung his head around to see that his wife had appeared, and, as was common with her, was about to make herself useful in a situation which was fraught with danger.

He strode over to lift her by the shoulders and drag her away from the horse. "No, wife," he ordered, his voice commanding, "this is no place for you. If you wish to be of use, there are women here who would benefit from your sympathy. Although they are not injured, they were thrown down when the coach and the wagon collided, and are badly shaken. Fortunate it was that we were right behind them and may help them. They, too, are on their way to take the waters at Buxton."

"But the poor horse is hurt," Bess began, trying to look back. Drew caught her again, and made her look forward.

"It is no concern of yours, madam, and will be taken care of. Come, these are friends of mine from London, Sir Henry Gascoyne and the Lady Arbell, his wife, who is most distressed, having sprained her wrist." So saying, he urged Bess gently along until they reached the shade of the largest tree where a splendidly dressed young woman was seated. She was leaning against its massive trunk, her eyes closed.

It gave Bess the strangest pang to discover that the Lady Arbell was the most beautiful woman she had ever seen, and that when she opened her lovely blue eyes it was to shine them on Drew, and speak to him, ignoring Bess on his arm, and his attempts to introduce her as his wife.

"Oh, Drew, dearest Drew, 'tis better than medicine to find you here in this savage wilderness." She pressed a large lace handkerchief to her eyes to hide them for a moment, before withdrawing it to stare at Bess, looking her up and down as though she were a servant she was about to hire—or dismiss.

"Your wife, you say, Drew? How odd. I thought

you unmarried.'' She took in Bess's practical brown travelling dress with a contemptuous glance. ''Well, well, madam, I see that *you* are well equipped to survive in the wilderness.''

Then, petulantly, ''Will someone not silence that stupid animal? I vow that it was he who caused this dreadful accident by his refusal to respond to the whip,'' for the injured horse had begun to complain again.

But not for long, since he was cut short in full cry by the crack of a horse pistol giving him the *coup de grâce*. At which the Lady Arbell gave a delicate shudder, and offered him a graceless epitaph by exclaiming, ''Thank God for that. I thought no one would ever silence the wretched creature. Why did it take you so long, Drew—and Henry—'' for her husband had come up to them ''—to dispose of it?''

She gave a great sigh and covered her face with her kerchief again. If, Bess thought, her wrist was damaged, it was but a slight hurt, seeing the extravagant play she was making with both her hands.

And it was Bess's turn to stare—at the Lady Arbell. She knew now why Drew had wanted her away from the horse, and that her commonsense should have warned her of what its fate must be. But it had been so beautiful lying there, and to think of one of God's own creatures coming to such a sad end, whilst its mistress wailed selfishly of her own minor discomforts, enraged her.

'''Tis a good thing we humans are not so harshly treated as horses, madam, when we are wounded,'' Bess told her bluntly, ''else a damaged wrist such as you sport might have your husband pistoling *you* down on the spot...''

"Wife! For shame," exclaimed Drew savagely, as the Lady Arbell, giving a great cry, fell back against the tree trunk, her kerchief pressed to her eyes again.

"This is not fitting," he told her. "You forget yourself, particularly since I have offered a seat in your coach to the Lady Arbell on her journey to Buxton, seeing that her own is beyond immediate repair. Pray ask her forgiveness at once."

He had grasped her right wrist in a grip of steel. The eyes which met hers were as darkly blue and sharp as a Damascene blade. He meant to be obeyed.

Bess wanted, oh, *so* desperately, to disobey him. Her anger at the languishing looks with which the lady had favoured—and was still favouring—her husband, whilst her own husband, whom she was ignoring, stood fatuously by, was overwhelming her. Commonsense prevailed. To defy him in public, over such a matter, would be foolish, even though her every sense revolted at having to apologise to the heartless trollop before her.

"Forgive me, madam, if I said aught to wound you. But it grieved me to see such a splendid creature destroyed, and in my grief, I forgot myself."

There, it was out. The Lady Arbell waved her kerchief at Bess again. "Oh, very well. I take you to be country bred, unschooled in the niceties of civilised life, and therefore must be forgiven. You must instruct your little wife, Drew, before you subject her to the scrutiny of the town, lest she bring mockery upon herself. And now pray lead me to the comfortable seat which you have promised me."

Detaching Drew from Bess, she took his arm, leaving her husband and Bess watching them as Drew escorted her away until the bend in the road hid them from sight.

The expression on Sir Henry Gascoyne's broad and pleasant face was so rueful that Bess took pity on him, saying robustly, "Why, sir, your wife and my husband were so distressed by her injury that they forgot to introduce us. Has my lord arranged a place for you in our cavalcade—or were you riding, as he is?"

"Riding? Why, yes, my lady. It was fortunate that I was ahead of the accident. The driver of our coach has broken his arm, and your husband has kindly lent us his physician, and promised the coachman a place in one of your carts, our remaining ones now being overfull."

Well, at least Drew hadn't been so determined to make eyes at the Lady Arbell that he had forgotten to do his duty by her servants, was Bess's somewhat acid internal reaction to that. But it was his wife, not Drew, who would have to pay for his kindness by enduring the spiteful tongue of the lady all the way to Buxton.

She would try to persuade him to allow her to make one of the party which was travelling there on horseback!

Alas! It seemed that Drew was determined that she was to entertain the Lady Arbell all the way to Buxton, so that the pleasure which Bess had been taking in her first excursion into the wide world outside Atherington was quite dimmed. Lady Arbell's first demand had been that Bess and aunt Hamilton's attendant ladies should be banished from the coach so that she might take up the whole of the seat on one side of it. Aunt Hamilton and Bess, she graciously conceded, might have the other seat between them.

Bess had had no opportunity to defy her, for Drew had told her in no uncertain terms that the Lady Arbell, being injured, must have all her wishes met. She thus, seething inside, was compelled to obey the Lady's slightest whim.

"For," the Lady told Bess as majestically as though she were the Queen herself, "I am not used to being cramped after such a fashion as to sit hugger-mugger with my inferiors. I wonder that you were happy to share your seat with your attendant lady—but, then, of course, I am forgetting that you are country bred and not accustomed to the finer manners of the town. Your good husband permitting, I shall be happy to instruct you—beginning with the task of reforming the manner in which you are dressed."

So saying, she patted her own heavily brocaded and farthingaled gown, with its tight and low-cut bodice, below a cartwheel ruff of giant proportions which was held up with whalebobe stiffeners. All of which left, Bess admitted, little room in the small coach for anyone else but a dwarf to sit comfortably by her. The Lady Arbell was apparently ignoring the fact that the skirts of her gown, and her fine shoes, had become lavishly smeared with mud from the track. She had also lost the high heel from her right shoe whilst tottering through the muddy turf to the Exfords' coach. Drew had therefore carried her the last part of the way.

He had looked uncommonly happy whilst he was doing so, Bess had noted, although the lady, being fashionably plump, must have been a heavy armful!

"The roads and byways between Atherington and Buxton are muddy and sometimes impassable so that one occasionally needs to get out and walk whilst the coach and wagons are pushed uphill," Bess said. "I therefore thought it best to wear the simplest clothes and the stoutest shoes I possess. Indeed, I have a pair of boots ready under the seat lest I have occasion to walk through a watersplash!''

''Dear child,'' said the Lady patronisingly, ''do not dwell so heavily on your country breeding. A true lady is known by her appearance, and so must dress accordingly. As for the mud—'' and she lifted her skirts disdainfully ''—why, I have a covey of attendant ladies, washerwomen and sempstresses to care for my clothes—so I do not trouble myself over any mishap which may befall them. You speak of watersplashes— why, the footmen will carry me through them, if necessary. No, no, I see that you must be properly schooled and I will do my old friend Drew the favour of taking you on.''

She preened a little as she finished, and then, before Bess could so much as open her mouth, either to thank her or to refuse her supposedly kind offer, she added, ''No, do not thank me. I could not allow Drew's lady to bring on him the laughter of the mob.''

Thank her! For what? For her infernal rudeness, and her unkindness to aunt Hamilton, to whom she had not addressed a single word, and to their two attendant ladies whom she had turned out to be squeezed among the occupants of the following cart when there was still plenty of room for them in the coach?

As for her injury, Bess did not believe a word of it. She was using it as an excuse to get her own way, something which she had doubtless been doing all her life. The sooner they arrived in Buxton, the better, when she could go her own way and cease to taunt Bess and make eyes at her husband—which she did every time Drew rode up to the coach and spoke to them through the opening in the coach door.

"You appear comfortable, ladies," he remarked approvingly. "It will not be long before we shall stop to eat at midday. In the meantime, continue to amuse yourselves. My wife will be pleased to have a new companion to talk to."

Bess gave him a watery smile whilst inwardly thinking, No, I'm not. For she does not allow me to speak and all she wishes to do is to patronise me.

From what Drew was saying, he appeared to think that they were having a splendid time together whilst the Lady Arbell prattled on about how she intended to transform his wife into a simpering copy of her own stupid self.

Around noon, as he had promised, they stopped. The footmen helped them out of the coach and led them off the track into a woodland dell where the servants had set up trestle tables and covered them with food and drink. They were far from any inn or hostelry, Drew had told them, and would entertain themselves. In the evening they would sup at Tutbury where they hoped to stay overnight.

A carpet had been spread on the ground and cushions were placed on it on which the ladies sat, whilst the men arranged themselves on fallen tree trunks, benches lifted from the wagons, or on their cloaks spread on the ground.

Through the trees the wooded hills of Derbyshire were mauve against a pale blue sky. Bess declined ale and drank water, fetched for her from a nearby spring. The Lady Arbell kept up a litany of charming complaint at the same time as she spoke movingly of eating in Arcadia. Mrs Facing-Both-Ways was Bess's sour verdict on her.

The servants brought to them pewter plates laden with pieces of chicken pie, slices of cold spiced beef with its attendant mustard, and thick trenchers of buttered bread to be eaten later with wedges of red Leicestershire cheese made in Atherington's dairy. Afterwards apple tart was handed around—to all of which Lady Arbell took exception as being not sufficiently refined for her delicate palate.

Drew, seated by her, opposite to Bess who was eating heartily of everything, said quietly, "Riding in the coach, madam, does not create the appetite which being ahorse in the open does."

Lady Arbell shuddered. "Oh, I would not wish to journey far on horseback—even if it made me able to eat such coarse stuff as this." She waved a fair white hand at her neglected plate which lay on the grass beside her.

"I am," Bess announced eagerly, through a mouthful of Dame Margery's good bread, "most willing to take horse and ride with you, husband, thereby seeing more of the fair Derbyshire countryside as well as making myself ready for the next good meal we shall eat at Tutbury."

Drew looked across at her happy smiling face. His wife was as different in appearance from the Lady Arbell as she could possibly be. Her hair had come down a little and the black velvet cap, which was supposed to cover it, had fallen to one side. Her serviceable brown skirt with its modest, highly laced bodice, was also askew, showing the white linen petticoat underneath it. He was surprised to discover that his wife's innocent disarray pleased him more than the Lady Arbell's careful finery.

This overset him a little, for he had long been one of Arbell's admirer's and had her husband not been his father's friend he would have made her his mistress. She had more than once hinted that she would not be averse to having him for a lover. He also found that his wife's hearty appetite both amused and pleased him—but he could not allow her to snub the Lady.

He shook his head at her. "Nay, wife. It seems to me that your appetite needs little encouragement, and I doubt whether your short excursions around Atherington have fitted you for a hard ride through difficult country. No, no, continue your pleasant gossip, and later, when we reach Buxton, allow me to arrange for some easier outings for you."

Bess tried not to look as unhappy as she felt. Her spirits rose a little when, later, Drew took the opportunity to walk her to the coach, leaving the Lady Arbell to her husband's care.

"You do understand," he told her, "that politeness alone means that I cannot permit you to ride with us. It is your duty to entertain our guest, for that is what she is."

"She seems to think that it is her duty to educate me, rather than mine to entertain her," Bess grumbled at him. "But I will do as you say. Do all fine ladies from the court resemble her? If so, I do not wish to be a fine lady!"

"She is very delicate, very much the young wife of an older man," admitted Drew. "She was the daughter of the last Earl of Frensham—hence she keeps the name of the Lady Arbell, being of a higher rank than a mere knight, rather than being called Lady Gascoyne. She was married to him against her will. More, she was of the Catholic faith and he is not, but her Protestant guardians insisted that she renounce her religion in order to marry him—that was the condition of her inheritance. You should feel pity for her.''

''She is so busy pitying *me* for my uncouth country manners,'' retorted Bess sturdily, ''that she would resent me if I tried to pity *her*.''

''Nevertheless,'' said Drew, handing her in to sit by aunt Hamilton, ''you will remember what my wishes are, I hope.''

He gave her such a winning smile that Bess's heart melted within her. She could forgive him anything if only he would look at her like that more often. Unfortunately the Lady Arbell had drawn level with them and saw the smile.

''What, still wooing your wife, Drew?'' she mocked at them. ''I thought that it was not the fashion these days for husband and wife to care for one another, once married. It is not like you to be other than in the van! You will be writing sonnets to her next, instead of to your mistress.''

His mistress? Did he have a mistress? Had he left her behind in London? Or did the Lady mean that now that he was married he ought to acquire one? Preferably herself, no doubt! Unless, of course, she was already his mistress.

Sir Henry closed his eyes in a pained fashion, but made no effort to reprove his wife. He opened them again, and said gently, ''Remember how young Drew's wife is, my dear, and that he has but lately met her again. She needs your encouragement—which I am sure you will offer her.''

Bess could not resist temptation, and said, mischief in her eyes if not in her face. "Oh, Sir Henry, you may rest assured that your wife is doing all that you might wish her to do. She has been offering me encouragement and advice ever since she became my companion on the journey!"

Sir Henry took this at face value and offered her a relieved smile, but Bess saw at once that she had not deceived Drew. He shook his head reprovingly at her behind Sir Henry's back, took him by the arm and walked him away before Bess could say anything more.

She had not deceived the Lady, either. "I see that you have a shrewd, if rural, wit, madam," she hissed at Bess, as she settled her elaborate skirts around her. "You may have cozened your husband and mine, but I know very well what you are at. Do not think that you may trick me at will."

Before Bess could speak, aunt Hamilton, who had sat silent ever since they had been compelled to share the coach with their unwanted guest, exclaimed indignantly, "My niece does not deserve your strictures, my lady. She has been the soul of politeness ever since we first offered you succour. You mock at her country manners, but I prefer them to the insolence of the town."

"No doubt," sneered the Lady, "since you share them yourself! If you are both so determined to carry the smell of the pig sty around with you, then I will leave you to your unfortunate preference, and say no more." She turned her head away from them, closed her eyes, and to Bess's great relief spoke no more until they reached Tutbury in the early evening.

## Chapter Seven

"With so many great ones visiting it, and so much spoken and written of it, I had not expected to find Buxton so small," was Bess's first remark to Drew when they rode into the village. Earlier that day he had relented a little, had given way to her pleas, and had allowed her to leave the coach so that she might ride into Buxton beside him.

Two nights ago whilst eating their supper at Tutbury before retiring to spend a blissful night in bed which went far, in Bess's estimation, towards making up for the disappointments of her day, Drew had told her of the book which a friend had lent him and which was full of the delights of the place—Buckstone, as he called it. It had been written by a physician, one Dr Jones. Drew did not tell her that Sir Francis Walsingham had passed it on to him so that he might know what to expect when he arrived there on his secret mission.

"Which is why I have brought a pair of musicians with us," Drew said, drinking his soup, "for the good doctor urged those who used the baths only to do so after they had spent several happy days listening to music. Music, he said, chases away melancholy.''

He cocked an enquiring and naughty eyebrow at her before adding, ''Can you think of another activity which might chase away melancholy, madam? And shall we engage in it when the meal is over? I vow I cannot wait until we have drunk Buxton water!''

Bess gave him a merry glance. One thing which she had not expected before his arrival was that she would enjoy Drew's lovemaking so much and join in it so heartily.

''And having read the book, and learned how popular Buxton has become amongst the nobility and gentry, I took the precaution of writing to the Earl of Shrewsbury to warn him that we should be arriving this week, and would require lodgings in his Great Hall. I had no mind to pleasure my wife in the barren wastes lost amongst the cold Derbyshire hills.''

So here they were, riding along a rough track by the River Wye into a large dale surrounded by the hills of the Peak. The hills were of a height such as Bess had never seen before. And in this dale was Buxton, a village so small that Atherington village seemed large beside it. It did not, Bess was to find, even possess a church.

What it did possess was George Shrewsbury's Great Hall of which Drew had told her. Four square, built of stone and four storeys high, it stood beside the spring which they had come to visit. Nearby were the Baths, and at the sight of them Bess shivered involuntarily. Even though it was summer, the Derbyshire wind was keen, and the Baths were open to the sky although one of them had a gallery around it, with seats and hearths in it, to warm the bathers and air their clothing when they had finished splashing in the waters.

Of course, the Lady Arbell, alighting from the coach which Bess had spurned that morning, allowing aunt Hamilton's elderly attendant to have a more comfortable seat than that in the cart to which the Lady Arbell had consigned her, immediately set up another litany of complaint. She shuddered theatrically, and no wonder, Bess thought, for she was wearing a low-cut bodice which revealed most of her bosom, exclaiming, "Is this what we have ridden so far—and in such discomfort—to see? We had been better advised to have remained at home.

"Husband," she called to Sir Henry who had just descended from his horse, "have we not mistook our destination? This surely cannot be the sacred well and the divine water of which we have heard so much!"

"Now, now, my dear," soothed her husband, slipping the cloak from his own shoulders to drape it around his wife's. "You will feel better when we are indoors before a warm fire."

He had evidently been reading Dr Jones's treatise, too, because he added, "We are recommended to take our ease for several days before we drink of the water. The air of Derbyshire is keener than that which we are used to, and we must grow accustomed to it."

Arbell allowed herself to be led indoors, leaving Bess, who was wearing a man's warm leather jacket over her sensible brown stuff dress, to dismount from her horse, and follow her in. Drew moved forward to take her hand. "You are not too discommoded by the cold, wife?"

"A little, but not so much as the Lady Arbell. Her

courtier-like clothing is no match for the winds which blow here.''

"No, indeed. I am pleased to see that you are dressed for any weather, wife."

Chatting together in such easy friendship enabled Bess to forget the annoying Lady Arbell and the worrying suspicion that Drew had been closer to her than he ought to have been. Hand in hand they entered George Shrewsbury's fine new building, to be welcomed by Thomas Greves who ran the Hall for the Earl. It contained, he told them, thirty rooms where the nobility and gentry might lodge, "As well," he added, "as those merchants and yeomen whom m'lord allows to stay here at reduced prices as an act of charity to those less fortunate than himself and his peers."

"Large though these rooms are," Bess whispered to Drew when they were at last left alone together in them, "they will not accommodate all of our people."

"Charles has arranged for half of them to lodge at the local inns," Drew told her. "Cease to trouble yourself, Lady Exford, about our arrangements. You are here to enjoy yourself, and forget the labour of running Atherington. You must be ready to break your fast, for Greves says that he is about to serve a midday meal in the Great Hall where all the lodgers eat together daily."

So she would have to endure the Lady Arbell at mealtimes, would she? No matter. She would enjoy herself, as Drew bade her, and be at last a lady of leisure—something which so far she had never experienced. Perhaps, if she were lucky, she would be far removed from Sir Henry and his wife at table.

Her luck held. She and Drew found themselves among a clutch of Derbyshire and Leicestershire squire's who were flattered to be thus seated among the great. The food was excellent. Timothy Blagg, who owned land not far from Atherington, advised her cheerfully, "Try this excellent ale, m'lady. The Earl of Shrewsbury has it sent here especially from Chatsworth, as well as the splendid cheese which graces our table today. Yesterday we ate fowls and rabbits which m'lord's servants had delivered in quantity for us. We are as well fed as any in England."

Drew smiled a little at this, but later acknowledged that Buxton fare was well worth the eating, and that the Earl had provided splendidly for his guests. "Not that he loses by it," he concluded shrewdly, "seeing that we pay him handsomely for his pains."

"Master Blagg said that they are expecting the Queen of Scots to arrive here any day now," offered Bess. "And since, like her, he is Catholic, he is longing to see her—although he drank to our present Queen right heartily at the end of the meal."

Unknowingly, Bess destroyed a little of the pleasure which Drew was beginning to find in her company and in this visit to a county whose rough beauties he had often heard spoken of, but had never seen. She had reminded him of his duty and of the promise which he had made to Walsingham, and for a moment the bright day grew a little dark for him. He could wish that all that he had to do was to pay attention to his wife's pleasure and his own.

His one hope was that the Queen of Scot's visit might be a little delayed so as to give him more time to woo his wife. In the meantime he would not only enjoy himself but would listen carefully to what his companions at the table were saying. They might be indiscreet in his presence since they knew him only as an idle courtier, not as one of the intimates of those who ruled England for the Queen.

"And Master Blagg says that it would not be wise for us to visit the Baths *after* we have eaten," Bess went on eagerly. "On the contrary, we must always do so *before* we eat—preferably in the morning."

"And again in the evening before supper," Drew continued for her, smiling at his wife's enthusiasm for everything she did, so different from the Lady Arbell's bored haughtiness, "and after that we shall be put to bed with bladders of hot water to make us sweat. I suspect that Master Blagg has also been reading the good Doctor's book!" He paused a little before whispering naughtily in her ear, "I think that we know a better way than that to make us sweat, eh, wife?"

Bess sparked back at him immediately. "You are a rogue, sir, to speak of such matters here…"

"But you agree with me, do you not?" Drew said wickedly. "For, after all, are we not husband and wife, and does not the wedding ceremony say that marriage is for the procreation of children, and how shall we procreate unless we enjoy ourselves in the marriage bed?"

There was no answer to that which Bess could usefully make, other than a feeble assent. "I suppose that if Buxton water improves both our bodies and our souls then the act of procreation may become more effective."

"Well said, wife, and I will remind you of that this evening, never fear—even if we have not yet qualified for the bladders of hot water by dipping into the cold Bath water!"

Which he duly did, and that night the moon streamed through the windows of Lord Shrewbury's noble hall on a husband and wife sleeping the sleep of the well and truly satisfied. Drew's worries over spying for Walsingham, and Bess's jealousy of the Lady Arbell, and any other lady who trained her arts on Drew, were alike forgotten…

"I had not thought that Buxton water would be quite so cold," Bess gasped several days later, as swathed in towels, she sat on a bench in the roofed colonnade surrounding the Bath, not far from one of the great hearths and its flaming fire.

"Rather you than me, m'lady," muttered Jess, her tirewoman, as she vigorously rubbed her mistress down. "I don't much like bathing—even when the water's warm. I wonder how m'lord is enjoying himself. They say that in wicked Italy men and women bathe together, but such rude manners have not reached here yet, praise be to God."

Bess was not quite sure whether she agreed with her woman. She rather thought that she might have liked to watch Drew swimming in all his naked glory—although she was also sure that she didn't really wish to see Sir Henry Gascoyne or some of the fatter squires unclothed. Drew had told her that on his visit to Italy with Philip Sidney they had both learned to swim in the warm Mediterranean.

"And a very pleasant pastime it is, too. When I take you to my home I shall have the pleasure of swimming with you in the river which runs at the bottom of the Park. We shall be like the gods of old, madam, sporting in Arcadia."

Take her to his home! Did that mean that he did not intend to leave her at Atherington, but would make her his true wife in every sense by keeping her by his side? Every one of Bess's newly awakened senses quivered at the very thought.

She had laughed her pleasure at Drew's enthusiasm, and told him, "Alas, husband, I need no teacher, for my father taught me when I was a child. But I shall join you with pleasure."

"There, m'lady. You are dry and your clothes are warmed. Do you wish me to dress you now?"

"Oh, yes, at once." Bess's eagerness was created by the appearance of the Lady Arbell and one of her hangers-on, Marian, the young wife of Master Blagg. Marian was monstrously pleased by the Lady's patronage, she never having met anyone half so grand before. Arbell, indeed, was singularly gracious to her, in contrast to the half-mocking manner in which she always spoke to Bess.

"Greetings, madam," she carolled in Bess's direction. "I see that you have taken to the water before us. A pity, we could have pretended that we were the Three Graces, or the three goddesses who appeared before Paris."

This parade of classical learning was obviously designed to put both Arbell's hearers down. Determined not to let Arbell patronise her, Bess asked, as Jess laced her into her overbodice, "And, pray, whom ought we to nominate as Paris? And where shall we find a golden apple?"

It occurred to her that apples had played a large part in her conversation lately and, pondering why this should be so, she almost missed Arbell's sulky, "Ah, I see you have read the classics, Lady Exford. Now, as to Paris, looking around our gentleman the choice must lie between dear Marian's husband—and your own. I wonder to which lady either of them might choose to give the apple?''

It had become plain to Bess that, by her slightly bewildered expression, Marian knew nothing of ''The Story of Paris of Troy and the Three Goddesses''. This belief was confirmed when, plucking up her courage, she asked hesitantly, ''And for what reason, pray, dear Lady Arbell, should my husband—or Lady Exford's— imitate Paris, whoever he was, by giving an apple to anyone?''

Before Arbell could answer Bess said rapidly, ''Why, Paris, the Trojan prince, was given a golden apple and told to hand it to whichever of the three Greek goddesses, Athene, Hera or Aphrodite, he thought the most beautiful. He chose Aphrodite, the goddess of love, and was rewarded with the beautiful Helen. But he also earned the undying hatred of the other two goddesses which, in the end, caused the Trojan War and the fall of Troy, and his own death.

''My advice to your husband—or mine—would be that he should take his golden apple to the nearest goldsmith and exchange it for some good English money. Thus we should all end up happy—and Buxton will not fall!''

The look with which the Lady Arbell rewarded Bess for this sublime piece of nonsense would have killed a man at ten paces! She had hoped that the obsequious Marian would have said that of the three of them the Lady Arbell must surely be the one to be rewarded with the apple. Instead, she was laughing at Bess's deflation of Arbell's mock heroics.

''Oh, I'm sure I should not like to bring about any such terrible thing,'' she exclaimed. ''You agree, m'lady Arbell?'' she added, unaware of that Lady's anger.

''How can I disagree? I see that your husband awaits you, Lady Exford.'' Arbell could not wait to be rid of Bess so that she might regain Marian Blagg's innocent worship, which had, for a moment, been transferred to the woman whom she regarded as her rival. ''Does *he* admire your pedantry, Lady Exford? I had not thought him to be attracted by female learning.''

''Oh, I think that he prefers it to female ignorance,'' was Bess's careless answer. ''Pray hand me my straw hat, Jess. The sun is strong today.''

''You have the air of the cat who has stolen the cream about you, wife,'' remarked Drew thoughtfully when Bess joined him, all rosy and refreshed from her bath and her sparring with the Lady Arbell. He had not seen the Lady and her companion, but he was beginning to learn his wife's ways—and read her looks.

''Have I, husband? Why, as to that, the sun pleases me, you please me, and my late companions have afforded me pleasure, the Lady Arbell most of all.''

Drew thought it wise not to pursue the matter further, but was much entertained over the next few days by the spectacle of the Lady Arbell trying to put Bess down, and being constantly foiled by her quick wits. More than ever he wished that it had not taken him so long to become reacquainted with the pearl who was his wife.

Unaware of the undercurrents around her, and that below the surface of her pleasant life there lurked those who would destroy it, as the pike lurks to feed on the lesser fish in the rivers and streams beside which she daily walked, Bess continued to take her innocent pleasure. It was not diminished on the day that the Queen of Scots's party rode into Buxton to be received as nobly as a once-reigning monarch ought to be.

Those lodging at Shrewsbury's Great House were waiting in its Hall to receive her and to pay her their respects. Prisoner she might be, but she was also the Queen Elizabeth's cousin, and her heir—which was the motive, Drew knew, for the plots against Elizabeth and on her behalf.

"She is not as beautiful as I expected her to be," Bess whispered to Drew. "But she has a right royal presence, has she not?"

"She is no longer young," Drew whispered back to her, "being nigh on forty years old. I had not expected to find her so tall." He had never seen her before, and although he had heard much of her beauty and her charm, no one had told him that she was as tall as he was, being all of six feet in height.

And here she was, being introduced to them—or rather they were being introduced to her by a servile Greves—as m'lord the Earl of Exford and his lady wife. They were now face to face with her, and could see every detail of her fading beauty and her unfading charm.

"Oh, but I have heard of you, my lord of Exford," she exclaimed in her pretty strangely accented voice in which French and Scottish inflections fought for dominance. "You are a friend of Sir Henry Sidney's son, Philip, are you not, and play at tennis with him?"

Now this was a surprise, and not a welcome one for Drew. He had thought himself almost anonymous, and he wondered who had made the effort to inform the

Queen of his friendships. And what else had they told her of him? Was there someone who knew what no one ought to know—that Drew Exford was more than a simple friend of those in Sir Francis Walsingham's circle?

No matter. He bowed and smiled, saying, "You do me great honour, your Grace, to remember such idle details of my life." The Queen made him no answer but, serene and cool, sailed by him in majesty to smile in her turn at Bess, and say, her eyes kind, but shrewd, "And a good day to you, Lady Exford. I had not heard that you were married, my lord," she said, turning her head towards him again.

"Long ago," he replied easily, "as children often are, but only recently have we claimed each other, now that the time for settling the future of the line has come."

"Ah, so that is why you are here, and not gracing my cousin's court."

"Indeed, your Grace. To take the waters—and secure the line." Drew hoped that he was not overdoing things, but no one appeared to see anything extraordinary in what was being said. Bess, however, who had spoken briefly to the Queen, praising the beauties of Buxton and the Peak, remarked to him afterwards, "Now, what was all that about, husband? How should she know of you—and tennis with Philip Sidney? You had not told me of that."

"Most remiss of me," smiled Drew, who was thinking up something innocuous to say to his wife, who was far too shrewd for her own good. "It is to be supposed that she was informed of who was lodging in Buxton and that one of her train knew of myself and Philip and took the trouble to mention it to her so that she might have something to say when she met us.''

Why did she not believe him? Bess only knew that, in the short time in which she and Drew had been husband and wife, she had come to learn the false notes in his voice; notes, she was coming to find, none other than she could hear. He was troubled, no doubt of it, by what the Queen had said, and why should that be?

A wise wife ought to say no more, and being a wise wife—for once—she fell silent. But, having been Bess Turville who had run Atherington by virtue of letting little pass her by, she put the matter at the back of her mind, not to be forgotten, but to be brought out again if a future occasion warranted it…

At the time, though, she listened carefully to what the Queen was saying to Sir Henry and the Lady Arbell who were standing beside them, but could detect no false notes there. The Lady Arbell was as overblown as usual in all that she said and did, and Sir Henry was as apologetic. The Queen spoke only briefly to them, passing swiftly on to young Timothy Blagg, whose day, nay, his year, was made by the Queen's graciousness and the length of time she spent with him.

So long was she with the squires that the Lady Arbell hissed her annoyance first at her husband and then at Bess. ''She behaves as though she were already our Queen, which, pray God, she may never be. Nor is she as beautiful as I was led to expect. Indeed, she is not beautiful at all!''

She preened herself as she spoke. And while Bess agreed with her, for she had heard much of the Queen of Scots's loveliness, and had not stopped to think that years of disappointment and imprisonment must have left their cruel marks on her, she also thought it tasteless of the Lady Arbell to make such a severe judgement on one so unfortunate.

And so she said to Drew later, when they were preparing to eat with the Queen and her companions. Drew hesitated a moment before answering her. At last, "She has brought most of her misfortunes on herself," he said slowly. "She made a most unwise marriage to young Henry Darnley, involved herself in his murder, and then married a brutal adventurer, the Earl of Bothwell. Everything which she touched turned to lead, and when that happens one must ask whether a person is unfortunate or has brought it upon themselves by their own misjudgement."

This, from Drew, was harsh. So far he had said little on matters of state, and when he had done so had spoken idly, as though little concerned. He must have read Bess's expression for he added, wryly for him, "Come, wife, we are here to take the waters and enjoy ourselves. I have ordered Tib to tell the musicians to attend us this afternoon when we visit the Baths. The day is fair, the sun is shining, and it may shine on us, as well as the Queen of Scots."

Something she had heard earlier struck Bess as he finished speaking. Something he had said. "You told me that the Lady Arbell had once been Catholic."

Drew stared at her, his eyebrows raised. "Aye, wife, so I did. But what of it?"

"That being so, husband, I am a little, nay, more than a little, surprised to find her so hot against the Queen of Scots, and so much for our own Queen."

"Hot against Queen Mary, was she, wife?" Drew was thoughtful. "That may not be as surprising as you think. Recent converts are always the noisiest for their new faith, I have found.''

''Oh,'' Bess was thoughtful in her turn. ''You are wiser in the ways of the wide world than I am. I had thought that perhaps she was jealous of the Queen's reputation for beauty—except that she denied that the Queen was beautiful.''

''Mayhap so. Let us forget them both. We have our own pleasures to follow—as they have theirs.'' He offered Bess his arm and they walked together down the main staircase and into the great room where yet another splendid meal had been prepared for them, and this time, the Earl of Shrewbury himself was there to eat it with them.

But despite what he had said to Bess, Drew did not dismiss what she had told him about the Lady Arbell from his mind. Warily he asked himself whether someone who wished to plot against England's Queen might not, as a blind, pretend to be hot for her, and hot against the person whom they really wished to serve.

Certainly the Lady Arbell would bear watching, and also the young Catholic squire Timothy Blagg, who could scarce eat his meal he was so busy staring worshipfully at the Queen. Bess, suddenly aware that Drew for some reason was distrait, saw that his eyes were on Arbell—and her heart sank.

Sat matters so? After only a few short weeks with his newfound wife, was her husband ready to dally again with the Lady? It seemed so. Her temper was not improved when, after the meal, the Earl of Shrewsbury approached her and asked her whether she was satisfied with her lodgings.

''Indeed, m'lord, most satisfied,'' she told him,

turning to Drew for confirmation. But he was no longer at her elbow—in fact, was not visible at all. Charles had taken his place and it was to him that she appealed for support instead. It was not, sadly, the first time that it occurred to her that since they had come to Buxton her husband's cousin and Comptroller was more assiduous in his attendance on her than Drew was.

Bess pushed the thought away. It was disloyal. She chattered animatedly to Lord Shrewsbury, who found that Lady Exford was a far more attractive young woman than report had said. Most attractive, but he would not tell his redoubtable wife so.

"And you are comfortable at Buxton, my lady? You find the waters agreeable?"

"When the weather is warm, yes." A reply which had him laughing before he released her to pay further attention to his prisoner, the Queen of Scots, who was seated in a corner of the room holding court, a bevy of young men and women about her. He had, he acknowledged to himself, a heavy burden to carry in making sure that she did not use these few weeks of relative freedom to instigate plots and treachery against his mistress, Queen Elizabeth of England.

Bess looked about her. Drew was not one of the party about the Queen, although Sir Henry Gascoyne was—but the Lady Arbell was not with him. She decided to go in search of him.

She walked through the double doors at the far end of the room. They opened on to a corridor which ran the length of the house. Tall windows, each with its enclosed seat, were set into its length, offering a view of Buxton and its surrounding hills. And there, in one of them, sat the Lady Arbell with Drew Exford by her side, his hand on hers. They were talking intimately, heads together.

What a cosy pair they made! A pity to disturb them was Bess's acid—and dismayed—thought. It was one thing to suspect her husband of marital treachery, quite another to find him at it.

She advanced on them, making no effort to keep her footsteps muted on the highly polished wooden floor. No matter! They were so engrossed in each other that they did not hear her coming. And when they did they sprang apart to face her, each of them smiling at her as though she were the dearest creature they knew.

"My dear," Drew said, rising to greet her. "The Lady has been giving me messages from my London friends. Master Sidney, she tells me, has not yet left for Wilton. The Queen, alas, is still not best pleased with him, and he intends to fly from her shade where once he lived in her full sun."

"I wonder," replied Bess, "that any of you can bring yourselves to leave her neighbourhood! And you, Lady Arbell? Is it her shade you fear, or her sun you enjoy?"

"Oh, her sun," smiled the Lady. "But, as I was telling your husband, my physician has recommended me to take the waters to restore my health, which too long a stay in London always impairs. My husband being so much older than I am, he requires an annual visit to a spa, and this year he decided to try what Buxton has to offer."

She turned her great eyes on Drew—needlessly—since he was already busily engaged in drinking in her manifold charms, and added, "To find old friends here is one of the delights of the place. It quite makes up for the grim hills which surround us."

Somehow her hand strayed on to Drew's silken thigh and patted it absently. She gave a great start, appeared to recall that she was in the presence of his wife, and removed it, saying, "Pray forgive me, I quite forgot that we are not at court and must adhere to country manners."

Yes, I might as well be a milkmaid, fumed Bess, from the manner in which she speaks to me, and Drew has apparently nothing better to do than behave as though she has bewitched him! Aloud she said, as sweetly as she could, for she would not let the Lady score any points off her by appearing openly jealous. "I thought, husband, that you were of a mind to make an early visit to the Baths—"

Before she could continue further, Drew said, also smiling at her, "Oh, my dear, the Lady Arbell has asked us to accompany Sir Henry, herself, and Master Blagg to St Ann's Well where we may drink the holy water. Tomorrow we may then all repair to the Baths."

"But the weather might change," protested Bess.

"Very unlikely, we are told," put in Arbell. "The old man who advises us on it hath said that it will be passing warm for the next week. Besides, the Queen of Scots will be going, and it would, Sir Henry says, only be civil for us to accompany her on her first outing. After that we may please ourselves."

So it was settled. Instead of a pleasant and quiet excursion to the Baths for the two of them, Bess found that they were to form part of a crowd attendant on the newly arrived Queen.

"It is always the same," Charles told her as he escorted her to where Drew—and the Lady and her husband—were waiting for them, since Bess had decided that she wished to change into stout shoes for the walk. "Whenever the Queen of Scots visits Buxton she becomes the centre of attraction. Even Lord Burghley, and the Earl of Leicester when they came here, danced attendance on her. So where the great and powerful of our world are content to lead, we must follow."

Bess could not tell him that her quarrel was not with the Queen, but with Arbell and her husband. It would sound too petty.

"You are not happy, wife," Drew whispered to her as they walked to the well together. Sir Henry had recovered his wife, and she had bade an unwilling farewell to Drew. "What ails you?"

"Nothing," lied Bess. "Except that I thought that we were going to visit the Baths privately this afternoon, not form part of the Queen's cortège."

"Oh, we must do our duty," returned Drew, who was well aware that it was his dalliance with the Lady which had disturbed his wife. But he had his other duty to do; that which consisted of trying to discover whether or no Arbell's visit to Buxton was wholly innocent. He wished that he might enlighten Bess as to what he was doing, but he was too old a hand to want to say anything to anyone about his mission. Even to his wife.

*Particularly* to his wife. He wanted to protect her, not put her at risk.

Bess was still complaining gently to him about their ruined afternoon. "I wonder that, being good Protestants, we are all so eager to visit a Holy Well which the late Thomas Cromwell ordered to be closed because it was an incitement to Papistry. I can understand the Queen of Scots wishing to go there, but for the rest…" She allowed her voice to die away.

Drew, well aware of the true reason for Bess's unhappiness, replied gently, "But the Well has been reopened and our present Queen puts no obstacles in the way of those who seek to find a cure by drinking of its sacred water. You may see the abandoned crutches of the lame who were healed hanging beside it."

He gave her a sly sideways look, adding, "And those who have difficulty in conceiving a child also come here to ask the Saint's blessing—as do the newly married who wish to bear their husband a child without delay."

"Oh, in that case," replied Bess, "I suppose I must drink of the water myself," and she returned his sly look with interest so that, forgetting himself, the Lady Arbell and all etiquette, Drew could not resist leaning towards her and kissing her on the corner of her mouth.

"Do not fret, sweeting," he told her. "There will be other days for us to sport in the water."

By now the whole party had reached the Well, and their lackeys were handing them small pewter cups to drink from. A group of villagers stood at a distance watching the great ones who had favoured these remote hills with their dazzling presence. The lads of the village ran forward to hold the horses of yet more visitors, come from Chatsworth, where they had been the guests of Lord Shrewsbury overnight before travelling on to Buxton.

Drew, on examining them with the benefit of his good long sight, exclaimed delightedly, "No, it cannot be! I vow and declare there is my good friend Philip Sidney."

He took Bess by the hand and walked her over to where a tall man with a high-nosed face, pale blonde hair and a delicate colour had just dismounted from his horse and was handing the reins to his groom.

"Philip! What fair wind blew you here? I had thought you long gone to Wilton and that if you were taking the waters, you were taking them at Bath."

Philip Sidney seemed to be as pleased at seeing Drew as Drew was at seeing him. "Good friend, my uncle Leicester recently rebuked me for never having visited Buxton. He swears that the waters are superior to those at Bath, so I thought that I would follow his example and discover whether he has the right of it. Had I known that you were here I should have speeded up my visit even further. As usual, you have forgot your manners and have not introduced me to your good lady. She *is* your good lady, I trust?"

This last came out in a serio-comic manner with much raising of fine eyebrows. Drew took the question in good part. "Of course. We have come on from Atherington to take the cure together. May I introduce my dear wife, Bess Exford, to my oldest friend, Philip Sidney? He invariably beats me at tennis, the dog, but I have been refining my skills in the bowling alley where I soon hope to gain my long-delayed revenge."

Philip was offering Bess his most courtier-like bow, all waving arms, bent right leg and down-hung head— much as though she were the Queen. "Ah, yet another Bess," he rallied her. "And are you as imperious as our divine majesty, or do you practise God's mercy on such poor mortals as myself?"

No doubt about it, he rivalled Drew in charm, but there was something melancholy about him. Now, whatever else he was, Drew was never melancholy. He possessed an effervescence of spirit which was never overwrought, always under control, and which served to inspire those he was with to believe that they, too, shared his ability to meet life head on and challenge it to do its worst, knowing that they would do their best.

He was effervescing now, but gently. "You have arrived just in time, my dear Pythias, to drink the water with her Grace of Scotland. A moment later would have been too late. Tib," he called to that young man who was offering him yet another cup of holy water, "pray give of Derbyshire's nectar to Master Sidney here, that we may convince him that Arcadia and its joys are not confined to the Southern counties, but may also be found in the Midland Shires."

Philip grimaced as he took the pewter cup which Tib held out and raised it high. "A toast to you, my Lady Exford," he offered. "I have drunk enough spa water in my journeyings to know that it seldom tastes like nectar! As for Derbyshire being Arcadia—well, as uncle Leicester says of most things, 'We shall see what we shall see.'"

He drank the water down with a flourish, saying as he finished, "Not so bad, nor so well, either, if I may be allowed to pun, my dear Damon. And if we are using our Greek nicknames, then pray tell me under what divine pseudonym your fair wife passes."

"Oh, he has not yet so baptised me," replied Bess, who had been staring in wonderment at the pair of them. "You call yourself Damon and Pythias, I suppose, because you are firm friends, as they were. But seeing that I am tall and brown-eyed and far from fair, being brown instead, I cannot be a goddess, but an alien sprite named—" and she hesitated "—Cleopatra."

Philip Sidney gave a great shout of laughter, all

melancholy fled. "So, she does not need you, my Damon, for she can speak for herself, your lady. And she is learned in the classics, and subtle too. For, in the same breath she names herself plain and yet awards herself the name of the beautiful Egyptian temptress who conquered both the great Julius Caesar and Marc Antony."

He dropped on to one knee, took Bess's hand and kissed it. "I salute you, Cleopatra, and one day you must show me your barge."

Bess laughed down at him, enjoying the jest. But suddenly she heard Drew give a short indrawn breath, and looked at him to discover, as Philip was doing, that the expression on her husband's face was not totally one of pleasure at his friend's jesting. For a fleeting moment jealousy rode there—and then was gone.

Bess's first response was one of a strange delight. For Drew to be jealous, even of his old and greatest friend, could only mean that he felt for her more than the tepid passion of mere friendship between man and woman. But she did not want her existence to mar what had obviously meant so much to him before he had met her.

She withdrew her hand from Philip's, saying, "Oh, I promise to tempt no one—except my husband, of course."

The awkward moment was gone. All three of them were laughing, and were presently joined by new friends, and old ones, who demanded to know what the jest was but were fobbed off by Drew announcing that it was one of Philip's learned ones which needed so much explanation that the jest disappeared in its unravelling.

"Then," drawled the Lady Arbell, no fool she,

"why was it amusing you so greatly? If the jest had disappeared?"

"Oh," smiled Philip Sidney, "the fact that the jest needed explanation was the jest itself!"

The laughter this provoked ended their private conversation and talk became general. Most of the company had drunk of the well water and were beginning to make their way back to the Great Hall. Bess found herself one of a group of wives whose husbands were making much of their new companions. Philip had already told them that he was taking lodgings at the Hall.

He took advantage of a break in the gaiety to slip an arm through Drew's and say, as though still jesting with him, "Remind me to pass on immediately a letter which I have for you in my saddlebags. It is from Walsingham; once he knew that I was making for Buxton, he was urgent that I deliver it to you as soon as possible. Which I will do. I had not known that you were so friendly with the old Fox."

"Oh, matters of business," responded Drew airily. He had no intention of telling Philip the truth of his relationship with Walsingham, the less people knew of it the better.

Besides, he was protecting Philip as much as himself by keeping mum. Which was all a great nuisance, for now he had two hostages to fortune instead of only one.

# Chapter Eight

Walsingham's letter was written in a double tongue—but was to the point.

"Know, dear friend," he wrote, "that my good wishes go with you and your lady to Buckstone. I have, unlike my lords of Burghley and Leicester, never visited there, but I am told that the waters are powerful and conducive to good health. That you should remain in command of yours is the wish of your old mentor and adviser. I fear that there is something in Buckstone's air which might bring on your melancholy.

"Know that all that glisters is not gold, and that there are many who affect a military stance who have never seen a battlefield. Know, too, that women make even better plotters than men, since to make up for their lack of bodily strength they frequently emulate the duplicity of Master Reynard the Fox himself.

"Know also that I have news of the greatest lady of all whom you have never pursued, but may be doing so by now. She is pursued by many for their own advantage—and for hers. My Lord of Leicester was hot for her once, but his common sense prevailed in the end and he fled the field. Others are neither so wise nor so expedient, and rumour hath it that more than one of the young squires at Buckstone may have drunk from tainted wells rather than the pure springs blessed by Saint Ann.

"This being so, take urgent care of your own health, and that of your good lady—to whom I hope that you are now reconciled. Do not yet stray from the straight path of marital virtue is the advice of your mentor. As with men, so with women, all that glisters is not gold. For your assistance I am despatching you a messenger, who will prove his allegiance to me by showing you the token of which we spoke in London.

"I send this by the hand of Master Philip Sidney, whose interest in Buckstone is confined to his friendship with you and his desire to compare its waters with those of Bath. Fail not to write me a loving letter in return. News from you always delights my old heart."

"Does it, indeed?" was Drew's sardonic comment, made aloud. He had waited until he was alone before opening the old Fox's missive, which he was now trying to decode. Someone pretending to be a soldier had arrived, or was going to arrive at Buxton and was, perhaps, involved in plotting for the Scots Queen, who was, he supposed, the lady whom he had never pursued but was pursuing now. He was to watch this man and his friends.

As for the squires—Drew could wish that his master in London had been more explicit, but he guessed that until the supposed military gentleman made contact with his target, or targets, he was not in possession of their names. He wondered who Walsingham's messenger might be: he doubted that he was already acquainted with him.

It was only when he was refolding the letter that he

saw that there was a hasty *postscriptum* scrawled on the back. "*Nota bene,* young friend, that every camp has its traitor…"

Now what did he mean by that? Drew puzzled. Was he saying that one of Drew's own entourage was to be suspected? And if so, if he knew his name, then why not give it to him, straightway, to act upon? Or was this simply one of the rumours that his other agents had picked up and passed on, which he thought that Drew ought to know of?

Reynard the Fox, indeed! Who should know better about foxes than the master of them all, sitting in his lair in London. He was waiting and hoping that Drew would discover who the conspirators were so that all their correspondence might be intercepted, read and passed on until the moment when, full details of the plot being known they, the hunters, became the hunted and Reynard would make the kill, instead of being killed himself.

Tickled by this fancy, Drew called for Charles, who was working on his books in the next room. He had been to the Well, but had left early. Drew had decided to begin his work for Walsingham without further shilly-shallying.

"Have you met any military gents in Buxton, Charles?" he asked. "I have a mind to talk tactics again. I have been re-reading Vegetius on the ""Art of War", and trying to reconcile what he says with my journeyings as a seafaring adventurer."

Charles looked up from his work. "Strange that you should ask that, Drew. A military man was in Philip Sidney's party, Captain Ralph Goreham by name. I spoke to him at the Well. He had drunk water at Spa, he said, and compared Buxton unfavourably with it."

"'True, there is no comparison," remarked Drew absently, "Spa being a bustling civilised centre, not a small village lost among hills. But Buxton has its own attractions, for all that. I suppose that Goreham practised his trade in Europe."

"In the Habsburg Empire, he said. Against the Turks."

"Ah, yes, the Turks. Odd how each country has its own favourite enemies. Now we scarce know how to choose between the Spanish and the French, but for the Habsburgs the Turks take the prize every time."

Charles thought that these comments were quintessential Drew. He had an imaginative turn of phrase and thought, rarely met. It was sometimes difficult to remember that he was more than a mere lightweight courtier, but was someone who had lived the rough life of a sailor aboard a man-of-war. His easy charm meant that one tended to underrate him.

Before Charles could answer his cousin, Bess entered. She had changed out of the sturdy clothing she had worn to visit the Well and, though she by no means rivalled the Lady Arbell in splendour, she was more like one's expectations of Lady Exford than usual.

Her bodice was tight-laced and thrust her breasts upward. Between them rested a black pearl on a silver chain. Her ruff was more of a cartwheel than it usually was, and her brocaded skirts were fuller. Her tiring woman had dressed her lustrous black hair high and had adorned it with another silver chain from which yet another black pearl depended onto her forehead.

She was even painted a little, although her creamy complexion, Drew considered, did not require paint—nor her cherry-red lips.

Forgetting Charles, Drew moved over to take her by the hand and kiss her on the cheek. "I shall," he murmured into her ear, "ask Philip to give me some much-needed lessons in the art of writing poetry so that I may hymn the praise of brown eyes and black hair, since all the poets I know of sing the praises only of blue orbs and blonde tresses!"

Bess raised the peacock-feathered fan which depended from her waist by yet another silver chain, to look at him over it. "You flatter me, sir. I know full well that I do not possess that blonde magnificence which men commonly call beauty—but if I please you, then I am content."

"Oh, you do more than please me," Drew muttered, and would have continued only Charles gave a loud "ahem'—which brought him down to earth again.

He moved away from the temptation which his wife presented to him, and recalled, a little wryly, the anger which he had felt when he had seen his friend admiring her. That he could not even allow Philip Sidney to jest with her so frankly had surprised Drew. Philip had called her beautiful, but her attraction depended on more than that. A better word for her would be charming, and charming in the deepest sense of the word, for there was a witchcraft about a woman whose looks were so unlike those which the world admired, yet who could draw the soul out of a man's eyes simply by looking at him.

Drew blinked at this unexpected revelation. And, of course, it was why the Lady Arbell paled beside her, which explained the Lady's antagonism to Bess. For she knew instinctively what Drew had just discovered by an act of reason. That her arts were exactly that, arts and artificial, whereas Bess's behaviour was artless, and therefore its effect was all the more powerful. Hence her constant scornful railing at what she was pleased to call Bess's "country ways".

He surfaced to discover that Bess had picked up one of the papers relating to Atherington on which Charles had been working, and was questioning him about it. Which reminded Drew that he ought to be questioning Charles. It was a moment's work to join his wife in inspecting the ledger which Charles was now holding out to her.

"You have absolute trust in your officers, madam wife?" he asked.

Bess nodded. "Most of my staff have worked for Atherington since before I was born, and I am sure that their loyalty is not in doubt."

Drew gave a careless laugh. "Well spoken, wife. Can you say as much, Charles? Is Exford's household equally exemplary in its loyalty?"

He was thinking of Walsingham's postscriptum as he spoke. Charles answered him equally lightly. "I wonder that you need to ask! Your officers also are notable for the long years during which they have served you."

It was an answer which Drew had expected, yet it disturbed him. If Walsingham were right, then someone around him owed allegiance to a faith and a cause to which the Earls of Exford had not subscribed since well before the present Queen had come to the throne. Like his predecessors, Drew valued the stability which the Protestant succession under Elizabeth had brought to England. And some one of his friends and servants was glistering like false gold—and he had no idea who it might be.

No point in questioning Charles further, however

lightly, for his wife's shrewd eye was on him, and he marvelled again at how easily she read him when he was being false.

Part of her witchcraft, no doubt.

No, he must not even think that. For a woman to be suspected to be a witch was always dangerous, and he must not put her at risk—even in his thoughts. And besides, was he not reading her? And what did that make him?

A double knock sounded on the door behind him. It was Philip Sidney come to ask them to walk to supper with him. Charles closed his ledger at Drew's command and all talk of business matters ceased. Like Drew and Bess, Philip was all magnificence. His huge cartwheel ruff was only held in place by wires, and its pale glory showed his fine-boned face to the fullest advantage.

Oddly, Bess thought, as the two friends stood side by side, Drew's Apollo-like good looks were enhanced, not degraded, by Philip's austerity. They were fire and ice, sun and moon, two sides of a valuable coin. For the second time that day she surprised jealousy on a man's face. This time it was Charles, whose normally good-humoured countenance fleetingly bore an expression which could only be described as malign.

So fleeting was it that Bess doubted her own senses. She even doubted that she had seen what she thought that she had seen. Charles's expression had not really changed—she had been in the sun too long, and the light had begun to play tricks on her.

She was more certain of this than ever when Drew began teasing both Charles and Philip, demanding that they play bowls against him before they ate. His two friends joked back at him, exchanging cheerful insults as was the habit of men when playing together.

"And you, wife," laughed Drew, turning to her as she walked, forgotten, between them, "must challenge the Lady Arbell to a game of *Troule in Madame*. You have a fine way with the ball."

"Oh," said Charles, "then I may wish for my lady to win—which is a favour I will not extend to my lord!"

More male laughter greeted this sally. Bess, who had no wish to challenge the Lady Arbell to anything, was compelled to smile when they met Sir Henry and his wife in the antechamber to the Great Hall, where Drew and Philip rapidly involved them both in their mutual folly. Bess had not seen her husband so light-hearted since they had reached Buxton.

Again, she sensed that there was something odd, something wild in his gaiety, but said nothing, smiling dutifully when Drew committed her to the childish game which was one of Buxton's specialities. Rolling little lead balls into holes at the end of a bench scarcely seemed a sensible occupation for grown-up women, so naturally the Lady Arbell was devoted to it.

On the other hand, if her Drew was determined to have her play with little lead balls, she might as well defeat the Lady Arbell at this silly game as not.

Which she duly did.

To that lady's great annoyance.

"I am glad that we had no money riding on this game," she exclaimed pettishly. "Although I find that I always play better when I wager something on it."

"Then I shall be sure to come prepared with my purse to challenge you, using the same odds as my husband used when challenging your husband and his friends in the bowling alley.''

The Lady shrugged her elegant shoulders. "As you wish.''

Bess uncharitably thought that her comprehensive defeat of Arbell had dimmed Arbell's enthusiasm for the game more than a little. She said nothing, however, other than, "I would wish to see my husband play bowls. I had not known that he was a skilled performer.''

"Oh, I have often watched him when we were at court together," said the Lady, staking her claim to have known Bess's husband longer than Bess had. "I will come with you.''

Which was not at all what Bess wanted, but she surrendered with a good grace, walking over to where the men stood, watching Drew demolish Charles on the bowling green as he had already demolished Philip and Sir Henry. There was another man standing with them, and ready to play, whom Bess had not seen before. He must have been one of the small party of gentlemen who had ridden over from Chatsworth. She wondered who he was.

As Drew had earlier done, when he and Charles had arrived at the green to find a stranger lounging on a bench, watching the squires who were engaged in an impromptu archery contest in the field nearby. He rose at the sight of Drew and his party.

"Ah, Master Sidney," he drawled, "you will do me the honour of introducing your friends to me, I hope.''

"Assuredly," Philip returned, bowing, "May I present to you, my most noble Lord of Exford, one Captain Ralph Goreham. My other friend, Lord Exford's cousin, Master Charles Breton, was, I believe, made known to you earlier this afternoon.''

Both men bowed most formally. Captain Goreham murmuring, ''Honoured, I'm sure, my lord.''

So this was Captain Goreham. Could he be the soldier of whom Walsingham had warned him to be suspicious? He was like every roving semi-mercenary captain whom Drew had ever met. He was over-dressed, over-mannered and full of himself. A man who, if Drew were being unkind, he would call a bully boy. Even the plume in the hat he was sweeping to the ground was over-large and shouted to the world, ''Pray look at me.''

Was it simply Walsingham's warning which was making him suspicious, or merely his own dislike of the parasites who attached themselves like leeches to those who frequented Elizabeth's court and thus might offer some kind of rich pickings?

Best to say nothing, to use his charm—as Bess was learning to use hers—and play a waiting game. Meantime there was a game of bowls to be won—in fact, a number of games of bowls, and he had a mind to win them all. Whether to prove himself to himself, or simply himself to Bess, Drew was not quite sure. He had the absurd notion that, like the knights of old, he ought to have asked her for some favour to carry with him when he went into battle—a handkerchief, perhaps.

This untoward fancy had him laughing to himself so hard that he missed a sally from the Captain which set Charles and Philip laughing out loud.

No matter, it was probably as empty as the bombastic Captain who had perpetrated it, and who now invited himself to become part of their game. For some reason, whether it was Walsingham's letter, or fear that Bess might find Philip—or even the Captain, the Lord forbid—more attractive than her husband, Drew played with a savagery foreign to him.

Bess's arrival, and the friendly arm she slipped through his, lightened his burden a little. "You won?" he asked her without taking his attention from Captain Goreham, who was the last person to play against him.

"Narrowly," she returned, not wishing to crow over her defeated opponent, however little she liked the Lady Arbell. Besides, Sir Henry was standing by and she did not wish to offend him. He gave her an approving—and somewhat surprised—smile. "You must be a good player to defeat my lady wife."

"I was lucky," said Bess untruthfully.

"Your husband, madam," said Captain Goreham "needs no luck. He carries all before him by his skill."

"This is Captain Ralph Goreham, to whom I now formally introduce you, wife," said Drew coldly for him. "He flatters me, but does not flatter you. My wife, sir, has a keen eye and a strong wrist and needs no luck to enable her to win a game."

The Captain bowed low. "My pardon, m'lady. I stand corrected. And now your husband has defeated me, as he has defeated the rest. See where his last wood lies against the jack, undoing me, for I have no more shots left. His eye is as true as he says yours is."

So, the mercenary Captain was bound and determined to flatter my wife, thought Drew, gritting his teeth. It seemed that all the world, after ignoring Bess Exford these many years, was suddenly bent on falling in love—or lust—with her. Perforce he was compelled to smile on the Captain, for, if he were the spy of whom Walsingham wrote, he had come to seduce more people than Bess.

The game over, they all strolled back to eat their supper. They had been provided, for once, with a meal of which Dr Jones would have approved: wheaten and leavened bread, and the flesh of goats and chickens boiled, not roasted. There was a great dish of pike, a platter piled high with boiled rabbit joints, and a quantity of fine ale. Wine had been banished, and more than one gentleman or lady's mouth was puckered as they ate fare which seemed exceedingly tasteless after the spicy roast meats to which they were accustomed.

"I had expected," Philip muttered somewhat morosely to Drew, "something better than this at Shrewsbury's table. Uncle Leicester always spoke highly of it, but I am sure that he would not have approved of this gutless fare."

"You are unlucky tonight, my friend," Drew whispered back. "One day a week we eat that which the great doctor says will not excite our stomachs. Tomorrow will be better. Greves has told Charles that m'lord has given orders that we are to have a pig roasted, and chickens, too—to make up for today's Lenten offerings. And there will be good wine on the table, as well as ale."

"Amen to that," Captain Goreham called across to them, raising his tankard in a general toast.

Bess, watching Drew, was suddenly aware that for some reason, the gallant Captain was not at all to his taste. Usually he was hail-fellow-well-met with everyone, however lowly in rank: it was one of his charms. She wondered briefly what ailed him.

No time to think of that, though, for Philip, who sat

on her left, was asking her about Atherington. "You live on the edge of the forest, do you not?"

Master Blagg, on her other side, chipped in in his usual eager fashion. Decidedly he had country manners as the Lady Arbell had frequently complained.

"Charnwood is beginning to be called a forest by courtesy only, sir. Is not that so, Lady Exford? My friend, Jack Bown, tells me that less charcoal is burned there every year, and that the deer grow smaller in numbers and leaner."

"Master Bown exaggerates, I fear," said Bess. "That is his habit. He constantly complains that the world is going to the devil." She did not add that this was partly because he was of the Catholic persuasion and he considered that all matters had gone ill since Elizabeth came to the throne.

"But it cannot rival Sherwood," smiled young Blagg. "Which is much as it was in the days of Robin Hood."

"That I do not dispute," said Bess.

Later, when she and Drew were alone again in their bedroom, Drew said to her, apparently idly, "This Bown, of whom Master Blagg spoke, who thinks that the world is going to the devil—of what persuasion is he?"

Bess, sitting up in bed, eager for the night's entertainment to begin, shrugged her shoulders. "Oh, it is not surprising that he thinks thus. He is staunchly Catholic, you see."

"Is he so? And he is Blagg's friend. But the Blaggs are Protestant I think someone said."

"They are now," explained Bess, "but only since Queen Elizabeth came in. Master Blagg's father knew

on which side his bread was buttered, my father said.
Are you coming to bed, husband, or would you prefer
me to offer you instead a roll call of the religious
persuasion of all the esquires and manorial lords in the
East Midlands?''

"Hussy," said Drew amiably as he jumped into bed
to land on top of her. "I shall think up a suitable
punishment for your impudence, Lady Exford."

And so he did. And it was one which had Bess
squealing with pleasure for, whether Drew loved her
or not, he was able to take her with him into those
fields of delight which she had never visited until the
day he had ridden through Atherington's main gates
for the second time in his life...

So, Blagg was a lapsed Catholic, was he? Like the
Lady Arbell and one or two others whom he knew
were frequenting Buxton in order—ostensibly—to enjoy its waters. And this Bown of whom Blagg had
spoken—would he suddenly appear to join this happy
little nest of possible traitors? Stupid, perhaps, to suspect that everyone he met might be a traitor, but, on
the other hand, perhaps not. And then there was the
problem of Captain Goreham, of whom Walsingham
had warned him—although he had warned him of no
one else by direct inference.

These gloomy thoughts ran through Drew's head as
he was being shaved for the day. Together with another one, which had only occurred to him recently.
Why had Walsingham recruited him for this mission
at all? He was not one of his inner circle of spies and
agents, that was for sure, and his previous experience
had been purely diplomatic.

Over breakfast, which today, at Drew's orders, had

been commissioned from a nearby inn and brought from thence to his private room, he was rather quieter than usual, so much so that both his cousin Charles and Bess privately remarked on it, and were disturbed for quite different reasons.

It was only when there was a knock on the door which heralded the arrival of the Queen of Scots's private secretary, Claude Nau, who was apparently inviting himself to break fast with Drew's party, that Drew came to life.

"Sit! Sit," he exclaimed. "Tib, a stool for Monsieur Nau, and see that he is provided with food and ale."

Claude Nau, a talkative man, devoted to his mistress, immediately launched into a lengthy explanation of his presence so early in the morning.

"Her Grace, the Queen of Scots, would count it an honour if you, m'lord Exford, and your lady, would consent to sup with her this evening in her rooms. She has already asked Master Sidney to join her and he has given his consent. At six thirty of the clock, after you have bathed, if that is agreeable to you." He rose and bowed as he finished his message, and then sat down again to drink the ale which Tib had poured for him.

Bess, watching Drew, knew that he was troubled by his invitation—but why should that be so? Even though he had treated Nau with perfect courtesy, she knew that he was ill at ease. Nothing, however, showed on his perfect face as he said all the right things to Nau, emphasising the honour which was being done to him by a woman who had once been a reigning Queen.

No one else seemed to notice anything untoward.

Charles passed Nau a platter of cold meat, and a large slice of bread, which he seized and ate greedily. "My mistress has a strong mind to see more of your lady, my lord Exford," Nau offered through a mouthful of food. "She misses the young company which she enjoyed when she lived with Lord and Lady Shrewsbury."

Following her husband's lead, Bess too, murmured of the honour being done her: an honour which she could have done without.

She said as much to Drew later, when they were alone, adding, apparently innocently, "I thought that you were none too pleased to be so singled out."

Drew offered her a half-truthful explanation. "Why, as to that, if her Majesty, my Queen, saw fit to treat her favourite, my Lord of Leicester, to a harangue about his lack of loyalty because he chose to favour the Queen of Scots with his presence at supper, what do you think that she will say to m'lord of Exford, one of her humbler servants, when she hears of this night's work?"

"Why, how should she hear of it, Buxton and London being so far apart?"

Her husband gave a short laugh. "My dear wife, before you go to London with me you must learn the ways of the wicked world you will be living in. Someone, somehow, will pass this news on to the Court—and thence to the Queen in order to gain favour. As one courtier goes up, another goes down."

Bess was not to know that, although there was truth in this, it was not the real reason for Drew's wariness, and for the moment his answer sufficed to reassure her. She worried later when she saw Drew single out the Lady Arbell for special attention, walking with her and Captain Goreham to the field where the men were engaged in an impromptu archery contest.

Philip Sidney, observing that her eyes followed Drew and his companions wistfully, said in his usual courtly manner, "I, too, have a wish to engage in some field sports, and would ask you to accompany me—if it so pleases you."

"It does." Bess was frank, and as Philip gallantly took her arm and walked her along, she asked him, "Tell me, sir, are all men the same? Do they all engage in competitions in which they seek to beat everyone against whom they strive? Is it a condition of being a man, as a tendency to sit and watch is that of a woman?"

"A grave question," was Philip's equally grave answer. "Except for one thing, my lady of Exford. I have been watching you as you watched us and by your expression I would have sworn that you would like to pull the longbow yourself. And if you do so, in competition, would you not wish to win? When you played at backgammon with me the other evening, your delight in winning was extreme, although courteously expressed."

Like Drew, then, he saw more into the hearts of men and women than he usually spoke of. She rewarded him with a smile. "To pull the longbow, yes. I have often wished to do that—but the pull may be too heavy for me, I fear."

"Nothing to that," replied Philip, smiling. "I have a light bow which pleases me, and which has come in my luggage. My man shall fetch it, and you may try your skill against me—for he shall also bring me my heavier one."

What a surprise for Drew, thought Bess gleefully—if he can bring himself to neglect the Lady Arbell long enough to know that I am even here!

While Philip's man ran off to do his master's bidding, she and Philip sat on one of the benches and watched Drew and the Captain practise. Before they began to shoot against one another in earnest, the Lady Arbell, smiling prettily, handed Drew her fine lace-edged handkerchief which hung from her belt as an ornament rather than for practical use.

"You must be my knight," she commanded him, ignoring her husband who hovered in her rear, and who seemed to be quite happy to have his wife admired by other women's husbands.

"My pleasure," replied Drew, the faithless brute, hanging over her hand, and placing the handkerchief in his belt. Yes, he was quite unaware that his wife was watching him, her teeth clenched.

Bess unclenched them, rose and, moved by she knew not what, walked over to where Captain Goreham stood watching this pretty pantomime, and handed him her own fair kerchief, saying, "Come, Captain, you must not be left out of this exchange of tokens. Here is my handkerchief, and for this round of arrows you must be my knight."

"Willingly, m'lady, most willingly."

It was Drew's teeth which were now clenched. But he could say nothing. He consigned both the Lady Arbell and his wife to the lowest pit of Hell. Was it not bad enough that he had to pretend to admire a woman whom he disliked and to be compelled in return to watch his wife favouring a fly-by-night mercenary who could conceivably be a traitor of the deepest die?

He was so distracted that his ability to find not only the gold, but the higher of the lesser colours on the target, deserted him, and he fell an easy victim to the gallant Captain in their first round. His temper was not assisted by having to watch Bess be instructed in the art of using the longbow by Philip Sidney. An art which consisted mainly of Philip putting his arms around his willing wife, meticulously aligning her posture as she was about to shoot!

"You are off the mark today, sir," remarked the observant Captain, who had a good idea of what was wrong with his opponent. He plucked Bess's handkerchief from his belt and waved it airily. "My lady's favour has a deal of magic in it today," he remarked with consummate impudence.

Bess, meantime, was beginning to enjoy herself, particularly when she overheard the Captain's baiting of Drew. She found Philip's light bow easy to use, and that she had, as he admiringly told her, a natural eye. The only thing which prevented her from achieving an even greater skill was her tendency to dissolve into giggles as she—correctly—read Drew's face and grasped the reason why *his* skill had also deserted him.

He deserved it, did he not? As the Lady Arbell deserved to pout as her champion failed so dismally where he had always succeeded before. If Philip noticed this by-play he made no comment on it, only challenged Bess to a contest. A contest which they both noisily enjoyed, adding to Drew's inward fury.

Except that, just when the Captain thought that he was about to overcome the known winner of all the male sports available at Buxton, Drew suddenly saw the funny side of the whole brouhaha. Who would have thought that he, the inconstant lover, should be so besotted with his wife that he fell the victim of a berserker rage when she became the object of the attention of others? It was a subject fit for the pen of Messer Boccaccio, no less, and this comic thought relieved him of his pain.

Furthermore, waiting his turn, he caught her eye—and the naughty minx winked at him! Oh, yes, she was winding him up, and he was fool enough to succumb to her cantrips. Chuckling to himself, he took his turn and started to shoot his arrows with such deadly grace that the Lady Arbell began to jump up and down and to squeak her approval. At which Drew, passing Bess on his way back to his mark, not only winked back at her, but also blessed her with a surreptitious kiss whilst pretending to frighten off a stray bee.

The Captain, unaware—or was he?—that his mockery of Drew over Bess's kerchief had almost certainly triggered off Drew's revival, watched helplessly as he was led to the slaughter.

Mournfully trying to hand her kerchief back to Bess, he sighed, ''Alas, your favour was not sufficient to help me to overcome your husband's skill. Had he not shot so poorly at the beginning of the contest he would have overcome me in quick march time, no doubt of it.''

''But you must keep my handkerchief,'' commanded Arbell of Drew when he tried to hand it back to her, ''seeing that it brought you luck in the end.''

Ever the gentleman, he bowed and took it from her, kissing it as he did so. Oddly, Bess watching him, felt no jealousy at the sight, for she was remembering both his wink and his kiss for her. She could not guess for what reason Drew was pursuing the Lady Arbell, but she was suddenly sure that his doing so was no threat to her.

For was it not plain that he had been unable to shoot properly until she had shown that she had forgiven him?

Paula Marshall

Drew saw Bess's puzzled [illegible] look at him, amused
and [illegible] at [illegible] he had said now. And
[illegible] his hand she [illegible] was present in the
purse... [illegible] the [illegible] again in his own
himself.

# Chapter Nine

"And exactly what game were you playing this morning with my so-called friend, Philip Sidney, wife?" Drew asked Bess once they were alone together in their rooms.

"Why, he was but teaching me archery, husband."

"Was he so, then, wife? From where I was standing, it seemed that he was teaching you quite a different game!"

Bess's eyes were as innocent as her voice as she answered him.

"Seeing that you were at some distance from us, husband, I wonder that you could tell whether we were playing at any game at all, let alone a particular one."

"Oh, a particular game, was it?" Drew's voice was half-joking and half-savage. "Let me see whether I can play it, too."

He strode over to where she stood, not far from the Great Bed, and put his arms about her, exactly as Philip had done when Bess had been encouraging him to tease Drew. He made as though to help her pull an imaginary bow, whispering in her ear as he half-turned her towards him, "Allow me to hold you so, dear madam, for I must raise your elbow a little so that you may better control the strength of your pull."

Bess made no effort to resist him, saying as she looked into the blue eyes so near to her own, "Like so, husband?"

"Nay, not so strong, wife, gently, gently. A subtle touch is best with the bow as in life," and he allowed his left hand to slip down from her shoulder where he had been caressing her neck so that he might caress her breast instead.

"Was this the game that you were playing, wife?"

Bess's first response was to shiver with delight, and then to spring away from him, her cheeks scarlet as the import of his words struck her.

"Nay, sir! You wrong both me and Master Sidney to think that we would play those games reserved only for husband and wife."

"Oh, but we all know that that last statement is not true, do we not? Many other than husband and wives play them," whispered Drew softly as he took her face in his hands and began to rain butterfly kisses on it, abandoning the pretence that they were engaged in mock archery, and engaging in the sport of love instead.

"It is true for me," faltered Bess, pulling her mouth away from his. "I could not bear for another man to touch me as you are doing now," for Drew's hand had strayed beneath the skirts of her gown and was stroking her in such a fashion that she groaned and shuddered beneath his touch.

"Shall we play the game of husband and wife here and now, wife? Before we join the busy world again?"

"Oh, but they are expecting us downstairs, husband."

"Then they must go unsatisfied rather than that I should, wife." He had manoeuvred the pair of them on to the Great Bed where he set about satisfying them both to such effect that Bess's protestations were lost in her cries of joy as he brought them to consummation.

Silence reigned for a time until Bess sat up, all her clothing awry, and her hair tumbled about her shoulders.

"How may I send for my woman now that I am in such disarray?" she lamented, trying to restore her crumpled ruff and her disordered hair at the same time. Drew, lazily lying on one elbow, his clothes in similar state, squinted up at her.

"Why, how should she object, seeing that we *are* husband and wife and may pleasure each other at any time. But if your modesty forbids, then I will restore you to order, and you, if you please, will restore me until we both look like a pair of Master Holbein's paintings rather than flesh-and-blood human beings."

Bess nodded her agreement, but she soon found that being dressed by Drew was nearly as arousing as being undressed by him! His hands seemed to be everywhere, and her hair became more, rather than less, unbound.

"I wonder how either of us is ever ready for the day," murmured Drew as he restored her bodice to its proper place and, as he said, "hid her treasures there from the sight of other men".

Straightening her ruff took some tedious time, and had him sighing. "Such a deal of calico, whalebone, wire and stiffening goes into our dress that we are nearly as constrained as the marionettes whom the Italians entertain us with. There, m'lady Exford, you are ready to dine—a little late in the day, mayhap. Now you may set me to rights.''

Setting Drew to rights was almost as teasing and tormenting and delightful as setting him to wrongs had been. And so Bess told him, which set him laughing and kissing her again, which began to undo all his earlier careful work, as well as hers.

Bess finally pushed him away. ''I, sir, am hungry. A morning spent first at the butts and then on the bed has served to whet my appetite nearly as much as a good early morning gallop.''

''There's nothing better than a good early morning gallop on the bed,'' proclaimed Drew. ''We must try it again soon. And now to break fast, but seeing that we are to dine with the Scots Queen tonight we must not overdo our eating, for it will be ill seen if we have no appetite then.''

''In that case,'' retorted Bess naughtily, ''a good early *evening* gallop on the bed might ensure our good manners in the Queen's rooms. We must not let it be seen that we are not mindful of the honour which she is doing us.''


''The honour which the Queen hath done us is none so great,'' Drew whispered to Bess after they had been received by Her Grace at supper that evening, ''for I note that Captain Goreham is also an honoured guest, as well as the Catholic half of the local gentry. We and Philip are Protestant fish out of water.''

''Perchance,'' Bess whispered back, ''she thinks that though we may not be Catholic, we may be sympathisers. But, look, we are not alone for here come Sir Henry and his wife.''

She offered the Lady Arbell a false smile even as

she spoke—and received one back. Her greeting from Sir Henry was bluff and sincere, the more so since Arbell immediately attached herself to Drew, and pouted her discontent on finding that when the meal was served she was compelled to sit by her husband at some distance from Drew and Bess, who were also seated side by side.

Bess had Captain Goreham on her left-hand side. He made a dead set at her during the lengthy meal, the chief subject of which was a dish of peacocks roasted in their feathers, to which Bess took great exception, seeing that the result was not only unpalatable, but unlovely.

Wisely, she kept her opinion to herself and concentrated on not encouraging the Captain to court her, which he seemed bent on doing. Unfortunately, what the Captain had seen at the archery butts had persuaded him that Bess, as a neglected wife, would be only too happy to receive his attentions instead of her husband's.

Fortunately, though, as the senior peer there, Drew was the focus of the Queen of Scots's interest, and she questioned him and Philip eagerly about their life at court, and their relationship with her cousin and captor, the Queen Elizabeth.

"If only I could meet her," Mary sighed, "I could perhaps convince her that I mean her no ill. These plots which are aimed at her person have nothing to do with me, you must understand. I neither initiate them, nor encourage them."

She turned all of her celebrated charm on Drew. "I am told that you are in favour with Her Grace, and I hope that when next you are at court you will convey that message to her. I have enthusiastic, but unwise, supporters who, because I am prisoner here, I am unable to restrain. You could perhaps pass that message on to her, too. And to Sir Francis Walsingham, who is her adviser on these matters.''

Did she know that he was Walsingham's friend and agent? Drew asked himself. Or was this idle conversation which was in truth not in the least idle, but was designed to convince him of her innocence—in which he did not believe at all.

The gallant Captain jumped into the small silence which followed before Drew could answer her. ''Oh, your Grace,'' he exclaimed, rising and bowing in her direction, his table napkin at his lips, ''no one who meets you could be other than convinced of your goodwill towards your cousin. Were I fortunate enough to be able to have an audience with the Queen's Grace, I would be only too happy to pass on your message!''

Would he, indeed? And what importance would Elizabeth place on the word of a hireling soldier who would be happy to say whatever anyone would pay him to say? Perhaps he was hopeful that the Queen of Scots would offer him a fee to speak on her behalf. If so, he would be disappointed since the Queen had virtually no money of her own, and was dependent on George Shrewsbury for the very bread which she was eating at table.

But his intervention had saved Drew from having to commit himself in any way to the Queen who was entertaining him. He gave a half-smile in the Captain's direction and left it at that.

His right-hand side companion, Marian Blagg, announced, her innocent voice louder than she had intended it to be, ''Only a person without a heart, Lord

Exford, could be content to see a good woman held prisoner, and not sympathise with the motives of those who seek to free her. Indeed, I have heard tell that Master Sidney's uncle, my lord of Leicester, not only wished to speak to the Queen on her Scottish Majesty's behalf, but was also wishful to marry her!''

This was to say the unsayable, and uttered in certain quarters the speaker might have felt her head loose upon her shoulders. Leicester had earned the Queen's displeasure for his temerity—and he was the Queen's favourite! What might Elizabeth not do to the powerless wife of a lowly country squire?

Marian's husband, Master Blagg, his face scarlet, murmured gently to her, ''Not here, my dear. This is no occasion for such a declaration, and might serve to place our hostess in peril should what you have said be repeated to her.''

''Oh!'' His wife flushed, and said apologetically, ''Pray forgive me, your Grace, if I have spoken out of turn. I meant no harm.''

''Of that I am sure,'' said Queen Mary, trying to comfort her. ''And I welcome the kindness with which you have spoken of me. But there are ill-wishers everywhere who might use your words not only against me, but against yourself. The path of virtue in my case is a narrow path indeed. We tread on eggshells—as I have cause to know.''

Silence fell. Everyone present knew of the Queen of Scots's sad story. Guilty or innocent of all of which she had been accused, she was paying a sad price for her unfortunate life.

Drew wondered whether Marian Blagg was betraying more than she knew. He also wondered whether her husband, in silencing her, was trying to retrieve what he thought that she might have given away: that there was a current plot on Mary's behalf, and that he was part of it. He would want no breath of suspicion cast on his loyalty. It was more than likely that his wife knew nothing of any conspiracy, but did know that her husband was sympathetic to Mary's cause.

The other question was: Did the Queen of Scots know of the plot? Her declaration of innocence was worthless. Neither could he take the word of anyone around the table—other than Bess's and Philip's—at face value. All present had an axe to grind and their attendance at this supper party might mean that their axe was a Catholic one!

Which begged the question as to why he and Bess and Philip had been invited. He sighed. He had always felt distaste at acting as Walsingham's amateur intelligencer, but as his feelings for Bess had begun to change so dramatically, his distaste for his task had grown too.

Had he known beforehand that he would come to care for his long-deserted wife he might have refused to play Walsingham's game. Common sense and loyalty to his mistress, the Queen Elizabeth, had him admitting that it was a task which he could not refuse—but that did not mean that he liked it. Ever since he had met Bess he had begun to change from the carefree young man who rarely questioned what he did—and how he did it. He remembered wryly what Philip had said to him recently about growing up, and no longer being a heedless boy.

And, of course, Walsingham had hinted at the same thing when he had told him, that last evening in London, that he was one of those who would carry on the responsibility of ruling England when he and Burghley and his fellow elder statesmen had gone to their last rest.

He shivered. Time was passing, and the easy Arcadia in which Philip and he had spent their early lives was passing, too. On the other hand, the life which he and Bess would spend together when this task was over had its own, different, attractions which were beginning to beckon to him.

Such as having sons and daughters to care for.

"You are silent tonight, my lord." This was Goreham, his sly face as probing as his voice, accosting Drew when the meal was over, and they were standing about the room, with the Queen seated on a small dais at one end of it.

"Aye, well, sir," returned Drew. "For one reason or another I have suffered a tiring day—not least when I took you on at archery."

Goreham took this as Drew intended, as a compliment. His smile was insufferable. "I must compliment you on your lady wife, m'lord. She is such a pearl as must soon grace her Majesty's court." He even had the effrontery to wink at Drew as though he were aware of the early evening gallop on the bed with which Drew and Bess had celebrated their return from the Baths.

Only Philip's hand on his arm prevented Drew from telling the Captain exactly what he thought of him and his innuendos.

"Her Grace would speak with you, as well as your wife, Drew," Philip said coolly—he had been surprised by Drew's quick show of anger at the Captain's impudence, and the Queen's rooms were not a fit place for his friend to lose his temper and provoke an unpleasant scene.

Drew recollected himself, stared dourly at the gallant Captain and went to join his wife who was admiring the tapestry on which the Queen had been working—a portrayal of the Babylonians in captivity—a referral to her own captivity, no doubt.

"I have my canvaswork with me," Bess was saying in reply to a question from Mary, to have the Queen answer,

"Then you must accept my invitation to work with me on those afternoons on which you do not go to the Baths."

Bess curtsied her agreement, saying as she rose, "I thank you for your kindness, your Grace, and will be happy to join you at your invitation. In return, may I bring my husband's musicians with me to play for us? I am sure that he would wish them to entertain you."

"Indeed, wife." Drew had arrived in time to hear Bess's last sentence. "You may have my blessing for that."

Mary's face betrayed her pleasure. Whether Drew felt any at his wife being singled out was quite another matter. But he allowed the Queen to question him about his life at court and also to confess to her that he had only recently met his wife again after ten years.

"Ah, a subject fit for a poem by Master Sidney," said the Queen, "seeing that you and she are now two lovebirds together."

Bess glowed and blushed at this, whilst Drew bemusedly wondered how much of their mutual pleasure must be showing, seeing that he had been compelled to listen to several knowing references to it already during the evening.

There was no doubt that they did not please everybody. Mary's patronage of Bess annoyed the Lady Arbell, who said shrilly to Drew as the Queen invited Bess to sit on a stool by her feet—a rare favour—"Her Grace is in a charitable mood this evening—she extends her patronage to all the world."

Drew chose to take this piece of nastiness in the wrong way, retorting with a smile, "I will pass your compliment on to my Countess, my dear Lady Arbell. She will be flattered to be compared with all the world."

This was not at all what Arbell had meant. She tossed her head and rewarded Drew's naughtiness with one of her own. "I suppose that, after all this graciousness from her Scots Majesty, you will be turning Catholic yourself and raising her banner in the Queen's court."

"Then you suppose wrongly, m'lady." Drew's voice was cold and grew colder as he continued to speak. "I do but use the occasion to practise my good manners as Messer Castiglione advises in his treatise, *The Book of the Courtier.* May I recommend it to you as useful reading."

Never before had he made his displeasure known so plainly. His easy charm, his refusal to be offended, had been a byword at Elizabeth's court. But he would not lightly suffer anyone to suggest that he might commit treason. Especially when that suggestion had been made before others, and even though he might make further cultivation of the Lady Arbell difficult by rebuking her.

Philip took him by the arm again to walk him away. It was strange, Drew reflected, that a man as high-tempered as Philip was so determined to act as a peacemaker for others.

"You grow short, dear friend, when your wife is

criticised,'' Philip told him once they were away from the crowd and they were standing alone in a window embrasure. ''The fair Arbell cannot forgive you for resisting her charms, and the gallant Captain is bent on troublemaking—for what reason I know not.''

Drew suspected what the reason might be, but could not say so to Philip. He shrugged. ''I had not thought that I would ever be a jealous husband,'' he confessed, ''but this morning I could even have cut *your* throat cheerfully when you sported with Bess at the butts.''

''Aye, so I saw.'' Philip was dry. ''But it will not do. She is a good creature and will not betray you, so you have no need to show the world the temper that no one knew you possessed.''

Well, that was true enough, Drew thought wryly. He was even surprising himself, so it was no wonder that he was surprising everyone else.

There, in the window embrasure, alone because Philip had left him, he faced a truth which he had been trying to evade ever since he had first opened his eyes to see the forest nymph above him: he was passionately in love with the wife whom he had deserted for so many long years, and could only grieve for what he had lost by that desertion.

He had mocked Philip gently for writing of love, claiming that it did not exist, was simply a poet's invention—and here he was, love's prisoner!

The Queen had at last let Bess go. She was walking towards him. She reached him. Drew put out a hand, took hers, looked into her eyes, and oblivious of the room, of anyone who might be watching, he kissed the hand he had taken.

''Come, wife,'' he said, still holding her hand and turning her towards the door. ''Let's to bed, and the rest of the world may wag as it will.''

## Chapter Ten

Drew had left Bess peacefully sleeping in the Great Bed in order to go riding on his own so that, far away from all distractions, he might think clearly about what dark plots were being hatched in Buxton—if any were, that was.

Early though he was, others were up before him. Or, at least, his cousin Charles was. Fully dressed, he was yawning and stretching himself in the corridor which led to the door to the stables. He stared at the sight of Drew in his riding clothes and boots.

"What? Abroad already? I thought that you were still enjoying the pleasures of the bridal bed." His tone was slightly mocking.

Drew ignored it. "I decided that an early morning ride would clear away the cobwebs of last night's supper."

Charles looked about him. "And Master Sidney? He is not to go with you? Would you care for me to act as your groom?"

"No, cousin. I have a mind for my own company this fine morning. Cicero's will do for me, and none other."

Charles shrugged. "No matter. I shall walk instead to the Baths and pleasure myself there—if ducking myself in cold water may be called a pleasure. I doubt me that I shall be more of a man afterwards than I was before!"

Drew left his striding away. All Buxton except himself and Charles, seemed to be in the arms of Morpheus, the god of sleep. No matter, he needed peace and quiet.

He found it by riding to the River Wye, travelling along it for a little time and then taking a narrow track which led up into the hills. He was quite alone, and on reaching a grassy plateau from whence he could see Buxton lying below him, small and unconsidered, he dismounted, tethered Cicero to a tree which he then sat beneath, and pondered on the puzzle which the little town, nay, village, presented.

His thinking was unproductive. He decided that the sooner the someone to whom Walsingham had referred in his letter arrived and presented him with the token which would prove that he was truly Walsingham's man, the better. They could discuss, in the light of the knowledge that he would bring with him, who might be the traitor.

All that sitting in the bright morning was doing for him was to cause him to admire the beauties of the wooded hills and the sound of birds calling. It was a pity that Philip was not with him. He would have been writing a sonnet to the day, for sure.

Laughing at himself, Drew swung into the saddle again to start for home. He had barely travelled a hundred yards when he heard a whirring noise. Immediately Cicero threw back his head...and slowly crumpled to the ground...taking Drew with him in such a fashion that he was thrown over Cicero's head to land, winded but uninjured, near him. Rising only to kneel and to shake his spinning head, Drew saw that poor Cicero had been struck in the neck by an arrow— which had surely not been meant for him, but for his master.

He had sufficient presence of mind to crawl around his mortally wounded horse and take shelter behind him, away from the direction from which the arrow had come.

His left wrist and shoulder ached abominably where they had hit the ground in his unexpected fall. He listened for any sound which might tell him where the archer was hidden, but could hear nothing. He dare not stand up and look around him for fear of presenting an easy target.

He flattened himself as much as possible and lay still, scarcely breathing. The birds were singing, the sun shone and the faint breeze blew as though there was no one on the hill who wished to murder Drew Exford. It was his own fault, he conceded ruefully, his head against Cicero's flank, for riding out alone and lightly armed.

His poor horse was lying quite still, possibly mortally wounded, for a stream of blood was flowing from his neck. He cursed his own folly that was killing, or had killed, his faithful friend.

The silence of the early day was suddenly broken. He could hear hoofbeats coming from the direction of the river. Someone was approaching him on horseback.

The murderer—or not?

There was nothing he could do, nowhere to hide. He dare not run towards the wood for if the horseman had a bow, or a pistol, he was a dead man. He had a horse pistol on his saddle but Cicero had fallen on to it. He only had the dagger at his belt.

The hoofbeats grew nearer.

Drew loosened his dagger and began to draw it.

The hoofbeats stopped.

The newcomer dismounted. A man's voice, familiar to Drew, called out, "Hola! Is anyone there?"

It was Captain Goreham. Was he friend—or foe? Had he a sword in his hand—or a bow ready drawn in order to deal Drew the *coup de grâce?*

"Yes," called Drew without rising. "It is I, Drew Exford. Come no nearer, until I know whether you mean me any harm."

The Captain took no note of him. He walked forward, stooped to look at Cicero—and saw the arrow in his neck.

"Ah, m'lord. I see why you are cautious. Shot at from ambush, were you?"

He said this as though it were the most natural thing in the world to find a young nobleman seated on the ground beside his stricken horse. Either he was innocent—or he was the most plausible sounding would-be murderer Drew could hope to meet.

Cautiously he raised his head. The Captain stood there, legs apart, unarmed, grinning down at him.

"Well, it was not I who shot at you, m'lord. I am a better marksman than your unseen enemy seems to have been—as you well know. And I have no reason to wish to kill you—but someone might think that he has."

Feeling a little foolish, and caught at complete disadvantage, Drew stood up.

"And how," he asked bluntly, "am I to know

whether you did take a shot at me, and when it failed, decide to try again another day?''

The Captain grinned, and spread his arms wide. ''Why, you may plainly see that I have no bow with me.''

''That makes nothing. You could have thrown it away when you saw that you had failed.''

''Oh, but I am an old soldier, sir. I would have made little of riding up and despatching you whilst you were still dazed. Someone who suspects that you are on the watch for traitors was doubtless your man, I dare hazard.''

Now how did he know that? But was not the Captain one of those whom Drew had suspected might be either the leader of the plot, or the go-between who was taking messages from the Scots Queen to the Spanish or French Embassy for forwarding to their masters at home? It still did not tell him whether Goreham was friend or foe.

The Captain saw him hesitate, saw that Drew had made no move to walk forward, but instead had drawn his dagger and was holding it at the ready in his hand.

''You do well to be cautious, young sir. I confess that I read you wrongly. I thought you a hothead, but you did, I suspect by instinct, the correct thing when you hid behind your horse, offering the bowman no target. And now, suspecting me, you hold on to your dagger. My apologies for doubting either your courage or your wisdom.''

Drew made a sudden decision. He sheathed his dagger and walked around poor Cicero.

''Whether or not you meant me harm a few moments ago, it is plain that you mean me none now.''

He deliberately turned his back on the Captain in order to kneel by Cicero who was bleeding to death.

"A pity," the Captain offered to Drew. "By all I ever saw, he was your faithful friend."

"Whom I killed," returned Drew bitterly.

The Captain shook his head. "When you are as old as I am, young sir, you will neither think nor say such things. But it does you credit. I will give you a ride home, but not yet."

Drew could not decide whether he disliked the Captain more when he was being greasily ingratiating or greasily patronising. On the other hand, it was possible that his arrival had scared off his attacker, and if so he owed him a debt of gratitude.

But before he could begin to pay it the Captain smiled benignly at him, and fumbled in the purse he wore at his belt, saying, "It is a doubly good chance that we have arrived here together where no man may see us. Not only have I put your assassin to flight, but I had need to speak to you privately."

The fumbling ended, he produced something from his purse, and handed it to Drew. "I think that you might recognise this, m'lord." Well, at least he had dropped the demeaning "young sir", was Drew's inward acid response as he took what the Captain proffered.

It was a small gold button with the letter *M* engraved on it, and it was the token of which Walsingham had spoken on his last night in London before he had left for Atherington. The *M* was short for the nickname which the Queen had given her faithful servant, "The Moor".

So, the Captain was Walsingham's agent and not

the Catholic plotter whom Drew had supposed he might be.

"My master said that you would recognise it," the Captain offered. "I have found no occasion for private speech with you before, and I am not wishful for my true allegiance to be known, you understand me, I'm sure."

Yes, Drew understood him. The Captain was doubtless pretending to be a Catholic sympathiser and by doing so hoped to gain access to the secret councils of possible plotters.

"And now, m'lord, with that in your hand, you may tell me what you have found, or think that you might have found, about the traitors in our midst."

Drew tossed the button into the air and caught it. "Little enough," he said. "I suspect Master Blagg, of course, and the friend Jack Bown with whom he keeps company, but whether they are active traitors or mere wordy sympathisers of the Queen I know not."

"Small fry!" The Captain was dismissive.

"So I supposed. But who is the Behemoth—the king of fish—who organises them? I suspect that the Lady Arbell is not innocent in this matter, but Sir Henry? Can one suspect him?"

"Oh, one suspects anyone," grinned the Captain. "That is a matter of course in this game."

Drew decided that a frontal attack might be useful. "And you, Captain, and your master. Do you know more—or less—than I do?"

"Oh, as to that, we know that there *is* a Behemoth, a leader, but who, we know not. Shortly after you left for the Midlands a letter destined for the French Embassy was found on the body of a go-between who was knifed in a London tavern—for quite other reasons than treason. It came from Buxton. It named no names, even the writer used a pseudonym. He called himself Leander. It said that a number of Leicestershire and Derbyshire gentlemen, led by Nemo, a man from outside the Midlands, were about to mount a plan to spring the Scots Queen from her prison and raise her standard. Help from both their Majesties of France and Spain was required for the plot to succeed. An invasion was suggested.''

"Nemo, eh?" Drew frowned. "A nameless gentleman? And that is all?"

"Aye, we are at sea here, with no sight of land. My master has known of Nemo for some time, but knows not his true name."

Drew suspected that Sir Francis Walsingham knew more than the old Fox was prepared to tell at this moment. He trusted no one, it seemed. Not even Captain Goreham—or the son of his old friend, Andrew, Lord Exford.

One last thing Drew had to find out before he said goodbye to his old friend who lay quiet on the ground. "Your master told me in the most cryptic fashion that every camp has its traitor. I am supposing that he suspects someone near me. You have no notion of who it might be?"

"None." The Captain's answer was unhesitating. "And now, m'lord, it is time I gave you a lift home; you have been absent for so long that your servants must soon become anxious. But before we leave we must destroy the evidence."

He bent down and wrenched the arrow from Cicero's neck. He looked up at Drew. "If we are to make this look like an accident and not an attempt at murder, we must cut your steed's throat, seeing that his leg was broken in the fall—but really to conceal the mark of the arrow. If you wish, I will perform the *coup de grâce.*"

"No!" Drew moved forward, his dagger in his hand. "He was my good horse, my old friend. It is I who must perform the last rites for him, you understand—hard though that may be. Leave me for a moment, and then you may take me back to report that Cicero has had an accident which cost him his life, but spared mine."

The Captain made no answer other than to move away. He heard Drew say as he knelt to perform his unwelcome task, "Oh, Cicero, before this is over you may be sure that I shall claim a life in exchange for yours. May you carry me again when we meet in the Shades."

"But you are not hurt, Drew? Only Cicero? Nay, not *only Cicero,* that sounds unfeeling, for Cicero was your friend, was he not?"

Bess was watching Master Todd, Drew's physician, examine his left wrist.

"He was, indeed, and I shall miss him. Never mind that he was growing old, I would not have had him leave me before his time."

Drew had given orders to Thomas, his head groom, to travel into the hills to recover Cicero's saddle—if that were possible. "Take Tib with you, and no one else," he had ordered, for Thomas and Tib were two of his men whom he was sure would be faithful to him and to Bess and who would not gossip if anything seemed out of the ordinary. Only the assassin must know the true reason for his horse's death.

Charles had met him as he left Thomas and Tib to carry out his orders.

"What's this I hear, Drew? That Cicero had an accident whilst you were riding in the hills above the town? How did that come about?"

"Quite simply," Drew lied. "As you know, Cicero was growing old. He stumbled and fell, breaking a blood vessel as he did so, as well as his right foreleg. I was lucky not to break mine, but I have hurt my wrist somewhat and bruised my shoulder. Master Todd is about to see to me."

"You should not have gone out without a groom," Charles scolded him. "Captain Goreham says that he came across you, quite by chance, and that you rode pillion with him back to Buxton. Had he not found you, you might have still been walking home. You had ridden a long way into the hills, he said."

"Yes, I owe him a debt of gratitude. Do not berate me, Charles, I have learned my lesson. I promise that I shall not ride out again without having half the grooms in Buxton in my train! Will that do?"

"Better that than fearing that you might have been lying one knows not where with a broken leg. Is not that so, Philip?"

Philip Sidney smiled agreement, thrust his arm through Drew's uninjured one, and asked to be allowed to escort him to his rooms.

"By the Lord God, Philip," retorted Drew testily, "I have but a small sprain of the wrist, my life is not in danger, and a fellow likes to be on his own occasionally without all England dancing attendance on him! Confess, Philip, you often feel the same."

"So I do. But you must remember that you are a married man now. Bess was beginning to fret over your non-return, and the news that you were seen riding pillion behind Captain Goreham did not relieve her of her fears until she found out that you had suffered but a minor hurt.''

What an unseemly pother, thought the disgusted Drew. And what would they all say if they knew the true reason for poor Cicero's death? And—more to the point—which one of the many who will offer me kind words of sympathy this afternoon is the person who tried to murder me this morning?

It was difficult to decide who might have wished to kill him since everyone whom he met expressed their distress at his untoward accident after such a fashion that it was difficult to believe that they were not sincere.

Even the Queen of Scots sent him a message through Nau, hoping that his injury was not so great that it would spoil his pleasure during his visit to Buxton.

Something which he had said to Captain Goreham on the ride back to Buxton stayed with him. ''You claim to be a man experienced in such matters, sir. Do you believe it possible that the arrow which killed Cicero this morning was meant to kill him, rather than me—a warning shot across my bows as my naval friends would say—to discourage me from further action?''

''Oh, aye, m'lord. Very like—although we have no means of proving the matter either way.'' So that was that—and altogether it left him in a most unsatisfactory situation. Particularly when Bess, in her usual thoughtful way, remarked to him as they prepared for supper that evening, ''Was there something odd about Cicero's death, husband?''

"Why do you ask?" Drew made his reply as lightly as he could.

"Nothing which I can put into words—except..." and Bess paused before continuing "...promise not to laugh at me if I explain why I might think so."

"I promise." Drew's tone was still light although he was inwardly cursing either Tib or Thomas if either of them had said anything to Bess which might have started her worrying about his safety

"It's this. I have come to know you very well, Drew, and your manner since you returned with Captain Goreham leads me to believe that Cicero's death was not quite what it seemed."

So, neither Tib nor Thomas had talked—which was as well for them. "And that is all, wife?" He smiled as he spoke.

"There! I said that you would laugh at me! And you have!"

"No, no, I am not laughing. But I am pleased that you should worry about me and poor Cicero. No need, my heart. Cicero is at rest—or perhaps galloping in the fields of heaven; and I am in perfect fig—except for a slightly damaged wrist. On the whole, matters went well for me, if not for my horse."

It was the first time Drew had experienced that strange phenomenon which can occur between lovers: that sixth sense which picks up the true feelings of the other rather than the ones which they are claiming to experience.

He realised at once that he was also beginning to read Bess's thoughts—although not as strongly as she was reading his. He did not think that he had deceived her and, although he disliked lying to her, he had done so as much to protect her as to keep her in the dark for no reason at all.

So when they sat down beside the Lady Arbell and Sir Henry at supper and they began their litany of commiseration over Cicero and his fall, nothing which Bess said revealed that she, for one, doubted that he had told the whole truth of what had happened on the hills above Buxton.

He would have to be careful in future, although he ruefully acknowledged that there was little which he could do to prevent his wife from being so sensitive to all his moods.

Looking around the table he tried to work out who his would-be assassin might have been. Which of his kind friends was it who wished to see him dead because of what he might uncover? All of them looked singularly innocent, and the one person whom he might have suspected by his manner was Captain Goreham—who had turned out to be the one person who wished to keep him alive—if only as a useful informant who could guide him to a larger payday. For Drew had not the slightest doubt why the Captain was such a keen patriot!

Drew's appetite had quite deserted him. A matter of comment for Arbell, who managed to inform the whole table of its disappearance.

"Small wonder," she said, with Sir Henry echoing her every word, "when you have endured such a harrowing experience!"

Much though he would have wished to retort that he was not harrowed at all, Drew desisted if only in honour of Cicro's memory. He tried to guide the conversation into other channels, but so little which was exciting ever happened at Buxton that the company would not lightly surrender such a juicy bone.

"I am beginning to wish that I *had* broken my neck this morning," he whispered savagely to Bess, "and then I should not have had to endure listening to all this twaddle. One might think that a man had never fallen off a horse before."

"Do not say so, Drew! Not even in jest. The unkind gods who might fulfil such a dreadful wish could be listening to you."

"Exactly," said Charles, who had overheard him, "You must not frighten your wife—and the other ladies, Drew. Their feelings are more delicate than ours."

"Then I would wish that their delicacy would extend itself to another topic," Drew ground out. He saw Philip reward him with an odd stare for his strange behaviour, and tried to control himself. He had to admit that what had happened earlier had shaken him. It was not only his fall and Cicero's death which perturbed him. The knowledge that he was as hunted an animal as the stag or the fox whom he had often pursued on Cicero's back was a strange and daunting thought.

But it behoved him to pull himself together and play the man, and not act like the spoiled darling of the court which Captain Goreham obviously thought that he was.

He saw the Captain's eye on him, and shouted mannerlessly down the table in his direction, "I have a mind to draw a bow against you tomorrow forenoon, Captain Goreham. Never mind that my wrist is damaged, it will need more than an unhappy fall to deter me from doing what I have a mind to do."

And if that was not a direct challenge to the unknown swine who had tried to kill him, then nothing was.

Bess stared at him—and his odd uncourteous behaviour. Philip leaned towards him and said, "Now, Drew, you should rest, rather than exercise, your wrist." A comment which Charles and Sir Henry both echoed.

"As an old soldier, I must advise you otherwise," boomed Sir Henry jovially, "and no more riding for a few days. You should not court another accident until you have recovered from the first."

With everyone so exasperatingly concerned for his welfare it seemed a miracle that anyone should wish to kill him! Even the squires joined in when the meal was over and they were standing about, drinking the last of the ale, the ladies disporting themselves on large settles before a blazing fire—the day having been cool and the evening cooler.

The only exception was the Captain, who followed him when he strode away from the company and out through the main doorway to stand on the steps in the open, watching the rising moon.

"Should you be showing yourself so partial to me?" Drew half-snarled at him. "Is it wise, considering everything?"

"Perhaps not. But that was a rare old challenge you flung at me and the rest of the company, and I told your crony Sidney that I was following you to make arrangements for the morning's match."

"Forgive my ill temper," Drew said. "You do not deserve it. If you must know, it is the inability to discover who my enemy is which is galling me. I had not half so ill a temper when I was engaged in a sea-fight against the Spaniards and we boarded their ship so as to make it our prize.''

It was the Captain's turn to be surprised. ''Ah, you have seen action, then, m'lord?''

''When I was nineteen I financed a ship to prey on the Spaniards' galleon run in the South Seas and persuaded my guardian to allow me to be an officer in the crew. So, yes, I have seen action. But at least I was face to face with my enemy then, and did not suspect that a friend might be stabbing me in the back.''

''Exactly so. I understand that you sent your grooms to recover the furniture on your horse. Did they suspect that anything untoward had happened?''

''If they did, they knew better than to say so,'' grinned Drew. ''They had orders to be as quiet as possible at what they found at the scene of the accident. I can only hope that they put it down to my wounded pride over being thrown.''

''And your good lady? She is not troubled, I trust?''

Drew was not sure whether he disliked the Captain more as a friend than as an enemy. His good lady, indeed! It made his young and pretty Bess sound as old and stale as her namesake of Hardwick. Nevertheless, he reassured the Captain that he had not told Bess of the true cause of his accident, so that consequently she was not too overset.

A fact borne out a few moments later when she joined them to admire the crescent moon, the surrounding stars and the clear sky.

''So this is where you vanished to, husband. Am I to suppose that you found the silence and peace of a summer's night more to your liking than the noisy fuss which your morning's accident has created? I hope,

Captain Goreham, that you have been discussing anything other than poor Cicero's misfortune with him. I have no mind to retire with a husband who is as sore as though he had spent the day as a bear being baited.''

The Captain's smile for her was one of admiration. "Exactly so, m'lady. We have been talking of sweet nothings, I do assure you; furthermore, it will be my pleasure to leave you alone to enjoy the moonlight."

He bowed and was gone.

"I find that I like the Capain more than I did," remarked Bess thoughtfully. "Now why should that be so?"

Well, not because he is given to telling the truth, was Drew's inward reaction to that. Instead he said, his voice grave and considering, "I suppose it is because he has the good sense, like yourself, to speak of other things to me. Tomorrow morning's archery match, for instance. We were mulling over the niceties of it."

A statement which made him as big a liar as the Captain! It suddenly occurred to Drew all over again that one of the drawbacks of being a spy—or even a humble intelligencer, which he was—was that one rarely spoke the truth, even to one's wife. He also thought that, his own attitude to the Captain having changed somewhat, Bess's intuitive understanding of his moods had resulted in changing hers, too.

He took her by the arm, "We had best return, I think. I would not have it thought that I was engaging in a lengthy fit of the sullens."

"No, husband. But you are allowed, I hope, to enjoy the evening with your wife."

The face Bess turned on him was so artlessly mischievous that Drew found himself giving a little groan and taking her into his arms. The sweet scent of her filled his nostrils. A passionate few minutes followed—until Drew released her from his demanding arms and stepped away from her.

"Not here, wife. Not here. It would not be seemly for us to be discovered enjoying ourselves in the open like a pair of country lovers."

Laughing, despite being full of the frustration of joy denied, Bess shook her head at him gravely. "Oh, you are right, Drew. Think what the Lady Arbell would say of you—that your wife, the milkmaid, had corrupted the finest flower of Her Majesty's Court. What can the world be coming to?"

He was so enchanted by her charming impudence that he took her in his arms again, and whispered into her ear, "You must not be jealous of her, wife. Think rather that she is jealous of you."

Bess pulled away from him a little. "But she is so beautiful in the way which our world accounts beautiful." The words were wrenched from her.

"Her face, yes. But her soul, Bess—what colour is that?"

Bess hid her face in Drew's hard chest—and his scent was now all about her. Horse, the open air, and the lavender in which his shirt and doublet had been packed in his trunk, were all mixed together with the characteristic musky aroma of a roused man.

Blindfolded, she would know him anywhere. Not to be united with him here, in the clean air, away from the gossip and the knowing eyes which followed them everywhere, was sweet torture indeed.

Nevertheless, she walked indoors with him, to endure for a little space the company of others until, alone together, they could end what the fair night outside had begun.

## Chapter Eleven

"Who would have thought that the gallant Captain would be late for this rendezvous?" complained Charles to Drew the following morning. "He was full of it last night. Swore that he would have his revenge on you. A strange revenge, not to turn up at all."

"Mayhap he is unwell," returned Drew, who had seated himself on a small stool placed behind the mark from which the archers shot. A number of other men were busily engaged in shooting against one another before they retired to the baths. Tib stood by, guarding Drew's bow and his quiver full of arrows. Philip Sidney, present to watch the match, was saying nothing, but his expression showed that he agreed with Charles.

Charles, indeed, was in a bad mood. He had just had word that morning that a courier carrying a satchelful of accounts, letters and instructions whom he had sent to the Comptroller at Drew's London house had been attacked at an inn on the London road, just north of the capital. The courier had been robbed of the small amount of money he was carrying, but the satchel had not been stolen, even though its contents had been strewn about the road outside the inn. The robber, or robbers, had not thought that they were worth making off with.

Drew, listening with half an ear to his lamentations, was looking towards the house, waiting for Captain Goreham to appear. Instead, he saw a page whom he recognised running in the direction of the butts.

"Ah, Charles," he said, "cease your pacing and your cursing. I believe that a Mercury is coming haste post-haste towards us with a budget of excuses from the good Captain, I believe."

Drew's Mercury was the Captain's youthful page, now advancing on them, an important look on his face.

"My master, Captain Goreham," he piped at Drew, bowing low before he spoke, "presents his apologies to you, my Lord of Exford, but he has awoken with the recurrence of an old leg injury which makes walking and standing difficult. He trusts that you will forgive him and, knowing that you may not have broken your fast, he asks you to do him the honour of breaking it with him in his room."

"Well done," said Drew. "To remember all that is a great feat, young sir. Tell your master that I will be pleased both to eat with him and to offer him my commiserations on his injury. We shall shoot against one another on a future day, I am sure."

"And if you believe that tale, Drew," grunted Charles, who had taken the Captain in acute dislike, "you are greener than I thought that you were. He is obviously regretting his challenge and taking the opportunity to avoid being beaten." Philip was nodding agreement with him.

"No matter." Drew stood up as the page ran off. "Civility demands that I wait upon him as he asks. To do otherwise would be too cruel a snub. You will both present my excuses to my wife, who has already gone with Sir Henry and his wife to break her fast.''

He could only wonder what game the Captain was playing now. Like Philip and Charles, he doubted the truth of the tale the page had told them, but not for the same reason as they did. No, the Captain wished to speak to him as soon as possible, and alone, and this was as easy a way of doing so without drawing suspicion on them that he could contrive.

The Captain was lying upon a settle, his leg stretched before him, and cushions behind his back. ''Which,'' he told Drew while pages and footmen finished setting out a meal for them, ''is also exceeding painful. So painful that I could scarce rise from my bed this morning. Was not that so, Tom?'' he asked the sturdiest footman of all.

''Oh, aye, master. In great pain you were. A-moaning and a-groaning. Should have stayed there.''

''Not I,'' said the Captain, looking manful. ''An old soldier such as I am must needs be out of bed, not lying in it like a foolish milksop. True, my lord?''

''Oh, very true,'' agreed Drew, wondering what was coming next when the Captain dismissed all his servants on the pretext that ''old soldier as I am, I do not need coddling. That will ruin me sooner than aught else.''

They were alone. Drew watched the Captain leap briskly out off the settle and begin to pile his plate with bread, butter, meat and cheese from the groaning table. No sign was left of his troublesome injury.

''Happy to see,'' Drew could not help remarking, ''that my mere presence seems to have brought about a remission of your agony.''

''Exactly so,'' agreed the Captain, his mouth full.

"Eat up, my lord. You will need your strength for what I am going to tell you."

Hardly a way to encourage a man's appetite; nevertheless Drew, too, filled his plate with the excellent victuals which Shrewsbury's kitchen provided, and drank his good ale.

"Now, m'lord," intoned the Captain, putting down his plate. "Attend to what I have to tell you. We— that is, Sir Francis and I—had no notion of how messages were being sent to the French Embassy by the plotters here. It was quite by accident that we discovered that there was a plot at all, but we could not find its conduit to the Continent. I have today received definite proof that a letter was secretly sent from Buxton to London during the last week."

He paused, before saying, "You will not like it when I tell you where it was discovered and who was carrying it, although we believe the courier to be innocent."

"Go on," Drew's voice was steady, though he knew that he was about to hear some bad news.

"We had word that the courier left Buxton on Monday, a week ago. One of my men knocked him on the head at an inn in Barnet, and found the letter in a secret pocket in the satchel carrying papers bound for your home in London. Yes, m'lord—" for he saw Drew's face change colour "—that is the right of it. And I am supposing that this is as great a surprise to you as it was to me."

"Then you suppose correctly, Captain. Although I find this news both unwelcome and difficult to believe."

"Nevertheless," said the Captain, "that is the truth of it."

"And did this letter give away who wrote it—and who the plotters were?"

The Captain shook his head. "Alas, no, my lord. False names were used. The letter was read, copied— so that those versed in codes might try to decipher it further—and then was sent on its way again when the courier recovered."

Drew knew who the courier was. A young gentleman of his household, Robert Nash by name. He was relieved to learn that the Captain thought him to be innocent. Except that two other persons were guilty— the man who had smuggled the letter into the satchel and the man who would remove it from its hiding place and send it on its way to the French Embassy.

And both men must be his retainers, his trusted servants.

"So, I am harbouring the traitors, Captain."

"Not all of them. Others are involved, but your men are the conduit through which the treacherous post to the Continent is directed."

This did not make Drew any happier. For it now seemed that it might be someone whom he trusted who had tried to kill him. He was aware of the Captain watching him as he stuffed bread, cheese, and sliced, spiced beef into his mouth.

He must say something, something full of common sense and determination as befitted his position. It came to him that what he would have liked most of all to do before he answered the Captain was to talk the whole thing over with his wife! Which was indeed a strange thought to have, except that she was level-headed after a fashion which he had never expected a woman to be.

"What then," he said at last, as the remainder of

the cheese disappeared down the Captain's throat, "ought we to do?"

"What we have been doing. Be patient and wait to see whether our men in London can uncover anything. Your home in London will be watched to try to find out who carries the letter to the Embassy. If and when we do so, then we can perhaps lean on him, and thus discover who else is involved. On the other hand, more might be gained by leaving him free so that we might learn who his associates are."

Lean on him! It would be Topcliffe, the torturer at the Tower of London, who would do the leaning— which was only what a traitor deserved when all was said and done. Still, he had to believe that the Captain knew his murky business.

Drew had small appetite for the food before him. Nevertheless, he ate as though he were hungry, the food ashes in his mouth. Who was it whom he trusted who was betraying him?

Later, in the evening as they talked after their meal, Bess was asking herself the same question. She was not concerned with spies and plotting but whether her husband was betraying her. She had come, thanks to his loving attentions to her, to believe that her suspicion of him over the matter of Lady Arbell was foolish, based on unfounded jealousy. In the last few days Drew had seemed indifferent to the Lady Arbell's attractions. His manner to her had become cool and indifferent.

But today he had changed again. Bess was not to know that Drew, driven by the need to discover exactly who was betraying whom at Buxton, had decided to encourage Arbell in her pursuit of him, in the hope that if she were involved in a Catholic plot, she would by some means give herself away when talking to him.

More wounding than that, Bess, who had spent the afternoon at the Holy Well with Marian Blagg, had walked back to her room up the great staircase and along the corridor which led through some of the bedrooms. She had heard voices; the voices of a man and a woman laughing together.

It was Drew and Arbell, standing before a window, talking intimately. Arbell was facing towards Bess, when she saw Bess coming, she flung her arms around Drew and kissed him on the cheek. From where Bess stood it seemed that Drew was encouraging her. In reality, Arbell, desperate to seduce him, thought that to make trouble between Drew and his wife was the best way to win him.

Drew heard someone coming. He detached himself—with some difficulty—from the clinging Arbell and turned to face his wife.

"Ah, there you are, my lady. You left the Well early?"

Bess was acid. "No earlier than I intended, my lord. Was there some reason why you wished me to be late?"

Arbell, who had now backed away from Drew, smiled sweetly at Bess. "I will give him back to you, Lady Exford, so that he may prepare himself for the evening meal."

I had not thought that she had me to hand back, was Drew's glum reaction, but judging by Bess's face, she believes what the lying bitch has just suggested.

His bow to Arbell before they left was as gallant as he could make it, although the moment that they were out of the Lady's hearing he said to Bess, without any apology, "Although appearances might seem otherwise, you are not to suspect that there is anything between the Lady Arbell and myself, wife."

"No?" Bess raised her eyebrows without raising her voice. "I wonder what you would say if I behaved as lovingly to your friend Philip—or Charles—or even Captain Goreham?"

Drew gritted his teeth. "I should say a great deal, believe me, but—"

"But I am not to say anything because I am a wife, not a husband. No, Drew, do not gloss over your behaviour. I would rather you were honest with me. I do not like deceit."

"Damnation, I am being honest with you, woman! I mean what I say, but…"

"But what? Do you mean what you do? And the Lady, does she mean what she says and does? That kiss she gave you, for example?"

"That kiss meant nothing. She forced it on me."

Bess began to laugh, genuine laughter, no bitterness in it. "Poor Drew, to be so assaulted by a woman. Shall I force a kiss on you, husband? Like this?"

And in a mocking imitation of Arbell she turned towards him, flung her arms around him and kissed him vigorously on the lips.

They had reached the privacy of their inner chamber. Drew's response was to take her in his arms, bear her down on to a fine Turkish carpet, and give her not one kiss, but many, before pleasuring her so vigorously that they both lay spent on the floor when their lovemaking had ended.

Panting, half-naked, his lips scarlet—as were Bess's with the force of their passion—Drew looked down at her, as she gazed up at him. "Now, woman, will you believe me? Do you think I could have treated you so lustily if I had spent the afternoon making love to *her?* I'd as soon make love to a…a…''

Words failed him. He couldn't think what it was that he didn't want to make love to… Instead, he began to stroke and pet Bess again, until she whispered into his almost unhearing ear, ''I think that the word you could not find for the Lady Arbell was 'pillow'. And if we are going to make the beast with two backs again, husband, do you think that I could lie on something soft whilst we do so? The floor, even with a carpet on it, makes a hard bed.''

''Assuredly.'' Drew picked her up again and carried her to the bed where they enjoyed themselves so heartily that they scarcely had time to clamber into their elaborate clothing before repairing to supper.

Even so, for the next few days, like Drew, Bess could not quite recapture the mindless happiness which she had enjoyed before she had seen Arbell kiss him so intimately. A shadow lay over her.

Drew's shadow was the knowledge of his household's involvement in the plot against the Queen. He saw and heard nothing to give him any clues which might help him to solve the mystery. By the end of the week, both Charles and Philip separately asked him what was troubling him. Was it so obvious? Plainly he would not make an agent if being a simple intelligencer was so hard to carry off!

And then a further blow fell. Captain Goreham challenged him to an archery match to replace the one which had been cancelled because of his supposed injury.

"But we must meet privately, you understand," the Captain said, looking solemn. "We need to be alone."

The next morning an early hour found them at the butts. They went through the pretence of a match, although neither man's mind was on the game. They spent the time between the rounds talking of what was paramount on both their minds, although a watcher from the windows of the Great Hall would merely have seen two men enjoying themselves in the cool of the early morning.

"I have news for you," the Captain said. They were standing at some distance from their two pages, whom they had encouraged to engage in a match of their own. "I have had a despatch from London which informs me that they have discovered the member of your household who is passing letters from Buxton to the French Embassy.

"One of your maidservants has a lover there, a man who poses as a senior footman, but is someone quite other. They are lovers, and she has been suborned into helping him by the promise of marriage. She does not understand quite what she is doing, but she takes charge of the satchel with the secret pocket after its legitimate papers have been removed and takes the letter from the pocket to give to her lover. Later he gives her a letter to Buxton which she must slip into the satchel before it goes north again."

Drew contained himself with some difficulty. He was astonished to find, after the Captain had passed on this bad news, that he could shoot at all, let alone shoot well.

"Can I believe you?" he asked, after he had shot into the gold again. "You are telling me that it is someone from my *own* retinue who is sending the letters from Buxton?''

Captain Goreham shot again before replying. "Indeed, m'lord. As you plainly see, it must be so.''

''And have you any evidence of who the spy at the Buxton end might be?''

The Captain pulled an arrow from his quiver. ''None at all, except...'' and he paused before looking quizzically at Drew ''...except that on the face of it, the traitor can be none other than yourself!''

The heavens reeled around Drew. So this accounted for Walsingham's odd treatment of him. That he thought Drew to be the traitor, and Goreham was obviously here to keep watch on him, rather than on anyone else.

He shot again. And hit the gold again.

From a great distance he heard the Captain behind him murmur, ''Well shot, m'lord.''

He was surprised by his own coolness when Tower Hill, hanging, drawing and quartering loomed before him. He stepped away to allow the Captain to take his turn, saying, ''I suppose that denial is useless, but deny it I must.''

''Failing any other evidence.'' The Captain was almost negligent in the manner of his reply.

Drew wanted to throttle him, and Walsingham, too. The Captain said, his own arrow having found the gold, ''The main plot here began after you arrived. Earlier we know that it was being run from London. And your grandfather was a Catholic.''

''Oh, rare, sir, rare,'' mocked Drew. ''Seeing that he was a young man in the old King's time when everyone was a Catholic. On that evidence you had better attaint and execute all the males in the kingdom.''

"I did not say that you are a conspirator, or even the chief one. Simply that the burden of the evidence lies in that direction. Convince me otherwise. Such are my orders.''

"Since my unsupported word of honour is not enough, only by unmasking the true traitor can I prove my innocence. Simply to shriek denials at you, and play the offended fool, would not have you believing otherwise.''

Without waiting for an answer Drew shot again—and struck the gold again. It seemed that his cold hauteur in the face of such a dreadful accusation disturbed the Captain more than it disturbed him, for from then on the match was downhill all the way for his opponent. Drew continued to find the gold whilst the Captain was doomed to the outer colours.

On his last hopeless shot the Captain put down his bow and turned to face Drew. His manner had changed completely. All its greasy unction had disappeared and the real man, hidden beneath it, appeared: the mercenary soldier completely sure of himself.

"The match is yours, m'lord. And I must confess that I have misread you again. True or traitor, you are not the soft, courtly creature I took you for. Your hand did not shake even at the moment of accusation. Rather than causing you to lose the match, from that moment on, your skill improved.''

"And what," asked Drew, "am I to make of that? That you think me a cold-blooded plotter—or simply cold-blooded—or that you said what you did to make me shoot badly?''

The Captain shook his head, "Why, as to being a conspirator, sir, I know not. Only time will tell."

Drew turned on his heel. "And now it is time to break fast. Forgive me if I do not accompany you back to the Hall. I have much to think of, and would prefer to do so alone."

He walked away in the direction of the Holy Well. His first thought was that he must keep watch for the courier returning with the satchel so that he might stop him and examine it before any one else did. What he found would determine his next action.

He also asked himself how serious the Captain's accusation had been. He thought that it might not be totally so, but the fact that it had been made at all explained Walsingham's odd behaviour towards him—and why he had been chosen to go to Derbyshire. Lacking evidence of any kind either about the Captain, who was conceivably a double agent, or who exactly the true conspirators might be, he could come to no real conclusion until he found some.

He only knew that he had grown hungry and that Bess might wonder where he had gone without telling her of his destination. She might even suspect that he had a secret tryst with Arbell—which would never do.

On reaching the Hall, he found Charles and Philip talking together in the entrance. About him, apparently, for Charles said, somewhat reproachfully, "Ah, there you are, cousin. A pity that you did not care to tell us that you and Captain Goreham had decided to engage in your postponed match this morning. Master Sidney and I would have enjoyed watching it."

"We met on a whim," Drew replied shortly, "and were bent on our own pleasure, not on that of others."

He was aware that he sounded surly, but he felt

surly, and in no mood to humour anyone. One thing he had decided on his walk: that he would treat all the members of his household as though they were the traitor—even Charles. He excluded Philip from suspicion, knowing that his hatred of Catholics was so strong that he had even lost favour with the Queen because of his opposition to her marrying the French Catholic, the Duc d'Alençon.

And Bess. He excluded Bess because he would have staked his life on her honesty.

"Forgive me," he said, brushing by them both. "I am hungry. I will talk to you both later when breaking my fast has improved my humour."

Charles said nothing. Nor Philip neither; he raised his fine brows and wondered what flea had occupied Drew's ear and spoiled his usual calm temper. He felt constrained to ask, his voice light to take the sting out of his words, "You lost the match, then?"

Drew, already on his way, turned back, and shook his head before he answered him. "On the contrary, cousin and friend both, I won it easily. May all such meetings for me end in victory."

# Chapter Twelve

Was he, or was he not, dallying with Arbell? If so, it wasn't making him very happy. On the contrary her husband, who had been in the best of humour when they had arrived at Buxton, was now in the worst of one.

Bess was preoccupied by this sad thought whilst she was being dressed for the day. Her maid was tying her sleeves on to her bodice and carefully arranging the little rolls which concealed the joins. Bess had refused to wear the huge ruff which her maid—and fashion—demanded, and had chosen a small one instead.

"But the Lady Arbell will be sure to be wearing hers," the maid wailed.

"All the more reason for me not to do so." Bess was crisp—and, for her, a little demanding. What she really wanted to do was put on her old coarse, brown dress and go riding with Drew across Charnwood Forest. She was growing tired of idleness at Buxton, of being pushed in and out of stiff clothes and being expected by her waiting women to rival the other ladies in the excesses of her dress.

Drew put his head around the door. "You are beautified enough to allow me in, I hope."

"Far too beautified." Bess was aware that she was being pettish but she could not help herself. "I have enjoyed my visit to Buxton, husband. It has been a happy change to be idle, but I am growing wishful to see my home again and go riding with you in something more comfortable than this."

"Ah, I suppose you mean that old piece of sacking you were wearing when I first met you," riposted Drew, kissing the cheek which Bess's maid had just treated with some sweet-smelling oil designed to make its user stay young for ever—or so the herbalist had said. "Couldn't you consider something between the two?"

"Only if it were comfortable."

"The Lady Arbell—" began the maid.

"No," ordered Bess. "Do not speak of her again. I have not the slightest wish to look like her. What are you laughing at, husband?"

"Anyone less like the Lady Arbell than my dear wife, I have yet to meet. Pray leave us," he told the maid.

"Now," he asked, "what has brought this fit on, wife?"

"Jealousy," said Bess bluntly, "and the fact that I wish to go home. We have been here long enough. Yes, I have enjoyed myself, but I find that I am growing homesick."

Drew would dearly have loved to accede to her wishes, but what he was unable to tell her restrained him. He could not leave Buxton until he had cleared his name and uncovered the real traitor. After a week of waiting and watching, he was still no nearer to doing that, for the courier from London had not yet returned. He did not wish to tell Bess the unhappy truth. He could only hope that the Captain's suspicions of him would be cleared up without her having to know of them.

Instead he remarked blandly, "I think that you deserve a little longer holiday, dear wife."

Bess was blunt again. "What keeps you here, Drew? Me, or the Lady Arbell?"

He took her in his arms, and said fiercely. "No, do not believe that. We must stay a little longer. I have my reasons for asking you to agree to this. Believe me, like you, I am wishful to be back at Atherington again."

This came out after a fashion which Bess could only believe was heartfelt.

But could she believe him?

"And your reasons are?"

"I cannot tell you—not yet, at least."

He only wanted to protect her, but by doing so he was in danger of losing her trust. He was going to lose it a little more when he made his next request.

"Sir Henry has asked that we make up a party of men to go riding along the Wye. He hopes to find deer, and we shall take our bows with us. He has permission to shoot from Lord Shrewsbury. He has asked that you keep company with the Lady Arbell whilst we are gone. We are like to be away until evening."

"Men, only men? Why cannot I accompany you? I can ride a horse as well as any man. And I do not wish to spend the day with the Lady Arbell. You may tell Sir Henry that I have a megrim and beg to be excused." Bess was unhappily aware that she sounded both unreasonable and petulant.

"Not all the men. Charles will not be going. He has accounts to do, he says, and Master Blagg is expecting his Steward today, and will only accompany us if the man arrives before we are due to leave. Nor will the Captain go. Like you, he has a megrim."

Which, seeing that he knew that she hadn't a megrim, thought Bess dolefully, could be taken any way you liked.

"Don't look at me like that," Drew told her. "I have no wish to go, either, but I have no real excuse to offer." Which was not the true reason why he wished to join the expedition. There was always the possibility that someone might say, or do, something incriminating whilst they were at ease. A slight possibility, but still a possibility.

"Very well, then. Go—I will entertain myself." She accompanied this with a kiss on his warm cheek to show that she forgave him for deserting her. "Do your duty—for I understand that you do not wish to snub Sir Henry by refusing his invitation."

Relieved, and after a kiss in return, Drew left her to sink down on a settle in her useless finery—for who was there to see it now? Except that Drew came back to put his head round the door again to say, "Do not sit indoors, dear wife. Tib may escort you should you wish to ride."

"But you know I must pretend that I have a megrim," Bess wailed.

"Then think of a better excuse," and Drew was gone.

I shall offer no excuse at all, thought Bess grimly. The kitchen shall pack us a picnic, and Tib and I shall pretend that we are quartering Charnwood Forest again. The maid must take off my fancy clothing and

I shall borrow some of Tib's, ride astride and pretend that I am virgin again and may do as I please! And what I please is to be as far away from the Lady Arbell as possible.

For Tib it had been like old times come back again. He and Walter, one of Lord Shrewsbury's grooms, had accompanied his lady on a ride into the hills. They had broken their fast on a grassy knoll among the trees, eating bread, butter and cheese with gusto. Once they had stopped to drink pure, fresh water from a stream. Bess was, for a brief space, the very young lady whom he had dared to love from afar.

They arrived back at Buxton in the middle of the afternoon, their small idyll over. For all her happiness that carefree afternoon, Bess could not truly wish herself maiden again; she had come to love her husband and would not have the old days return.

Tib cared for their horses, helped by Walter, after watching his mistress walk cautiously back into the Hall lest anyone see her in her boy's garb. Walter wanted to talk about the day, and the girl he hoped to marry who lived and worked at Chatsworth, being part of Lord Shrewsbury's immense household, but Tib did not want to hear of the happiness of others.

He excused himself, and decided to look for one of m'lord's dogs which had wandered off that morning and had not been seen since. It was as good an excuse as any to be alone. He set off whistling to keep his spirits up and occasionally calling Ranter's name.

After a time Tib no longer needed to whistle to be happy. He had become resigned to the fact that, now that Bess was married to m'lord Exford, she was forever out of his reach. He had come to the edge of the

Great Hall's demesne, where a wall separated it from the scrub and brambles which surrounded it. Near a rude gate which opened on to the wilderness stood a small stone building in the shape of a classical temple, which overlooked the view towards the distant hills.

Was it possible that naughty Ranter had hidden himself away there again as he had done a few days ago? Tib walked over to it and up the steps which led to a small verandah and a doorway which gave access to an inner room. The door stood slightly ajar.

He was about to shout Ranter's name when he heard voices and muted laughter. Someone was using the little temple for a secret tryst, no doubt about it—the voices were both male and female, and their tone was loving and confidential.

Tib smiled to himself, and turned to leave—and then stopped. One of the voices, the woman's, was speaking his mistress's name after the most derisory fashion, and he recognised it as that of the Lady Arbell.

Now, who could she be with? Stableyard gossip held that she and m'lord Exford were lovers, but Tib had never believed that, and she could not be with m'lord now, for he was far away on a deer hunt with the Lady Arbell's husband.

And then he heard the man's voice—and the sound of it shocked him, not only because it told him who the Lady Arbell's lover was, but even more because of what he was saying.

"Oh," he laughed, "we have foxed them properly, my love. And, the cream of the jest is that, with any luck, we shall have the whole world believing that Exford and his wife are conspiring to set Queen Mary on the throne of England, something which will bring great profit to us both, whether we succeed in our enterprise or not!'' The woman's laughter which followed was hard and cruel.

No! Tib was almost beside himself on hearing this, for no less was being joked about than a conspiracy to condemn his master and mistress to a cruel death on Tower Hill!

His shock on hearing such treachery—and who was planning it—was so great that he forgot to be cautious as he ran from the temple to find Lady Exford immediately to tell her of what he had overheard. Alas, someone had left a pail in the lee of the steps and his foot caught it and sent it clattering.

The man's voice called, ''Hola, who's there?'' and on receiving no answer, there was the sound of following footsteps. Tib realised too late that he must not be discovered and began to run as fast as he could, but his pursuer was fleeter of foot and was upon him before he had gone many yards. He spun Tib round so that they stood face to face.

They were quite alone; Tib was unarmed and the other man held a dagger in his hand. He laughed at the sight of Tib, standing there with no saviour, no one in sight to whom he might call for help.

''Oh, the faithful servant,'' he jeered. ''Not someone to bribe to keep quiet, I fear,'' and before Tib could comprehend that his doom was upon him, he drove the dagger into Tib's breast.

Tib fell and lay still. His murderer bent down and dragged him to the edge of the undergrowth where, with luck, he might not be found for some time. He wrenched Tib's small medallion of St Christopher from around his neck, and cut his half-empty purse away to suggest that the man who had shot at Lord Exford might have found easier pickings.

And then he returned to the Lady Arbell to tell her that they were safe, but that they must, separately, return to the house at all speed so that no one might suspect that they had aught to do with the murdered man outside.

Behind them, Tib, half-conscious and not quite dead, pressed a lax hand to his wound to stem the flow of blood and began to drag himself free in the direction of the Great House…

Bess, dressed in her finery again, visited the Baths, something which she had not done for several days. Afterwards, refreshed, and feeling the need for exercise, she decided to take a turn in the grounds which surrounded the Hall. Hardly had she done so before she saw Philip Sidney coming towards her across the grass, a book in his hand. He greeted her with a smile.

"I had thought that you were with the deer hunters," she rallied him.

"Well, so I was, but I grew weary of the chase after we had eaten, and the poetic fit being on me, I stayed behind to indulge it—I always carry a small notebook with me, you understand. Then, the Muse being satisfied, I decided to return early to Buxton, only to find that the others were home some time before me, having gone by a shorter route! On learning that you had gone to the Baths, Drew decided to walk there."

Beth gave a little groan. "Alas, we must have crossed with each other. I returned by the longer path. We could have met and taken a walk together."

Ever gallant, Philip sought to console her. "In his

absence, will you do me the honour of walking with me a little instead, madam?''

''Only if you promise to read me your latest sonnet when we have done so,'' returned Bess gaily. Despite missing Drew, she was feeling at peace with all the world, and could even have been civil to the Lady Arbell if she had suddenly appeared.

''To the temple then, that haven of peace away from the noise of the Hall,'' Philip said, ''and there I may read you my new sonnet, and after that talk philoso-phy—if it so pleases you.''

''Oh, everything pleases me this afternoon, Master Sidney. Yes, I will walk with you.''

Afterwards, Bess was to think glumly that every time she thought that she might have found Arcadia, something dreadful happened to ruin it, and to remind her of the cruel harshness of the real world in which she lived.

They were almost at the little temple when they saw something lying on the ground before it. It appeared to be a heap of discarded clothes, but no, it could not be that, for it was moving. Nearer to, the pathetic heap turned out to be a man stretched on the ground, who tried to lift his head a little as they approached him.

''Stand back, Bess,'' Philip ordered her, for like Bess he had seen the trail of blood behind the fallen man. ''I do not think that this is a sight for you.''

''No,'' exclaimed Bess feverishly, disobeying him and running forward. ''Oh, sweet Jesu, I do believe that it's Tib,'' and before Philip could stop her, she was on her knees beside her poor servant who was covered in blood and plainly dying.

He was trying to speak to her, but when he did so

his voice was so faint that she could not hear him properly, nor could Philip, who knelt on his other side.

She took his hand. "Oh, Tib, who has done this to you?" Her voice broke as she spoke.

Tib only knew one thing: that he had found his beloved mistress again and that he must warn her before death claimed him. "Betrayed," he managed to choke out. "You are betrayed by the Lady Arbell and—" and even as he began to choke out her lover's name there came a gush of blood from his mouth and he fell headlong into the darkness of oblivion and death.

"No!" Bess could not believe it. Tib had been her playmate and later her friend and protector and now he was gone.

"Come," said Philip, rising gently after closing Tib's eyes. "We can do no more for him. We must return to the House and make arrangements for—"

"No, I shall stay with him until those arrive who will carry him to his last resting place before he is decently buried."

"It might not be safe," Philip began, to have Bess say passionately,

"I have known him all my life, and this is the least that I can do for a faithful servant."

She was not to be moved, and Philip, respecting her wishes, left her there alone, to wonder numbly who it might be who wished to betray her and why. She was sure that the Lady Arbell had not murdered Tib, but the man who must have been with her in the temple and whom Tib must have unfortunately surprised.

But she would speak of his last words to no one for she knew that Philip had not heard them. Besides, how could she accuse Arbell—whom everyone must know she disliked—lacking any evidence to support her, without appearing stupidly spiteful? Nor could she yet speak of this matter to Drew, for, things being as they were, it might be him of whom Tib was trying to speak.

No, that could not be! Drew was no murderer, she was sure of that. And, after he had overcome his first anger with Tib because he had been a witness of his behaviour to Bess, he had been consistently kind to him.

It was all too much. Bess dropped her head and, still holding Tib's hand, began to weep for him and for the happy days which were gone.

# Chapter Thirteen

Tib's murder did not create quite as much commotion as the attempt on Drew's life, for as the Lady Arbell tastelessly remarked, "He was only a servant, after all."

It was as well that she did not say that in Bess's hearing—or in that of the Queen of Scots, who had once seen a faithful servant, her Italian musician Rizzio, murdered in front of her.

Bess had never liked the Queen so much as on the first occasion when they met after Tib's death when she commiserated with her on it. "Such a terrible thing to happen, and here in the depths of the country where we are alone, and where we must fear that someone we know might have done such a dreadful deed."

This unhappy thought was on a number of minds, Drew's and Captain Goreham's among them. The Captain found occasion to whisper to him, "Do you suppose that your man was in league with the traitors, m'lord?"

"Unlikely, I would have thought. Unless he was

recruited after he had arrived here—either by someone
in my retinue, or another's.''

Drew would have expected Bess to have been distressed by Tib's awful end and the fact that she had
witnessed it, but the depth of it surprised him. He was
not to know that Bess's unhappiness was magnified by
her lonely worries over who Tib's murderer might be,
since she had told no one of his last words. One other
thing which kept her silent was that if she reported
them, the finger of suspicion would be sure to point
at Drew, who was thought to be attracted to the Lady
Arbell more than he should be.

Her fears haunted her for the next two days, until,
quite suddenly whilst reading her Bible, she had a revelation. She did not compare it with St Paul's on the
road to Damascus, for that would have been blasphe-
mous, but it was a revelation all the same.

Why was she doubting Drew? Nothing he had ever
said or done to her—or to others—gave her any reason
to believe that he might do anything as dreadful as kill
Tib. And certainly not just to stop him from revealing
that he was enjoying a secret tryst with Arbell in the
little temple.

She loved Drew, and love, they said, or as poets
like Philip said, was blind, but she was not so blind
as to allow love to destroy her better judgment. And
another thing had begun to trouble her. Tib had coupled Arbell's name with betrayal and her first thought
had been that Drew might have been betraying her by
trysting with Arbell—to put it politely.

But suppose that Tib had meant something quite
different from that? Something which might explain
why Drew had been shot at—that he was being betrayed, as well as herself? The thought seemed fanci-

ful...and yet...and yet... Were they not in the neighbourhood of a woman for whom many men had plotted, might be plotting even now, and would surely do so in the future?

But how could she and Drew be involved in this? Devious plotters might wish to kill the Queen of England on behalf of the Queen of Scots, but why should they wish to kill Drew?

One thing she must do, and at once, as soon as they were safely alone. She must tell him of Tib's last words.

So it was that later that night, once their servants had left them and they were alone in the Great Bed, Bess gently put aside Drew's attempts to make love to her and said, as composedly as she could, for she did not wish to sound like a hysterical fool, "Drew, there is something of great importance which I must tell you and no one else."

He leaned back on his pillows, his arms crossed above his head, laughing up at her as she sat there so still and so solemn.

"Come, wife, what is it that has you putting on such a Friday face? I know Tib's death has disturbed you, but life goes on and, knowing him, I do not believe that he would have you grieving endlessly for him."

Bess said, still calm and reserved, "Three days is hardly endless, Drew, but yes, it is of Tib's death that I wish to speak. That afternoon, when Philip and I found him lying on the ground in his blood and trying to crawl to the house, he spoke to me."

Drew sat up, his face changing from a comic mask to a tragic one like an actor in buskins interpreting a

Greek play and lifting one mask from his face to replace it with another.

"He spoke to you? Philip said nothing of this, nor have you—until now. Why, wife, why? For what he said might be of such import that we might be able to identify his murderer."

Bess closed her eyes, and then opened them again as she took his right hand which lay lax on the counterpane.

"Listen to me, my lord of Exford, and you will know why I have said nothing—not even to you until this secret moment. Philip could not hear him. I was bent over him, and it was to me to whom he spoke, and to none other. He said, and you must believe that I heard him aright, although his voice was choked with blood…"

Her own voice faltered and died, as Tib's had done. Drew pressed her hand lovingly, and she found strength to continue.

"He said, 'You are betrayed. By the Lady Arbell and…' And then he spoke no more, for blood gushed from his mouth, and so he died before he named a name. I have thought long and hard. I do not believe that Arbell killed him, but I believe that she had a secret meeting in the little temple with a lover, a man who did kill Tib. Why he should do so drastic a thing, I cannot think…?"

Her voice still thick with unshed tears, Bess stopped.

Drew stared at her, his brain whirling. Finally he said, his voice nearly as unrecognisable as his wife's, "Did you say nothing because you thought that Tib's murderer might have been me? That the word betrayal, coupled with Arbell, might have meant that? And then kept quiet to protect me? Or did you not believe that I was Arbell's secret companion, but that others would?''

''Oh, Drew, heart of my heart, I knew not what I thought when Tib died in my arms. Forgive me for that. Later, knowing you, I could not believe that you would kill Tib, nor could I think why Arbell's secret lover should wish to do so, either.''

Drew took her by the shoulders, ungently for him, and looked deep into her eyes. ''I shall not try to defend myself. You said that you believed that I was not responsible for Tib's death, and I can understand why, for a moment, you thought that I might have been. No forgiveness is needed. You were right to say nothing of his last words, and you must continue to be silent. Now I must question you. Was that all he said? Think carefully before you answer.''

''He said nothing more, alas! He tried to speak when he first saw me, but could not, and I fear that when he did, the effort killed him.'' She gave a little sob.

Drew pressed her hand again and said, ''Bear with me whilst I ask you one more thing. How near was Tib to the temple when you first saw him?''

Bess thought for a moment before answering. ''Quite near. This morning, on pretence of going for a walk, I followed the track he had made and it led to the undergrowth not far from the temple where the fence meets the wilderness beyond—and that is all I know, Drew, and God help me, I wish I did not!''

Drew loosened his hands from her shoulders and kissed her in mercy and pity, not in passion. ''And, knowing this, you have said nothing, but carried this burden on your own.''

It was almost a question, and Bess answered it as such. "I have spoken to no one, not even to Philip who was with me, and whom I trust. A secret is not a secret if one talks of it—but I owed it to you to tell you the truth."

"For which I honour you, wife. Now, lie down beside me, not to make love but to be comforted. I thought that you were brave, but you are braver than I knew."

Bess turned into his arms. A great weight had rolled from her shoulders. It had not gone completely, but the knowledge that her burden was shared had lightened it.

Presently she said, "Drew? Who could it be? I have thought and thought, but I can come to no conclusion. I cannot believe that it was anyone we know, but consider, would the Lady Arbell be trysting with someone we do not know?"

"I wish," began Drew, stroking and petting her as he spoke, "but that is foolish of me—to wish that this had never happened. I fear that Tib's murderer is among us, smiling as he speaks, and it behoves us all, especially yourself, to be careful. In future you must never be alone. I know that you often prefer your own company, but you must forfeit that for your own safety. Consider that the man who killed Tib did not intend him to crawl away and speak to anyone.

"Now let us sleep, for tomorrow is another day."

After a little space, Bess, emotionally drained, fell asleep in his arms, but Drew could not find oblivion for, on hearing of Tib's last words, he was sure that the Lady Arbell's lover must be the spy whom he and Captain Goreham were seeking—and he still had no notion of who he might be.

\* \* \*

"So, your brave lady heard what her servant said as he died, and told no one but yourself of it. Forgive my frankness, but she is a shrewd piece, and no mistake. Most women would have run about Buxton blabbing of what they had been told to all and sundry."

Drew was secretly pleased by this flattery. "Yes, I am a lucky man, Captain. She has had a hard life, and that perforce makes her wary, you understand. She has never been pampered."

"Exactly so, and this puts a new complexion on things. We now know one conspirator, the Lady Arbell—but not the important one—the one who takes the letters from the satchel and hands them to Nau."

He thought a moment. "You still have no notion of who that might be—and whether he is the Lady Arbell's lover?"

"None, and you are not to ask me to use Bess to find out. I will not have her put in danger."

"Oh, agreed as to that. But we are in the dark, and have no means yet of finding light."

"Except that I shall try to intercept the courier carrying the satchel when he returns so that I may examine it before anyone else does. With luck it may contain a letter."

Goreham nodded. "Good, very good—we shall make an intelligencer of you yet."

"God forbid," riposted Drew fervently. "I have had a deal of trouble in thinking of an excuse for me to intercept the courier myself—pray God it works. The sooner this wretched affair is over, the villains are found, and my name is cleared, the better."

"Oh, my master will want this plot to continue for a little while longer in order to net as many traitors as possible."

This news singularly failed to cheer Drew. Rightly or wrongly, he believed that there might be more to this affair than the Captain thought. It seemed to him that he had become a target for the plotters and for the life of him he could not think why. They could have no way of knowing of his involvement with Walsingham, for according to the Captain only he, Walsingham and Drew himself knew of that.

"Plays his cards very close to his chest, does Sir Francis," had been the Captain's comment when telling Drew this. "No one is allowed to know of anyone else's complicity and God help the poor devil who talks out of turn. He might soon lack a tongue."

Another cheerful thought. But that aside, all that remained for him was to try to reach the courier before anyone else did. Which might be difficult, since no one would expect m'lord Exford to hang about the stables waiting for one of his servants to arrive from London. One of his many underlings would be expected to do that for him.

No one watching Bess and Drew could have guessed from their behaviour that between them they harboured a number of secrets which might have been expected to leave a shadow on all their doings. Drew never ceased to marvel at the resilience and common sense of his wife. She said nothing further to him on the subject of Tib. For some days she wore a black dress in his memory and attended his funeral at the little church in a nearby village.

Aunt Hamilton remonstrated with her over her brief mourning. "Whatever will people think, my dear? After all, he was only an underservant. The Lady Arbell…"

"Do not tell me what the Lady Arbell is saying," Bess retorted. "I have no wish to hear it. And you, of all people, know that Tib has been my friend since childhood, and was more of a true gentleman than half the men boasting that title in Buxton. My husband approves of my behaviour and that is enough for me."

Aunt Hamilton said no more. Bess wondered wryly what aunt Hamilton's reaction would be if she knew the true story of Tib's death—which she was determined to avenge. But for all of her and Drew's care in listening to what was said—and half-said—they were no nearer to solving the mystery.

No matter. Patience was all, and to soothe her troubled spirit she decided that when she next met Philip she would ask him to read some of his latest poetry to her.

Yet the mystery might be nearer to being solved than she thought.

Later that afternoon, alone in his room—for Bess had finally snared Philip and was seated in the open at the back of the Hall, gilded by the sun and listening to his latest poem—Drew stared at the courier's satchel which he hoped would give up his secrets to him.

By pure chance—that chance of which Machiavelli had often written, and which the gods were said to favour mere mortals with—he had been in the stable-yard when the courier had arrived from London.

It had been the easiest thing in the world to take the heavy satchel from him and declared that he would deliver it to Charles, whilst the courier refreshed himself in the kitchen after his long ride north. But

Charles, out somewhere in the grounds, would have to wait until his master had inspected the satchel himself.

Drew began to loosen the buckles of the bag. It was full of letters and papers which he carefully removed before inspecting an inner pocket which was sewn into one of the bag's sides.

It was fastened by a button which Drew undid before putting his hand inside to find—nothing.

Nothing, it seemed, was straightforward in this Machiavellian game in which Sir Francis Walsingham had ensnared him. Of course, an almost open pocket which the courier—or anyone else—could easily inspect, would not carry a secret letter. It must be elsewhere—but where?

At the bottom of the pocket was a piece of fine linen, a lace-edged kerchief. Drew pulled it out and felt it carefully. Nothing.

Disappointment rode on his shoulders. He put his hand deep into the pocket and felt around it carefully before examining the outside of the satchel again. To notice something odd about it. The external stitching of the pocket continued to the bottom of the satchel, but the pocket he had been examining stopped halfway down it.

There must be a pocket beneath the obvious one—but how would one open it? Drew ran his fingers carefully along the pocket's bottom. Its seams were thick. Inspiration struck. He pulled one of the seams back a little and found three tiny buttons set between the seam and the bag's side. He undid them carefully to reveal a long thin opening, inside which a sheet of paper lay.

It was the secret letter contained in a version of what was commonly called a poacher's pouch.

He had started well, but his task was only half done.

The letter must be copied, and carefully replaced before he passed the bag on to Charles with some witless joke to the effect that he was becoming one of his own servants these days, but the poor devil of a courier had looked quite done up, so he had saved him the stairs.

Again he considered telling Charles of what was passing, but he remembered what Captain Goreham had said to him of the wisdom of Sir Francis Walsingham in playing his cards close to his chest by telling as few as possible of his suspicions—or his knowledge—and desisted.

I am become a true intelligencer, Drew thought wryly when, later, after copying the letter and replacing it, he joined Philip and Bess beneath the trees and laughed and talked with them and promised to take Bess to see Wilton, Philip's beautiful home, before the summer was over if their circumstances allowed.

But he did not fool Bess. As he had walked towards them she had, for a brief moment, espied a hagged look on his face, but at the sight of her it had vanished as though it had never been.

Whether Philip had seen it or no, he ceased to read the poem he had embarked on, and welcomed Drew as he sat down on a grassy bank facing them.

Drew waved an idle hand. "Continue, Philip. I would hear your latest tropes."

Philip obeyed. His beautiful voice soothed both Bess and Drew as he spoke of requited and unrequited love. So absorbed were they both that the arrival of Sir Henry and the Lady Arbell went unnoticed. They sat by Drew until, on Philip pausing for breath, Arbell interrupted him to exclaim, "Oh, fine, oh, passing fine, Master Sidney."

"Even finer, madam," remarked Bess coldly, unable to stomach the sight of the woman who must have stood by and allowed Tib to be murdered—and then said nothing, "if you had waited until Master Sidney had finished his poem!"

"Oh, had you not done so? Pray accept my apologies, sir, and continue." This was said with a gracious simper as though she was conferring on the poet a favour of the greatest magnitude.

Still seething, Bess welcomed the sight of Charles arriving. He, at least, sat down quietly beside the Lady Arbell, and allowed Philip to finish before joining in the general applause when he did so.

"Bravo, Master Sidney," was Sir Henry's contribution, echoed by the rest of the party, including Charles who asked for another verse to be read, if the poet had another with him, that was.

Arbell's simper became a pout. Listening to poetry was not her notion of a pleasant way of passing an afternoon. She placed a light, proprietary hand on Charles's knee. "Come, Master Breton, your admiration of the Muse does you credit, but I have had sufficient of sitting about. Perhaps you would do me the honour of taking a turn about the garden with me."

Something about Arbell's familiar manner to Charles, and his easy acceptance of it, grated on Bess. Which was perhaps, she thought wryly, not surprising since nearly everything the lady did grated on her.

Charles, apparently her admirer, like all the other men in Buxton, sprang to his feet and obeyed her command with "You will allow?" to Sir Henry, who waved a complaisant hand at him, apparently pleased that every man below the age of sixty admired his wife.

Which made it all the more difficult to decide precisely which one had been with her in the temple!

Their going broke up the party. Drew, his copy of the letter burning a hole in his pocket, excused himself from escorting Bess back to the house, leaving Philip to do so. He strode off in urgent search of Captain Goreham with whom he said that he had business, watched by a puzzled Bess.

Yes, there was something afoot, no doubt about it, something which had Drew making an unlikely confidant of the Captain. But Drew was not telling her what it was. She was so intrigued by this new mystery that she scarcely heard a word Philip spoke to her. When she reached her room she bade him farewell most absently in a manner not at all like her usual effervescent self, so that Philip began to wonder what was wrong with *her!*

Still musing, Bess walked over to the window which overlooked the grounds, to see Drew talking intimately to Captain Goreham. Stranger and stranger, particularly when he took the Captain by the arm in a familiar way and walked him away from the house, out of sight of its windows. Towards the butts, she supposed. But he had not taken his bow with him, nor any attendants, so he could scarcely be about to challenge the Captain to yet another match.

Almost before they had disappeared into the trees Charles now came into view, escorting Arbell, and talking animatedly to her—yet another poor fish whom she had hooked and was drawing in, no doubt.

The oddness about them which had troubled Bess earlier, troubled her again. They were plainly about to part when Arbell said something at which Charles laughed, bowed his head and took her hand—to kiss it most reverently. Before he could lift his head again, Arbell leaned forward and carelessly ruffled his hair. He caught the caressing hand and kissed it again, passionately not reverently, his eyes hard on the face of the woman before him.

The hairs on the back of Bess's head stood on end. There was something so revealing in the little scene before her that it was apparent that this was not the first occasion on which they had exchanged similar intimacies. It was as though a flash of lightning, arcing in the dark, had displayed before her, not the landscape which she had always known, but one so different that all her understanding of the world about her was completely altered.

Not Charles! No, it could not have been Charles who had killed poor Tib! But, yes, there was little doubt that Charles was Arbell's lover. A thousand small things, half-seen, half-heard and half-understood, told Bess that she was not wrong in that assumption. She had believed from the moment that she had heard Tib's last words that Arbell's secret lover had killed Tib, but did that mean that, if Charles was Arbell's lover, *he* had necessarily done so? She could well have more than one.

Which was unlikely. Given the open circumstances of their life at Buxton, to run one secret lover demanded the powers of a Machiavelli—to run several would be impossible.

Her next problem was a grave one. How to tell Drew? She had no real evidence of Charles's guilt, and Charles was the cousin with whom he had been brought up, and who was his closest, nearest friend.

Yet the more Bess thought it over, the more convinced she became that Charles *was* Arbell's secret lover and therefore, inevitably, Tib's murderer. He had not gone on the deer hunt, but had asked to stay behind—to tryst with Arbell in the temple, no doubt. But why had it been necessary to kill Tib? Surely no one would be very surprised or shocked to learn that Arbell had a lover—even Sir Henry didn't seem to care greatly whether his wife was faithful to him or not.

Whilst she was worrying over these new and painful thoughts, Charles and Arbell had walked out of her line of sight. She was left to wait for Drew's return when she must decide whether she ought to tell him of her suspicions.

Drew was wrestling with his own suspicions. Once they were out of the sight of the house, he had handed to Captain Goreham the copy of the letter from the satchel. The Captain had grunted after giving it a quick cursory glance.

"I need more time to examine it," he had said, "although it's written in a simple code. But from what I can see it tells us nothing that we do not already know. Only that the conspirators are urged to continue, and that, at the appropriate moment, the French will provide them with aid. There's mention of a possible attack on Queen Elizabeth—but no names, and no dates. We shall have to keep this correspondence going in order to learn who is involved—and we must continue to keep careful watch on the Lady Arbell."

So, if Drew had hoped that the letter might reveal his innocence and bring the whole affair to a conclusion he had been mistaken! They were no further on.

"And you still have not yet discovered the name of the Lady Arbell's lover?"

Drew had shaken his head. "As I gather you have not?"

It was the Captain's turn to shake *his* head, saying, "I think that you are in a better position to discover that than I am."

Which was a damned ambiguous statement, and left it open that the Captain might still consider Drew to be the guilty party!

Altogether he was not in the best of tempers when he joined Bess again, and the sight of her worried face served to depress him even further. "What is it, wife?" he asked. "What new horrors have you for me?"

"Do you read me so easily?" Bess shook her head. "Nay, Drew, that is not important. I hardly know how to tell you what is important."

She sat down, her face away from him. Improbably, there had been tears in her voice. She could feel them and Drew could hear them.

He sat down beside her on the settle. "Nay, sweeting, do not cry. I know that Tib's death has overset you, but it is not like my brave girl to go on grieving for what may not be mended."

Bess pulled her handkerchief from the purse at her girdle and wiped her eyes with it. "No, Drew, it's not that. I hardly know how to tell you of my suspicions because I have no real evidence to offer for them. But tell you I must. It has been borne in upon me by their behaviour that Arbell's lover is none other than your cousin Charles!"

Drew sprang to his feet. "No, never. I would as lief suspect myself!"

Bess could not help it. She, who never cried, now began to cry in earnest. "There," she said through her sobs, "I knew that I should have kept quiet. But, oh, husband, the feeling is so strong and grows stronger.

So strong that I had to tell you of it. If you think me wrong, or mistaken, you must forget what I have said.''

Drew stared down at her. Not long since he had been admiring her courage, her resilience and—face it, Drew—her cleverness. Why had he denied what she had told him with such speed? Why had he answered in a manner which precluded further discussion? Was it because, if one looked at it coolly and logically, the person most likely to be the one who placed the letter going to London in the satchel, and took out the one coming from London, must be no other than his cousin Charles?

Was that the explanation for his own recent ill humour with the world? He had been enraged that the Captain could consider him a traitor. Was he so enraged with himself for thinking that Charles might be the traitor that he refused to contemplate the evidence which showed that he must be? And was that why he was so angry with Bess? Because she had said the unsayable?

He sat down beside her again, put his arm around her shoulders, and kissed all that he could see of her cheek.

''Forgive me, wife, for being overhasty in my answer to you. What is it which makes you think Charles might be Arbell's lover?''

He did not add, And the traitor who is plotting against the Crown, for if Charles was guilty it explained why it had been necessary for him to murder Tib. It also explained why Tib's last words had been of betrayal.

Bess turned her tear-drenched face towards him. ''Everything and nothing,'' she said, before telling him what she had seen that afternoon, and had half-sensed on previous occasions.

"You see," she explained, "Charles excused himself from going on the hunt—which gave him and Arbell a good opportunity to be together. You, and the rest of the hunt, had scarce time after you had returned to meet her in the temple, pursue an amour with her, and then murder Tib. So, it seemed to me, as doubtless it did to you, that it must have been one of the men who stayed behind who was with her. I cannot believe that it was someone unknown from outside who killed him."

"Nor I," said Drew sadly, for the more he thought about it, and the more Bess had told him of her vague inklings which had brought her worries about Arbell and Charles to a head when she had seen them alone together, the more he considered that the most unlikely suspect of all was the most likely.

After all, Charles had every opportunity both to play the traitor and to run the secret correspondence between Nau and the London Embassy. And how many others were involved? Both in his household and outside it?

Drew's face was so grim that Bess put a tentative hand on the arm which had fallen away from her shoulders. "Drew? What are you thinking? Have I been a complete fool?"

"Alas, I fear not. But you must understand that we have no evidence, no evidence at all, that Arbell and Charles are either guilty lovers, or that Charles killed Tib. We should be laughed at for accusing them on such flimsy evidence. And supposing that we were proved to be wrong? Charles was my childhood's friend and playmate as Tib was yours. Am I to kill a long-standing love between us by accusing him of murdering Tib—and then discover that he was not the murderer at all?''

Oh, dear God, how hard this was. He could not tell Bess why his suspicions had begun to match hers. He had kept from her the knowledge of the plot against Queen Elizabeth and the knowledge that, if Charles was the traitor, he was not only Arbell's lover, but also her fellow conspirator, and that by some mischance Tib, overhearing them talking had had to be killed to silence him.

Worse than that, if Tib's words about Arbell and betrayal were true, then it was Charles who was arranging matters so that he, Drew, appeared to be guilty.

He could understand Bess's tears only too well. He wanted to scream at the sun and the moon, at the Christian God and all the gods in the Pantheon, his rage and terror on learning that the man who was trying to consign him and Bess to the block on Tower Hill was none other than his old friend and playmate.

Every camp has its traitor, Walsingham had said, doubtless believing that he, Drew, was the traitor. Or did he? Did the wily devil who masterminded Queen Elizabeth's security know more than he was telling Goreham and himself? Had he, perhaps, chosen Drew to unmask Charles because it would have been almost impossible for anyone else to do so?

He tightened his arm about Bess, who had ceased crying and had turned her head into his chest for comfort.

''What are we to do, then?'' she asked him.

''Nothing. Lacking evidence, we can do nothing.''

Which was not quite true, because now he and Goreham must find evidence by trapping Charles, not only to prove that Drew was not the traitor, but also because he must avenge Tib's cruel death.

This led him to draw another unhappy conclusion from these latest revelations. Was it possible that Charles had been the man who had shot at him and killed Cicero? But why should he do that? If he wished Drew to be suspected as the traitor, then why kill him? Or was the shot to warn him? But of what?

Mystery upon mystery, and all of them defying logic. There was only one sane thing left in this mad world and that was the woman who lay so confidingly in his arms. The woman whom he had once rejected and who was now the centre of his being.

# Chapter Fourteen

What gave him, and his knowledge of the plot against him, away to Charles, Drew never knew. Later he was to ask himself whether it was something he—or perhaps Bess—had said or done. Or was it Captain Goreham, who had known it was Charles all the time, and who had hinted of it to him, in order to force an ending to the matter? Drew thought not, for Goreham's instructions were to the contrary. Sir Francis wished to keep the plot in motion.

On the surface, indeed, everything went on as before. The three of them, Drew, Bess and Charles, Philip sometimes with them, patronised the Baths, drank water from the Holy Well and practised at the butts. Bess even brought herself to speak civilly to Arbell, to play at *Troule in Madame* with her as though Tib had not died and her and Charles's treachery was unknown.

Philip Sidney, indeed, was the only person to note that something ailed Drew and he bearded him about it. To be told shortly that he "was over-exercising his poetic imagination" annoyed him more than a little, for Philip was emerging from his prolonged state of calm melancholy into that of fervid excitement in which he found difficulty controlling the hot temper which went with it. He had been subject to these mood swings from childhood.

It was Charles who was agitated. He had need to be, for although Drew had replaced the letter most carefully in the satchel's hidden pocket, on fetching it out, once he was alone, Charles had had the strangest sensation that someone had been there before him.

The Bible says that the wicked flee when no man pursueth. Charles was being pursued, but did not know it, and wished to flee all the same. Ever since he had killed Tib, his guilt had begun to haunt him. On the spur of the moment fear of what Tib might have overheard had driven him to commit murder, but he had regretted his hasty action ever since, for as a result he lived in the shadow of an even greater fear.

The fear of being revealed not only as a murderer but as a traitor. Every word spoken to him seemed to carry a hidden, hideous, meaning. Every joke, every sidelong glance, seemed to say to him, Thou art the man. He knew how Cain felt after he had killed Abel, and his self-love had turned to self-loathing.

Down in the stables, after his fit of unreasoning fear over the letter, he met the courier who was helping Walter with the horses. Fear had him saying abruptly, ''Come here, man. I know that you were attacked on the way to London, and lucky you were to survive it, but was there aught amiss on your return journey? Did anyone try to stop you? Did anyone but yourself handle the satchel you carried?''

A little bewildered, the man stared at him. ''No, sir. Nothing untoward at all. No man but myself touched the satchel until I reached Buxton when m'lord himself took it from me. Most particular he was that I should give it to him for safekeeping so that he might hand it directly to you.''

So, Drew had been ''most particular,'' had he? And why was that? It was not in Drew's habit to act as a messenger boy. The black imp which had sat on Charles's right shoulder since that dreadful afternoon when he had murdered Tib, whispered in his ear, ''And why should Drew be 'most particular'? Is it possible that he suspects something?''

But if so, why and how? Had any other of Drew's habits changed recently? The imp whispered, What of his friendship with Captain Goreham? Well, what of it? Simply that, first of all, he had plainly detested the man, but, quite suddenly, his manner to him had changed, and he had become friendly—if not intimate—with him. But why not? After all, the Captain had helped him home again after the abortive attempt on his life.

And only Charles knew that it had not been an attempt on Drew's life at all. Instead, in a fit of anger that fate had given everything to Drew, and nothing to him, he had on an impulse shot to kill Cicero. At worst, he was destroying something which Drew loved, at best Drew might have broken his neck when the horse, in falling, brought him down, too.

The imp grumbled at him all the way back to his room. It muttered, You are forgetting something important. Drew must have done something which might throw light on why he should suspect you.

Oh, be damned! He was no Walsingham, to be seeing plots everywhere.

Walsingham! That was it. Drew had visited Walsingham before he had decided to go north to see his wife. He had even told him that his real reason for going north at all was to visit Buxton, which he had often longed to see.

And be damned to that, too! Drew, he uncharitably thought, was hardly the kind of world-weary grandee who needed to refresh his ageing mind and body by drinking stinking water in a damned dreary village! Never mind that it had suited him to have Drew there. He had even remonstrated with him a little, saying that the place would bore him, which statement, to Charles's great relief, Drew had dismissed with a laugh.

And it was Walsingham who had invited Drew to supper, not the other way round. And Walsingham was the Queen's spymaster.

Nothing for it now but to test Drew. To listen most carefully to him, and alas, to his wife—whom Drew did not deserve. And also to voice his suspicions to Arbell.

Neither Bess nor Drew was sleeping well. Soon after she had told him of her suspicions, Bess had awoken shortly after midnight one morning to find herself alone in bed. She sat up and looked about her.

Drew was standing in the window, with his back to her. He had parted the heavy curtains so that the moonlight shone on him, gilding his hair. He was motionless, one hand holding the curtain. His whole stiff posture told of his distress

Bess slipped silently from the bed and walked to his side to take the lax hand which was not holding the curtain. "What is it, Drew? Are you finding sleep difficult, too?"

As though her words had broken some spell which

was holding him in thrall, he turned to take her in his arms, burying his head in her soft bosom after a fashion which was almost childlike. It was, Bess knew without being told, the posture of every babe seeking comfort from its mother.

"Oh, Bess," he said, his voice muffled, "simply to touch you gives me ease, and that is why I have been standing here, debating with myself. For there is something which I know that you do not, and which I have now persuaded myself that you should. I have been trying to shield you from the evil deeds of the wicked world, but I know that I have married a strong woman, and so I will share my burden with you. You may even be safer if I do."

What in the world was he about to say? Bess stroked his head gently. "Do not tell me if it distresses you. I have every faith in your judgment."

Drew looked up at her, his eyes tender. "And I in yours." He took a deep breath, and without further ado told her of Charles and his treachery, and his involvement with Walsingham and Captain Goreham.

He ended by saying to her with the most passionate conviction, "From now on you must be even more careful than you have been. To share such knowledge with me is to share the danger which I am in."

Bess was silent when he had finished. "Alas, that explains what Tib was trying to tell me. I am glad that you have confided in me. You should not have to bear this burden alone—whatever danger it puts me in."

In one passionate movement Drew stood up and lifted her into his arms. "You are my treasure," he told her hoarsely, "and had not Walsingham asked me to go to Buxton I should never have met you, never have known you. Oh, Bess, you are my heart's darling, the other half of myself whom I never hoped to meet. You are the only good thing to have come out of this tangled mess.''

Kissing and petting her, he carried her to the bed. This was neither the time nor the place to discuss the meat of what he had told her. Rather, Bess thought, before thought ceased altogether in the throes of their mutual passion, it was the time to give him surcease from the pain which Charles's treachery was causing him.

But he, and his treachery, had to be faced, and at the same time life had to go on. Drew had made it plain to Bess that her life, as well as his, lay in the balance if he could not unmask Charles and present Captain Goreham with enough proof to convince him of their innocence. He had urged Bess to caution, bidden her to take no risks, but he had privately conceded that, strong-willed as she was, she might dare to do and say more than he thought wise.

He was right. The very next morning Bess confronted the Captain. ''You are a bigger fool than I took you for,'' she said bluntly, ''if you think that my husband could ever be a traitor.''

Captain Goreham could not have been more surprised if a pet rabbit had bitten him. He gave a short laugh. ''Oh, I honour a woman who supports her husband, dear Lady Exford, but do admit it, it takes more than a wife's word to convince a court of his innocence.''

''Nothing to that,'' retorted Bess spiritedly, ''for you know that my husband could not have killed Tib and that Charles Breton most certainly did.''

''There is that,'' the Captain agreed, ''and perhaps

you could now tell *me* exactly what the poor young man said to you when you and Master Sidney found him.''

"Assuredly,'' and presently they were engaged in as eager a tête-à-tête as he and Drew had shared. The Captain tactfully complimented Bess on her memory and on her *savoir-faire* when she had found her playmate dying.

"Well, I shouldn't have been much use to him if I had engaged in a fit of the vapours or fainted, or done something equally stupid.''

"Exactly so, m'lady. I see that your husband is coming in search of you. Need I tell you that whatever is said between the three of us over this sad matter must remain a secret?''

"I am not a fool, sir. And I must tell you that my eye will now be secretly upon the Lady Arbell and all her doings. One false step and I shall loose you at her throat!''

A spirited lady, indeed, was Drew's seemingly demure young wife. The Captain briefly envied him his bedmate. In his experience, high spirits in one area of life were like to be found in another!

"So, wife, I looked for you in our room to be told that you were gone, and behold, I find you dallying with the Captain. Go to, you should be dallying with me!''

M'lord Exford's voice was jovial, but the look he gave the Captain was a hard one, and probing. The Captain knew why the look was there.

"No dallying. M'lady and I were speaking of matters of state. Was not that so, madam?''

Before Bess could answer him, Drew was speaking

again. "I thought, wife, that I had advised you to speak of matters of state to no one but myself."

This time it was the Captain's answer which was forestalled. "Why, husband," Bess said, her face aglow, "I thought that for me to listen to the opinions of a fresh mind on the subject would be most useful."

"And useful to me also," added the Captain. "For it was most enlightening to hear from m'lady's own lips the last words of her unfortunate servant."

"I can think of two other people who might be unfortunate if I had my way," growled Drew, "and neither of them is above ten paces from me."

The Captain took him by the sleeve in the most familiar manner. "Come, m'lord, seeing that m'lady has been involved in this wretched business by accident and by her ability to read the minds and acts of others correctly, there is no way in which she can be returned to her previous situation of fortunate ignorance. That being so, it would be stupid for us not to take advantage of her abilities. By doing so, she will be in no more, and no less, danger."

"So you say." Bess was fascinated to note that Drew was still growling. "But seeing that we are about to be discovered, I will say nothing further to either of you. At present, that is. Later, why, later, will be quite another matter."

They were being approached by the Lady Arbell, who was escorted by the two squires, Masters Blagg and Bown. Sir Henry was in the rear, attended by Claude Nau and Charles. Charles, on seeing Drew, exclaimed cheerfully, "Oh, there you are, cousin. I have received two letters this morning, both by special messenger and both of which need your urgent attention."

"Not so urgent that they cannot wait upon my pleasure." Drew's annoyance with Bess for involving herself with Goreham still held him in thrall and was making him short with everyone.

She had no business putting herself at risk, none at all, and that coarse schemer, Goreham, had no business to be taking advantage of her ignorance of the danger in which she might be.

"Come, wife," he said, seizing her by the hand and half-dragging her away, "I have a mind to refresh myself in the Baths. I will do the honours with you all later. Until then, adieu."

*Exeunt* left, m'lord and m'lady Exford, he thought grimly, remembering the plays and masques he had seen when he had been at Oxford University with Philip Sidney, as he walked Bess rapidly away.

"Now what bee has lodged itself in his bonnet?" queried Arbell, her brows raised as she watched the pair of them disappear rapidly from sight. Two people were not surprised. They were an amused Captain Goreham and an alarmed Charles Breton.

So, thought the Captain, m'lord Exford's Achilles' heel is his clever young wife: that is a thing to remember, whilst Charles concluded bitterly that Drew's odd conduct was one more piece of evidence to lead him to conclude that Drew was suspicious of him and that it was affecting his behaviour.

As Bess, tactlessly, was busy warning Drew once they were safely out of sight of the others. "What ails you, husband, to be so short with everyone? You are in danger of starting your fox by warning him that the hounds are after him."

Without letting go of her hand, Drew stopped short suddenly, so suddenly that Bess almost fell over.

''I will tell you what is wrong, madam wife. It is wrong that you should run to the Captain at the first opportunity and begin to meddle in this matter, something I most expressly told you that you were not to do! *That* is what is wrong.''

Bess gave him her most wounded stare. ''You forget, husband, that it was I who alerted you to the possibility of Charles's treachery and that, being your wife, I am thus in as much danger of ending up on the block on Tower Hill as you are. Since I assume that the Captain had feared that you might be the traitor, I assured him most solemnly that you were not.''

''A most valuable ploy, wife, seeing that a wife's word about her husband has no force in law.''

''But Captain Goreham is not the law...''

Her face was so rosy and indignant, so alight with a combination of love and determination, that Drew was quite overset. He gave a little cry of thwarted indignation mixed with lust, and pushing her into the shade of a small dell, sheltered from observation, he bore her to the ground.

''Is this the only way in which I can silence you, madam?'' he groaned at her, stopping her mouth with a kiss.

Bess struggled her mouth free, ''I will not be silenced...'' she began, then, as Drew began to pull her skirts up, ''No, no, we shall be seen. Drew, think where we are, what you are doing.''

''I *am* thinking of what I am doing. I am pleasuring a naughty wife and silencing her—if only for the time that I am doing so! And if you keep quiet whilst I am about this happy business, no one will know that we are here because no one will be able to see or hear us.''

It was impossible to try to prevent him. He had but to touch her and she was on fire. And, despite what she had said, he had been right when he had said that they were not likely to be seen. But to keep quiet when all her senses were alive and thrilling was almost impossible. And when she reached climax and opened her mouth to shout her joy, his hand was over it, silencing her—so she bit him. Not hard, but enough to break the skin slightly.

Drew reared up, and hissed at her after he had inspected his damaged thumb. ''Vixen! I shall punish you for that this night when we are quite alone.'' But he was laughing quietly after he spoke, all his recent ill humour gone, whilst Bess, happy that he was not irredeemably angry with her, began to laugh too, her head in his chest to muffle the noise she was making.

Sitting up, they clung to one another as they heard the party which they had left behind them walk past their hiding place. Arbell was trilling, the Captain was booming, and Charles's light baritone was acting as counterpoint to him.

''And now to the Baths, else I am foresworn,'' laughed Drew, watching Bess set herself to rights again. ''But confess, wife, love in the open is a fine thing.''

''Not so very open,'' retorted Bess saucily. ''Another day we must go alone to the hills and play at nymphs and shepherds there—when all is safe again, that is.''

''Aye, if that happy day ever arrives.''

Which was a sombre note on which to end, but as Bess said to him when they walked sedately along to the Baths, ''We are not really nymphs and shepherds but, like the lovers in Philip's poems, we may pretend to be—if only for a short time.''

Charles, despite his outward calm, was in ferment. He was sure that Drew knew of his treachery, and sure also that Captain Goreham had a hand in the game. There was something present in Drew's eye when he spoke to him, as well as something lacking in his voice. The quiet confidence which had always lain between them had been shattered.

The only question was, How soon would Drew move against him? That question haunted him. If Drew had discovered the secret compartment and the strange letter in it, one way of allaying his suspicions might be to ensure that when the satchel went south again in a few days time, the compartment was empty. But Arbell had already told him that Nau would have another letter ready before it left.

That letter must be stopped, and the only way to ensure that it was, must be to tell her that for their own safety's sake it would be necessary for it to be held back for the time being. So sure was he that he— and possibly Arbell as well—was being watched that, meeting her by chance in the Baths on the day before the courier was due to leave, he asked that they might meet privily for he had something urgent to tell her.

''Privily, sir? Why privily? Ah, I see you mean in the little temple.''

Charles shuddered. ''God forbid.'' The place was anathema to him—how could she make such an insensitive suggestion? Had she no remorse? No feeling for the poor dead boy? And what a hypocrite he was to mourn over having killed Tib when he was so busy trying to consign his cousin to a brutal death!

But all he said was, "No, not there. I have reason to believe that we are being watched. This afternoon, let us ride separately and secretly to the hills above Buxton, for I have somewhat to tell you that might alter all our plans."

The Lady's beautiful eyebrows arched in surprise. "How so? Our enterprise has gone well so far—save for the unfortunate episode of which you know. But if it will make you happy, then I will give way. Although I shall find it difficult to ride out without an escort."

"This afternoon, then, at two of the clock, at the Holm oak beyond the brow of the hill where the footpath forks. We shall not be seen from the village."

She was late, of course. She would be, would she not? The festering anger with which Charles was beginning to view life was ready to transfer itself to Arbell. Particularly when she rode into his view and he saw that she was accompanied by that complaisant and cuckolded clown, her husband.

Charles tethered his horse to a tree and walked towards her, his face thunderous. It was not until he was near to her that that he saw that she looked rather less than her usual haughty and impudent self. She also read his angry face correctly, and began with an uncharacteristically nervous rush of words. "My husband, I must now confess, is party to our enterprise and has insisted that he accompany me."

This put a totally different complexion on things. When Arbell had recruited him earlier in the year, having become aware of his dissatisfaction with his life with Drew, and also that he had secret hankerings after the restoration of the Catholic faith, she had said noth-

ing of her husband's involvement and much of her
recluse brother's.

Did she ever speak the truth? Sir Henry, who had
also dismounted, waved a hand to silence her for she
would have continued. He stared Charles coldly down.

"You have matters of urgency to tell me relating to
our noble enterprise, Master Breton. Pray speak on,
my time is valuable."

He was quite unlike the amiable fool and nonentity
whom the world thought it knew. Charles began
slowly, "The Lady Arbell..."

Sir Henry waved a contemptuous hand. "Oh, we
have no time for that—or her. Arbell, my dear, pray
ride a little way into the nearest copse and admire the
scenery from there. I would talk privately with Master
Breton."

He smiled at Charles. "She has been a useful—and
pleasant—go-between, you will allow."

Oh, he had been roundly tricked into this murky
business, had he not? It was becoming plain to Charles
that he had been bought with Arbell's body. But there
was no time to think of that. He had to consider instead his own safety, and theirs.

"He suspects," Charles said slowly. "My cousin
Drew suspects that I am involved in the plot on behalf
of the Queen of Scots and may even know that I killed
his wretched servant."

Sir Henry said dispassionately, "And a careless fool
you were to put yourself in the way of being vulnerable to such an underling. For once I have not chosen
my tool well. What, may I ask, makes you believe that
you are blown?"

"I have no direct evidence, but I am sure of it. I
have come to ask that the letter from Nau to our allies

in London shall not go south in the Exford courier's satchel. If it does I believe that my cousin will intercept it, read it, and send it on, thus enabling Walsingham to monitor our doings and prove that he is innocent of wrongdoing when one of our aims was to implicate him if the correspondence was discovered.''

''*Our* aims, Master Breton? *Our* aims? You are mistaken. That was *your* aim, and yours alone. *I* am not interested in Exford's fate or future.''

Charles's face was ghastly. ''You have tricked me...''

Sir Henry smiled sweetly at him. ''No, no, sir, you tricked yourself. And the letter will go south to London. I order it so done.''

''Then I shall not obey you.''

''How fortunate that I discover your cowardly folly thus early on in this great enterprise,'' said Sir Henry, still sweet, ''for I can dispose of you as neatly as you killed that poor fool of Exford's—and with less chance of discovery.''

He had moved closer and closer to Charles, until, on his last words, he drove the dagger he had taken from his belt into Charles after the same fashion as Charles had despatched Tib.

Without a sound Charles fell forward. Sir Henry stared down at him. ''A pity,'' he said to himself, ''that that had to be done, but necessary. Now to dispose of the evidence.''

Arbell had not dismounted. She had found a small plateau from which there was a view away from Buxton and she rode round and about it until Sir Henry, leading Charles's horse and riding his own, came into view again.

"Where is Charles?" she asked, her face fearful.

"Now that, my dear, you do not need to know. Suffice it that he will not be returning to Buxton and that we shall need to use another messenger. He had grown fearful and tiresome, and therefore dangerous."

He paused. "You are sure that no one knew that you were meeting him here?"

"Quite sure—but his disappearance will be most remarked on. He is, after all, not a nobody of a groom, but a Breton and an Earl's cousin."

"Oh, my dear, think nothing of that. Remember, Exford has been shot at, the groom was killed, and all, you must understand, by the disaffected who roam these parts, who frequent the hills and the woods looking for victims to kill and rob. They have grown bolder of late, one must admit. Now we will loose his horse— to gallop home riderless, and puzzle everyone."

"But the letter? With Charles gone, how shall that be sent south?"

"No matter. I have another who will do the business as well as yon poor fool. In these enterprises one must always be ready to change one's plans."

Arbell stared at the husband whom everyone believed to be her dupe, when the matter was quite otherwise. Oh, he thought of everything, did he not? And disposed of everyone who stood in his way. Now and in the past. It did not do to ask how two of his older brothers had died in accidents before him and he had inherited all. His pretence of being a kindly, bumbling cuckold had been the ploy of a cunning man who had allowed his wife to betray him only with those he wanted to use. It also allowed those whom he wished to betray to underestimate—nay—to pity him.

For the first time Arbell, who was not quite so stupid as she seemed, asked herself a question. How safe am I if he comes to think that I stand in his way? Thinking this, she sniffled miserably all the way back to Buxton. But it was for herself that she grieved, not Charles.

Halfway down the cliff from which Sir Henry had thrown him, caught on bushes before he had reached the ground, still alive and still hoping to be saved, Charles prayed for deliverance from the nightmare which his life had become, but not a deliverance which would end in his death.

He could hear woodsmen far below him, felling trees, and began to shout feebly in the hope that he might yet be saved…

## Chapter Fifteen

"Drew?"

"My love?"

Bess decided that she would be daring. After all, she had nothing to lose. "When this is over, may we go back to Atherington? We could enjoy ourselves there, nearly as well as we have done this afternoon."

Drew looked over to where she sat, looking out of the latticed bedroom window towards the hills.

"No baths?" he suggested naughtily.

"What? Oh, you mean that we have no baths at Atherington. But there is a lake but half a mile from the house. We could take our pleasure there."

"So we could. And if you look at me like that, wife, I shall take my pleasure now—and yours, I hope. But I dare not since I have been expecting Charles's arrival this last hour." He frowned. "It is not like him to be behind time. I trust…" He fell silent.

"Yes?"

"I trust that he has not discovered that we suspect him. His manner to me has been most constrained these last few days."

"The bell will chime for supper shortly," Bess said

somewhat slyly. "He will be sure to be there for that, and you may speak to him then."

But he wasn't. And it was as they were leaving after one of Lord Shrewbury's less interesting meals that Walter, the Great Hall's chief groom, came up to them, his face grave.

"I would, if you please, have a word with you alone, m'lord."

Drew was about to reply that anything which Walter had to tell him could be said before his wife, when something in Walter's steady look stopped him.

"Forgive me, wife, if I ask you to go to your room. I will join you there later."

Walter waited to speak until Bess was out of earshot. "It's Master Breton, m'lord. I fear that some accident may have befallen him. He took his horse out when the tower clock chimed two, and rode off towards the hills without a groom and never returned. But—and this is the troublesome part, m'lord—at the hour of five by that same clock, his riderless horse returned, all of a lather."

"And no sign of Master Breton?" Which was a stupid question, Drew owned, but was forced from him by the serious nature of Walter's story.

"None, m'lord. But, knowing that an unknown marksman had made you a target, I took the liberty of sending two of the grooms into the hills to look where I knew he might have ridden by the direction he took. They are not back yet, but I must humbly urge you to send another party out in the opposite direction as soon as maybe."

"Do that, Walter. I will come to the yard myself. Was there anyone with you when Master Breton set out?"

"Only one of the lads, Jem by name."

Drew thought a moment. Charles, the potential traitor and the possible murderer of young Tib, was now missing himself. Which could mean that he, Bess and the Captain were mistaken as to his treachery...but he thought not.

He followed Walter to the yard where the boy Jem was caring for Charles's spent horse. "Tell me, lad," he ordered, still abrupt—Walter thought that he had never seen m'lord so disturbed—"did anyone join Master Breton when he rode out."

"Nay, m'lord. I watched him ride off towards the hills. He was quite alone."

"Nor did anyone follow him?"

"Not in my sight, m'lord, no."

Drew looked around at the grooms and servitors of Lord Shrewsbury's other guests. Philip had just ridden in, late for supper, and on seeing Drew, he dismounted and walked over to him.

"What's amiss?" he asked. "You look troubled."

Drew told him. "And it seems that he was alone. Jem here says he rode towards the hills."

Philip frowned and said idly, "He was not the only one. What time did he leave?"

Walter told him. "Hmm." Philip thought for a moment. "It must have been some short time later that I saw Sir Henry and his wife set off in that direction. Best ask if they caught a glimpse of him."

"Arbell? The Lady Arbell set off in that direction?" Drew was so eager that Philip stared at him.

"Aye, with her husband," he repeated.

"I shall question them forthwith. And you, Walter, send out another party and let me know immediately if there is any news."

He swung round. "Forgive me, Philip, if I leave you on the instant but I must away. Some accident has befallen him, and the sooner we order things so that he might be recovered, the better."

He found Sir Henry and his wife in the Great Parlour next to the dining hall, Bess was with them. It seemed that they had stopped her on the way to her room and asked her to join them in a jug of mulled wine. Arbell was, for once, being civil to Bess. Drew was not civil to any of them.

He interrupted Arbell's long-winded welcoming of him by waving a hand at her. "No time for that. My cousin Charles went riding early this afternoon into the hills. He has not returned but his horse has—riderless. Some accident must have befallen him. Philip Sidney believes that you might have seen in which direction he went since you set out shortly after him…"

He got no further. The Lady Arbell gave a strangled cry and covered her face with a fine lace-bordered handkerchief, emerging from it long enough to say, "Oh, no, not another terrible mishap after your's and that poor boy's—I forget his name."

"Tib," Bess reminded her sharply. "His name was Tib." She was not in the least deceived by Arbell's meretricious goings-on. She would have been equally overset if she had spilt wine down her elaborate gown. "And did Charles take no groom with him after all he said to you about the folly of riding out alone?" she asked Drew.

Bess could plainly see that this aspect of the matter had not struck him before.

"I had not thought of that," he replied. And, indeed, it suggested to him immediately that Charles might have set off on an errand to meet someone in secret. Someone whom he did not wish his groom to know of.

Bess meantime watched Sir Henry clumsily comforting his wife in his usual kind manner. ''There, there, my dear, we must hope that his horse threw him, and that he will be found safe and sound.''

To no avail. Arbell continued to sob bitterly, shedding the mock tears for Charles which she had not offered Tib, being Bess's cynical thought. Yet when her husband neglected her for a moment to ask Drew grave questions about search parties, and she dropped her handkerchief again, Bess was surprised to see that she had been weeping real tears, not the pretend ones which she usually went in for.

Another unwelcome thought struck her. If she and Drew were right, Arbell knew of Tib's murder even if she had not actually watched the deed being done, and now here she was, placed not far from Charles before he disappeared. This was either an unfortunate coincidence, or something worse. But surely Arbell couldn't have killed Charles, or engineered his death, could she? No, it was her tongue that was long and strong, not her body.

Further thought was stopped by Arbell suddenly descending, or ascending, Bess was not sure which, into real hysterics. Aunt Hamilton, who had been hovering whilst all this was going on, looked reproachfully at the men for talking so frankly of death or injury before the women. She put an arm around Arbell and said comfortingly, ''Let me help you to your room, my dear. We are not needed here.''

She seemed to be asking for Bess to help her with the stricken Arbell, but Bess shook her head. She felt that she needed to speak to Drew at once, if not sooner.

"Oh, you do not need me, Aunt. See, here is Arbell's woman. Drew may need comforting, too. After all, Charles is his cousin."

Sir Henry, beneath his outward appearance of loving care, was beginning to be annoyed with Arbell, fearing that she might yet say or do something incriminating, and was only too happy to have her led away to collapse in private. It was as though what might have happened to her late lover had only become real to her when Drew had spoken of his riderless horse.

Once she had been removed, the men, for Philip had joined them, began to plan how they might yet recover Charles, either dead or alive, injured or non-injured. Drew finally took Bess by the arm to lead her to their room so that he could change into clothes and boots suitable for riding out himself.

He also knew Bess well enough to be aware that she was big with something which she wished to tell him in private!

"Drew," she said breathlessly the moment that they were alone. "Arbell was crying real tears over Charles, I know she was. She must know that something serious has happened to him, and that is why she was crying."

Drew stopped in the middle of pulling on his boots. "That's a big jump to make, wife, although I give you that she seemed genuinely distressed."

"So?" Bess challenged him.

"So, I believe that one of two things occurred. Either Charles had a genuine accident, nothing to do with any plot, or else he met someone who is also in the plot and something went wrong, resulting in Charles disappearing.''

"Well, we do know that Arbell was in the plot, so perhaps she was meeting Charles."

Drew stood up. "But, Bess, can you see Arbell killing Charles and disposing of his body?"

"No. But think, she was riding out with Sir Henry. Suppose he was in the plot all the time and it was he who…disposed, as you say, of his body. And that is why Arbell is so upset. She knows the truth about Charles's disappearance."

Drew sat down heavily on the bed. "You are sure that she was crying real tears?"

"Quite sure."

"She could have been pretending—and still crying real tears."

"She has never cried real tears before. I know that because I have been watching her like a hawk ever since I first met her. In the beginning because I thought that either you were already lovers, or that she was determined to seduce you, and later when we suspected that she was with Charles when Tib was murdered."

What a woman! She was as shrewd as the Queen was said to have been when she was Bess's age. A true Bess, indeed!

"Yes," he said slowly, "it make more sense to believe that Sir Henry is running the plot, using Arbell to tempt Charles into helping them; and keeping secretly in touch with Nau and enlisting the other conspirators who are here. They would scarcely follow a woman. We have been thinking of Charles as the leading conspirator. Suppose that he was Sir Henry and Arbell's dupe?"

"And," said practical Bess, who was not remembering with sorrow, as Drew was, the days when he and Charles had been happy boys together, "suppose their bait was that they would pretend you were the organiser so that if Sir Francis discovered the plot he would go after you, not them? Charles must have thought that either way he gained. If the plot succeeded, he would be rewarded with your lands and title; if it failed and you were arrested and convicted, he is your nearest relative, even if on your mother's side, and he might gain what was left over after your attainder—since you would leave no heir."

"True. And if we are right, then whilst Philip and I are searching for Charles, you must go to Captain Goreham and tell him of our suspicions. And, Bess, remember that they are suspicions only. We have not the slightest scrap of hard evidence which would convince Sir Francis or a High Court of their guilt."

And so Captain Goreham also told her when she found him. "No, m'lady, I believe that we may have reached the truth of the matter, but nothing can be done until we have some hard proof, which at the moment is missing. Do you go back to the house and watch the Lady Arbell lest she and her husband commit some action or some folly which might enable me to act. Until then we must bide our time."

Which was roughly what Drew had said to her. He said it again when he returned from searching for Charles. "We have not found him," he told her sadly, for he still had a faint hope that his cousin might not be the traitor he thought him. "But we have found this," and he handed to Bess the small gold medallion showing St George killing the dragon which Charles had worn on a chain around his neck.

Bess took it, her own face as distressed as Drew's. "Where was it?" she asked.

"Caught on a bush, on the edge of the cliff which faces away from Buxton. The odd thing about it was that there was no sign of hoofprints there. Just the faint impression of a pair of boots belonging to a larger and heavier man than Charles."

He decided to tell her the worst of it. "There was also the tracks made by a man being dragged along the ground, a man who must have been Charles. We rode to the bottom of the cliff, but there was no sign of him there. Which, all things considered, is passing strange, for he could not have survived the fall. After that we searched around, but could see no other sign of him. There were some evidence that woodcutters had passed that way, but we could not discover where they had encamped. By then it was growing so dark and the terrain so treacherous, that we decided to return and try again tomorrow."

He fell silent before bursting out with, "Oh, Bess, I do not know whether I wish to find him. To do so would help to clear us, but if he were alive, what is his end likely to be—given all that he may have done?"

Bess put her arms around him. "Oh, Drew, you are magnanimity itself, seeing that he has tried to kill you—and you must remember that he did kill Tib. To that extent he deserves what is coming to him."

"He was my childhood friend." Drew's voice was muffled.

"True. And there is the other thing. We now know that it must have been Sir Henry, not Arbell, who dragged him to the cliff and threw him over. She could not possibly have done that. Have you told the other searchers of our suspicions?''

''No, for I remembered Captain Goreham's dictum, 'The less said the better.'''

He looked so tired that Bess said gently, ''Let's to bed, my love, to sleep. Remember that tomorrow is another day.''

''You are my comforter and my strength,'' he muttered into her ear as they lay quietly down, ''and come what may, together we shall face down the world—and bring down Sir Henry and Arbell into the bargain, praise God.''

It was true that the less said the better, but there were those who were shrewd enough to read a puzzle and Philip Sidney was one of them.

Eating his poached eggs at breakfast, the eggs which the good physician Jones had recommended to those who took the waters, but over which both Philip and Drew had pulled wry faces, Philip remarked, apparently casually, ''Would it be wrong of me to assume that there is rather more to the recent odd events than meets the eye? After all, it is not every day, nor even every month or year, that one hears of an attempt to kill a man—yourself—an actual murder—that of your page—and the disappearance of a man of substance—like your cousin Charles. London itself would be proud of such record of crime over such a short space of time!''

''True,'' Drew replied, as, to his profound disgust, egg yolk dribbled down his chin. ''But these things happen.''

''Aye, mayhap. But when they happen in the vicinity of a lady around whom countless plots have been hatched, a man of sense might find himself asking question."

"True again, but that does not mean that another man of sense might be able or willing to answer them."

"Oh, that is an answer in itself, is it not?" Philip smiled. "For were nothing untoward happening you would be willing to speak the truth to me, but seeing that you are not, then I must believe that there is more to all this than mere coincidence, sent by the gods. Take my kerchief, Drew, and use it before the egg yolk leaves your chin and stains your ruff. It is a most devilish stain, very difficult to remove—or so my valet tells me."

Drew wiped his chin clean, and grumbled, "You are a damnably persistent fellow, but I am an obstinate one—and that is all that you learn from me."

"Not even if I tell you that I have reason to know that Sir Henry is a secret Catholic sympathiser and that is why Arbell's relatives allowed him to marry her?"

Bess, sitting on Philip's left, said brightly, "Goodness, we are serious today, Philip. Must we discuss religion at breakfast? I had much rather not."

As a ploy to silence Philip this was singularly unsuccessful.

He waved a long-fingered hand at her. "You are, m'lady, as devious as your husband. Else you would not have watched the Lady Arbell this last week as keenly as a dog watches a rabbit hole, waiting for his prey to appear."

"Dear me," said Bess, a trifle mortified, "was I as obvious as that?"

"No, I doubt whether any others saw. But Drew will tell you that I have more senses than five."

"Amen to that," and Drew clapped Philip on the back. "And will pay for that one day, no doubt. Forgive me, old friend, if I say no more."

"Indeed—If you will bet with me over whether Master Charles Breton is alive or dead, and that the question of religion, with deference to you, m'lady, is germane to the matter."

"No, not even with you will I bet on my cousin's life." Drew threw down Philip's stained kerchief. "And now I must go to the stables to begin the search for him again. Will you accompany us?"

"And will you ask Sir Henry…?" Philip paused significantly.

"Ask him what?"

"Why, whether or no he wishes to join us, what else?"

Philip's smile was so oversweet, Drew thought, that it bordered on the rancid. *He suspects a plot. Why else would he tell me of Sir Henry's secret Catholic leanings? And how many others are beginning to guess the truth? Say what you will, murder and treason smell to high heaven and will not be suppressed.*

He kissed Bess openly, so that all the world might see that he loved his wife. She was looking pale this morning. The strain of her secret knowledge was beginning to tell, even on her brave spirit.

Bess watched them go. Moved by some urge that she did not understand, she decided to follow them, even though it was plain that Drew wished her to remain behind. To watch Arbell, no doubt.

Instead, despite wearing thin slippers, she walked to the stable yard. The day was a dull one, and a light drizzle was falling. Their golden summer had turned as dark as the day's news. In the bustle of the yard

Drew and his fellow did not see her as horses were brought out, grooms shouted and the business of the day began. Others were also riding out, although not to look for Charles. Sir Henry and Arbell were not among them, for even as Bess had left the dining-room they had passed her on the way into it.

Drew's party were all mounted and ready to start. A great train of grooms was going with them so that they might search more places than one at the same time. But, at the very last moment, Walter, at the head of them all, shouted "Hola, someone comes. Stop a moment, m'lord."

Through the arched opening to the yard walked a small party of artisans and peasants. Most of them were shouldering axes, some carried large wicker baskets. One of their number was leading a donkey on which a man was slumped. The man was only just identifiable as Charles Breton, so torn and stained was his clothing. The worst stains of all were of blood. His head and chest had been bandaged with dirty cloths, and he had been roped to the donkey to keep him on it. Even so, every now and then one of the peasants steadied him so that he might not fall off.

The leading man said, speaking with an accent that was barely understandable, "Be my lord of Exford here?"

Drew dismounted and walked towards him.

"I am Lord Exford. What would you have with me?"

The man waved a hand at Charles. "We found this fellow halfway down the cliff late yesterday after we had finished our work. We brought him down and tended him overnight. He seems like to die. He can speak, but would not give us his name. All he would say was that we were to bring him to Lord Exford at the big house in Buxton. Here he is, and if he dies of his journey we are not to blame.''

''Indeed not.'' Bess watched Drew walk over to where Charles sagged in the arms of the man sustaining him. He said in a low voice that none but Charles could hear, ''Is this truly what you want, Charles?''

''Truly, yes, truly,'' Charles mumbled. ''Sanctuary.'' He fell silent.

This last word came out so loudly that all present heard it. Captain Goreham had joined Drew, and spoke to him briefly ending with, ''Agree to his wishes, m'lord.''

Drew waved a peremptory hand at Walter, who had also dismounted and had come over to him. ''See that he is carried to his room, and a physician sent for.''

Charles must have heard him, for he gave a moaning sigh and fell into Walter's arms, unconscious.

Bess had slowly advanced until she was in Drew's line of sight.

''You should not be here,'' he told her, but he did not sound angry.

''He is not dead, then?'' Bess asked; which was a stupid thing to say, to be sure, but Drew did not seem to think so.

''Almost, by the look of him,'' he replied. ''He is not conscious, nor, I think will he recover himself soon. It is useful that you are here, for you may go and tell Sir Henry and his wife that Charles has been brought back alive, but is unable to speak. That should give them food for thought. They may try to leave, but they will be stopped.

''I shall give orders that no one is to leave until my cousin recovers sufficiently to tell his story. Captain

Goreham tells me that he has already sent word to the High Sheriff of the county, asking either that he comes to Buxton himself or that he sends his senior officers and tipstaffs here as soon as possible. He has given no reason beyond the simple one of the recent criminal acts which have taken place and which need investigating.''

Bess needed no second bidding. She ran back into the Hall to find that Sir Henry and the Lady Arbell were already leaving the dining-room.

Arbell caught her by the sleeve, her voice high and stammered out, ''Is it true? Is it true that Charles Breton is alive and has been brought back to the Hall?''

''Quite true,'' said Bess, and then, naughtily, but in order to see how Arbell responded. ''With him being such a friend of yours, you will doubtless be greatly relieved and will wish to see him as soon as possible. But, alas, he is gravely injured and is at this moment unconscious.''

The conflicting expressions of apprehension mixed with relief on Arbell's face when she heard this last piece of news told Bess everything.

''Oh, no,'' she said swiftly. ''Now that we know that he is safe and sound we may leave at once. Sir Henry has had urgent news from home which requires his presence there immediately. You may give Master Breton our best wishes for his speedy recovery, of course.''

Bess was about to inform them that their leave-taking would not be possible, for no one would be allowed to leave until the High Sheriff or his officers arrived, and then only with their permission, when Drew came in and saved her the trouble.

"This is preposterous," Sir Henry exclaimed, speaking at last. "What possible reason could you have for detaining me and my wife?"

"What, indeed?" said Drew smoothly. "But take heart. You are not alone in this. All now present in the hall must remain, including those who were about to set out this morning and must now delay their journey.

"The claims of justice are strong—as are those of your safety—who knows what murdering outlaws may be hiding in the hills?" he ended as Sir Henry opened his mouth to challenge him again.

Arbell's face was ghastly. She appealed to Bess. "Can you not persuade your husband to change his mind, m'lady? It is imperative that we leave immediately."

Indeed it was! For was not the game now up? Bess was not averse to playing cat and mouse with the woman who had stood by when one man was murdered and another was sent to his probable death.

"If you have aught to argue, madam, that would enable m'lord Exford and the High Sheriff to look kindly on you, then say it now."

This was a direct invitation to her to confess and, by her expression, Arbell took it as such. But before she could answer Bess, Sir Henry seized her wrist in a grip of iron.

"I will not have my wife beg on my behalf," he said, still playing the mild and amiable buffoon. "I can speak for myself, and she can surely have nothing to say that I cannot say for her."

"Truly spoken," answered Drew, who was also beginning to enjoy playing the cat and watching the mice wriggle. "For the meantime I have ordered the stables closed until the High Sheriff and his officers arrive and have sent word to Lord Shrewsbury at Chatsworth as to what has passed here. I am determined to smoke out those who have treated my cousin so cruelly.''

No word had been spoken of plots or treason, but like Philip Sidney, who had arrived to stand at Drew's elbow, lending him the weight of his powerful family name, Sir Henry knew full well why Drew was behaving as he did. As did Arbell, whose face was ghastlier than ever, and who was now caressing the wrist which Sir Henry had twisted when it was behind her back but had now freed.

Bess's hawk eye could see bruises on it, and she wondered what Sir Henry would say to his wife when they were alone.

The unofficial meeting was over. Sir Henry, muttering, ''I know not who gave you authority to be in charge at Buxton, Exford, but of course, I will do my duty and remain here,'' walked away, his dignity still intact. He was grasping Arbell firmly by her other wrist and her face was set in a rictus of pain which passed as pity for Charles among those who were watching and were not in the know.

''Well done, wife,'' said Drew quietly. ''You almost frightened Arbell into giving herself away. Philip,'' he added, ''I should like to speak to you privily.''

Captain Goreham had agreed with him that, under the new circumstances of Charles's return, it would not hurt for another person to be aware that there was a conspiracy brewing. Besides that, Philip would be available to keep another watchful eye on Sir Henry and his wife, lest they try to escape.

''All will be over for them,'' he said to Drew, ''if

your cousin recovers sufficiently to be able to tell us who attacked him. His room must be guarded so that none might enter secretly and dispose of him and his evidence.''

''I have already arranged for that to be done.''

''Good, good.'' The Captain nodded approvingly at Drew. ''And guard yourself and your good lady, too, for there are others here besides our chief suspects who may be in the plot, and might wish to take any action designed to save their necks from the block or the hangman's noose.''

Bess shivered at his words. Both then and later, when she sat at an early afternoon repast, she looked at those around her with new eyes.

Drew was telling Philip and Captain Goreham that he had spoken with the wood cutters and although they had told him in detail where they had found Charles, halfway down the cliff with a great wound in his chest, they had no notion of how he came to be there.

''So that is a dead end, my masters. I have seen the physician caring for Charles, and he is hopeful that he may live and speak to us, but for the moment he is out of his wits.''

Philip lifted his goblet. ''I'll drink to that. For the rest, Nau has had the impudence to commiserate with me on the assault on a friend, and bade me pass that message on to you, Drew, which I now do. He also said that his mistress, the Queen of Scots, was shocked to hear of such barbarism being practised in this fair country. She also asks you to attend her so that she may offer you her sympathy in person.''

''Does she so?'' Drew's voice was savage. ''The same sympathy, I suppose, which she offered her own murdered husband, Henry Darnley!''

"Come, come, Drew. That remark goes under the heading of those which are thought but never said. The lady was a Queen—you must swallow your just indignation and go through the forms of ceremony which imprison us all."

Bess put a quiet hand on Drew's arm to quieten him. They were no longer beleaguered, no longer suspected of monstrous treachery, so there was no need for him to lose his temper.

Drew shook his head as though to clear it. "You are right, Philip, and I am wrong to rail at you. I must do my duty and visit her, but I shall not ask Bess to join me. You, wife, will need to be ready to go to Charles's room should he regain consciousness during my absence, and wish to speak. Since we are telling no one of the conspiracy, it would not do for us to behave as though Charles were a prisoner."

So it was agreed, and Drew, changed into his most magnificent attire, repaired to the Queen of Scots's quarters to receive her lengthy commiseration with a straight face. Bess, an anxious aunt Hamilton by her side, remained in her room. Her aunt had just returned from caring for Lady Arbell who, she informed her niece, was most distressed.

"You were somewhat unkind to her, my dear," she reproached Bess. "It was not like you at all."

Bess could make no reply that would satisfy her aunt, so, surprisingly for her, she kept silent, stitching away at her canvaswork, her head bent, listening for the messenger who might come to tell her that Charles had regained consciousness.

She shook her head at Drew when he returned and looked questioningly at her.

"Philip came, not ten minutes ago, to tell us that

Charles was still unconscious, but that he showed signs of returning to life.''

''Good,'' said Drew, but his approval was not, as aunt Hamilton thought, for Charles's showing signs of improvement, but rather for the hope that he might soon be able to tell them who had tried to kill him and why.

The bell rang for the midday meal, but Bess had ordered food from the Talbot Arms to be served in their room. Before they could begin to eat, Charles's page ran in, shouting breathlessly, ''The physician has sent me to tell you that my master has regained consciousness and has asked to speak to you. He is very weak, and the physician told me to warn you that he might swoon again before you reach him.''

Drew was out of the door like a scalded cat, all his ceremonial lordship forgotten in his urgency, was Bess's irreverent thought.

He found Charles propped up against pillows, his face ghastly, his breathing shallow. The physician stood by him, looking anxious.

''He wishes to speak to you, m'lord, but I have warned him that overmuch exertion might prove fatal.''

''Be damned to that,'' whispered Charles. ''If it is the last thing I do I must speak to you at once, cousin, privately.''

Weak though he was, he stressed the words cousin and privately.

The physician immediately began to warn him against doing any such thing. ''I need to be with you,'' he said.

Drew shook his head at him. ''You heard my

cousin," he said. "If he wishes to be alone with me, then Amen to that."

"I must warn you—" the physician began.

"You have already done so." Drew's voice was stern. "For once, let the patient decide. If you continue to defy us, I shall have my footmen remove you."

Grumbling, the physician left at last. Charles gave a weak smile. "It would not do for him to hear what I have to tell you."

"Nothing to that, cousin. Speak."

Charles's smile was now deathly weary. "I never thought that you would call me cousin again after what I have tried to do to you."

"Nothing alters our relationship, even treachery." Drew was as cool as he could be.

"True." He sighed. "Now let me tell you all of my wicked folly—even unto this last."

Haltingly, stopping occasionally to allow Drew to hold a goblet of water to his cracked lips, Charles told his whole sad tale. Drew, Bess and Captain Goreham had already guessed the gist of it. He named the names of those whom he had contacted both in London and in Buxton. Drew was a little relieved to hear that young Master Blagg was not one of them—he had taken a liking to him and his wife. Master Bown, however, was involved and several others with whom neither Drew nor Bess were intimate.

"I thought that I was the prime player in the game, using Arbell, not being used by her. And all the time that apparent dotard and cuckold, Sir Henry, was pulling the strings. He used Arbell as bait, no doubt of that…I thought that she loved me. We were to marry when the plot succeeded after her marriage to him was annulled. It was forced on her, she said."

This last confession set off a fit of coughing so strong that Drew, out of pity, was constrained to hold him up, finally lying him back on the pillows.

"But why, Charles, why? I know your family were devout Catholics so I can understand your wishing to restore the faith, but why did you try to betray *me* so cruelly? We were close friends from boyhood on. I thought that you loved me, as I loved you."

Charles lay silent and spent, moving his head restlessly on the pillows. Drew rose from the seat he had taken by the bed. "No, do not answer me if it pains you. I have no right to—"

Charles reared up and caught him by the wrist. "No, stay, and I will try to explain. Was I not merely the poor relation of the wrong religion, lucky to have you as a patron? You always had so much and I so little. You were Earl and I was nothing. Everything which you touched turned to gold. Every woman I ever wanted fell into your arms, not mine. Every game I played, you could beat me at. Even at University you outshone me.

"And your wife, she whom you had named monkey and vilely deserted for ten long years, proved to have turned into a beauty. Worse than that, she took one look at you when you arrived to claim her and became yet another worshipper of the god named Andrew Exford. She never looked at me, although when I looked at her I would have worshipped *her,* not required her to worship *me.* Even if I had not already begun to betray you, I would have done so after we came to Atherington…"

He stopped to cough, to turn his head away before beginning to speak again. "Oh, God, how I grew to hate you. I would have done anything to bring you low, anything. But I could not even do that properly, but fell victim to another who used me only to throw me away. And then, today, knowing what you do, you speak to me kindly, call me cousin. You will, I'm sure, even offer me forgiveness—as much as you can with that man of Walsingham's after me, that is. And what does your kindness make me but an even worse cur and traitor than I already am?"

What could Drew say? Nothing. He had his duty to do, and that entailed handing over to Walsingham and the State not only Sir Henry, Arbell and the others, but also Charles, who, now that he had confessed all, might earn a little, a very little, in the way of mercy.

The urgent knocking on the door which had begun whilst Charles was speaking, and which Drew had scarcely noticed, became even more urgent, and only stopped when Captain Goreham entered the room.

The Captain took one look at Drew, saw him nod, heard him say that Charles had confessed all, and now must give all the details to the Captain as Walsingham's representative.

"Not now," he said. "There's no time for that now. Sir Henry, aware that his game is up, has made a run for it. He has bribed one of the grooms to get him a horse and you and I must be after him."

"And Arbell?"

"Not to be found. She was not with him. The thing is, he must be captured secretly, for this whole business must be kept undercover until we are ready to tell all—if we ever do have to tell all. Do you post guards on this room and come with me. I have told Master Sidney to begin a search for the Lady. She cannot have gone far. He will also speak privily with the High Sheriff's officers if they arrive in our absence.''

Drew took one last agonised look at Charles, who was now lying back with his eyes closed, called for his page who had been lurking anxiously in the corridor, and then set off for the stables—this time still in the court finery he had worn to visit the Queen of Scots.

Bess, although anxious to know what was passing in Charles's room, stitched steadily on. Aunt Hamilton excused herself after a short time. Bess was, for once, pleased by her absence, mostly because she could not speak the truth to her aunt, and she was growing tired of dissembling.

I would not make a conspirator, she decided, it's too much like hard work! What I want to do is to go home to Atherington with Drew, and then, later on, perhaps, visit Wilton, which Philip has persuaded me is as near to Arcadia as any place on earth.

To think of Philip was to bring him into the room, enquiring hastily, without a by-your-leave or any of his usual courtier-like gravity, ''Have you seen the Lady Arbell lately?'' and immediately that she said him nay, he was gone again, and she could hear him running down the corridor.

Straightway after that, which was odd enough, aunt Hamilton almost fell into the room. She had a great bruise on her face and her farthingale's hoop had been knocked awry. She was breathing so shortly that when Bess ran at her, asking ''What's amiss, Aunt?'' it took her several minutes to regain the power of speech.

''Oh, Bess,'' she said at last, ''you were right about Arbell all the time. I have just met her in the lower corridor outside the Great Parlour and stopped to pass the time of day with her and tell her the good news, that dear Charles had recovered his senses again and that Drew was with him. You may imagine my surprise when she immediately shouted, 'Out of my way, you silly old woman. I've no time to lose', and struck at me so hard that I fell to the ground, before she ran off with her skirts held high like any rustic milk-maid!''

Poor aunt Hamilton's senses were even more confounded when her niece, throwing down her canvas-work, shot past her through the door, hurling at her as she went, ''Forgive me, but if that is so, I have no time to lose, either.''

The poor lady collapsed into a chair, exclaiming, ''What, has all the world suddenly run mad?'' before shouting in her turn, this time for her woman to come bathe her face.

So that was what Philip had been about, thought Bess, running down the corridor, looking for Arbell. And her silly aunt had had nothing better to do than tell her that Charles was likely confessing everything to Drew.

Where could she have gone? Escaped with Sir Henry, perhaps. That notion was knocked on the head when she met Philip in the Entrance Hall.

''Have you seen Arbell?'' they both asked together.

Bess shook her head, ''I only know that she is not to be found. Perhaps she and her husband are trying to escape.''

''No, he has escaped on his own, on horseback. Captain Goreham and Drew are after him.''

So he had deserted Arbell; left her to her fate. Which was all of a piece, coming as it did from a man who had callously used his wife as bait to catch careless and greedy fish like Charles.

"Useless to stand here talking," said Philip. "She cannot have gone far. I will go to the stables; she might be trying to bribe a groom. You had best return to your lodgings, my dear, and wait for Drew. This is no work for you."

Was it not? Bess did not argue with him. She tried to think what she would do in Arbell's shoes. The trouble was that she was so unlike Arbell she had difficulty in doing any such thing.

Suppose Arbell thought that now Sir Henry had deserted her, one way of escaping from imprisonment and death was to go into Buxton itself and try to hire a horse, or a carriage at the inn. She could then make for the home of a Catholic family in the area who might be ready to hide her. She would probably think the gamble worth the taking.

Moreover, Bess was sure that the villagers did not know of the secret goings-on in Lord Shrewsbury's Great Hall and therefore they would not try to stop her from leaving. Both Captain Goreham and Drew wanted to keep the conspiracy from public knowledge as long as possible.

What to do? There was no time for her to find grooms or pages in order to send them into the village, for if she took too long Arbell might yet escape. There was only one thing for it. She must go after Arbell!

No sooner thought than done. If she did not exactly raise her skirts like a milkmaid, Bess half-ran, half-trotted into the village street and made for the Talbot Inn...

# Chapter Sixteen

Meantime Drew and Captain Goreham were on Sir Henry's trail. He was not so far ahead of them that they might not catch him up. He would, the Captain guessed, make for the byway which led to the road to Derby, not only because it ran south to safety, but because he would need fresh horses which could only be found on a road with post houses on it.

Reaching the byway, which wound uphill out of Buxton, they could see Sir Henry ahead of them, riding hard. For a time they could only match his speed, but gradually they began to gain on him, until he could hear them close behind him. He turned once to look at them when they were almost on him, and seeing who it was following him, he realised immediately that he was like to be the victim of a relentless Nemesis.

He reined his horse in, leaped from it and ran off the road and into the scrub and forest which bordered it, in the hope that he could somehow elude them in it.

Drew and Captain Goreham followed suit, only staying to tether their horses to a nearby tree. Both of them had armed themselves before leaving the stables, and found, as they ran through the undergrowth and between the trees, that their swords were a drawback in such conditions. They had little difficulty in tracking Sir Henry, although they were unable to see him, since it was impossible to run quietly through such rough terrain.

Slowly the forest began to thin out until, finally, Sir Henry found himself on a large plateau, covered in scrub and heath, with the forest continuing again some half a mile away. Wishing to regain its shelter, he ran swiftly towards it, following a track which ran parallel with the edge of the cliff which had created the break in the forest. Far below him he could see the road to Derby winding into the blue distance.

Drew, with Captain Goreham, a much heavier man, labouring in his rear, was almost upon him, his youth and strength giving him an advantage over both the older men. He caught up with Sir Henry at the point where the scrub met the forest.

"Hold," he cried, drawing his rapier. "I bid you stop and surrender yourself in the name of the Queen."

Realising that he was cornered, Sir Henry turned and drew his own sword, "No. For you hold no office which gives you the right to arrest me."

"I have the right of a trueborn Englishman to arrest anyone he suspects of treason and murder and you have committed both. Be sensible and surrender so that you may throw yourself upon the Queen's mercy."

"Oh, I know right well what *her* mercy might be," retorted Sir Henry, advancing on him, rapier at the ready. "I see that your ally has fled the field. If you wish to take me you must kill me first,'' and drawing his dagger, he thrust at Drew without delay.

Drew only had time to draw his own dagger before Sir Henry was upon him. He had no doubt at all that Sir Henry meant it to end in the death of one or other of them, and he defended himself vigorously against a man who had been a master swordsman in his youth. He could only hope that his own youth, and his skill, would sustain him.

And what had he meant by saying that the Captain had fled the field? It was true that he had not appeared to help him in his fight with Sir Henry. Where could he have gone?

He was soon to find out.

In the to and fro of the duel he was turned until he was facing the direction by which he and the Captain had come and, true enough, there was no sign of him. Drew could not believe that he had been left to deal with Sir Henry alone, but he had no choice but to act as though that he had.

Youth and strength at last began to prevail. Sir Henry, almost overcome by the ferocity of Drew's attack, was compelled to retreat backwards towards the forest. Twice Drew caught him, first with his sword and then with his dagger, drawing blood, but he could not quite follow up his advantage. So engrossed were both men in their struggle for mastery that neither of them realised that the path of the duel had brought them dangerously near to the cliff edge.

And then Drew saw Captain Goreham. He was down on his hands and knees in the scrub, advancing slowly towards the pair of them. Drew, by measured feints, kept Sir Henry in front of the approaching Captain so that he should not espy him until, seeing his enemy beginning to falter, he prepared to deliver the *coup de grâce* which would kill him.

But he was never to do so. Captain Goreham, having crawled and slithered to a point immediately behind Sir Henry, suddenly rose and gripped him round the waist. Surprised at this attack from such an unexpected quarter, Sir Henry cried out and dropped his sword, preparatory to tackling this new threat.

The Captain, his face savage, gave him no chance to launch a counter-attack. He whirled his prey round and, with one mighty heave, flung him over the cliff's edge.

Drew, dropping his sword, joined the Captain where he stood, looking at Sir Henry who lay still, some hundred feet below them, his neck broken. He had suffered the fate which he had destined for Charles.

He took the Captain by the arm and said half-angrily, "Why did you do that? I was about to finish him off."

The Captain answered him softly, "Do but think, m'lord. This matter must not become public—which it would have done if you had killed him in a duel. Now there are no marks of a sword or dagger on him, only those of his fall. An accident, was it not? You are safe and innocent of causing another's death, and so am I, for you'll not talk, I'll be bound. My master Walsingham would not approve of that. No, no, this was the better way. We are not even here. We rode out by quite another route. Others shall find him for us."

"But Charles and Arbell—what of them and the other conspirators?"

"Why, m'lord, we shall speak of that later. Now we

must return to Buxton and pretend to have enjoyed our ride.''

Drew sheathed his sword. He would have liked to have had his revenge for Tib and the duping of Charles, but life was not necessarily arranged for the benefit of those who lived it. He listened to the Captain as he outlined their next steps.

Philip Sidney's errand to the stables in order to find whether there was any news of Arbell turned out to be fruitless. It occurred to him that she might not have tried to escape at all, and that it would be as well to go to Bess's lodgings to discover whether she might have seen her.

He bounded up the stairs like a very greyhound to visit her. Alas, when he shot into the Exfords' room, he found no Bess, but only a dishevelled aunt Hamilton, who was being tended by one of her ladies who was holding a wet cloth to her bruised cheek.

''Tell me, madam,'' he asked, breathless, without any of his usual elaborate courtesy. ''Is Lady Exford here—and have you seen the Lady Arbell?''

''Questions, questions,'' returned aunt Hamilton crossly. ''The world is full of them today. The Lady Arbell I do not wish to speak of, and as for Bess, when I told her that Arbell had run off after attacking me, why, what must Bess do but run after *her*, incontinent.''

''But where, madam, did they go?''

Aunt Hamilton murmured, ''I have no idea, none in the world,'' before she lay back and closed her eyes, seeking some relief from a day gone mad. But she was not destined to find it. The door opened again. This time to let in one of the pages. ''Oh, Master Sidney, the grooms told me that you would be here. They said you were looking for the Lady Arbell. Not ten minutes ago I saw her run out of the gates and down the road to the village. I thought that was strange, indeed, but stranger still, not long after that, I saw m'Lady Exford running in that direction…''

He was not allowed to finish. Philip pushed past him without a word and ran down the stairs even faster than he had come up them, shouting for his horse and grooms as he approached the stable.

Aunt Hamilton opened her eyes and said faintly to her lady, ''Child, fetch me a tisane. I must try to sleep at once and try to recover from the insults of a world turned upside down. I thought that Master Sidney was the most courteous of men, but he is no better than the rest, alas.''

Watched by curious eyes, Bess ran down the village street towards the inn. And there, just as she had supposed, was Arbell, arguing with the landlord and a groom who was holding a flighty horse. It seemed that her ladyship having no money or servants with her they were loath to let her leave on a valuable horse.

In the middle of their noisy bickering Arbell turned and saw Bess running towards her, calling her name.

''No!'' she cried, before pulling up her skirts. To the astonishment of the landlord, who was still refusing to let her mount his horse, she turned and ran, away from Bess, away from discovery and ruin, down the village street towards the road out of Buxton and the river which ran beside it. Where she thought that she was going, the good God alone knew. Panic had Arbell in its grip and flight was her instinctive response.

Panting with effort, Bess ran after her. Her heavy clothing hampered her, and, oh, how she wished she was in the boy's clothes which she had always worn when she rode out with Tib.

Tib! The very thought of him was a spur to her tired legs. She reminded herself that Arbell was similarly hampered, took no exercise and was doubtless finding flight even more difficult than Bess was finding pursuit.

She was slowing down and Bess was visibly gaining on her. They were soon out of the village and on the road, or rather the track, which ran by the river. Sobbing, tears of fear and rage streaming down her face, Arbell turned to face her pursuer. She could run no more.

"What do you want of me? In the name of heaven, let me go." Her voice was a croak; her whole appearance was of such utter despair as to invite pity.

Bess felt no pity for her. She thought of Tib and, yes, of Charles, traitor and dupe though he was, and her heart hardened against the woman before her.

"No," she said sternly. "Come back with me and face your fate."

"Never," shrieked Arbell, and turned to run again, but she only managed a few yards before Bess was upon her. She caught Arbell round the shoulders to stop her, but Arbell, desperate, twisting, tore herself loose and tried to run away again. Bess, fired by rage and revenge, caught her again, this time around the waist. They struggled together for a few moments before Arbell lost her footing and fell to the ground, dragging Bess with her.

Side by side, entwined, they rolled down the bank towards the river—and into it, Arbell giving one last agonised shriek as she entered the icy water, Bess, silent, still grimly holding on to her prey. She had swum in cold water before and was by no means as shocked as Arbell was by its cruel clutches.

"Dear God, save me, I cannot swim. Oh, help me, help me." Arbell's cries were for anyone, even Bess.

The summer had been a dry one, and the river was low, but their heavy skirts encumbered both women. Bess, realising that their summary ducking had ended Arbell's resistance, made for the river bank, dripping water, leaving Arbell behind her.

Why should she not leave Arbell to her fate? Just think, she told herself, of all the trouble that would save Drew, and the state. But she could not. To do any such thing would make her as bad as Arbell, whom she so despised. Wearily, Bess returned to help her out, a task rendered difficult by Arbell's refusal to help herself in any way.

Somehow Bess dragged and hoisted her out of the water, and laid her on the grass, gasping and panting, all her resistance gone, destroyed by her involuntary ducking.

Bess, trying to wring the water out of her skirts, said, her voice as severe as she could make it, "If you try to get up and run, Arbell, I shall either sit on you, or push you back into the river, so you had better behave yourself."

Even as she spoke she could hear hoofbeats and voices shouting her name. Help was at hand. Help in the shape of Philip Sidney and a couple of grooms.

Bess thought that the long day would never end. Philip had escorted her and Arbell back to the Great Hall, each of them riding pillion and dripping wetly over an unlucky groom. Arbell had been handed over to her ladies, and Philip had bid a pair of grooms guard her door so that she might not escape again.

Bess's ladies had stripped her of her wet clothing, and then bathed and dressed her in all her best finery. All the time poor aunt Hamilton had moaned and clucked over her as though she were twelve again.

The tisane her waiting woman had brought her had barely had time to take effect before Bess's arrival in such disarray set the seal of unlikeliness on her already unlikely day.

"I cannot imagine what you think you have been doing," she wailed as though Bess were a child again.

"Saving Arbell from the river," returned Bess briskly, but somewhat unhelpfully. She didn't think that it would be wise to inform her aunt how Arbell had come to fall in.

She was still being chided and wailed over when Drew came in from his ride.

"Such a pother as we have been engaged in today, you would never believe. You were well out of it," aunt Hamilton told him. "You have missed all the excitement," and she gave him her version of Bess's heavily laundered tale about following Arbell and rescuing her from the River Wye.

She ended by complaining of Master Sidney's sudden loss of courtesy, and by demanding that Drew reprimand his wife for being such a hoyden.

"Seeing that she is in your care now, not mine! Oh, what a day it has been! I am like to die of excitement and shall need a holiday to recover from this one."

"Yes, indeed, I have certainly missed all the excitement," Drew told her gravely and untruthfully. "And you would scarcely have me reproach my wife for carrying out such a noble deed. She almost certainly saved Arbell's life.''

Something in his voice alerted Bess. She said to her aunt, ''My dear, I think that it is you who ought to take a rest, not me, and recover from the exertions of your day.''

Still grumbling, her aunt left them. As the door shut behind her, Bess took Drew by the hand,

''And now, husband, is it not time that we told the truth to one another?''

''No hope of deceiving you, my dear, I see,'' and he launched into the tale of Sir Henry's attempt to escape and his subsequent death, before listening to Bess's story. Philip had already told him the gist of it.

He took her into his arms as she finished. ''Dear heart, you are never to do such a thing again. You should not have followed Arbell at all, let alone ended up in the water with her, but, all things considered, it was for the best,'' was all that he had to say.

Bess, who had been waiting for him, a little fearful that he might disapprove of her headstrong goings-on, was mightily relieved. Drew laughed a little as her face brightened visibly.

''But you are never to do such a thing again,'' he repeated, kissing her. ''You were lucky that neither of you drowned.''

''Little likelihood that I should, seeing that I am able to swim!'' Bess was dismissive. ''Arbell, now, was quite another matter for she could not. Have you had time to see Charles again? The physician says that he is fast recovering.''

Drew shook his head, ''No, alas, and this afternoon must be given over to help the Captain concoct some sort of explanation for the wild happenings of the last few days. We may have to call on Philip's lively imagination.''

''But even he could scarce have foreseen Sir Henry and his plotting.''

''No, indeed. And a search party will have to be sent to find him since he has not returned from his ride. And, of course, Captain Goreham and I have said nothing of what actually happened to Sir Henry on the hill beyond Buxton. Needless to say he had not informed his servants or grooms that he had no intention of returning at all!''

Bess shivered, her face solemn again. ''He might have killed you, Drew. Now *you* must promise me that *you* will never do such rash thing again.''

''My answer will be the same as yours—which was no answer at all!''

''And in the end he found the death he would have given Charles. There's a kind of divine justice about that. Arbell does not know, of course?''

''Nor anyone else.''

''But when the High Sheriff's men arrive, everything will come out, will it not?''

Drew began to laugh. ''Which was my thought, too. But, no, the Captain says that they will be given an explanation which will have nothing to do with any conspiracies against the Queen's Majesty. He has, he said, already prepared the ground for that. Do not ask me how—he is to tell me later.''

''I would not like him for an enemy.''

''Nor I.''

''And Charles and Arbell—if all is to be kept quiet, what will happen to them?''

''I don't yet know. Now that I have found you dry, rosy, and as impertinent as ever, with no need of succour from me, I am to meet the Captain and Philip for a final council of war. He will advise us on how best to explain the odd happenings of the last few days in such a fashion that no one will ask any further questions."

"Although they might think a lot," Bess added, "and, Drew, when we are finally alone together tonight, there is something I must tell you."

"Now, lady wife, you have whetted my appetite, I shall hurry back as soon as possible."

But as soon as possible for Drew was a long time coming. First of all there was the council of war to attend, and when that was over, the search party arrived back with Sir Henry's body, which caused more than a little to-do. Not long after that the High Sheriff's men arrived and joined in yet another council at which the Captain produced witnesses who gave evidence that there was a party of bandits, landless men of straw, roving this part of the Peak District and who were preying upon those who were foolish enough to ride out alone.

As for preventing any of the guests from leaving until the High Sheriff's men arrived, the Captain explained that as a precaution against further attacks until action was taken against them. It was agreed that a party of armed men would be assembled as soon as possible to scour the district and rid them of this plague.

"And, of course," the Captain had said privately to Drew and Philip, "they are bound to find some sturdy beggars playing at Robin Hood, and will hang them out of hand, even though they will deny all knowledge of the deaths of your page and Sir Henry and the attack on Master Breton. So everyone will be happy.''

Drew told all this to Bess when he finally arrived back in their rooms at midnight, having had an audience with the Queen of Scots and her secretary Claude Nau in order to tell them the unlikely story which the Captain had concocted.

''Whether the Queen knew aught of what passed is a moot point, but her secretary undoubtedly did. Nevertheless he smiled and congratulated us, even though he must have known that we were lying in our teeth. Dear God, Bess, I shall be glad to see the back of this vile business. This is the last enterprise I shall undertake for Sir Francis.''

''And Arbell and Charles, what will happen to them—seeing that they cannot be accused of treason?''

''Arbell will be confined, as the Queen of Scots is, in the care of a distant relative who is a loyal servant of the Crown. It will be given out that her health has failed. She will not argue against her confinement— she knows that she is lucky not to be sent to the scaffold on Tower Hill.''

''And Charles, will he go to the scaffold? After all, he did murder Tib most cruelly.''

Drew shook his head in sorrow, thinking of his boyhood friend who had been willing to use disaffected Catholics in order to injure him. He also thought of the many loyal English Catholics who quietly practised their faith in secret, who did not deserve to be persecuted for the actions of the few.

''Not so,'' he said, ''since all is to be kept secret. No, if he recovers from his wound, he will be taken to the Tower of London as soon as he is fit to travel.

Once there he will be offered a choice between a secret death in its dungeons or working as a double agent for Walsingham.

"I think myself I would prefer the first choice—but that is up to Charles. He and Arbell are both fortunate that the Captain's orders were to keep this plot, and the identities of the plotters, secret, if he could, for there have been too many plots lately. Since this one was so feeble in execution, and involved so few persons of any consequence—apart from Sir Henry, who is conveniently dead—the Captain is able to carry out Walsingham's decision. He will keep an eye on the minor members like Master Bown, you may be sure."

"So, it is over, Drew?"

Drew, who was lying in a great armchair, exhausted, nodded his head in agreement. Bess was already in the Great Bed, and had been there for some hours, waiting for him.

"Yes, dear wife. It is over. Thanks be to God."

"And we may go home—soon?"

Drew came over to sit beside her. He clasped her face in his two hands and asked her gravely, "Home, wife? And where is that?"

"Why, husband," she told him, looking deep into his eyes, "it is where *you* are. But I like to think that you could call Atherington home."

He relinquished her face and lay down beside her, clothed though he was.

"Dear wife, until I came to Atherington I never had anywhere which I could call a true home. My father's house in the country which I inherited is half a ruin, left over from the Wars of the Roses. The other half is new built, but bleak and bare. My mother died early and no woman ever made it comfortable. I have a small house in London and some rooms at court—when I attended there.

"The only home I have ever known is Atherington. For that I would bid God's blessing on Walsingham for sending me north on this mission, and for suggesting that if I visited Buxton with you no one would think that I had an ulterior motive. Without that we might never have met again. The few days I spent at Atherington with my new wife were the happiest I have ever known—once you and I came to terms."

Bess's face was rueful. "Came to terms, Drew? Is that all that we have done?"

He pulled her down beside him. "No, indeed, my darling hussy. Let me say the words to describe that which I once thought existed only in the imagination of poets like Philip. I love you, Lady Exford, more than I ever thought to love any woman, and I wish to live with you, where you will, whether it is at Atherington, or Exford House when we visit it. I am tired of Queens and courts, of intrigue and jockeying for position. Something which Charles said to me, when he explained why he became a traitor, made me ask myself whether, in the pride of my rank, I rode roughshod over the wishes and desires of others, as though only I existed in the world. My one wish now is to raise a family and safeguard the interests of the people who serve Exford and Atherington."

He fell silent. Bess kissed him on the cheek. A friendly kiss, not a passionate one. She had just gained her heart's desire—the knowledge that he loved her as she loved him. It was true that he had only come to claim her because of the suspected plot, but that meant nothing in the light of what had passed between them since. She gave a quiet little laugh.

"Why, husband, it is my turn to say that I love you, and happy I am that your monkey wife turned out to be the one woman in the world with whom you wish to live. And as for raising a family, then I have to tell you that you may be nearer to achieving that wish than you might think. I have reason to believe, my Lord of Exford, that I am already increasing, and that, boy or girl, your first child is on the way."

Drew sat up and clasped her in his arms again. "Oh, my darling, what a clever wife you are! And what a naughty one, to follow Arbell into the river knowing that."

"And no harm done, husband. I have observed that the wives of my humble people at Atherington who continue to work have easier births than the fine ladies who live about me and do nothing for nine months. So do not expect me to sit at home with my feet up."

"No, indeed, I would never expect that of you! But neither must you be rash. And we shall certainly return to Atherington now, for it has all the comforts for a breeding wife that Exford lacks."

Bess lay back on her pillows as Drew began to pull off his clothing preparatory to coming to bed—to celebrate her news, no doubt.

"I promise to behave myself on one condition," she said, as he jumped in beside her.

"Anything, I will grant my dear wife and the future mother of my child, anything."

"That next year we visit our good friend, Master Sidney, at Wilton."

"Oh, is that all! I had expected you to demand the equivalent of the Crown jewels at least."

Which had Bess laughing as they prepared to enjoy the first of many happy nights together, now knowing that each truly loved the other, and that their love was strong enough to sustain them through good times and bad.

The deserted bride was deserted no longer.

\* \* \* \* \*

Historical Romance™

4 brand new titles each month

...rich, vivid
and passionate

Available on subscription every month
from the Reader Service™

GEN/04/RS2 V2